DAUGHTER OF WAR & WITCHCRAFT

Jenn Lynn Adams

Apollo	god of truth and prophecy, twin brother of Artemis, son of Zeus and Leto, Hecate's cousin
Artemis	goddess of the hunt, twin sister of Apollo, daughter of Zeus and Leto, Hecate's cousin
Asclepius	god of medicine and healing
Athena	current queen of Mount Olympus and ruler of all the gods and goddesses
Castor	Pollux's twin, son of King Tyndareus and Leda, Hecate's husband
Charon	ferryman of the Underworld
Circe	goddess of sorcery, daughter of Helios
Clotho, Lachesis, Atropos	the Fates
Despoena	nymph daughter of Demeter and Poseidon
Dione	mother of Aphrodite, oracle of Dodona
Gaia	goddess of the earth
Hades	king of the Underworld, husband of Persephone, brother to Zeus
Hecate	Titan of witchcraft
Helen	queen of Sparta, wife of Menelaus, daughter of Zeus and Leda
Helios	Titan of the sun
Hephaestus	god of the forge, son of Hera, foster son of Thetis
Heracles	son of Alcmene and Zeus, foster son of General Amphitryon
Menelaus	king of Sparta, husband of Helen
Persephone	queen of the Underworld, wife of Hades, daughter of Demeter
Rhadamanthus, Minos, Aeacus	judges of souls entering the Underworld
Thetis	foster mother of Hephaestus, mother of Achilles

PROLOGUE

In terms of my life's journey, time is measured in *before Melinoe* and *after Melinoe*. My life on the island of Crete with Zeus as my childhood companion. And then reincarnating myself as Melinoe, daughter of Persephone and Hades. Daughter of the Underworld.

Standing in the small hut I call home with my husband Castor, I stare outside at the giant oak. The tree has now grown to a monstrous height. Its massive boughs sway in the warm breeze. The leaves bristle and hum with anticipation.

If I'm honest with myself, I miss Melinoe.

I miss her innocence. The simplicity of the life she had as nothing more than the heiress to this kingdom. I miss that her problems were small. Always black and white

Never gray.

My problems, inevitably in varying shades of ash, have been left untended. I've avoided them. Ignored their presence on the horizon. And thus, they have festered and become aggravated, spreading like a rot from this vibrant oak tree. I take a sip of the warm liquid in my mug, a potion concocted to drive away the migraines that have plagued me for the last several months. But nothing can calm my mind, my visions, which have seen what's coming.

"O goddess, O queen of those below,

I beseech you

to banish the soul's frenzy

to the ends of the earth . . ."

-hymn to Melinoe

POLLUX

"Harder, harder!" the brown-haired woman demands as she rides my cock. Her heavy breasts bounce up and down. I reach for them, wanting to roll the nipples between my thumb and forefinger and make her scream with pleasure. But she pushes my hands away and instead interlaces our fingers. She pulls me to her, my face full of her luscious assets, and we roll over as one.

On top, I plow into her.

"More, my prince!" she demands breathlessly.

My legs and lungs burn from the exertion. Unwilling to stop with my climax just beyond reach, I grit my teeth and pump faster.

Her squeals of rapture intensify, and I join her with a mighty roar of passion just as a loud and unwelcome knock at the door interrupts us.

"Prince Pollux?" the deep baritone on the other side of the barrier questions.

I don't bother responding. My brain is mush as I chase my release.

Harder.

More.

"Prince Pollux." The man's voice is louder. More demanding. "Prince Pollux!"

"In a moment!" I manage as I continue the battle atop the bedding. Even if I haven't seen a real battle in an age, at least I can continue to pillage the willing women of Sparta.

"Prince Pollux, the queen demands an audience. *Now*."

"I said *in a moment*!" I'm so close my toes curl and my vision goes hazy. Just a few more thrusts and—

"Open the door, sir," my sister orders the servant, her voice a shocking ice bath after a hard day of training. The door swings noisily on its hinges, banging against the wall. My cock instantly shrivels. I pull out of the woman. She mewls in disappointment.

"Fuck," I hiss, covering my bare ass with a blanket while my companion grabs a pillow.

I turn, my face on fire with embarrassment as my sister enters. Her eyes are cold. Her lips curled into a grimace as she turns her back to the scene. Bedclothes in disarray. The smell of sex and sweat permeating the air.

"You would make your queen wait while you fornicate with a washer-woman?" Her clipped tone leaves no room for a lovingly snide comment or sarcastic retort, so instead, I lower my eyes and offer a contrite head bob. Not that she can see me with her eyes fastened on the open door.

I hope she regrets barging in.

Behind me, my bedfellow scurries to the adjoining bathing area, her pin-straight hair discreetly covering her reddened face.

I edge backward on the bed, wrapping a throw around my waist, and run my hands through my now silvery-white locks. The years of pleasure seeking have aged me like a fine Chian wine, but without the requisite wars and life of constant soldiering there's been no need to keep my hair clipped short. I grab a leather cord from the side table and tie back the length before dragging a long linen tunic over myself.

Moving to the small table near the hearth, I pull out a chair for my sister. Hearing the scrape of the wood, she turns and makes her way over. She lowers her heavy form with a weary sigh, a palm coming to rest on the bump beneath her chiton.

"Bring the special tisane from Hecate and a plate of biscuits." She flicks her wrist at the servant, dismissing him. Once we're alone, her eyes wander over my face, a small wrinkle forming between her eyebrows. "You look like *kaká*."

"I do not look like shit," I retort through gritted teeth.

"You've done nothing except fight and fuck since Father's death. It's unbecoming of the queen's brother to behave thusly." We're quiet as the refreshments arrive, and she nibbles a biscuit before taking a dainty sip of the acrid liquid.

"It's not fighting if there's no war. I'm training our country's soldiers in case—"

"In case of what? We're finally at peace. Menelaus has ensured that."

I refrain from rolling my eyes and instead nod at the cup and sniff. "What's in that stuff anyway?"

She shrugs and swallows another mouthful. "I have no clue, but I trust Hecate with my life, and if she says it's healthy for the babe, then I'll drink a thousand cupfuls."

I pour myself a pint of wine leftover from the previous day and greedily gulp down the entire contents at once.

Helen eyes me from across the table, her lips thinning.

"What?" I ask innocently. "I'm thirsty after my . . . exertions." I offer her a wry smile and a shrug.

"This is exactly what I'm worried about."

"What precisely are you worried about, dearest sister? Your opulent lifestyle of lying around and becoming a brood mare for your king?" The wine, mixed with the lack of a release, has loosened my tongue. "Or is it the fact that your husband stole our family's throne? A position that should have passed to me once Castor abdicated in my favor?"

Her cheeks redden. "Enough is enough, brother. I'm sending you to the Underworld. Let Castor deal with you and your lackadaisical lifestyle for once. Menelaus and I have enough to worry about without you moping around."

"I'm not moping," I grumble as I shove a biscuit in my mouth. "And I don't believe this is your decision, Helen. You'd never rid yourself of your favorite brother." I smile sweetly at her and then widen my eyes and cock my head, reverting to the lovable goofy brother I know she adores.

"This *is* my decision," she responds with a shaky voice. "And Menelaus's too."

"Ah, the new king of Sparta is tired of his brother-in-law already." I huff in annoyance and rub my jaw. Whether it's sore from the tension I hold there or the tongue-fucking I gave my paramour last night, I'm not sure.

"We both agreed this is for the best. You've been doing nothing but fornicating with anything that walks, unceasingly training for hours a day with no war on, and refusing to sleep or nourish your body with anything beyond wine. It's not healthy, and I won't have your death on my conscience. Are you even listening to me?"

"No," I answer honestly. I've heard it all before. From Castor and Hecate when they were last home and from the constant rotation of women I spend my nights with. Maybe Helen's right. Maybe a change of scenery is just what I need. Plus, I haven't seen my twin or his wife since Tyndareus's funeral.

"Castor will meet you at the Cape of Taenarum in two days' time. Say your goodbyes to Pieris."

"Who?"

Helen stands and shakes her head. A noise of disgust escapes from her throat. "The woman you were fucking, Pollux. Her name is Pieris."

As she stalks from the room, I don't bother asking how she knows my partner's name. But a coldness settles over my bones as I traipse into the bathing room and discover Pieris luxuriating in a bubble bath, her tits peeking through the scented foam.

Pushing aside my misgivings, I pull the tunic over my head, my cock already standing at attention.

"We should probably finish what we started." I smirk as I climb into the warm water and her waiting arms.

• • • • • • • • • • •

"Thrust deeper!"

"Harder! Harder, I say!"

"No, not there."

"Have you ever done this before?"

I release an exasperated roar at the Spartiates, the royal guardsmen who would normally accompany the king in battle. Their form is pitiful, but seeing as we've had no battle or war in an age, it falls on me to keep the men trained.

"Just in case," I was told when assigned the duty. It's simply one more menial chore that Menelaus has tasked me with. As though I need to earn my place here at my family's court.

As if summoned through thought, the king appears. He climbs up steps into the raised viewing pavilion and takes a seat in Tyndareus's throne. An entourage of his childhood companions surround him, all just as portly as he. I holster my blade as the hoplites salute.

"Prince Pollux, a moment of your time!" the king calls from his lofty position. I gesture to my second-in-command. He is more than capable of running them through the daily drills, which again raises the question of why I've been given this task.

Rolling my eyes, I take my time walking the length of the arena. If Menelaus is annoyed with my pace, he hides it well behind a bushy beard and equally unruly eyebrows.

Before I ascend the dais, a servant stops me. He beckons to my blades.

"Royal protocol states one must hand over his weapons in the presence of the king, Prince Pollux. Even *you*."

I raise my gaze up the steps, and I catch Menelaus turning his head back to the arena. *Fucking coward.*

I swallow the anger and unfasten my belt, handing the heavy contraption to the servant who proceeds to buckle under the weight. I snort and climb the steps, my fists clenched at my sides.

"Brother! How goes it?" The king clasps my forearm. He tightens his grip, and his long nails press into the leather, leaving half-moons embedded in the material. "Tell me how my guard fares."

"They're itching for a battle, Menelaus." His eyes darken at my refusal to address him by his kingly title.

"Yes, well, my people enjoy a life of peace and prosperity."

I fight the urge to tell him that *my* people are fighters. It's in our blood. And as for prosperity . . . The man need only to leave the safety of the castle to see for himself that inflation has increased and beggars line the streets, hungry and out of work.

Ignoring my silence, Menelaus continues. "I wanted to make certain you understood the message from the queen."

I bristle, clasping my hands in front of me to avoid ripping out his eyes. "I'm uncertain of the reason behind the message, Menelaus." Why the fuck do I need to leave *my* kingdom?

"You see, I had no issue with you fucking your way through the staff. In fact, with your ability to train my soldiers so well, I encouraged it. After all, I understand that every man has his *urges*." He winks as his companions laugh uproariously.

My stomach sours.

"Unfortunately, you've finally stuck your prick in the one servant who does not belong to you."

The coldness returns to my bones, a warning I had ignored in favor of a good lay. "She doesn't belong to you either, and she came to *me* willingly," I blurt out before I can stop myself.

Menelaus launches out of his throne and pulls a long blade from the sheath at his belt. He points it directly at my cock as two of his footmen grab my arms. Weaponless and surrounded by those loyal to the king, I wriggle to hold my hands up in supplication.

"I meant no disrespect, brother," I spit out the words even as my molars grind together. "I had no idea she was spoken for."

He returns his blade to its home along his outer thigh and settles back onto the throne, the ancient wooden chair creaking under the bulk of his body. I imagine the delicate washerwoman buried beneath him and immediately beg the gods to wipe the image from my thoughts.

"I won't be a cuckold in my own kingdom. You'll pack your things and be gone by nightfall."

"You cannot be serious!" My fists clench, and in my mind my knuckles connect with his meaty jaw.

Menelaus gestures to his bodyguards, men whom I personally trained for service. Together they hoist me away from the king and down the stairs, where I'm roughly deposited on my ass in the dirt.

"Gone by nightfall!" Menelaus hollers down at me, his beady eyes gloating from the throne that should've been mine.

Hecate

"My lady, thank goodness you're here!" Selene bows low, her face nearly touching the aged granite steps of the palace.

"Enough of that." I flick my wrist and scurry up the stairs, bypassing her completely. She quickly rises and follows behind. Her footsteps move quickly before the distinct sound of fabric tearing hits my ear. A hiss of pain rips through clenched teeth.

"Selene!" Worry knitting my brow, I retrace my path and pull her to standing, assessing her for injuries. The length of her chiton hangs uneven and exposes a reddened knee, but nothing more. Satisfied she's free of broken bones, I pull her along as I continue to ascend.

I must hurry.

"Slow down, Melinoe!"

I freeze midstep. Turning, I meet her widened eyes with my own. It's been years since I've been called her name.

"I-I'm so sorry, my lady." Looking mortified, Selene raises her wrinkled hands to her mouth, as though she could draw the moniker back into her body and trap it inside.

Like I was trapped for so long.

Remembering the importance of my visit and the urgency surrounding it, I bring myself back to the present and, thighs burning and chest heaving, push onward. I reach the summit of the palace stairs and turn toward Hades's private chambers. The basket of bottled herbs and medicinals clangs at my side, and while I'm wary of breaking something, it doesn't slow my gait.

"My lady, please!" Selene, on my heels, finally catches up to me and, grabbing my wrist, pulls me to a stop. My chest heaves as I push the fly-away curls from my sweaty brow.

"There's no time for pleasantries, Selene. The note stated that—"

"The note stated that Hades wished to see you immediately," Selene interrupts. "What is all this?" She glances at the basket.

"The missive was signed by Thanatus. Why would Father's minister sign the letter unless something was horribly wrong?"

"Nothing is wrong, my darling daughter!" Hades's voice booms from behind me and I turn, taking him in from head to toe. I smell the blood before I spy a bandage across his left palm. I rush toward him, pulling the fabric away from the cut.

"What have you done, Father?" Despite the years I've now spent as Hecate, Hades will always be my beloved *patéras*. The man who raised me.

"As I've already told you. It is nothing. A simple flesh wound from my morning training with General Rhadamanthus."

I tut and shake my head. Reaching into my basket, I pull out a healing unguent. "I don't know why you won't allow me to be your healer. Who treated you?" After slathering the ointment onto the wound, I rewrap the binding and secure it tightly.

"Your husband treated the scrape, my dear."

I blush and drop his hand, returning the salve to my kit and wiping my hands on my chiton.

"Besides, I can't have my princess working as the royal healer when she has so many more important duties. Mainly, assisting me in running the realm while the queen is away."

"You know I enjoy sitting as a minister in Persephone's absence, but I am capable of more. Whatever you need of me, I will do it."

"You do enough, Hecate."

I fall in step as he descends a steep staircase that leads to the throne room. Selene follows quietly behind, offering to carry my basket. I pass it over to her with a nod of thanks and link arms with Hades. He moves slower, and I know his bones ache with the approaching wet autumn weather, even if he says nothing. We arrive at our weekly appointment, and as we wait for the guards to announce our entrance, I look up and notice something is missing.

"*Emfanízontai os stémma.*" The crown of the Underworld appears in my outstretched hands, and I pass it over to Hades.

He rolls his eyes and huffs in annoyance, refusing to take it. "You know I dislike wearing the regalia, Hecate. It pokes into my skull and weighs heavily on my neck after sitting here for so many hours listening to the souls' concerns. I only wear it for state events because Persephone makes me."

Smiling deviously, I wink and then press my lips together, blowing out a gust of air. The crown disappears into dust. I rub my hands free of the remnants. Looking up at Hades, my smile cracks, and we begin to laugh as we are finally announced and enter the throne room to the applause of our subjects.

· · · ● · ● · · ·

The knock at the door startles me and I drop my concoction onto the floor, uttering a curse aloud.

"A moment!" I call as I move carefully to clean up the mess. I'm meticulous with the glass shards and dump the remains into my waste bin with regret blooming in my chest. I've been working for days on a salve that will ease my migraines. As they've become more pronounced, the need for a treatment has become crucial.

I curiously ease the door open, wondering who could be visiting unannounced at this hour. I like to get an early start and awoke before the red dawn crested over the Elysian Fields. Careful not to wake Castor or Cerberus, who has taken to sleeping at the foot of our bed, I tiptoed out of the bedroom and made my way silently to the adjoining room that housed my studio. With Persephone's imminent return and my duties at the palace, my time to work unimpeded is limited.

"Selene?" I pull the door open and step aside, inviting her in. She's wrapped warmly in a woolen shawl and carrying a basket of pastries. She sets them on the table and I eye them greedily, my stomach grumbling with a reminder that I've not broken my fast yet.

"My lady, I was hoping for a moment of your time."

"Of course, Selene. We could have spoken this evening at our family dinner, though. There was no reason for you to come all this way." I reach for a carafe of watered wine and pour us each a cup. Grabbing a pastry, I tear off a hunk and savor the buttery flavor as it melts on my tongue. No matter how many times I've tried, I've been unable to replicate the palace cook's recipe. I surmise I've been given an incomplete list of ingredients so that I'll continue visiting for breakfast.

"Perhaps we could have discussed this at dinner, but what I need to say must be done in private. I'm afraid I've disrespected you, Hecate." She lowers her eyes, and I see a blush of embarrassment creep up her neck.

My brow furrows and I set down the half-eaten cake. I reach across the table, pulling her hand into my own. "In what way could you have possibly done this, Selene?"

"When you visited the palace the other day, I called you Melinoe, and for that I am deeply sorry."

"Oh." I sit back, unsure how to continue. While I'm not upset at being called Melinoe—Castor frequently interchanges the name as a joke—Selene and I have never spoken about my journey. Or the truth she kept from me for twenty-three years.

"My lady, you once saved my virtue from Zeus, and I will never be able to repay you. And now I've offended you, and I can't forgive myself for that."

I sit forward abruptly and smack my hand on the table, shaking the dishes. "Enough, Selene!" She flinches and I soften my tone. "I'm not upset about the moniker. It's just a name, and Melinoe was an enormous part of my journey."

She visibly relaxes and sighs in relief.

"And furthermore, there's no need for you to repay me for rescuing you from that beastly Zeus. You allowed me entrance to the Underworld. You brought me to my home—to all this." I indicate the modest hut around us. I swallow. "But, there are times when I wonder why you never told me the truth. You had me as Melinoe for twenty-three years, and nary a word or clue as to who I really was."

Her eyes well with unshed tears and her chin wobbles. "Hecate, don't you remember? You bound me with an oath spell. I physically couldn't speak the words, my child."

My fingertips tremble. Bile burns the back of my throat. I bound a *friend* with a spell? The memory hits me like an ocean wave. I'm sucked down, unable to breathe as my actions become clear. Meeting Selene's eyes, I see the tears streaming down her ashen cheeks.

I remember now. What I did to my friend. "You didn't agree with my plan because you didn't want to lose your only friend in the Underworld. And instead of listening to you, I bound you with an oath spell, taking your decision from you because of my own desires." The realization weighs heavily on me and I sag against the table.

Selene nods solemnly. "But, Hecate." Now it's her turn to reach across the table and take my hand. "I understand why you did it, though at the time I hated you for it. It was selfish of me to think I knew better than you when it came to Zeus." She stands and comes around the table, kneeling before me. "What matters is that you're back here in the Underworld. You're safe. We're all safe." She pulls me into a hug, and for just a moment, I close my eyes, inhaling the familiar scent of the woman who raised me. But just as quickly, my eyes flick open and I glance out the window behind her at the oak tree, its massive branches reaching toward the reddened sky. I wonder at her words.

Are we really safe?

POLLUX

Thanks to my sister's cunt of a husband, I arrive in the town of Taenarus a full day early. My body servant, a man likely appointed by Menelaus to spy on me, finds suitable lodgings for us both and disappears to the servants' quarters, leaving me completely and utterly alone. Tossing my traveling pack near the unlit hearth, I sigh heavily as I drop to the fur-lined bed and run my fingers through my silvery locks.

I can't believe I've been banished from my own home.

After Menelaus's ridiculous demand that I leave immediately, I went straight to Helen's quarters and, in a rage, made the situation that much worse.

"Did you know he fucks your servants, Helen?" I roared. The color drained from her face.

She bent in half over her belly as a scream echoed through the halls of the castle. "Get out!"

Her servants ran for help, judgment in their eyes, and a midwife was rushed in. I was subsequently ushered away so as not to agitate her delicate condition any further while she was placed on bed rest for the remainder of her pregnancy.

Needless to say, there was no happy send off as I left Sparta.

Looking around at the dismal room, I wonder how everything has fallen apart since Tyndareus's death. I put my elbows on my knees and drop my head into my hands as the panic surfaces.

The night Tyndareus, my foster father and the man who raised me, died. Unable to save him.

My fault.

I pinch my eyes closed and abruptly stand. I need to get out of this room and get a drink in my hand. It's the only way to avoid the memories.

I stomp down the stairs of the inn, and as soon as I've escaped outdoors, I inhale deeply. The scent of the town calms my tormented mind. I focus on the bustling people, the clear sky, anything but the contents of my mind.

Turning left, I spy a sign for a tavern and my spirits lift. I cross the lane, dodging a group of children playing a game of ball, and push open the heavy door. The darkened interior soothes my soul and my shoulders relax as I enter. Taking a seat at the bar, I beckon to the barkeep and down the first libation that's placed in front of me in one gulp. The dark thoughts are already a hazy memory fading away.

"Another," I order as I blow out a breath. The barkeep sets down a second and, before he can turn around to assist another patron, my cup is empty.

"Again."

He eyes me with a frown. "You'll need to slow down. I've got other customers to serve."

I toss a heavy bag of coins onto the bar. It lands with a thud that matches the throbbing vein in the barman's forehead. "Close up early and just serve me then."

A feminine *tsk* from the neighboring stool pulls me from the bartender's wrinkled face and sour breath. Turning slowly, I sweep my gaze over the source, a breathtaking woman. That I missed her when I entered the bar is beyond belief, but here she daintily sits with a murderous look on her gorgeous face. She is tiny, smaller than most women I've met. I wonder idly if she is a nymph, one of those troublesome creatures of nature, but I don't have the courage to ask. Thick honey-blond hair falls down her back in loose waves as green eyes glare at me through heavy dark lashes. I lick my lips as my eyes travel down to her ample cleavage.

Fuck me. I truly am blessed by the gods.

"*Diastrevló*," she mutters under her breath, just loud enough for me to hear.

I quickly raise my eyes as I certainly don't enjoy being called a pervert, let alone by one so beautiful. Instead, I turn to the barkeep and toss another bag of coins between us. "Close up early and serve *us*," I say with a flirtatious smile and a wink at the nymph.

Her lips twist in disgust, and with a snort, she drops to the ground and walks to a table in the corner.

Lucky for me, the bartender pockets the bags and hollers to the other patrons, "Closing up! Out! Out!" The few customers grumble on their way out, shooting me murderous glances and curses. One man even spits in my direction. I shrug it off amiably and continue drinking, raising my cup and nodding at each one.

The beauty at the corner table doesn't move.

The barman scurries to the door and locks it behind the last patron. Then, he returns to his serving post, digs around under the rail for a full jug, and sets it on the wooden bar top before disappearing into a darkened room in the back.

With a heavy hand, I pour myself another mug. Turning on my stool, I hold the bottle aloft. "Care to join me? There's plenty here." I direct my offer to the corner.

"No, I don't care to join you, but I do need a top off." She stands and saunters over to me, setting her own cup on the bar.

I fill it to the brim with a pathetic nod. I can't even pay a woman to spend time with me. Turning back to my libation and my own sorrowful existence, I spin my mug in silence. After a few moments, I notice she's returned to her original stool and is watching me with blatant curiosity.

She tilts her head and presses her lips together as I turn my body toward hers. Her eyebrows raise, waiting for me to speak first. Fortunately for her, I'm impatient, and I always give the ladies what they want. "What brings you to Taenarus?"

"That's what you want to ask me? What brings me to this town?" She rolls her eyes and looks away, shaking her head in what appears to be disappointment.

I'm taken aback by her bluntness, and frankly, it turns me on. As a prince, I'm certainly not used to a woman who doesn't instantly throw herself at me. I clear my throat, ready to try again. "Are you married?"

"Do I look married?" She waves her ringless hand in my face. "Why? Are you?" Her face pales.

I snort, nearly spitting out the ale I'd just swallowed, and release a belly laugh.

"Is that a no?"

"That's a fuck no, *mikrí nýmfi*."

Her lip curls in disgust, and I see a flash of anger pass over her features. "I am nobody's *little nymph*," she snarls in my face. Turning away from me, she slugs back the last remnants of her drink before dropping to the ground and moving swiftly toward the door.

I mirror her movements, from tossing back my own drink to stalking across the sticky floor. I reach her just as she grabs the door handle. I grasp her elbow and tug her gently away from the exit, and she twirls straight into my chest, hardly reaching my sternum.

"Don't go," I beg, my voice thick with the dregs of the ale. "Please."

Her eyes narrow as she assesses me. She's quiet for a moment, and then she sucks her bottom lip between her teeth and chews on the plumpness. "I'll stay," she finally says, "but on one condition."

"What's that?" I raise an eyebrow, uncertain of the demands this miniature despot may make of me, but curious nonetheless.

"We switch to something a little stronger. And you tell me your name." She adds the last as an afterthought.

A smirk pulls at the corner of my lips, and I hold out my palm. She tentatively takes my hand in hers and we shake, sealing the arrangement. "I'm Pollux."

A flicker of something flashes over her features before she dazzles me with a smile.

"Time for that stronger drink, Pollux." I like the sound of my name on her tongue.

I jog behind the bar like an obedient dog and dig around. She returns to her stool and leans her elbows on the counter, watching me search. Finding a nearly full bottle, I pop the cork, take a whiff, and wince. "This should do." I pull our two empty cups closer and start to pour when she holds her hand out, stopping me.

"Let's play a game."

"What kind of game?" I set the bottle down between us and lean my hip against the bar as a devilish grin lights up her face. I'm directly across from her and have the perfect view of her pert tits as she starts to fiddle with a pouch at her waist.

She takes a coin from the belt and places it on the bar top. "Call it," she says as she picks up the disk and flips it into the air, catching it deftly in her small hands.

"Heads."

She turns the coin onto the back of her hand. "Tails." She smiles triumphantly. "Drink," she nods to my cup. I laugh and fling the liquid back. It burns a streak down my throat and I hiss, trying not to cough.

"Your turn." She passes me the coin. It's warm from the heat of her touch.

I flip it as she calls out, "Heads." Swiping the circle out of the air, I turn it onto my own hand.

"Heads," I chuckle softly. I shake my head and place the piece into her waiting hand. I brush my fingertips along her palm and notice a blush creep up her neck.

She winks at me and my cock springs to life, which is a bit of a surprise considering the amount of alcohol I've imbibed so far this evening. "Do you wish to continue?"

"Of course. I'm nothing if not persistent."

She hums as a smile plays at her mouth. "I could tell." She glances around at the empty tavern and then turns back to me, one single eyebrow cocked.

I nod to the coin that she's been fingering. My mouth goes dry as I watch her lazily play with the disk. "Again. I'm sure I'll get it this time."

She brings her palm to her lips and blows seductively on it. "For good luck." Her voice goes husky as her eyes meet mine. She holds her hand out to me and I mirror her actions, my lips pressing together and blowing lightly onto her skin. Goose pimples break out along her wrist.

"Tails," I call as she flips the coin and catches it before quickly turning it to her hand.

"Heads." She holds in a giggle. I groan in frustration and sling back the drink. When my eyes refocus on her, everything is spinning.

"I'll make a deal with you," she says, finally coming into focus. "If you get the next one correct, I'll take two drinks."

I stick my hand out to shake in agreement, but completely miss and knock over the bottle. Liquid coats the bar, and my face heats in embarrassment. What type of man can't hold his liquor against a tiny woman?

"I'm sure there's another." She pats my hand and drops to the ground before stepping behind the bar to join me. Standing next to her, I am baffled by how small she is compared to me, barely coming up to my chest. She drops to her knees, her eyes on me as she dips and begins digging around. "This will do!" she exclaims as she pops back to her feet.

My eyes can't focus enough to make out the label, so I shrug. I sway as she walks back to her stool. She pours a measure and sets the cup between us. Taking a deep breath, she places the coin between her thumb and forefinger and flips it high into the air.

My eyes work to track the coin in the air. I start to call out, "Ta—"

And then something heavy smashes into the side of my head, and everything goes dark.

HECATE

"Cerberus, heel!" Castor shouts as we walk the narrow path to the castle proper. With his tongues hanging from his mouths, the giant three-headed dog obediently lopes to Castor's side.

"I can't believe how much he's improved since you first began working with him." I link my arm with Castor's and nestle into his side as a chilly breeze blows through the pomegranate trees.

"He's gotten tame in his old age."

I sigh, the anxious feeling of unease creeping into my thoughts once again.

"Another headache?" Castor slows his pace and pulls away, looking at me with a worried frown.

"No, not today. I find that dinner with Hades is very refreshing, but with Persephone returning from the Land of the Living in two days' time, I wonder how our weekly feasts will change with her presence."

"You two have made such great progress in the years we've been here. I'm sure she'll be delighted to see you, and you can speak about Demeter and the other Olympians."

"Perhaps," I say, presenting a confidence I don't necessarily feel. Even as the Underworld has remained my home, my relationship with Persephone is still fragile. Hardly solid.

We continue our peaceful walk, Cerberus emitting various grunts and snorts as he trots by our side, until the castle comes into view.

My eyes linger on the window of my childhood bedroom before Castor nudges me and directs my gaze to the unnaturally long line of souls waiting outside the gates.

"I've never seen this many souls waiting before, wife."

I stop in my tracks and shift from foot to foot, my scalp prickling.

"Maybe it's nothing—"

"Or maybe it's something. The something that we've been waiting for," I clarify as I meet his eyes. The worry and uncertainty in them matches the feeling in my gut.

Castor releases me and I hurry over to the line, searching for someone—any-one—who can tell me their story. How they came to be in the Underworld. What happened in the Land of the Living? Maybe it's something as natural as a volcano eruption or flood. I nurture the small hope, but as I follow the crowd closer to the palace gates, I'm met with soul after soul, corpse after corpse, too debilitated to speak or even acknowledge my presence. Necks are slashed. Skulls are crushed. Limbs are missing. Entrails hang from gaping stomach wounds. There's nothing natural about these deaths. I cover my mouth in horror until I come upon a young girl and her mother. They seem out of place in this group of gore.

I approach slowly, squat down to the little girl's level, and speak softly. "Please, tell me what has happened. What has brought you here?"

The girl looks up with shiny brown eyes slick with unshed tears. She holds out a husk doll and I tentatively take it. "How did you come to be here?" I repeat.

"You did this," she hisses at me, just as clotted blood begins to seep from her nose. Her tiny hand snaps out and grabs my wrist.

I recoil in horror, but her grip grows tighter.

"You did this, Hecate, Titan of witchcraft. It was you who brought this curse upon the Land of the Living."

I'm too stunned to speak, to comprehend what the child is saying, so I shake my head in dismay instead.

"It was *you*."

· · · · ● · ● · · · ·

We arrive at the Cape of Taenarum two days later, Castor and I on horseback and Selene riding in a carriage to attend Persephone. This is the first time Hades has been unable to accompany me on the trip to collect his bride. He'd stepped in to serve as an additional judge of the souls crossing into the Underworld, and his face was gaunt and tired as we bade him farewell this morning. Even now the line of souls remains as long as ever, with more added by the hour.

"What in the Land of the Living is going on out there?" Hades roared when Castor brought me, shaking and nearly catatonic, into the castle. I couldn't get the little girl's words out of my mind.

"You need to send for Rhadamanthus. Hurry," Castor said as he handed me over to Selene. In my mother's absence, she frequently joined our weekly dinners, and I was grateful for her presence now.

"He's out there judging the souls," Hades responded, just as Rhadamanthus himself stalked into the chamber. His face was ashen and his fists were clenched. "Ho! General, what news?"

"My king. My princess." Rhadamanthus's gaze flicked warily to mine as he arose from his genuflection, and my breath caught in my throat. Even after all these years, Rhadamanthus continued to address me by my old title and treat me like the stubborn daughter of his liege.

"What's causing the influx of souls?" Castor ran his fingers through his hair, a habit I had learned throughout our years together meant that he was frustrated, worried, or even scared.

Rhadamanthus cleared his throat and clasped his hands together. "Ah, it's hard to say, Your Highness." He avoided meeting my eyes.

I stiffened at the affront. From training me as magicless Melinoe to teaching me the methods the Underworld judges imposed to protect our kingdom, Rhadamanthus had never lied to me. Until now.

"There's something you're not telling us, General." As though she could read my thoughts, Selene voiced what I was unable to. We collectively turned to her, the hunched elderly handmaiden. Her chest puffed out and her chin lifted.

Even though he could reprimand her for her outburst, Rhadamanthus respected Selene and her position as part of our family too much to do so. Instead, he sighed and eyed the exit.

Hades, his patience worn thin, bellowed, "Enough, Rhadamanthus! Tell us the cause of this deluge of souls!"

The general's gaze finally landed on mine and I flinched inwardly. "W-We believe that Hecate has caused this by imprisoning Zeus, Your Highness."

"What?" Hades roared at the same time Selene gasped, her hand covering her mouth.

My shoulders sagged as my head dropped.

It was you, the little girl had said. *It was you who brought this curse upon the Land of the Living.*

That night, back in our warm cabin, Castor paced back and forth, his footsteps shaking the small abode. "I don't understand how overthrowing a-a-a monster led to thousands of souls on our doorstep."

I quietly rolled and unrolled a scroll as I sat by the fire, my mind in chaos as I watched the flames for a sign, a message, anything to help me understand the path forward.

Pulled from my thoughts, I found Castor watching me intently. "What are you thinking, my love?"

I brought my hand to my temple and rubbed at the throbbing that had grown painful.

"You have another migraine? How many is that this week?" He scrunched his brow as the concern transformed his face.

"Three," I responded breathlessly as I continued to massage the painful region. A bright white light flashed before my eyes as the ache intensified into an explosion. A shriek ripped from my throat as I fell to the floor. Castor rushed to my side.

"Hecate! Hecate!" I heard him yelling as he shook my rigid body, but my mind was lost in a vision. The pain swept from my temple through my bones, and I watched from outside myself as the oak tree in the distance ignited in a burst of flames.

POLLUX

I wait patiently on the cliff of Cape Taenarum for Hecate and Castor. Checking the sun's position in the sky, I dismount from my horse and hand the reins to the servant who's accompanied me. The same one who ushered Helen into my room two nights ago and then ditched me to drink alone in a tavern where I was subsequently assaulted by a tiny nymph. My lips thin as he takes the mount and turns to ride off, leaving me to wait alone with only my thoughts and a goose egg the size of my fist on the side of my head as my companions.

"Prick," I mutter under my breath. I wince as the dull throbbing in my head sparks to life.

"What was that?" I startle as Persephone appears behind me. From atop her own horse, her blood red curls appear on fire in the sunlight. Her green eyes, normally the color of spring grass, are dimmed to more of a chartreuse as autumn approaches.

"Your Highness." I bend a knee and lower my head. Before I can raise myself from the obeisance, I hear her sandaled feet hit the ground. Looking up, my heart skips a beat as rose petals rain to the dirt. The horse is gone.

"What the fu—" I start before realizing I'm in the presence of an Olympian and immediately clamp my mouth shut.

"Do not worry about my mount, Prince." She responds to my horrified expression with a smirk. "He came from the earth and now he's returned to the earth."

I say nothing but swallow down my rising gorge. Persephone has always left me feeling a bit uneasy, what with her unearthly stillness and moods so closely tied to the seasons. Even now, in the early days of autumn, her behavior is closed off. Chilly.

"What happened there?" She indicates the tender wound on my temple, but before I can respond, thunder shakes the ground.

We turn in tandem as the portal to the Underworld sparks open. Hecate stands on the other side, her hands thrust out and her jaw set. I begin to take a step through before Persephone reaches out, her arm blocking my path forward.

"We wait."

I halt as though an ivy vine has my legs in a vise.

"A moment, my little witchling," Persephone yells through the doorway.

Hecate flinches, a look of annoyance passing over her features, before her shoulders roll back. Even from here I can see a sheen of sweat beading on her hairline as the exertion takes a noticeable toll. "I can't hold this much longer. I don't have the power of Hades's bident to keep the portal open indefinitely."

I turn my gaze to Persephone just as a familiar young woman rides up at full speed, her honey hair flying behind her. Breathless, she reins in her mount and leaps from the horse. Standing to the side, her hip cocked and a single eyebrow raised, she watches with indifference as Persephone snaps her fingers, the horse falling to the ground in a flurry of rose petals.

"Sorry I'm late, sister," she finally says to Persephone as she rolls her lips. "Mother really struggles with goodbyes."

• • • • • • • • • •

My eyes widen in horror at the sea of souls standing outside the gates.

"I warned you," Castor murmurs from the seat of his horse. Hecate rides in front of him, her face stony. She remains silent.

Turning in the saddle, I watch as Persephone draws back the curtain of the carriage window, her mouth falling open at the sight.

"What can I do to help, brother?" My gaze returns to my twin. If I'm to be banished to this desolate place, I might as well make myself useful.

"We'll go around to the back gates," Castor instructs our party, ignoring my inquiry. I swallow down the affront and, with a backward glance, follow. We gallop at a pace, Hecate in front while Castor and I fall to the rear. Without needing to speak to our mission, we protect the carriage like the trained soldiers we are, the Underworld queen and her mysterious evil sister seated comfortably inside.

I frown, thinking about the look the little she-demon had given me as she jumped effortlessly from her horse. Her eyes, the color of the cape, sparkled with mischief as a devilish grin touched her pink mouth.

"I'm Desy," she said, sweeping her hair from her face and addressing me as though we'd just met.

"Do you remember knocking me out cold in a tavern last night and stealing my gold?" I wanted to ask, but my courage failed me. Instead, the throbbing at my temple sharpened and I hissed in pain.

As she climbed up into the carriage, her pert rear pulling at the thin fabric of her gown, I had to adjust myself to keep from tenting my linen traveling pants. Just as I reached to rearrange myself, she turned around, caught my eye before dipping her gaze to my crotch, and let out a throaty laugh at my expense.

Diastrevló, she mouthed to me before escaping into the darkness of the carriage.

"Pollux?" I'm pulled from my thoughts by Castor. He eyes me curiously, waiting for a response to a question I didn't hear.

"Yes, of course," I respond in an attempt to cover the fact that my heads—both of them—were focused on the enigmatic guest riding with Persephone.

"Good. We wouldn't want an uncomfortable situation on our hands, what with Demeter's animosity toward Hecate and, by association, us."

I swallow the lump in my throat, wondering what I've inadvertently agreed to while daydreaming. Unfortunately, I don't have much time to ponder the thought as we are ushered into the palace proper. The gate clanks closed behind us, and we are immediately surrounded by Tartarusian guards.

Castor dismounts and assists a still-sullen Hecate from the saddle. I frown, my brow creasing as I realize Hecate hasn't said more than a handful of words since we left Taenarum. She must simply be worried for her kingdom and the souls who have overrun the Underworld.

I shrug and turn toward the carriage, waiting for Persephone to disembark with the help of her servant before I scurry to help Desy. The nymph ducks her head and steps down onto the carriage block before daintily pressing her hand into my waiting one. I offer a slow smile and a dip of my chin. Two can play at this game.

"Oh my!" she exclaims as she throws herself awkwardly into my arms.

I catch her gracefully, careful to keep my fingers from holding her too tightly, and promptly set her on the ground as I step away.

"I'm so sorry! I must have caught the hem of my chiton and stumbled. Thank the gods you are so strong." She winks and, with a glare from Persephone, follows her sister up the steps of the castle.

"What the fuck was that?" Castor is beside me in an instant. He grips my tunic in his fist and hauls me closer, his face an angry shade of red.

"She tripped," I shrug indifferently. Did he want me to drop her?

"You promised you'd stay away from her, Pollux!"

I cock an eyebrow. "I don't remember agreeing to that."

"You just did before we entered the gates!"

"Hm . . ." I mumble evasively. "I wasn't really listening." If he can choose to ignore my question about helping the line of souls, I can choose to ignore his warning against the intriguing nymph.

Castor emits a low growl and loosens his grip before grabbing Hecate's hand and nearly pulling her up the steps.

I release a huff of amusement. My banishment just got interesting.

HECATE

Persephone's celebratory return aligns with the autumnal equinox, and as Castor and I make our way through the crowded ballroom, I flash him a loving smile. It was many years ago that Hades and Persephone brought him to this very event and presented him as my intended groom.

Before I can take another step, Castor has swept me into his arms and, with his hand sliding deliciously lower on my back, leans into my ear. "This celebration always brings back the best memories of us, sweetheart."

My heart flutters for the first time in days, and I feel a lightness that's been missing ever since the incident with the young girl and Rhadamanthus. "I can't imagine my vomiting on your shoes was a fond memory, Cas."

"Every day I've spent with you has been wonderful, and I wouldn't change a thing. Even the way we first met."

Bats flutter in my stomach, and a delicious warmth tingles in my core. I press closer to my husband, the man I once thought had betrayed me to Zeus for a chance at immortality. As the old king of the gods' name sparks to mind, the heaviness returns, weighing me down, and I stumble over the steps of the dance.

"Until we know more of the situation in the Land of the Living, keep him from your thoughts." As though he knows my innermost musings, Castor nuzzles into my neck and softly presses his lips to the tender skin. My nipples harden through my gown, and goosebumps prickle along my throat.

"Distract me then," I whisper against his scruffy jaw. Even after all this time, I desire my husband with a thirst that isn't easily quenched. I quickly glance around, ensure we aren't being watched, and run my fingers down the length of his tunic. As Hades's master of horse and hound, Castor has taken to wearing the more formal deep purple himation at courtly functions. I emit a low growl when I realize I'm unable to simply sink my hands into his leathers and stroke him.

"Damn this garb. Next time you're wearing your Spartan leathers," I command.

"Next time I'll wear nothing, if you'd prefer."

I release a guffaw as his mischievous grin turns serious. His body stiffens, and the muscles in his jaw twitch. Turning to follow his darkened gaze, I spot Pollux and Despoena wrapped around each other in a shadowy corner, their faces inches from one another.

"I thought you made him promise to stay away from her."

"I did, although he probably wasn't listening with the right head."

I snort in agreement. "Nothing good can come from the two of them together."

Castor's eyes return to mine as he tilts his head.

"She's just as much trouble as he is."

"Apparently, he's been nothing but a problem since our father's death. Helen had to send him here or Menelaus was going to get involved."

I tilt my lips in a bemused smile. "Castor, Pollux isn't the one I'm worried about."

"What do you mean?"

I loose a heavy sigh and pull him off the dance floor and into our own darkened corner away from the ears of the courtiers. "She's a wild child. Even more so than Pol."

Castor huffs out a laugh and rubs the back of his neck. "There's no way that tiny little nymph is more of a mess than Pollux, Hecate." He glances warily at his twin.

"I'm telling you the truth. Despoena spent most autumnal equinoxes here in the Underworld. The first time she didn't visit was when you arrived for our betrothal. I spent my youth with her, and I promise she's a handful."

He's openly staring at them now as he scratches his scruffy jaw. "I just can't imagine how much trouble someone that small could be."

I cock an eyebrow and place my hand on my hip, ready to watch him eat his words. "Exactly. She uses her innocent appearance as a weapon. Pollux must stay away from her if he's to remain here. There's absolutely no way Persephone, Demeter, or Helen would believe *she* was the problem."

"Persephone believes her sister an innocent too?"

"Of course," I retort. "Despoena is nothing if not sly. It's puzzling how she tricks everyone around her into believing she's some wide-eyed ingenue."

"Fuck. This is not what we need right now," Castor mutters as we both look over. And that's when we realize both Despoena and Pollux have disappeared.

POLLUX

"**I**'m glad to see you're upright, Prince Pollux."

I sigh and turn around, coming face-to-face with the evil nymph who assaulted me over drinks and a game of coin toss. My jaw hardens, which only makes the bruise on my temple throb painfully, and I wince.

Her eyebrows draw together and she reaches up, tenderly placing her cold glass to the dark purple wound. I lean into the cool cup, and her arm, and close my eyes. The loudness of the party, combined with the brightness of the sconces along the tapestried walls, only adds to the pain in my head.

"Come with me," she whispers over the din of the musicians. My eyes flash open and I lower my brows, my face surely showing my utter confusion.

"Why would I trust you to take me anywhere? You knocked me unconscious and stole all my gold. Which, by the way, I'd very much like returned. What do you need with so much money anyway?" I narrow my eyes at her.

Desy emits a growl of frustration and ignores my question. "Come on. You know I'm more fun than this stuffy soiree." She holds her hand out to me. "Plus this music is abysmal." She tosses back the liquid in the glass and sets it atop a passing servant's tray.

I glare at her. "It's probably best if I turn in for the night, what with the giant goose egg on the side of my head. And, to make matters worse, I've no money for drinks, *mikrí nýmfi*." I shrug and turn away, scouring the party for the type of woman who won't knock me upside the head with a thick bottle of booze.

She sidles up to me. Her height, or lack thereof, affords me the perfect view of the tops of her creamy breasts. "Keep looking, Pollux." It takes me a moment to realize she's speaking of the women at the party and not her perfect cleavage. "You won't find a single one who keeps you on your princely toes like I do." Sending me a crooked smirk, she huffs and flounces away in her deep green ball gown, the color setting off her tan skin and sun-streaked waves. It's like she was born in a forest and lived her life completely naked. Kissed by just the sun and the stars. I bite my lip, wondering if there are tan lines under that dress.

"Wait!" I stalk after her, catching up and falling in step. "So tell me about this place. It must be more exciting than this, no?"

"Oh, you have no idea." She pulls me through a side door and out into the crisp air, and I follow like the fool I am.

• • • ● • ● • • • •

"How do you know of this place?" I ask as Desy tugs me into a rowdy tavern in the valley below the castle.

"I spent much of my childhood here in the Underworld during the autumnal equinox, my friend," she shouts over the roar of the patrons. I've heard Castor's tales of the lavish celebrations that occur on Persephone's return from the Land of the Living, but I've never experienced them. Until now.

The party inside the tavern rages on despite the never-ending line of souls waiting at the gates for entrance to the realm. It's as if the souls inside the kingdom have no memory of life outside.

"To the return of the queen!" one inebriated drinker shouts as he hoists his drink in the air. Some liquid spills, sloshing onto the bar top, but the drunk seems not to care a bit.

"Hear, hear!" The crowd cheers as other toasts are made to the beloved Queen Persephone. Desy rolls her eyes, a scowl transforming her face.

"Do you want to leave?" I ask over the din.

She shakes her head and stands on her toes to look around. "I'm supposed to meet my friend Orphne. It's been an age since we've seen one another." She takes my hand and pulls me farther into the crowd. We stay close, our bodies brushing against one another. Our hands still entwined, we're jostled toward the dance floor where revelers twirl and twist to the lively music.

"Desy!" A shrill shriek pierces my ears through the music, and an equally tiny nymph throws herself into my companion's arms.

"Orphne!" The two friends embrace and kiss cheeks before they both look to me.

"And who is this?" Desy's friend cocks an eyebrow as her ink-black eyes trail me from head to toe. A slow, seductive smile lifts her lips.

"This is Pollux, prince of Sparta." Desy's eyes meet mine as Orphne pulls me in for a hug, and I swear I see a flash of fire within their green color.

"Come dance with us, Prince." Orphne uses one hand to tug me onto the floor as she grabs Desy around the waist with the other, pulling her close. She whispers something into Desy's ear, and they both turn to me, conspiratorial smiles on their pink lips.

The beat of the music picks up, and Orphne lifts her hand. She's bedecked in a short, shadowy dress. The fabric seems to reach out to me, beckoning me closer as it licks against my exposed forearms.

"What's this material?" I ask as I twirl Orphne in front of me while Desy grabs me from behind, pressing her buxom chest into the small of my back. I tower over both women, but that doesn't stop them from gyrating around me in a seductive dance. Orphne's straight black hair whips from her face as she whirls away from me, but I reach out and pull her back. She straddles my leg and arches her back. As the foggy fabric shifts, her breasts are exposed. The dark brown nipples are hard. My palms ache to touch, but I don't get to linger too long as Desy grabs my chin and yanks my attention to her. She turns around and grinds her rear into my thigh. From this vantage point I can lean over her and make out the top of her cleavage, the tan flesh heaving as she breathes in the celebratory spirit.

The song ends and a slower tune begins. We continue our group dance, the women switching positions from my front to my back. When Desy's in front she runs her hands up my abs and along my throat. Orphne, from behind, slides her fingers around my waist, cups my ass, and slithers down my thighs. I'm rock-hard.

"I need a drink!" Orphne finally yells over the music. She takes hold of Desy and me and pulls us toward the barkeep.

"Three melogions!" Desy shouts to the bartender and then turns to me, her face and neck flush with color. She raises to her toes and I lean down, her voice loud in my ear. "Have you ever tried this drink, Prince?"

I shake my head as three small, shallow cups are laid before us. We each grab one and raise it up. "*Stin ygeía mas*!" We toast to our health and down the honeyed wine. The flavors explode in my mouth. I immediately want more.

"Another round!" Orphne exclaims as she slams her cup on the bar. "This drink is much more potent than wine. We must be careful, Desy, or else . . ." She trails off as she licks a drop of liquid from the corner of her mouth.

I lean down and shout to be heard. "Or else what?"

"Or else Orphne and I will fuck you. Together," Desy adds with a whisper in my ear. The music is so loud I can't be certain I've heard her correctly, but when she and Orphne turn to each other and laugh as they begin reminiscing of another night of debauchery, I am certain that my cock is ready for whatever the night holds.

I slug back a second cupful of the sweet nectar and send a quick prayer of gratitude to Helen and her hideous husband. Perhaps I'll stay banished in the Underworld forever?

Hecate

Despite the celebration still raging in the throne room, Castor and I have been called to Hades's private chambers. I take a seat near Rhadamanthus and smile in greeting, showing that there are no harsh feelings between us. Castor stands behind me, his hand protectively on my shoulder. The other two Underworld judges, Minos and Aeacus, enter and quickly find seats. While I'm not very close with them, they both nod at Castor and me. Minos lowers his ox-like body onto the nearest couch but refuses to relax. Instead, his back is ramrod straight. I don't know that I've ever seen the Underworld judge recline in peace. Aeacus situates himself on a stool. Tinier than the other two judges, he folds his legs under his lithe body easily and winks at Minos, who only grunts in return.

We collectively turn as Hades enters from his bedroom. The judges make to stand, but my father shakes his head and encourages them to stay put. "There is no need for frivolous manners at a time like this." I look around the room and notice the others with raised brows and questioning looks on their faces.

"What news, sire?" Rhadamanthus cuts to the business at hand. I've always liked his forthrightness.

"I sent inquiries and have finally received a missive from the Land of the Living. It doesn't look good."

Castor's hand flexes on my shoulder, steadying me for the news I've known was coming.

"What's causing the influx of souls then? And, more importantly, how do we stop it?" Minos's voice rumbles the room as though he were a raging bull.

Hades rubs his chin thoughtfully, and in that moment, I finally notice how drawn and haggard he appears. This ordeal has taken a toll on him, on all of the judges. They're weary, run ragged by the long hours and never-ending line that, even now, stretches beyond the Archeron River.

"According to my information, a breed of giants now roams the Land of the Living. They're terrorizing—slaughtering—the humans and threatening the Olympians by throwing boulders and burning oak trees at the gates of Mount Olympus as they attempt to take the castle there."

Burning oaks, just like in my visions. I stiffen, but Castor's hand moves from my shoulder to my arm, caressing it gently and bringing a sense of calm to my nerves.

"How can we help?" My husband's voice echoes my thoughts.

"I must stay here and oversee the judging of the souls, so I need you and Hecate to travel to the Land of the Living and meet with Athena. See what she needs and help her find a way to neutralize the threat."

I glance behind me at Castor. A gleam of something flashes in his eyes. I'm sure he's eager to get back to the Land of the Living, back to fighting and soldiering after spending so long in the Underworld, but I cannot muster the excitement he feels at returning to Mount Olympus. Not when my gut tells me these giants will not be dealt with so easily.

As I turn back toward the judges and my father, I meet Rhadamanthus's gaze. The uncertainty and worry I see in his eyes surely matches my own. I gulp down my fears and stand, plastering a smile on my face. "We'd be happy to travel to Mount Olympus, Father."

· · • • · • • · • · ·

"Why are you so quiet, wife? It's unlike you, especially after imbibing so many cups of Persephone's famous pomegranate-flavored wine." Castor pulls me toward him and sweeps my hair behind my back as his fingers trail along my neck. Shivers of pleasure break out along my skin, but the heat I should feel at my husband's touch has gone cold for the night.

I flick my gaze through the window to the domineering oak tree in the distance, its branches wavering on the crisp evening breeze. The image of it bursting into flames flits through my mind, and I swallow the lump that's formed in my throat at the memory.

"Hecate?" Castor's voice breaks through, and I snap my eyes up to his. A frown pulls at his mouth.

I leave the warmth of his arms and move into the bedroom, where I pull a woven bag from under the bed. I turn to open a chest of clothing and run into Castor's broad midsection.

"Hecate, what is wrong? Are you not eager for this journey? Have we not been planning for this invasion—this very moment—since we returned to the Underworld?"

I eye him warily, my eyes going blurry with unshed tears. "Eager? For war? No, Castor, I'm not eager for this. I'm not a soldier, and I am not excited about this journey to Mount Olympus."

He purses his lips as a furrow wrinkles his brow. "You've prophesied this war for years, wife. Aren't you ready to finally see it through?"

I press my palms to my eyes and inhale deeply, my emotions running amok. The wisp of a migraine throbs at the base of my skull, and I sink to the bed. Tightness spreads through my chest, and I struggle to breathe. My lungs feel as though they're devoid of air. I gasp, my mouth gaping like a baby bird's. "Cas, I-I can't breathe!" My body rebels against me, and a sob escapes from my throat. Adrenaline courses through my veins, and I begin to tremble.

"Shh, sweetheart." He drops to his knees and runs his calloused fingers through my hair and down my arm. "Open your eyes and focus on me."

I follow his command and, though my vision is blurred, I blink up at him.

"Inhale as I count to five, and then exhale as I count from six to ten."

Still struggling to breathe, I nod. My chin quivers and my teeth chatter loudly in the quiet hut.

He takes my hands in his and counts. "One."

I part my lips and inhale.

"Two. Three."

Our eyes locked, my chest expands.

"Four."

My lungs reach their peak capacity, and I hold the air.

"Five. Now you're going to exhale as I count to ten," he reminds me. "Six."

My lips part, and I release the breath.

"Seven. Eight."

My chest shrinks and the tightness in my chest starts to abate.

"Nine."

Empty, my shoulders sag as my body stills.

"Ten," he whispers as his thumbs caress circles on the underside of my wrists.

My body feels as though it's been through a battle. Everything aches and my face feels puffy and swollen. The migraine at the base of my skull has spread to the back of my eyes.

"Keep inhaling for five and exhaling for five." Castor joins me on the bed, and I immediately crumple against him, my head landing in his lap. "Talk to me, my love. Tell me what you're thinking. If you keep this all bottled up inside like one of your potions, it's bound to bubble up and break you."

"I used to think nothing could break me," I whisper, my eyes closed as Castor traces my features. He runs his finger over my forehead, down past my temple, and around my cheekbones. He follows the laugh lines that have deepened in the years we've spent together in the Underworld and curls under my lip and back up over my chin. The movement calms me, and I can finally breathe deeply as I continue counting in my head.

"Nothing can break you, my Titan witch. You are the strongest person I know."

A small chuckle escapes from my mouth, and my eyes flick open in surprise. "I used to be stronger."

"What's changed?"

"I found you."

His face falls. A softness creeps into his eyes, and the apple on his neck bobs as he swallows. "Hecate . . ." My name is a whisper on his breath. We lean into each other—he bends and I rise—until our mouths meet in the middle.

As our tongues collide, and I wrap my arms around his neck, I know that what I said is true. Finding him, and then losing him, made me weaker. It showed me, even for a brief moment, what a life without love, without him, would feel like. It's a life I refuse to accept, no matter the price I have to pay.

POLLUX

"Oh, Orphne." A moan escapes from Desy's lips as we walk in the door of the small hut. "I love what you've done with the place since I was here last!"

Looking around at the cozy cottage, I would have to agree with Desy's assessment. Orphne has decorated her abode in bright fabrics that shimmer against the hearth's light. The teal and white paint on the walls remind me of Sparta's beautiful oceanic views.

My broad shoulders barely fit through the tiny doorway, and the inside isn't much bigger, which means we're all three nearly sitting atop one another on the lone bed, the one piece of furniture in the cottage. Desy giggles absently to herself and almost falls off, but I'm able to catch her. I pull her toward me.

"I'm a bit drunk off the melogions, Pollux." She attempts to whisper as she lies across my lap, but instead nearly shouts in my face. The smell of the fruity nectar on her breath invites me in for a taste, but it feels wrong to take advantage of someone this intoxicated.

I am a gentleman, I mentally remind myself over and over.

"That doesn't mean we can't have a little fun, Prince." As if she can read my thoughts, Orphne crawls on her hands and knees over to us, her rounded ass swaying behind her as the shadowy material of her dress shifts away, exposing her entirely. Her gaze is sultry, and as she licks her lips, her small breasts pop through the fog.

"He likes it," Desy adds as she slides her hand down to my crotch. My lip trembles at her touch. She gasps, her eyes widening, as my hardness twitches against her hand. "He really likes it, Orphne." Desy palms my cock through the thin fabric as Orphne presses her chest against my back and runs her hands through my hair. The shadows tangle around my throat.

"Do you like it, Prince?"

I hum in assent.

"Tell me," Orphne whispers in my ear. Then she glides her tongue in, licking the whorl and biting me gently.

"Yes, I like it. Very much," I hiss in agreement. Orphne pulls my shirt over my head and tosses it on the floor. She runs her long nails down my back, and a shiver of desire goes straight to my cock. I slide my hand down Desy's spine and cup her ass as she continues to grip me.

"You're making my mouth water, Pollux," Desy groans, releasing my hardened length. She rises on her knees to straddle me and presses against my chest. Her tits are at eye level. I could stare at them for hours, and now *my* mouth is watering as I imagine running my tongue over the sun-kissed skin. Licking the salty sweat from her cleavage. I palm her ass—she's got an amazing one—and pull her against my cock. The friction from my pants and the sensation of her breasts flattened against my bare chest has me panting. Orphne, not to be left out, strips off her shadowy top and wraps it around my eyes. The foggy fabric steals my vision.

"Let's have a little fun with him, Desy," Orphne's sultry voice comes from behind.

While I don't love the idea of not being able to watch what's happening around me, my other senses heighten with the loss of my sight. Each girlish giggle sparks an infinite number of images in my head. What they might be doing. What they might be doing to *each other*. I feel Desy raise her arms and shimmy out of her dress. It lands next to my lap in a heap just as something soft and round is pushed against my lips.

"Lick her," Orphne whispers in my ear, and I obediently open my mouth and pull Desy's nipple in, flicking my tongue over the tightening bud. My hands splay up her back, pulling her closer. She inhales sharply and writhes against my cock.

The mattress dips as Orphne sits next to me. She guides my hand to her mouth and inserts a finger, which she licks and sucks. I run the fingers of my other hand through Desy's hair. She leans into my neck and plants kisses along my jaw. I want nothing more than to whip off this blindfold, flip her over, and drive into her. My mind is mad with desire for Desy. Orphne's just the icing on the cake.

Desy emits a high-pitched moan just as a loud knock stops all three of us, but it's the voice outside that has me seeing red through the darkness of the fog.

"Pollux! Open up!" What the fuck is Castor doing here?

"How did he know where to find you?" Desy hisses as I rip off the blindfold. The shadows dissipate. Desy's nostrils flare. The whites of her eyes the only thing I see. I can't imagine telling her that twins have odd ways of communicating, so instead I just shrug.

"Maybe he's come to join us?" Orphne suggests with a giggle. But I know better, and as I reach for my shirt, the door shatters off its hinges.

"What the fuck did you do that for?" Orphne screams at my brother as her hands cover her bare breasts.

He rolls his eyes, ignoring her completely. "Pollux. Desy. Let's go." He doesn't look surprised to find us together, nor does he seem at all taken aback by the rumpled bedding or topless Orphne.

Chastised and slightly embarrassed, I gulp down my anger and move to stand beside him. Like the rebuked dog that I am, I won't bark or bite. I fall in line. Desy, on the other hand, puts her hands on her hips and squints at Castor. "I'm not leaving." Even with her heavy breasts on full display, her gown askew and lip tint smeared, she glares daggers at my brother. I fight a smirk and watch with besotted amusement.

"Yes you are. Something's come up. Persephone expects you back at the castle. It's time to go." Castor clenches his fists at his side. He's definitely mad but trying his best to control his anger.

Desy snorts and flips her hair over her shoulder. "Tell my sister I'll return in the morning." She smirks at Orphne, whose wide eyes bounce back and forth between the two. "When I'm finished here."

Castor's anger flares to life, but before he can react, I step across the tiny hut and hoist Desy over my shoulder like a sack of grain. I won't allow my twin to flounder or lose this battle. "Put me down!" she screeches as she flails, her arms pummeling my back. I restrain her legs before she lands a kick to my balls.

Ignoring her cries of frustration, I follow a chuckling Castor through the missing door.

"Who's going to fix my door?" Orphne shouts after us.

"I'm sure one of your other lovers can help you out," Castor replies as we step into the darkness.

• • • • • • • • • • •

After carrying an angry—and topless—Desy the entire way from the village to the castle, my back aches with the beating she rained down on me. There's nothing that kills sexual tension and a good time like a woman who threatens to shove her foot up your ass if you don't put her down. I quickly deposit her in the care of Selene, Persephone's most trusted handmaiden, and then Castor and I make a hasty retreat to the kitchen for a nightcap.

"You're telling me that an actual race of giants has overtaken the area around Mount Olympus and are threatening the Olympian gods?" The entire tale sounded ridiculous the moment it left Castor's mouth, but his stiff posture and rigid jaw tell me he's serious.

"They're not just threatening the Olympians, Pol. You saw the line of souls still waiting at the gates. These giants are hurting people. *Our* people. The people of Sparta." He pours a dram of something strong and slings it back without flinching. I hold the drink up to my nose and sniff, the smell burning my eyes. I almost retch, but gulp it down with a shudder. My brother always could drink me under the table.

"I'll help in any way that I can. What does Hades suggest we do?"

"The message that arrived today begs for help from the Underworld, but with the influx of souls, Hades is needed here. So we will head to Mount Olympus and offer any support we can." He rinses the glasses in a bucket of soapy water and dries them off.

While I'm sad to leave the Underworld so quickly, and the ladies I'd certainly hoped to spend more time with, I nod in agreement. A soldier's job is never done. "I'll be ready to depart in the morning, unless you need me sooner? My blade could use a good polish, but perhaps that could wait if you're hoping to depart—"

Castor doesn't meet my eyes as he returns the glasses to their places before interrupting me. "When I said *we*, I meant Hecate and me. You won't be coming to Mount Olympus, Pollux."

"Oh." Gulping down the disappointment, I clear my throat and glance around at the opulent kitchen. "So what purpose do I serve in all this, brother?" I try to make my voice light and airy—effortless—when deep inside I feel as useless as I did in Sparta.

Inhaling deeply and placing his hands on his hips, Castor pauses for a moment. Looks at the ground. Sighs heavily and squeezes his eyes closed.

"I'll do anything to help. You know this. Just tell me what I can do—how I can serve a purpose here."

He slowly inhales again and releases the air through pursed lips. Then finally makes eye contact. "We need you to take Desy back to Demeter."

"What?" Of all the useless tasks I've been asked to do as a soldier, escorting a spoiled nymph back to her evil mother has to be the winner. "I'm a trained soldier, Castor. I can fight. I can lead. I can be of assistance in a million different ways."

"I know," Castor responds, running his hands through his short silvery hair. It's the only difference between the two of us. That and he's actually a productive and revered member of the Underworld. "Unfortunately, Persephone really needs someone to see her sister home safely, and Hades will deny his queen nothing."

"So why can't *you* take her?"

Castor's eyes harden and his face turns red. "My task, brother, is to assist my *wife* safely to Mount Olympus as an emissary to the Underworld."

"Psh." I roll my eyes. "Everyone knows Hecate can travel safely without you by her side." As soon as the words leave my mouth, I know I've fucked up, especially when Castor's fist connects with my jaw.

"Watch what you imply about my relationship, Pollux. We wouldn't want to discuss your shortcomings, now would we?" He eyes me darkly, wringing his hand as I rub my jaw.

Berated and feeling like a complete ass, I decide to be the bigger man. I hold my forearm out and Castor grasps it in forgiveness. "I'm sorry. That was uncalled for. Your wife is more powerful than you, but I shouldn't have thrown it in your face. I understand why she'd want you with her instead of me anyway."

"What's that supposed to mean?"

Before I can restrain myself, the emotions breach the dam I've constructed to keep myself in check. "It means nobody wants me around, Castor. Not Helen. Not Hecate. Not even you. Everyone has moved on and found a purpose, but mine still remains up in the air. Ever since Father—"

"I know, brother," Castor says as he leans against the counter. "I miss him just as much as you do." He's quiet for a moment, likely remembering all the times we spent with our *pater* hunting, training, and riding. Finally, he exhales loudly. "Pol, you're my brother and my best friend. And you have a place here in the Underworld with us when all this settles down." He claps me on the back as he moves past me toward the kitchen doorway. "And as for a purpose? Well, getting Desy home to Demeter is a pretty important purpose, especially if you have to carry her the whole way there like you did tonight." He chuckles and blows out the remaining candle, leaving me alone in the darkened room. With only my thoughts and the empty kitchen for companionship.

HECATE

The courtyard is full of courtiers wishing to see us off to the Land of the Living. Noticeably absent, though, are Hades, Rhadamanthus, Minos, and Aeacus. With the line extending as far as the eye can see, their never-ending duties judging the souls keep them from attending our send off. My mouth is too dry, and I reach for the wine carafe in my saddlebag, taking a nourishing swig.

"It's never too early for a little nip, is it sister?" Pollux eyes me conspiratorially with a slight smirk. Against my better judgment, I pass him the skin. He makes to take a drink, but lips flattened and brow furrowed, he shakes his head and passes it back to me.

I tuck the carafe back in the saddlebag and glare daggers at the castle door.

"What's the hold up?" Castor hollers at the guard on duty.

"We're awaiting the queen and her sister, sir."

Castor, Pollux, and I exchange knowing glances just as the door opens and Selene slinks out, her face firmly set. She stomps over to us, bypassing her usual *good morning* to the guard who closes the door behind her. We circle our horses as she approaches.

"I've never met such a-a"—she pauses, and I notice identical knowing smirks on Castor's and Pollux's faces—"spoiled brat!"

My husband and his twin burst into laughter while Selene's face morphs into outrage.

"What do you mean?" I quickly dismount and toss my reins to Castor, who continues to cackle with glee.

"She's refusing to leave, the *paidáki*!"

I suppress my own giggle and school my features. "You're not wrong about her being a disrespectful child, Selene. But can't Persephone do something?"

"The queen refuses to hold her sister accountable for her actions. She's as bad as Demeter, allowing the nymph to behave however she chooses. She tasked me with getting Despoena packed and out the door, but I've been locked out! What am I to do?"

Seeing my stand-in mother distraught lights a fire in my belly, and before I know what's happening, I'm now the one stomping through the courtyard.

Raising my palm as I mutter a curse under my breath, the heavy wooden door flies off its hinges and shatters into pieces.

"Oh fuck," I hear Pollux behind me, his voice high-pitched with glee.

"Hecate, no!"

I glance backward as Castor dismounts and runs after me, but I continue my path into the castle. Turning into the stairwell, I run up the steps two at a time and then follow the well-trodden passage to the guest chambers. I arrive just as Castor yanks my arm back, his chest heaving with exertion.

"Don't get involved," he warns, his tone dropping to a hiss.

"I'll not have Selene disrespected in her own home. Someone needs to teach this girl a lesson on manners." I turn toward the locked door, press my hand to the wood grain, and closing my eyes, recite a quick spell. "*Xekleidóste to frágma.*" The lock clicks and the door swings open.

Raising a brow at Castor, I sweep in, my eyes settling on the covered lump on the bed. I grit my teeth and advance, reminding myself to temper my anger else we have another soul to deal with. I fling the fur-lined covers off Despoena, only to find a bundle of pillows instead.

The growl of anger simmers in my belly and eventually bursts forth from my mouth in a howl of rage.

"I'll find her," Castor responds, turning and running down the hallway. My fists clenched, I turn the opposite way, toward Persephone's chambers.

I storm past the guest rooms and finally enter the royal family wing. I stop abruptly at my childhood bedroom. The anger in my blood is already threatening to boil over. Pressing my palm to the door, I begin to recite the unlocking spell before realizing that the door is already ajar. It creaks open, and I find Persephone sitting on my old bed, a worn and ratty blanket clutched in her hands.

"What are you doing in here?" I ask incredulously.

She turns away from me, her face pointed to the window. "I was looking for Desy. She can't be found." I hear the tremble in her voice and step through the doorway.

"She's clearly not in here," I mutter under my breath.

"No, the door was locked."

"Oh . . ." I bite my lip, confused about how to proceed with an obviously upset Persephone. We've never been close, especially now that I've become an adviser to Hades. Even when I was a child, when I was Melinoe, she was gone so often, and for such long periods of time, that we both held ourselves aloof.

She pulls the worn fabric through her fingers. "I found this in Demeter's things while I was in the Land of the Living."

"What is it?" I frown and wrinkle my nose, wondering at the importance of a tattered old blanket.

"It was yours. Or rather, it was Melinoe's." My stomach drops.

"I see." I edge toward the bed and tentatively sit on the corner, reaching my hand out. She hands it over and I examine the wrap, the fabric now thin and musty.

"I wanted a child so badly, Hecate." She juts her chin toward the window, refusing to turn to me. "So badly, I would've done anything to make it happen."

"I remember." I fold the remains of the blanket and set it between us on the bed.

"Do you?"

I nod my head. "You came to my hut daily for a potion. I was waiting for you when . . ." I don't finish the sentence. *When Zeus arrived.*

She winces, her fists clenching in her lap. A silence falls over us, and I itch to get up and continue looking for Despoena, to return to preparing for the journey to the Land of the Living.

She tilts her chin toward the window. "I suppose the souls out there are my children now."

My throat tightens, and instinctively, I reach for her hand, pulling it to my chest. "Persephone, you helped raise me to become who I am today." While not completely true, the lie flows off my tongue, if only to ease her sadness.

She finally meets my gaze, her eyes shining pools of tears. "I wish that were true, Hecate, but we both know it's not. I knew from the first time I gazed on Melinoe's tiny infant face that something wasn't right, that this baby wasn't really mine."

My muscles tense, and I pull my hand back. "So why didn't you ever tell me the truth? All those years I believed there was something wrong with me, that I was worthless because I had no magic and my own mother didn't love me."

"I thought it was better to keep up the ruse, that maybe if I lied to myself long enough, it would come true. That you would stay my Melinoe forever."

Disgust rolls over me and I stand, needing to put space between us. "You lied about so much, Persephone. Who my father was. Who I was." I shake my head at her, my lip curling.

"You don't understand, Hecate. All I ever wanted was to escape the confines of my overbearing mother. But when I made my choice to marry Hades, it was a scandal. I couldn't let all those people know the life I chose was ruined, a complete lie."

"So you lied to me instead?"

"Yes." As quickly as the words leave her mouth, her face reddens as she finally admits the truth.

My throat burns, and I feel the blood drain from my face as my fingers tingle. I look up at the ceiling and then around at my childhood bedroom, now tainted by Persephone's words. I turn toward the door.

"Hecate, I didn't mean—"

"I need to find Despoena so we can be on our way," I state flatly. I don't even bother to close the door behind me as I flee from the room, the tingle of anger spreading all over my body.

POLLUX

Hecate dismounts from her horse and, after tossing the reins to Castor, proceeds to situate herself in the mouth of a dark cave. Raising her arms, she closes her eyes and loudly recites the spell to unlock the entrance to the Land of the Living.

"*Anoixe tin pórta. Fos anamméno. Xekleidóste tin pórta. Steílte to fos.*" She throws her head back, the last word dying on her breath. Ever since she stomped out of the castle, Castor following with a sullen Desy in his wake, Hecate's been unusually quiet. Her face, though, says it all. Even from this distance, I can see her jaw tightening as she grinds her teeth.

Desy peeks out from the carriage window, her lip curled in disgust. When she catches me looking, she flings the curtain closed.

"What's her problem?" I ask Castor, whose eyes haven't left Hecate since we departed.

"I'm not sure. She's been having migraines more frequently. I'm sure the stress of this mission isn't helping."

I shake my head. "Not Hecate. What's wrong with Desy?" I clarify. He finally breaks his fixation on his wife and meets my eyes.

"Where do I begin with that one?" He flicks his gaze to the carriage and rolls his eyes. "She doesn't want to return to the Land of the Living. I found her cavorting with one of Hades's guards."

I snap my head in the direction of the carriage, my lips pressed firmly together. "Sh-She was doing what?" My voice rises an octave, and my twin crinkles his brow as his gaze hardens. Something tightens in my chest. Is it anger? Jealousy? I rub my sternum. Clear my throat and look away from my brother's silent and judging expression. Why wouldn't she be interested in a soldier in Hades's guard? After all, I've nothing to offer her. My chest pain increases, and I wince.

"We're clear to enter the Land of the Living." Hecate returns to our side. "Do you have a chest pain, Pollux?" Worry touches her features.

"No, just a little indigestion. Must be from something I ate earlier," I lie. She narrows her eyes, and I'm certain I've been caught fibbing to the all-knowing witch, but she abruptly turns and makes her way toward the carriage.

She flings open the door, which slams against the side of the wagon. "It's time, Despoena." Hecate's tone brooks no disagreement, but to nobody's surprise, Desy refuses to leave the carriage.

"I'm not going." From my vantage point, I see a sandal-clad foot cross over a suntanned leg, the chiton riding up enough to expose her sleek calf. I can only imagine that she's crossed her arms over her ample chest and has an adorable frown touching her kissable lips.

The tightness returns to my chest and I gasp. What the fuck am I thinking, imagining Desy's tits and mouth? She's clearly unstable and likely to be a burr in my side as I escort her to Demeter's home, yet I can't stop thinking about her.

"You're going. Now get out of the fucking carriage, or I'll drag you out myself." Hecate's fingers brighten, as though her digits were made of candles.

"I can stay and help. You can't make me return to Demeter! I won't go!" The carriage jostles as Hecate climbs inside.

"Fuck, this can't be good," I mutter under my breath to Castor.

"I think I'd rather deal with the giants terrorizing Mount Olympus than that one," Castor replies as he quirks an eyebrow at me.

I huff in annoyance, wondering how I'm supposed to get this wild creature back home with both of us in one piece.

• • • • • • • • • • •

"Quit touching me," Desy snarls as she whips her head around, smacking me in the face with her hair.

I release the reins from one hand and clear the strands from my mouth. "I'd let you take control of the horse, but as you've no idea where we're headed . . ." The retort falls flat as Desy rips the reins from my other hand and flicks her wrist. My body lurches as our horse takes off at a trot, our bodies fluidly flowing with the increased gait. My chest rubs against her back, the friction giving way to a delicious heat that spreads straight to my cock. She squeezes her thighs around the saddle and her ass tightens, the horse's trot turning into a full gallop. I secure my hold around her waist, driving my pelvis into her backside.

"Where are you taking us?" I inquire lazily. I'm enjoying the trip too much to care that we've left Hecate and Castor behind.

"Just enjoy the ride, Prince."

I smirk and thrust my hardened length into her ass. "Already am, *mikrí nýmfi*, as you can surely tell."

"Funny." She turns slightly, the side of her mouth quirking at the corner. "I can't feel a thing."

I growl in frustration and grab the reins from her hands, yanking the horse to a stop. Quickly dismounting, I pull Desy from atop the beast, a yelp breaking free from her surprised face.

"Put me down!"

I'm more than happy to oblige and plunk her to her feet in front of me. I tower over her, and as she glares up at me, I'm overcome with pure lust—a lust that sweeps through my body and lights it on fire.

Her emerald-green eyes stare up at me through thick lashes, and I completely lose control. We both reach for one another at the same time. As she slams her full lips into mine, I grab her around the hips and haul her up my body, caressing her round backside. She wraps her legs around my waist. The sweetest sigh of pleasure escapes from her mouth, and as I hold onto her ass with one hand, I bring the other up into her hair, fisting the tangles as my tongue parts the seam of her lips.

We feast on each other, tasting and sucking until we're both breathless.

She pulls away slowly, reluctance flashing in her eyes. She blinks and then swallows, her throat begging to be licked. "Wait here. I want to show you something." I lower her to the ground, feeling every inch of her body creep along mine. She bites her lip as she walks backward into a nearby copse of trees. "Stay right there." She then turns around and, hips swaying, disappears into the shadowy tree line. "I'll be right back," her voice calls from within the darkness.

I rub my chin and smile to myself. Fuck, but this one is different from the others. She drives me wild, and as I continue to watch the trees, waiting for her to reappear, I adjust myself in my leathers. My cock throbs with need, and an uncomfortable heaviness settles in my balls. I'm not used to going this long without female companionship. My foot taps the hardened ground impatiently.

Behind me, the horse blows out a breath and releases a stream of urine. Frowning, I take the reins and move the both of us a few paces away to dry ground. I keep my eyes trained on the spot where Desy disappeared. The horse leans down and pulls at a few weeds, his teeth crunching contentedly as the sun beats down on us.

"Desy?" I call out and then crane my neck to listen. What could be taking so long?

A bird flies overhead, its caw startling me. I watch it fly into the trees, disappearing within the foliage.

"De-sy?" This time I cup my hand to my mouth, elongating the syllables of her name.

Nothing.

Sighing, I click my tongue and tug on the reins, the horse chuffing irritably at leaving the weed patch behind. I dawdle, hoping that Desy will reappear.

A noise from the road stops me in my tracks. The horse's ears perk up. He's heard it too. I quickly mount up and turn us toward the beaten path, my breath quickening as my heart rate increases. The beating in my chest matches the thoughts running through my head.

Where has Desy gone?

Was she taken by bandits?

Is she hurt?

I'm going to kill someone for this.

The last one gives me pause, and as much as I want to close my eyes and calm myself down, I keep my gaze trained on the road as the sound of hooves grows louder. A set of riders appears over the hill and my breath catches in my throat.

Hecate and Castor.

Thank goodness I think, forcibly blowing out the breath I'd been holding.

My eyes widen as I realize that, without Desy, Hecate's going to be angry.

Very angry.

HECATE

"You must be delirious from the sun, Pollux." I pull a rag from my saddlebag and dip it into the skin of water on my hip. I attempt to dab the cool cloth onto his forehead, but he pushes me away.

"I know what I saw, Hecate. Desy went past the tree line into the forest just over there." He points into the distance, except there are no trees. No forest. No shadows. Instead, an area of shrubland dotted with lavender, sage, wild thyme, and stunted holly oaks glares back at us. Disappearing among such scrubby flora would be nearly impossible.

I bite my lip and furrow my brow, holding out the cool cloth to Pollux. He shakes his head, so I fold and return it to the satchel. "Despoena has always remained very tight-lipped about any abilities she had. I spent my childhood as Melinoe convinced that we were alike—two powerless young girls." I squint into the distance and release a heavy sigh, followed by a small chuckle.

"What's so humorous?" Pollux's gaze narrows at me, but the hilarity of the moment hits me like a strike of lightning, and I double over with glee as the laughter racks my body. "Hecate, are you laughing at me?"

I straighten up and attempt to take a deep breath to calm the giggles, but the tears begin to flow instead as the mirth courses through my veins. I haven't laughed like this in days, and it feels good to smile, to release the tension I've felt daily since the meeting with Hades and his generals.

"Why are you laughing at me, sister?" Pollux places both hands on his hips and glares at me, his lip curling in anger.

"I-I'm not laughing at *you*, Pol," I respond as I come down from the high. "I'm laughing that Despoena would rather run away than return to her mother Demeter. It's the same for Persephone. Everyone assumes she was abducted by Hades, but—"

"But anyone who's met them knows they're completely in love," Castor completes my thought, his eyes falling warmly on me. I reach out for him, taking his hand in my own, and rub my thumb over his palm.

"Desy doesn't want to return to her mother," Pollux repeats. "And all this time I thought she was running from my company."

I snort. "That could also be it, but I truly believe she'd do anything to get out of Demeter's clutches."

"Even run away." Pollux grins, nodding his head. He stands a bit taller, puffing out his chest. The realization that she wasn't running from him means something, and I narrow my eyes at him.

"You haven't fallen for her, have you, Pollux?" I stick my pointer finger directly into his chest, shoving it against his leather tunic. Castor clears his throat behind me, and I turn, my vision flaming red as my fingers tingle. "I told you to warn him away from her!"

My husband holds up his hands in defeat, a look of surprise on his face. "I did, but you know Pollux. He never listens to anyone!"

Turning back to my traitorous brother-in-law, I assess him through shrewd eyes. "You haven't been with her, have you?"

He snorts and looks everywhere but at me.

"Have you?" I ask again, louder.

"Of course not," he responds with a shrug. "Not like she hasn't tried." I see the cocky look he passes Castor over my head.

"Pollux, do you know what happens if you're with a nymph?"

The knot in his throat bobs as he swallows heavily, his smile falling as the color drains from his face. "No. What happens?"

"They entrap your heart and mind. You belong to them; you live to serve them in all things."

He smirks wickedly. "That doesn't sound so bad, Hecate."

I shake my head, trying to impart the seriousness of the situation. "Pollux, this isn't one of your pranks or a game. If Despoena successfully seduces you, you're no longer your own man. You belong to her." I fold my arms and lean back, waiting for him to realize how close he's come to destroying his life.

His mouth gapes like a fish out of water, and I'm finally satisfied that he understands the seriousness of the situation. "So what the fuck am I supposed to do now? Just let her go and be glad that I'm not ensnared in her evil sexual clutches?"

I shake my head. "No, we have to find her and return her to Demeter. But once you've made sure she's back with her overbearing mother, you hightail it out of there, Pol."

He nods silently, a look of shock still etched in his features. "So where could she have gone?"

· · · · ● · ● · · ·

"What do you mean, she's with Menelaus's men?" Pollux's anger emanates from his pores, smelling of charcoal and burned wood. I crinkle my nose even as my eyes widen in surprise. I'm normally the one with the uncontrolled fiery passion.

"Would you like me to repeat the spell and check again?" I tap my foot impatiently as I cross my arms over my chest.

"That won't be necessary. We must hurry." Pollux climbs atop his mount with an ease only seen in his twin. I bite my lip and press down a smile as Castor hoists me onto our shared horse. Pegasus was thankfully returned to me when

Athena became reigning queen of Mount Olympus, and his presence on our journey is a boon.

Pollux clicks his tongue and we take off, riding with a breeze at our backs. "I thought Menelaus was a good king and husband to Helen, brother," Castor shouts from behind me. I hold the reins tightly and squeeze my thighs as the white beast leaps effortlessly over a fallen log.

"Whatever gave you that idea?" Pollux pulls away from us, his pace bordering on dangerous for both him and his horse.

"Helen's letters always speak so highly of him."

Pollux throws his head back and laughs, the sarcastic mirth hitting us like a slap to the face.

I would twist in the saddle to assess Castor's features, but I'd surely fall and break my neck. "So what's he really like then?" Pollux doesn't answer right away, and I'm sure my question's gone unheard.

He suddenly pulls on the reins and calls, "Whoa!" We nearly collide with him, but Castor's expert horsemanship saves us as he reins in Pegasus. The horse shakes his head angrily at the leather straps pulling against his mouth.

"Sorry, sweetness," I whisper as I lean into his neck and pat lovingly.

"Why don't I ever get those kinds of strokes from you, wife?" Castor mutters from behind me.

I turn, my mischievous smile matching the fire in my belly. "Because you prefer it rough, my love."

He chortles, but a snort of disgust from our companion cools our lust for one another. "If you two are done?"

I feel a blush creep up my neck, surely matching Castor's reddened cheeks, and we nod at Pollux.

"Menelaus is anything but faithful to our dear sister, but it's not just that that bothers me. He'll fuck any pretty little thing, throwing it in Helen's face as he parades his most recent paramour about the court."

"And Helen accepts this behavior from her consort?" My voice is incredulous as I recall all the growth Helen went through to become the queen she is today.

"He's no longer just her consort. He's padded the court with his supporters, who named him king in his own right. Our Helen no longer has any real power. She's reverted to her childish nature of surrounding herself with pretty frivolous things, allowing her husband to run Sparta while she maintains her reputation as 'the most beautiful.'"

Castor's lips thin, and I feel his body stiffen in anger. "We must ensure Desy is safe from Menelaus. We don't need to add an additional war with Demeter and Persephone; our focus must remain on returning Desy to her home and then traveling to Mount Olympus. Then we can deal with Menelaus and Helen."

"Then there's no time to waste." I snap my fingers and wings spring forth from the back of Pegasus and Pollux's horse. Pegasus whinnies happily at the return of his wings. Pollux's horse, however, begins to buck wildly, as though to shake the new appendages from his back.

"Whoa now." Pollux strokes the horse's neck and eyes me angrily. "You could've warned me, Hecate."

"Where's the fun in that?" I ask innocently. "They won't fly with the extra weight, but the wings will assist us in setting the pace we need to arrive quickly. Follow us." I kick my heels into Pegasus, who stretches his wings and glides gracefully along the path. His hooves hardly touch the hardened earth, making the ride smoother and less painful for all.

Castor stretches and turns in the saddle. "Pol is doing better than I thought," he tells me. I, too, turn and hold in a laugh as Pollux's horse flaps his wings awkwardly, smacking Pollux in the side of the head.

"Hm, I suppose it could be worse." Returning my gaze forward, I click my tongue and Pegasus speeds up, taking us closer to Menelaus and Despoena.

POLLUX

"Thank the gods!" I cry as Sparta comes into view. My head is throbbing, and I've bitten my tongue at least a dozen times as this newly winged beast thrashed his way to our destination.

I catch up to Hecate and Castor, who've stopped on a hill overlooking the city. As my horse and I approach, Hecate flicks her wrist and the wings disappear. My mount neighs in gratitude while their white creature chuffs in frustration.

"I know, sweetness. I'll put them back when it's time to depart for Olympus," Hecate coos into her horse's ear. In any other situation, I'd poke fun at her baby voice, but now's not the time.

We gallop down the hill and enter the castle proper with a nod from the guards at the gate. "Remember," Castor voices sternly, his gaze boring into mine, "we're meant to spend the night here before splitting up and going our separate ways. You need to keep cordial relations with Helen's husband, despite your personal feelings."

I grind my teeth, hating that I'll have to put on my princely mask for the evening. But if it gets Desy safely away from that brute and keeps our focus on the true war, I can control my emotions. We dismount, handing our horses to the stable boys, and enter the palace.

"Please let the queen know we've arrived," Castor directs the nearest servant. I narrow my eyes, recognizing the bastard who abandoned me in Taenarus. My former body servant.

"Be quick about it," I add, just to be a prick. The servant's eyes go cold, but he bows nonetheless and departs.

A second servant takes us to our quarters. The rooms Castor and I used for years have now been turned into guest housing, but luckily, they still adjoin with a door. I chuckle inwardly as Hecate tests the sliding bar across the wooden frame.

Helen appears, a diaphanous chiton trailing delicately behind her sandal-clad feet. She squeals in delight and rushes straight toward Hecate, the two embracing over Helen's enlarged belly. Hecate pulls away and coos over the bump, Helen blushing as she bites her lip. Castor slides in for a hug. It's a wonderful reunion, to be sure.

"Ahem," I cough loudly as I glare at my family. Helen's smile falters, but she reaches out her arms nonetheless, and I am thusly wrapped in her warmth. She pats my back affectionately before pulling away, a look of consternation crinkling her brow.

"What are you doing out of bed?" I inquire as my eyes dip to her belly.

"I was made aware that your . . . friend . . . was taken captive by Menelaus's men earlier this afternoon. I've had to deal with your mess once again." Helen eyes me warily, but I sigh with relief.

"Despoena is actually Demeter's daughter and Persephone's sister. Pollux has been tasked with returning her home while Castor and I journey to Olympus." I'm grateful for Hecate's emotionless explanation, as I feel my face heating as my sister eyes me suspiciously.

"She attempted to disarm one of the guards and steal his blade and horse, you know."

"Where is she?" I demand. If Menelaus has touched her, I'll have his head.

"She's resting in the room across the hall. When they discovered who she was, we certainly didn't want to anger the goddess of the harvest or her mysterious daughter."

"As an emissary to the Underworld, I can assure you that Persephone and Hades both appreciate your care and discretion, Helen." Hecate diffuses the situation effortlessly and, as she pulls a jar from the pouch at her waist and hands it to my sister with instructions on applying it to avoid stretch marks, I tune everything else out.

More than anything, I need to speak with Desy.

· · · · ●·●· ● · · ·

Rather than sit around catching up with my family, I angrily stalk across the hall, fighting the urge to throw open the closed door. Instead, I take a fortifying breath, count to five, and gently turn the knob. The curtains are drawn, shutting out the fading early evening sun, and a small form is buried under the furs on the bed. Candles twinkle from the sconces, casting an eerie glow about the chamber.

Thinking Desy is asleep and that I'll leave her to rest, I start to turn and see my way out when a sniffle stops me in my tracks. I pause, listening, as a sob disrupts the silence.

"Desy?" I close the door behind me and pad softly to the edge of the bed.

"Leave me, Pollux." I'm surprised she could tell it was me. Surprised and touched, actually.

I clear my throat and perch on the bed. She keeps her back to me, but I speak my mind, nonetheless. "You see, I can't leave you. Your sister would have my hide. You, on the other hand, seem Hades-bent on leaving me."

She stays silent, but the sobs continue to rack her body, shaking the bed. I reach out my hand and place it on her blanket-covered shoulder. She hisses in pain and scoots away from my touch.

My body stiffens. "Are you hurt?"

"I-I'm fine. Please. Just leave." She snuggles farther into the blankets. Sighing, I stand and, in two strides, make it to the window. I whip open the curtains, allowing in enough of the setting sun to brighten up the room.

Turning back to her, my mind goes wild with anger as I see the extent of her injuries. Her lip is swollen, and there's blood crusted in her hairline. "Who the fuck did this, Despoena?" I climb onto the bed and raise her from her position. She winces, teeth clenched, and the blanket falls away to expose her black-and-blue shoulder.

"It's nothing."

"It's anything but," I bellow. She flinches at my anger. "Who. The. Fuck. Did. This?" I manage to get the words out as she collapses into my arms, her tears wetting the front of my tunic.

"M-Menelaus. It was Menelaus who did this."

* * *

My rage echoes through the entire castle as I call his name.

"Menelaus!"

I smash open doors, my blade drawn.

"Menelaus!"

I take the steps two at a time down to the dining hall, throwing his name out like a battle cry.

"*Menelaus!*"

He's nowhere to be found, but my outburst has alerted all the necessary guards, as well as Hecate, Castor, and Helen, who follow in my wake with an obscene number of questions.

"Where is he?" I round on Helen, my blade drawn. Her eyes widen in surprise and she holds one shaking hand over her mouth. The other over her belly.

"I-I don't know, Pol. What is wrong?"

Castor steps in between Helen and the blade, his gaze icy with warning. "Put down the blade, brother. We will find Menelaus and figure this out. Together."

"The fuck we will, Castor. He hurt her." I snarl at my twin, the desire to drive the blade into Menelaus's gut like warm bread overtaking my senses.

Behind Castor, Helen's face pales as Hecate hisses inwardly.

"I'll ask again, sister, where is your dearest husband?"

"Here I am, Pollux! My servants tell me you're running about and disrupting the entire palace with your obscenities." I turn as Menelaus's enormous form enters the dining hall, his arms aloft in joviality. "Well, I repeat. Here I am, Prince." His gaze darkens as his rosebud mouth curls in disgust.

"You've injured an innocent nymph, Menelaus. A daughter of Demeter." I point my blade straight at his thick neck, my gaze narrowing.

He laughs uproariously, the sound echoing throughout the cavernous chamber. "That *innocent nymph* attacked me and three of my guards in an attempt to steal a blade and a horse. It wasn't until she was adequately subdued that I realized who she was. It caused quite the stir." His eyes gleam with utter evil, as though daring me to challenge him. He has an army of Spartan soldiers at his back, ready to slice into my belly and feed my innards to the royal pigs for attacking their king.

"As emissary to Persephone, queen of the Underworld, an attack on the queen's sister would be seen as an attack on the queen herself." Hecate's voice rings out from behind me, and I don't have to look to know that her magic has surfaced. I can see the glow of fire reflected in Menelaus's eyes.

"Yes, well, perhaps you can inform the queen that her sister attacked me and my men first, witch."

Hecate's gaze narrows and a vein in her neck throbs. "It took how many men to restrain the tiny nymph?"

"Four," Menelaus grunts.

"And the bruises and injuries? Is it common practice among your Spartan guard to harm helpless women? Or is that something you've enacted since banishing Pollux from the realm?"

A growl grows from the back of Menelaus's throat. He clenches his fists as his eyes dart to Helen's. She withers beneath his gaze.

"Our party will be on our way to find suitable lodgings in town. And be certain I'll be speaking with Hades regarding our alliance when I return to the Underworld." Hecate turns, her steps echoing up the stairs. Castor follows, but Helen's frozen form remains just out of eyesight.

"Pollux, please . . ." Helen begins, but falls silent with a glare from her husband.

Narrowing my eyes, I sheath my sword and, finally breaking eye contact with the beastly king of Sparta, follow my twin and his wife up the stairs to pack our bags and be on our way.

HECATE

"**G**et off me!"

The words echo off the chamber walls as Castor and I lock eyes across the room. I rush to the door and, throwing it open, find several soldiers restraining Pollux.

"Release him!" Castor's voice booms as he pushes past me. Another set of soldiers grabs my husband's arms and holds him back.

"Enough!" I yell as my fingers grow hot. "What exactly is going on here?" My veins throb with the energy coursing through my blood. It begs to be released, but I tamp it down with a harsh reminder of my ambassadorial duties to Hades.

"I suggest you control your witch, Prince, else we do it for you," a soldier sneers at my husband. He pulls an adamantine chain from a pouch at his waist and coils it around his knuckles, all while eyeing me with bloodthirsty hunger.

Castor's eyes go dark with rage. "What is the meaning of this?" His gaze bounces back and forth between mine and Pollux's.

"The king has challenged Prince Pollux to a duel. We have come to take him to the arena. Should he refuse, he'll be locked below the castle in the dungeon." The soldier's beastly smile stretches his face and shows his blackened teeth.

"This is nonsense! The royal family does not duel with one another," Pollux spits through a busted lip. His tongue works the skin around the wound.

"Psh," replies the soldier. "Our king's been waiting for this moment." He crouches low and hisses in Pollux's face. "If I were you, Prince, I'd lay down my arms before the match begins, else you lose the only appendage you bother to use anymore." His lips quirk.

Pollux thrashes against his human restraints before the soldier's foot lands square in his gut. Castor lunges while I reach forward, my digits growing so hot as to be painful.

"Castor? Pollux?" Helen's shrill voice pulls everyone from the melee and we freeze. The soldiers immediately drop on bended knee, while Castor and I pull Pollux to standing. "What? What has happened here?" Her gaze travels over her brother's bloodied lip and then lands on my hands. I clench my fists and open my mouth to respond when Pollux interrupts.

"Your husband has finally gotten his wish, my queen." His eyes are cold. Dead. The love for his golden sister gone.

Helen's lip trembles as tears well in her eyes. "Wh-what do you mean precisely?"

But it's too late. Pollux has stalked into his room. From the open doorway I watch as he sheaths his short sword, throws his leather vest over his thin tunic, and ties his hair back with a cord.

"What is going on here, Castor?" The queen's voice rises at least three octaves, bordering on hysterical.

My husband simply looks down at his sister and shakes his head. Then he stalks into Pollux's room and slams the door behind himself.

• • • ● • ● • ● • •

"Prince Pollux. Brother. How nice of you to join me this afternoon." Menelaus stands in the center of the arena surrounded by his entourage of lackeys.

"Can't you do something to stop this farce, Helen?" From our station on the raised platform, I whip my eyes to the queen. She sits stoically on her throne, not

73

a muscle moving. Dejected, I shake my head and stand, ready to run down to the dirt-packed coliseum and put an end to this once and for all. Beyond the city of Sparta, there are giants terrorizing mortals and killing innocent people. And here we are watching Menelaus have a pissing match with his wife's brother? "This is outrageous."

"Don't go." Her plea is so soft, so quiet, that I'm uncertain if she spoke or I simply imagined it. It's only when she pulls her gaze from the arena—when I see the anguish on her face—that I know she uttered the words. "You don't know what it's like. Living here with *him*."

I return to my seat and pull her hand into my lap. "Come with us, Helen. Flee this place. Flee him."

She shakes her head and stares down at her other hand. The nails are bitten to the quick. The skin torn and bloodied along the nails. "I can't. The throne belongs to our family. I can't just . . . leave." Her gaze goes flat as her eyes narrow. "I'm not Castor."

"What's that supposed to mean?"

She swallows and looks out onto the flattened ground, where her husband laughs jovially with his men. His rounded belly jiggles as his beady eyes find his wife's. "The throne was never meant to be mine. Or Pollux's. It was always meant for Castor. Until—"

"Until I came along," I finish for her. My lips thin and I grip the armrest of the chair, my nails digging into the wood. Tired of the absurdity of this situation, I stand and turn my body to the queen's. "He will destroy you, Helen, if *you* allow it." I'll not say anything else, for it will only fall on deaf ears. Until Helen decides to become the strong woman I know she's capable of being, she'll never stand up to Menelaus.

I take the stairs and find Castor just as Pollux draws his blade from its scabbard. "You didn't want to be his second?" My knitted brow surely conveys the confusion at Castor not backing his brother.

"He refused me. Said he needed to do this alone." Castor's jaw works, and I know his brother's exclusion has hurt him. My palm finds his shoulder, and I run my fingers along his collarbone. Feel the tension and knots working as he watches Pollux.

"You didn't think to fight me, your king, did you?" Menelaus's gruff voice reaches our ears just as he steps aside, revealing a hidden door in the dirt. Pollux's throat bobs as he gulps.

"Wha—?" My voice fails me as a bald beast of a man climbs from the cavern. He's chained. The smell of adamantine burns my nostrils, and I wince.

As the sun moves from behind a cloud, Castor gasps. My eyes widen. The man's body is not made of skin, but carved of metal.

"Let me introduce you to Talos. Crafted by the god Hephaestus, his body is made entirely of bronze." Menelaus chortles as Pollux's eyes travel up the metallic man's chiseled form. Even from this distance I can hear his heart beating wildly.

Castor makes to move, but I grip his arm, holding him in place. "We have to help him."

I shake my head. "He wants to do this alone." My husband's jaw works, the noise of his grinding teeth as loud as the bronze man's chains dropping to the dirt. I bite my lip and clench my fists as Pollux raises his sword and slashes, hitting the beast in the thigh. The metal-on-metal sound ricochets around the circular arena, drowning out our collective gasps. Pollux dodges and slices once more, this time going for the stomach, but again his sword merely screeches along the bronzed material.

"He can't be cut," I whisper to myself. My eyes dart over the figure, his body a miracle of metalwork. I don't know much about forging or working with metals, but I do know that every weapon has a weak spot. The trick is finding it.

With the sun shining brightly now, it's hard to keep my gaze trained on the creature as he dodges and slashes with his own weapon, but I'm finally able to spot it.

A nail.

I inhale giddily, a smile coming easily to my face, and turn to Castor. "The weakness!" I point toward the beast. "It's the nail. See it?"

Castor squints through the sun's rays, his eyes searching for the spot on the man's arm. When he finds it, his own face lights up and he raises his hand to his mouth. "The arm, Pol! The weakness!"

It takes only a moment for Pollux to understand and find the nail. He parries right then left, crouching and rolling under the bronzed man's leg. As he comes up from behind, he manages to dig the tip of his sword under the head of the nail and spring it loose.

As the fastener falls to the ground and the man collapses in a river of metallic blood, Menelaus's rage echoes throughout the arena.

"Get out! Get out of my castle and out of my city!"

We don't need to be told twice, and with one last glance at Helen's tense form on the dais, we dash to find Despoena.

POLLUX

I escort Desy to the stables where our horses await. Hecate tightens the girth on Pegasus, cinching the leather strap around his belly with stiff movements and a frown of anger tugging on the corners of her mouth.

"I'll saddle my own horse," I mention as I drop mine and Desy's bags. Hecate eyes me and lets out a derisive snort.

"Wife." Castor's tone is calming, and I watch as the witch's shoulders soften. Shaking my head, I toss the saddle blanket over my horse and then hoist the saddle up over the beast's back.

It is quiet while I focus on tacking the horse, but the peace doesn't last long as Desy opens her mouth. "I'm sorry about all this," she drawls at Hecate. I watch as her beautiful moss-green eyes widen in contrition.

I smell the ozone in the air before I see the spark ignite on Hecate's forefinger. "Desy, look out!" I dive in front of the tiny nymph, taking the fire directly to the chest. The flame hits me, but I'm able to stay upright even as I stumble, the wind knocked from my lungs. Coughing and patting my leathers, I ensure the flame is out before stalking toward my sister-in-law.

"What the fuck was that about?"

Her eyes flare with anger, darkening to an ominous shade of deep navy. "You shouldn't have stood in my way, Pollux."

"That was unnecessary, Hecate." I edge closer to her, my fists clenched as I glare down at the powerful witch.

"Despoena running off and then attacking Menelaus's men was *unnecessary*. You getting us involved in a pointless duel with Menelaus was *unnecessary*, Pollux." Hecate's lip curls in disgust as she speaks the nymph's name, and my insides boil with rage.

"What Desy did, or didn't do, was no reason for Menelaus's men to strike her, and you know it." I stand my ground, my jaw clenching and my body rigid with adrenaline and anger. I narrow my eyes at Hecate, willing her to remember.

As though she immediately recalls our journey to avenge Persephone against another man who also hurt women, she grits her teeth and finally breaks eye contact, sighing heavily. "You're right. Despite what Despoena did, we cannot condone the actions of a brute like Menelaus. Castor and I will ride ahead into town and find lodgings for us for the night. But come morning, we part ways." She eyes Desy, who gulps and nods, her teeth chewing her bottom lip.

I move to help Hecate mount Pegasus, but she swats me away and nods toward Desy. "Deal with that one, brother."

• • • • ● • ● • • • •

"What do you mean there are only two rooms left?"

"I suppose you both should've thought of this before we were forced to leave the accommodations of the castle, Pollux."

Desy and I stare at Castor, our mouths agape as we realize we'll be forced to share a room together.

"And just to be clear, Hecate can't—?"

Before I can even finish the sentence, Castor's uproarious laugh cuts me off. "No, Hecate *won't*. My wife and I need a decent night's sleep before we make our way to Mount Olympus, and there's no way either of us is watching that devious nymph all night."

Desy rolls her eyes and sucks her teeth as Castor slaps my back. Grabbing his bags and hoisting them over his shoulder, he takes the stairs two at a time, leaving us alone.

I jut my chin toward the stairs and follow as Desy leads the way. Turning at the top, we are led into a spacious room with—of course—a single bed.

Setting her bag on the floor, Desy turns to me, her eyes sparkling with malice. She crosses her arms and eyes me up and down. "You'll take the floor."

"Like fuck I will, *mikrí nýmfi*. You're more than welcome to sleep on the floor, but I'll be in the bed—with or without you." I throw my gear on the floor and leap onto the feather-filled mattress.

A snarl escapes her pouted lips, and I fight the urge to laugh. Two can play these types of games.

I lie back, my hands going behind my head in a mock-relaxed posture. Desy glares at me, her eyes turning to emerald slits. When I flash a toothy smile back, she groans in frustration and drops to her knees, digging through her luggage. She tosses items all over the place until she finds what she's looking for—an oversized man's tunic.

"Thanks for thinking of me, but I prefer to sleep in the nude." I stand up from the warmth of the bed and begin disrobing. I unhook the sheath for my blade and then unlace my boots, setting both neatly in the corner. On second thought, I leave the shoes there and move the weapon next to my side of the bed as I eye Desy. Watching me intently, her cheeks flush and she rolls her eyes yet again. A flash of those deep green eyes rolling back into her head while I feast between her thighs flits through my mind, and I suddenly worry about disrobing with a hard-on.

"This nightshirt isn't for you." She hugs the tattered garment close, its presence clearly giving her comfort.

My jaw tightens as I continue to undress. I unroll the sleeves of my shirt and pull it over my head, folding it neatly and then laying it next to my boots. "You steal that shirt like you stole my money? Let me guess, you got another unsuspecting fool drunk and took the clothes right off his back, yes?" I shake my head, reminding myself of Hecate's warning. *You'd no longer be your own man. You would belong to her.*

Is this her ploy, her game? Am I just some chump she's attempting to entrap to do her bidding?

"I didn't steal this from anyone." She fingers the material. "It was my father's. I always take it with me when I travel." Glancing up, her glimmering eyes shoot me a look of disdain.

"I'm sorry. I didn't know," I respond stupidly. I swallow the lump in my throat as she rises to her feet and turns away to a darkened corner of the small room.

Looking over her shoulder, she sees me watching and glares. Heat creeps up my neck. I avert my gaze and clear my throat. She turns back to the corner and begins disrobing. I, too, unlace my leather trousers, tossing them quickly on my pile, and climb into the bed.

Reverting to my faux relaxed position, I watch, mesmerized, as Desy undresses. She unhooks her sandals and then undoes her belt before coiling it up. The way she wraps the leather around her hand has me imagining tying her up. Using the strap on her soft backside to punish her for running from me. I gulp and blink away the fantasy. She pulls her long honey locks to the side and quickly braids the length, securing the end with a cord from her wrist. I swallow slowly, my body warming, as she glances over her shoulder one more time and catches my eye. Her gaze travels the length of the bed to the tented blanket over my midsection.

Keeping my eyes locked on hers, I readjust, rolling to my side. A gentleman would avert his gaze, but I'm no such thing. My mouth waters as she turns back around and pulls her long chiton over her shoulders, exposing her calves and round ass. Her shoulder blades roll under browned skin as she folds up the fabric and, bending over and affording me a perfect view of *everything*, sets it with her sandals. Then she pulls the nightshirt over herself.

Even with her fully covered from shoulder to kneecap, my cock is at full attention. She turns and struts toward me. As hard as I try to stay focused on her face, I can't help myself as my gaze slides down. I think I'm likely to come the second she slides into the bed. Her tits bounce under the sheer fabric as she covers the distance, and I sigh in frustration as she quickly extinguishes the candle on the side table.

"See enough, Prince?" she asks as she climbs under the furs. My body tenses as her bare leg brushes against mine.

"Not nearly enough, *mikrí nýmfi*."

She snorts and turns to me, our faces inches apart in the dark. "I told you once before to stop calling me that."

I don't respond but smile in the darkness. I love agitating her. I want to reach out and run my calloused fingers over her soft body, to feel each and every one of her curves.

Instead, I decide to open my big mouth.

"Who's your father anyway?"

"Oh, you didn't know?" She yawns and rolls over, yanking the covers with her. "It's Poseidon."

Just my luck.

HECATE

"I cannot believe we are in this situation." I glare at the small bed, the fur blanket matted and smelling of feet.

"It certainly isn't as comfortable as the guest rooms at the palace, my heart." Castor advances and wraps his arms around me from behind, his weight a calming presence after this awful day. "But anywhere with you is perfect."

I turn into him and wrap my arms around his neck. "I suppose we'll have to make do, husband." I rise onto my toes and press a soft kiss to the corner of his mouth. His hands span the width of my back and pull me closer. I feel his need between us, and the warmth of our love soothes me.

"You know, it reminds me of those lodgings we once shared on our way to the Oracle of Delphi. Do you recall?"

I sigh wistfully. "I do. I had the most glorious bath and you gave me an amazing massage."

"Which you fell asleep in the middle of." He smiles ruefully. "I know there's no chance for a bath," he mutters, eyeing the empty copper tub filled with cobwebs in the corner, "but I think a massage might do wonders for your migraines. If you can stay awake?" He wiggles his fingers and I squeal with glee, eager to feel his muscular hands kneading the tension from my flesh.

"I'm sure there are a few additional knots of stress after dealing with Despoena and Pollux," I add as I turn toward the bed. Castor follows and pulls my tunic over my head from behind, discarding it on the floor and pressing his lips to my bare shoulders. A shiver runs up my spine, and my nipples harden.

"I prefer not to think about them right now, wife."

Still facing away from him, I moan in agreement and loosen my hair from the pins.

Castor uncoils it, running his fingers through its length. "Turn around."

I spin, hiding my bare breasts behind my arms with an impish grin. "I think I'd prefer you also not be wearing a top, Cas." I draw out the *s* sound, hissing like a snake. He groans in agreement, and I help him shed the shirt. Dropping it on the floor with my own, I press myself into his naked chest. "That's better."

We ease our way onto the bed. I sit and he follows, towering over me and straddling my lap. I reach up and pull his mouth to mine, finally tasting him. Even after all these years, I still desire him. Still want to feel his face pressed between my thighs as he feasts on me. Still enjoy making him hard.

"This is an interesting massage," he mutters as I part the seam of his lips, my tongue darting in to caress his.

I pull his hands to my breasts and, with my own fingers, show him how to touch me. I roll my hardened nipples in between my thumbs and forefingers, motioning for Castor to follow my lead. He takes over, dipping his face to take a pink tip in between his lips. He pulls with his mouth, and I gasp in delight as warmth spreads to my clit. I reach around his back and run my fingers along the groove of his spine, and a shudder racks his body.

His hardened length presses against the fabric of my skirt, the friction heating me more than the fire in my veins. "I want to touch you," I whisper into his hair. He releases my nipple from his mouth with a pop and looks up at me, a devilish grin transforming his face. I love that look, the one of no expectations and pure surprise. "Loosen your leathers," I demand greedily. My mouth waters for the taste of him as my fingers itch to stroke his length.

He rolls onto his side and unties the laces of his pants, pulling his hard cock from the depths. Pushing him onto his back, I climb onto my knees and take him in my fist. I start to stroke him slowly. Gently. But my touch becomes more frenzied as the desire to taste him takes over. I give in, leaning down and taking him in my mouth. I suck deeply down the length, my saliva coating his velvety skin.

"This is a wonderful massage, but I want to taste you, Hecate."

"Not yet," I respond before I swallow him deeper. I graze my teeth gently along his length as I pull him out, then flick my tongue along the tip. His hips grind into the bed and a hiss of pleasure escapes from between his lips.

Releasing him from my mouth, I use my saliva to stroke him from root to tip with my hand and give a soft squeeze on the head of his cock. His legs shake and toes flex, his breathing increasing.

"I need you now, wife." He raises up on his elbows and pulls me in for a deep kiss. I think he's going to part my lips and thrust his tongue in my mouth, but instead he grabs my shoulder and, with a force that sends sparks of desire straight to my cunt, shoves my face into the furs. He grabs my hips and hoists them into the air, smacking my bare ass and then caressing the same spot.

I moan and swirl my hips, my pussy certainly dripping wet for him. He swipes a finger from my clit through my folds and along the seam of my ass. I turn and watch as he licks his finger, his eyelids drooping with pleasure.

"Fuck me like this." My pendulous breasts graze the fur blanket, my curls are wild and untamed, and my bare ass is in the air, but I've never felt sexier. My fingers tingle with unreleased energy, and I dig my hands into the bedding. "I need you to fuck me hard. *Now.*"

He responds by smacking my behind and pulling my hips toward his. I feel him notch his cock at my entrance before swirling it in my wetness. I push back into him, demanding and needy.

"So impatient."

I growl in frustration and spread my knees. He continues to tease me, so I lean into my shoulder and touch myself. My fingers slide easily into the valleys of my cunt and it's not long before I'm rocking against my own hand.

"Enough of that. My turn," Castor growls as he finally enters me. I see stars and cry out, my fingers stilling for just a moment before continuing their slick assault. He grinds into me, pulling my hips up. I'm gushing now, the wetness running down my thigh and spraying onto my back as he thrusts harder into me. "I need to taste you," he growls as he pulls out and then proceeds to lean down and lick me from front to back.

I moan in ecstasy as he reenters me, but he goes only as deep as the tip. Over and over he sinks just the head of himself within me, and I whine and squirm for more.

"Fuck me. *Hard!*" I shout as I sit up. He finally fully sinks into me, and I bounce up and down on my knees. He grabs my hair and coils it around his fist, pulling it back. My gaze goes up, my throat exposed, and he leans around and licks my neck up to my ear.

"I could do this all night," he whispers against my skin. When he releasing the strands, I plummet back down to the bed, catching myself with my hands as he traces a gentle finger along my spine. I arch my ass higher and he pumps faster. Harder.

I reach once more for my clit, my fingers sliding along the slick skin, and see stars. My moans of ecstasy match his roar of release, and we climax together in a mixture of cries and grunts. Our pace slows, the aftereffects sending tremors through my bones. I'm still full, even as he withdraws.

I collapse on the bed and Castor pulls me to him, the remnants of our lovemaking all over our sweat-soaked bodies. I sweep my hair out of the way and he nuzzles into my back.

"I love you," I breathe out into the room as I catch my breath.

"I love you, Hecate," he responds, his breath tickling my shoulders.

But even as his breathing deepens and we fall into the silence of the night, I worry if our love—what we have—is enough to make it out of this war alive.

POLLUX

"Your only job is to get Desy safely to Demeter and then head north and rendezvous with us on Mount Olympus," Castor reminds me as he tightens Pegasus's girth. The horse swings his tail around and smacks my twin with a swat. "Gods-damned horse! Cut it out! Hecate isn't riding without a saddle, so deal with it or I'll send you to the butcher to be meat for Sparta's poor."

I chuckle to myself and adjust the stirrups of my own saddle. "Why not just have Hecate open a portal or something and spirit yourselves to Olympus? Seems it'd be much easier than all this." I indicate the tack littering the ground.

Castor's jaw clenches, and I know there's something he's not telling me. "We have a few stops to make along the way. Besides, I miss traveling atop a horse. Seeing the sun's light." His gaze shifts away as he grabs a brush from a bucket and begins grooming his mount.

"Oh? Does Hecate know about this additional detour, or are you keeping secrets from her again?" I don't like antagonizing my brother, but I won't let him forget about the last time he and his wife traveled to Olympus. Castor endangered all of us by refusing to share that he had been blackmailed by Zeus. It almost cost him his life, as well as his marriage.

"I don't need to be reminded of that right now." He grinds his teeth together and angrily whips the brush into the bucket. It lands with a clatter as the canister tips over.

I'm quiet for a moment, mostly to give my brother a chance to cool off. "So where are you stopping then?"

"Hecate wants to return to Delphi." His lips thin as he stares at me, challenging me, but I remain silent. "She's hoping the oracle will have some advice on how to win this war against the giants."

"She's worried, then." I remember the last time we visited the oracle. How nervous Melinoe—now Hecate—was as she searched for answers to her true identity.

Castor's eyes meet mine, the question answered in simply a look. "I'm worried about her. She's been getting these painful migraines and—" His mouth snaps shut as Hecate and Desy exit the inn, their bags in hand. Hecate's long black skirt, with a slit up either side, and leather tunic with gold forearm cuffs could not be more at odds with Desy's floaty gown. Castor rushes to his bride and takes her gear. She smiles at him, but as she sees me her face drops.

I approach Desy, and as she thrusts her own luggage into my hand, Hecate turns to her, a sharpness transforming her features. "Despoena, Pollux has his orders from your sister to return you to Demeter. If you know what's good for you, you'll give him no more trouble." Turning to me, her eyes soften and her voice drops. "Pollux, I wish you luck and safe travels. We will meet in Olympus." We clasp forearms. Just when I remember that Hecate's never been one for affections, she pulls me toward her and whispers something inaudibly in my ear.

"What's that?" I ask, turning toward her.

"Nothing, just wishing you safe travels, brother." She hugs me once more before pulling away and nodding with finality.

Castor assists Hecate while I help Desy mount our horse, and as the inn is already a distance from the castle, it's not long before we arrive on the outskirts of the town.

"Safe travels, brother," Castor shouts as Hecate mutters something under her breath. Pegasus, with an excited whinny, sprouts wings from his back. I snort and shake my head, glad that Desy's home in Arcadia is near enough to ride without magical help. I don't think my stomach could handle another flight.

I wave as Pegasus gallops along, his flapping wings and hooves leaving a cloud of dust behind.

Turning back to Desy, I snap the reins and look to the road ahead.

· · · ● · ● · ● · · ·

"Desy, we've been riding for hours. Aren't you going to answer a single question I've asked?"

In response, she dramatically shakes her head back and forth. Her hair snags against my scruff and I bat it away, deliberately swiping my hand down her back as I smooth her locks. She stiffens against me, holding her body erect.

I sag dejectedly and roll my neck from side to side, the strain of riding double not one I'm used to. The last time was with my sister, Helen, as we traipsed from Aphidna through the countryside to the Calydonian boar hunt. I smile fondly, remembering the sweet camp maid I tumbled with in a deserted bunk while my sister snored soundly in our shared tent with her new pet ferret, Galinthias.

Missing the feel of a willing woman in my bed, I groan in annoyance. Instead of spending my evenings feasting on a beautiful maiden, I'm stuck delivering a bad-tempered nymph to her hostile mother.

"You don't have to groan at me. You're forced to take me home, not make conversation."

I'm not sure if Desy's heard my thoughts, but I blush regardless.

"You know, if you'd simply agree to take me to Olympus with you, I'd be much more pleasant."

I sigh in relief, glad that she can't actually read my mind. "I'm a soldier, *mikrí nýmfi*, just following orders."

She growls in frustration and whips her head around, her hair once again tangling in my unshaven stubble. "You're a prince. Your father was Zeus. Grow a pair already." She glares at me, her nostrils flaring. When I don't take the bait, she huffs in annoyance. "That's what I thought."

"Just because I won't break my promise to see you safely to your home doesn't mean that I'm not brave or that I don't . . . have a pair." I whisper the last part in her ear, my voice sounding gruffer than I mean to.

Turning back to meet my gaze, her eyes quickly dip to my lap before returning to my face. "That's not what I meant. I just wish I could have stayed in the Underworld or traveled to Olympus. I've never been, and it's unlikely I'll ever go."

"Why not? Doesn't Demeter ever bring you with her?"

Her shoulders rise to meet her ears. "Since Athena took over, Mother isn't needed much." Remembering what Hecate shared of her own tetchy relationship with Demeter, I can imagine why the goddess of the harvest is not invited into Olympus to assist with the new regime. As a condescending and uptight woman who treats others horribly, her behavior certainly wouldn't be tolerated in the modern Olympus that Athena rules.

"What about when Persephone comes to visit?"

"Mother doesn't like to be alone. If Persephone is called to Olympus, I have to stay and keep Mother company."

"But you've traveled to the Underworld. Who keeps Demeter company then?"

"My brother, Philomelus, visits from time to time, usually around the harvest in early fall, so I'm able to visit Persephone."

My lips thin as I realize why Desy desires to be free. She's been shackled, locked up in a life of loneliness. "I wish I could take you with me to Olympus, but it wouldn't be safe."

She sighs, sagging against me. "I know. That's what Mother always says too. I was only a babe when Persephone left, but she's terrified I'll be stolen away from her just like Persephone was."

"You can't believe that old lie, can you?" I snort. Demeter shamed Hades and Persephone's love to anyone who would listen, and for years the gods and goddesses of the Land of the Living believed her lies. It's only in recent memory that the truth has spread, likely by Hecate and her correspondence with Athena and Artemis.

"I did once. I thought Hades was the ogre my mother claimed. But when I started visiting, I saw the truth. Hades loves my sister, and she loves him. I tried to tell my mother, but she wouldn't believe me. She told me that was part of Hades's ploy." She chuckles to herself. "As though Hades were that deep and diabolical."

I let out a guffaw as well. Anyone who's met the god of the Underworld knows he's nothing if not a lover at heart. He uses the darkness of the Under-world to feed the rumors of a terrifying and abominable disposition, when in reality he's a wise and just ruler.

"Do you . . ." I pause, taking a gulp as I formulate the correct way to ask such a personal question. "Do you hope to find a love like that one day, Despoena?"

She's quiet for a moment. I lean to the side and watch the flutter of her heartbeat in her neck. Her chest rises and falls steadily, but her gaze stays straight ahead.

"Des—"

"Love has only ever confined me, kept me prisoner. I don't want that kind of love." Her chin tilts higher and she swallows. Squaring her shoulders, she sits straighter in the saddle, pulling away from me.

HECATE

I scrunch my eyes closed as Castor performs the necessary sacrifice of the goat.

"The meat will feed the people of the village," he reminds me—and himself—as he cleans his hands. We stand together outside the oracle's temple. It's surprisingly empty and lacking the crowd that was present the last time we were here.

A shiver runs through my body.

"Where do you think everyone is, Hecate?" Castor swipes the bloodied blade on his leather trousers as he returns to my side. The air crackles with an uneasiness, and the hair on the back of my neck stands up.

"Let's get inside and speak with the oracle so we can be on our way." I interlace my fingers with his, and we take the steps slowly, the lack of an overeager crowd contributing to the apprehension I feel.

As we approach the entry to the temple, the door is slightly ajar. I swallow and, glancing at Castor, nod my head as we both reach out and push into the darkness. The smell of incense is thick and heavy. "Is this how it looked to you . . . before?" Castor whispers as we carefully toe over the jagged stone floor.

"No." I glance around and am appalled at the change. Where once stood an airy forest full of lush trees and babbling fountains now stands a graveyard of twiggy timber and soot-covered weeds sprouting between the stone path. I release Castor's hand and snap my fingers, a spark of light flaring into the depth.

A small figure sits huddled in the middle of the temple. Her black shroud blends in with the darkness. Castor and I glance at one another and move forward. "Pythia?" I call stoically, my voice echoing through the temple.

She looks up and I gasp. While I've never seen the true Pythia, Castor and I spoke at length of her appearance. The figure I saw was merely a figment of Hera's trickery, but Castor witnessed the true Pythia. Her diminutive frame remains the same, but where once her eyes were milky, they now flash as yellow as her skin, as though a poison has overtaken her body. Can I trust that this is the true oracle?

"My lady, are you well?" I inch closer, but Castor stays rooted in the spot behind me.

The smell of urine permeates the air, and I'm certain that something isn't quite right, but I press forward, nonetheless. "Pythia? It is I, Hecate, Titan of witchcraft and vassal to Hades and Persephone of the Underworld." I bow low, showing the respect due to a seer.

I hear her lips part, a gummy sound that tickles my ears, and glance up as her tongue swipes along the cracked skin. "Come forward, Hecate." A long, crooked finger beckons me closer.

I glance back at Castor, his eyes dazed as he sways on his feet.

"Your mate is in a restful slumber, for only you and I may hear what is spoken within these walls."

I reach out to release him, but a hiss of warning flies from her lips, and I recoil, my hand stinging as though it's been slapped.

"If you wish to end the onslaught against your people, you will do well to listen to what I say, witch."

I gulp down a snarky retort and approach her, my fingers tingling in warning.

"Kneel before me." The Pythia pushes her wispy arms into the chair and rises. I drop to my knees as my heart thuds in my ears. "You will light the burner and I will reveal your future," she says as she places an herb-filled basket before me.

I recall the last time I was here. As Melinoe I was unable to harness my powers and only then discovered my true self. As the oracle adds a thick liquid to the basket, I gulp down the apprehension that simmers in my gut. My life changed so drastically when I consulted my future once before. Will the same happen again?

"It is ready." The Pythia sits back on her haunches and places her gnarled hands in her lap, her eyes studying me. Does she see the girl I once was, the one who was scared and searching for answers to her powerless life? A part of that terrified girl still resides within me. I feel her beneath the surface. Telling me to tread lightly. To beware. Or does the oracle see the me I present to the world, the witch who will stop at nothing to restore order and punish those who harm the helpless?

"Light the burner, Hecate."

• • • ● • ● • • • •

I open my eyes as a luscious breeze fills my nostrils. It's the smell of home. Bergamot and pomegranate. Safety and security. I inhale deeply and a smile lifts my lips. Stretching, I find my fingers interlaced with Castor's, and blinking sleepily, a shiver of delight runs through me. I lean over and press my lips to his, but his face remains closed off as though he's asleep. Except that we stand outside our home. My brow crinkles at the strangeness.

The sky suddenly darkens to a deep maroon. The hair on my arms stands up. Lightning flashes in the sky. I breathe in again, but the smell has turned sour. I taste it in my mouth. It's the smell of rancid meat and burned flesh. My gorge rises, but I swallow it back down as something sinister slithers down my spine. Castor's eyes spark open, and in their reflection, I see flames. I whip around; the daunting oak tree stands in front of me. The leaves roar alive as the fire consumes it. I back up, pulling Castor with me, but he remains standing in his spot.

"Castor!" I yell as I claw at his forearm, but he's immoveable. The fire lights up his features and dances in his eyes. "Cas, we need to go!"

He doesn't flinch, doesn't acknowledge me. I try to lift him around his waist, but his weight is too solid. I try shoving into him with my shoulder, but pain flares through the joint. The heat of the flaming tree licks at my back, the smell of burned hair assaults my nostrils. This isn't right. This isn't right at all.

That same sinister shiver slides along my spine, a serpent's tongue flicking along each individual vertebrae, and I feel his presence behind me. My heart pounds in my chest, and I watch as Castor's eyes widen, the fear shining through even as his face remains frozen.

"Hello, Hecate."

My bowels turn watery, and I whip around as a hand snakes out and grabs Castor by the throat, hoisting him high into the air. My demigod husband is no match for the king of all gods, the villain my fellow immortals and I imprisoned in the Underworld.

"Let him go, Zeus," I roar as rage burns through my palms.

He says nothing, his gaze cold and devoid of emotion, as he crushes my beloved's throat. Castor's fingers claw at the hand encircling his neck, but it's no use. Zeus smiles, his teeth sparkling, bright white even as the flames flicker behind him. My husband falls to the ground, his body lifeless as his eyes stare into the abyss. My heart shatters, and I fall to my knees. I claw at my skin as a scream of grief rips from deep within my body.

And the whole world collapses around me.

* * *

I gasp and my surroundings reappear.

The decrepit temple.

The oracle.

The burner and its fragrance wafting through the air.

My head is pounding, and I swipe the tears from my face. My fingers come away coated in blood. The torn and bloodied skin lodged beneath my fingernails evidence of my vision, yet my body is free of the marks.

"You know what you have to do, witch." The Pythia's voice is low, more a growl as her sad yellowed eyes meet mine.

I shake my head vehemently. "I won't bring him back. I'll never set him free." My breathing becomes ragged as the incense smoke fills my nostrils.

"It is not for you to decide these things. She has already decided by unleashing the giants upon the earth."

"Who is she?"

The Pythia is silent, her gaze cold.

"There must be another way, there has—"

"There is no other way. Look around you." She waves her papery-skinned hands through the air. "This is just the beginning." She reaches across the small flame and takes my hand, examining it. Her palm is cold while mine burns hot. "You have seen the lives already stolen, the crowds in the Underworld, the souls taken far too soon."

The image of the small girl and her mother appears in my mind and I blink, tamping that memory down. "If you do not stop this, we all cease to exist."

Salty tears leak from my eyes, stinging as they form trenches in my tender skin. "Anyone but him, Pythia. Please," I beg as I hunch over her hand. She pulls away from me and tips up my chin with her bony finger.

"You cannot fight fate, Hecate. It can only be him." She leans down and blows out the flame, and as the warmth seeps from my body and I sag onto the floor, it's Castor's arms that are finally there to lift me and carry me away.

POLLUX

"Hello? Mother? I'm home!"

Desy's voice echoes through the large limestone abode. Fluted columns line either side of the entryway. A table filled with a cornucopia of breads sits in the middle of the foyer.

My belly grumbles, and I approach and grab a biscuit before biting into it. "Ah, what the fuck?" I howl, and Desy bursts out laughing.

"Pollux, those are painted rocks. They're decorative." She doubles over, her face turning pink as tears of mirth stream down her cheeks. "Did you really think we just leave food out in the entryway?"

Rubbing my jaw, I set down the faux food and frown. "Your mother is the goddess of the harvest, and we've been riding for hours. I'm delirious with thirst and hunger."

"Why didn't you say so? Follow me." She reaches out and grabs my hand, pulling me through the hallway and into an open kitchen. My skin burns at her touch. Is this a means to ensnare me through touch? The heat creeps from my hand up my arm and settles in my chest.

The room we enter is large and overlooks a patio but is itself covered to protect from the elements.

Desy disappears into an adjoining pantry and quickly returns with an armful of treats. She lays them out on the counter, and my mouth waters as I take in the loot before me. Thick orange carrots and shiny olives sit next to juicy figs, plump dates, and sweet almonds. She saunters back into the pantry and then returns, pulling a carafe of wine from behind her back, a glint of mischief in her eye.

"Mother usually forces me to water down the wine, but it doesn't appear she's home at the moment." She points across the room. "Cups are in the top cabinet." I grab two and help her uncork the bottle, pouring us each a healthy measure. We work in silence, cutting the carrots and arranging the food onto a wooden board, and then I follow Desy to the patio.

We sit in silence as we both dig into the feast. I release a sigh of contentment as I bite into an olive, its juice dribbling down my chin.

"Mother's always had the best harvest in Arcadia," Desy says as she pulls apart a fig and plucks out the purplish flesh.

I raise my glass of wine in mock salute. "To Demeter's bountiful harvest!"

Desy clinks her cup with mine as a smile blooms on her face. "Hear, hear!" I lift my wine to my lips and take a greedy pull of the liquid, emptying the contents. Desy, on the other hand, takes a small sip before setting down her mug.

I refill my cup and hold it aloft again. Desy follows my lead, her eyes wide and an expectant look lighting up her features. "And let's not forget, to returning you home and to a safe journey onward!"

As though a cloud covered the sun, Desy's face falls. She slams her mug onto the table and rises abruptly.

"Des—" I start, but she turns on her heel and runs from the room, leaving me with a tableful of uneaten food and an empty jug of wine.

• • • • ❋ • • • • •

"Desy?" I call out as I walk through the home. I'd taken my time finishing the cup of wine before cleaning up the uneaten food and putting the kitchen to rights. I'm not used to seeking out women. If anything, they normally come to me. But for whatever reason, the desire to let the nymph stew in her own emotions before coming to her senses isn't as strong as I thought it'd be. If anything, I find myself wanting to comfort her. To hold her and apologize for whatever I've done to upset her. A tightness takes hold in my chest, and I rub at my sternum to ease the discomfort. *It must be the olives,* I tell myself.

The sun has begun to set, but I'm able to find the atrium, the center of the home, and I pass through it. Even within the open air of the inner garden, Demeter's ability to grow lush plants is evident in the beautiful aromatic flowers and waxy-leafed shrubs. I glimpse an empty bench and, with no Desy in sight, continue my journey through the darkened halls of the home.

I come to a closed door and knock softly. "Desy?" I wait, but there's no answer. I jiggle the knob and, finding the door locked, decide to move onward. "Desy?" I raise my voice slightly, hoping she'll finally answer. I stop to listen.

A soft sniffle tickles my ear, and I press forward to the next door, finding it slightly ajar. "Desy?" I gently push it open, the creak of the hinge giving away any idea I had of entering quietly. Her tiny form is curled on a simple bed.

"Leave me alone," she whispers from the corner.

"I can't do that." I gulp and lean against the frame of the door, keeping my distance as is appropriate for not only a prince of Sparta, but also a daughter of Demeter. Plus, I'm scared what I'll do in an empty house with this gorgeous woman before me. I may be a demigod, but I'm no god, and even the honorable Hades himself wouldn't be able to tamp down the urges heating my loins right now.

"Just go, Pollux. You've seen me home and now you can be on your way, like you said."

I sigh. "So that's what this is about. You can't bear for me to leave." I smirk into the darkness, my ego swelling to the size of this castle-sized abode.

She snorts into her pillow and then turns her eyes toward me. Even without the light of a candle, they flash brightly, shining with unshed tears. "I can't wait for you to leave," she clarifies, wiping her nose on her forearm. Her hair is unruly from the pillow, her face is tear-stained and red from crying, and her clothing is rumpled and askew. But nonetheless, she looks beautiful.

"That's the thing, though." I push off the doorframe and move farther into the room. Slowly. "I can't just leave you here unattended." I stop near her bed and stare down at her, my arms hanging uselessly at my side when all they want to do is grab her around the waist and bring her down onto my hard cock.

"I'm a big girl. I don't need a nursemaid to watch over me. You should go." Her eyes turn to the window.

I shake my head. "No, it's too dark to ride now. I should stay." I reach out and tuck a stray curl behind her ear. I allow my finger to trail down the side of her neck to her collarbone.

Her eyes close and she inhales deeply, a shudder racking her body.

"Do you want me to stay, *mikrí nýmfi*?" Gravelly and low, my voice is barely a whisper into the darkness. My heart pounds as I await her answer. My cock throbs painfully in my leathers, begging to be released.

A breath passes. Then another. I'm certain she's going to kick me out on my ass, tell me not to call her little nymph, and make me sleep in the stable, or worse, on the floor. After all, there's only one bed in this room, and I can't very well keep an eye on her from a separate room. But she finally—finally—looks up at me. Those emerald eyes sparkle in the dark. Her lips part as her tongue pokes out and licks along the seam. My heart stutters in my chest.

"Yes, I want you to stay," she finally answers. "Stay with me." And I collapse into her as she pulls me down to the bed.

Hᴇᴄᴀᴛᴇ

"**W**hat do you mean we must free Zeus, Hecate? This is absurd and absolutely impossible!" Athena rises abruptly from her throne and stalks down the steps, coming to stop right in front of Castor's and my prone position on the floor. As reigning ruler of Olympus and queen of the gods, I am more than happy to show respect to my liege. Unfortunately, I refused to participate in the silly banter and proper court etiquette, and instead just blurted out the news the second I was presented to Athena.

I rise from my genuflection and glance around at the appalled faces of my brethren. Artemis remains seated in her throne at Athena's side. As lead adviser and favored goddess, my cousin's position at court is secure. She's done a great deal to better the lives of young girls in the various city-states, including providing training in childbirth to midwives. While most believe it's just in her kind nature, only I and her brother Apollo know it's in deference to their mother.

The remainder of the gods and goddesses in attendance watch me warily. I scan the familiar faces of Ares, Aphrodite, Apollo, and Demeter. My breath hitches on the last one, as I imagine Pollux and Desy have already arrived in Arcadia and discovered Demeter missing. The goddess of the harvest glares daggers at me, likely wondering where her impish youngest daughter is, but I tilt my chin up and turn my gaze back to the queen.

"We spoke with the Oracle of Delphi, Athena, and—"

"Apollo, approach!" Athena beckons him over with a jerk of her hand. Artemis tenses in her seat, her fingers digging into the wooden throne. As Apollo's twin, I can only imagine she's experiencing the same nerves as him at being called to speak before the court on such a delicate matter.

"As god of prophecy and oracles, we must verify that what your Pythia in Delphi spoke is true." Athena retreats and nods firmly as she clasps her hands behind her back.

Apollo steps forward and holds out his palms. I glance at Castor, not wanting to share what I saw in the vision, but Apollo only smiles at me and urges me forward. Taking a strengthening breath, I place my hands in his. His grip tightens and his eyelids flutter closed.

"*Oi aiónes mas eínai deménoi metaxý tous. Kai tha se akoúso*," I mutter under my breath. As the spell takes effect, I feel the memory of the vision bubble up from the depths in which I'd buried it.

The fear sapping my breath.

The heat of the fire at my back.

The hiss of his breath on my neck.

"Hello, Hecate."

I rear back with a yelp as Apollo's eyes fly open. Castor reaches for me, and I bury myself in the safety of his arms, just as I did when he carried me from the oracle's temple.

"What did you see?" Athena steps forward, her owlish face inquisitive and curious.

Apollo blinks once. Twice. His gaze never leaves my face. From my place in Castor's embrace, I shake my head ever so slightly, hoping he won't share everything he witnessed.

The gods and goddesses around the room remain on edge. The tension is thick. Apollo swallows, the lump in his throat bobbing as he finally opens his mouth.

"The oracle was correct. Zeus must be set free, and Hecate must be the one to do so."

· · · ● · ● · · ·

"I won't stay behind like some—some mortal!" Castor growls, his finger pointed in my face. I glare right back, my jaw clenched with fury.

"You will do as I say and stay here where it's safe." I'll not watch as Zeus destroys my lover for a second time.

My husband approaches me, his shoulders squared and eyebrows lowered. I narrow my eyes and curl my hands into fists at my side, ready to send him flying on his ass or tie him to the bed if he refuses to follow orders.

"I don't take orders from you, wife." His forehead lowers, and his body is pressed up against mine.

Heat flares in my belly. Whether it's from anger or desire, I'm not sure, but I grit my teeth and tilt my face up to meet his murderous gaze. "Let me remind you of what I am—and what I'm capable of doing—should you disobey me." I curl my lip and trail a finger down his leather-clad arm. "*Kápste to fos,*" I murmur, my head tilting as a tiny flame erupts from my finger. I sear a line in Castor's attire, from his bicep to his wrist, and then pull away and blow seductively, extinguishing the flare.

Castor whips his arm out and grabs me around the throat, his large hand encircling my neck with ease. Instead of being terrified, I'm turned on. My nipples tighten under my tunic. My undergarments grow damp and the desire to ravage my husband, to show him who's in control, surges from inside my core.

"*Schoiniá ton dénoun,*" I hiss as he grinds his body into mine. There's a rustling from the chaise behind us, and I hold still as the blankets and bedding tear themselves into thick cords. He releases my throat and looks behind him just as the fabric wraps around his middle, pulling him away from me and toward the divan. I stalk toward him as he's pulled down to a seated position and then secured to the seat.

"You cannot be serious." His biceps ripple under the leather tunic as he strains against the knots, but it's useless. My magic is much stronger than simple shredded sheets.

"I must do this alone, Castor." I kneel before him and push his knees apart, my fingers splayed over his thick thighs. He continues to pull against the restraints, and I tsk and shake my head. "You can struggle all you want, but you'll not be set free until I'm safely in the Underworld. Standing outside our home, the one we made together." I inch my fingers higher to the tie at his waist. Unlacing it, I loosen his pants and do my best to tug them down, even a little, and free his hard cock.

"I won't put what we have, what we've built together, in danger just to suit your ego." I fist him, and he inhales sharply. His struggling subsides, and he spreads his legs wider, sinking into the chair, as I pump him harder. "I'm the one that put Zeus there, and I'm the one who must set him free. The oracle prophesied it, and so it must be done." I release the king of the gods' name from my mouth, then suck my husband down. I lower to the base, hitting the deepest part of my throat, and tears spring to my eyes. I sniff and blink them away, promising myself not to cry, not to show Castor how scared I truly am at releasing my sworn enemy.

As though he can read my mind, my husband caresses my shoulder with his restrained hand. I look up at him through wet lashes, his thick cock still between my lips.

"Come up here," he whispers, and I oblige. I sink into him and he catches me with his mouth, his tongue diving into me. "Release me so I can feel you, love."

I shake my head and push away from him. "I can't do that." I reach between us and ruck up my skirt, pushing the wet fabric that encases my nether area aside. "But I can do this." I guide him to my entrance and impale myself, taking his erection inch by delicious inch. His fingers claw at the seat and I can feel his leg muscles flexing beneath me, but I keep going until I bottom out, my juices slicking him the entire way down.

Now eye level, I start to slowly move up and down. "I need to see more of you," he indicates, eyeing my chest. I untuck my tunic and unfasten the cords binding the leather vest I wear for additional protection. Discarding the vest, I pull the tunic down just enough so my bare breasts are exposed. I lift one to his mouth, and he pulls it in, biting gently with his teeth, as his tongue flicks over the hardened nipple.

I moan and continue to ride his cock harder, grinding into him. He pushes up into me, his bound fingers grazing my thighs. Releasing my breast from his mouth, he locks his eyes with mine. He holds my stare, his cold gaze at odds with the desire heating our bodies. But I'm angry too. Angry that he isn't trusting me to oversee this task alone. Angry that he's not thinking of his own safety, of what losing him would do to me. I bounce faster now, letting my rage take control, and he growls and grunts, matching me thrust for thrust. Our breathing is heavy, our bodies sweating. He squeezes his eyes shut just as I throw back my head, our release coming fast and all at once.

Our bodies stiffen together as we reach a crescendo, both of us ignoring the argument as we lock eyes and fall back to earth.

I slow my movements, gasping for air. I finally lower my head and pull my hair away from my face.

His expression is tight with fury as the lump in his throat bobs up and down. His knuckles are white as his muscles work to break the restraints.

"I have to do this alone, Castor."

The coldness seeps from his skin, and I shiver as I lace up my clothing and step away from him. His warm seed trickles down my thigh.

"I'm sorry," I add before fleeing the room.

POLLUX

"**I** 've wanted to sink my cock into you since we met," I growl into Desy's ear as she pulls me down onto the bed. Moaning in response, she rolls her hips up to meet mine. I dip my mouth to hers; I want to devour her whole. She meets me halfway, nipping at my lips. She digs her fingers into my scalp as I wrap her legs around my waist and pull her closer.

"Tell me you want this, Despoena. Tell me you've thought of me all this time. That it's all just been a game—that you've been teasing me so this moment would drive us both mad."

She's silent but bites my lip. Hard. She draws blood. I smell the coppery tang, taste the sweet explosion, but I'm too hard to be anything but turned on. I sink my bloodied mouth to her throat and suck, pulling her skin in between my teeth, ready to mark her as mine.

"Wait," she relents, gently pushing against my chest. I pull back, my breaths coming in gulps.

"We've waited long enough, *mikrí nýmfi*. It's time we both enjoyed ourselves." I reach for her, but she bats me away with a smirk.

"If we do this, I want to go to Olympus with you." Her jaw is set, her gaze challenging.

I'm aghast, blinking in confusion. How did we go from nearly fucking to bargaining? "You'd trade yourself for a trip to the palace of the gods?"

She swallows, her steely eyes meeting mine. "I would."

I huff in annoyance. I can't believe I've been had again. First she steals my money, and now she's working me up just to push me away. I adjust myself and shrug my shoulders. "I'm afraid I can't oblige. My orders were clear. Deliver you safely home. No more, no less."

"Are you certain about that, soldier?" She stands from the bed and then unhooks the pin holding up her chiton. It drops to the floor revealing her completely naked body.

Fuck.

I gulp. She's fucking beautiful. My eyes go wide and my breath hitches. My fingers itch to touch her soft skin, to pull her full breasts into my wet mouth one at a time. To lick my way from her shoulder to her . . .

She raises her hands to her hardened nipples and rolls each one between her thumb and forefinger. Her mouth falls open as her eyes darken, and I watch. Transfixed. Aching to touch. A groan rumbles from my chest, and I reach for her. She walks toward me, one hand falling to her stomach and tiptoeing downward. I follow the path farther south with my eyes until her fingers are buried deep within her brown curls. She stops in front of the bed and, placing one foot on the mattress, spreads herself wide before me. Her head tips back as she slips a finger into her heat.

"I'll do whatever you want—take you wherever you want—so long as you come here. *Now*," I demand as my voice cracks. I rise to my knees and unlace my leather pants. Pulling myself free, I stroke my length in front of her. Her gaze dips down, and her eyes flash with desire as she watches me fist myself. I grab her hips and drag her to me. She knees her way onto the bed, and I release my cock and wrap my hands around her ass, cupping both cheeks. My hard length presses into her belly. I lay her on her back, then sink down and nuzzle her hand aside.

"It's my turn to touch you," I growl.

She arches her back and I nudge her knees apart, exposing her glistening pink folds like a meal on a platter. I'm starving.

I lower my face to her sex and tongue her clit. At the same time, I maneuver a digit to her entrance and part her flesh. I flick my tongue quickly over her bundle of nerves, and she moans, her knees falling farther apart. I easily sink another finger into her, then curl both digits inside as her hips start to buck against my face. "That's it, *mikrí nýmfi*. Show me what you like." I nibble at her tender flesh and thrust farther into her, circling my fingers, as her cries of ecstasy grow louder.

"Come on my face," I beg as she raises her head and releases a string of curses. She grinds into me, soaking the bedclothes. Her breasts bounce, and the spasms rock her body until she finally slows, her breathing heavy.

"Get up here," she demands, pulling me to her. She licks at my lips, tasting herself on my tongue, and reaches for the head of my cock. "I've wanted this, Pollux," she whispers as she notches me into position. My body pushes roughly into her, and she gasps, adjusting her hips. "Go slowly."

"I'm sorry." I reach down and drag my length up and down between her sex, wetting myself with her arousal. I push into her slowly this time, and she inhales deeply, her breasts rolling up into my face. I pull one fleshy mound into my mouth and tug on the sensitive flesh. Her muscles relax, her slickness drenches my cock, and I slide all the way home as we both roar to life.

Desy throws her head back into the bed, her long neck exposed, and claws her fingernails down my back. She grabs my ass and pulls me farther into her with each thrust. "More," she demands, wrapping her heels around my legs and arching into me.

"You're so fucking wet." Her breasts bounce against my chest. I reach up and run my thumb along her bottom lip. She moans through heavy breaths, and I know I'm not going to last much longer. "Fuck, Desy, I'm already almost there. I promise next time I'll last longer."

In response, she takes my hand and drags it down her body to her swollen clit. With her fingers guiding us, she presses both our digits into her flesh. "Ah, right there," she moans as our hands entangle. Her inner walls start to spasm, choking my cock, and she gasps for breath as her eyes close. "I'm coming, Pol, I'm coming!"

I grunt, pounding into her harder, as my own muscles contract. I grip the bedding behind her head and grit my teeth, roaring in one final thrust. My vision swims and my body shudders before I collapse. Rolling onto my back, I bring my hand to my chest and attempt to catch my breath, mentally slowing my pounding heart. Desy stays still beside me, her breathing coming in shallow spurts.

"Are you well? Did I hurt you, *mikrí nýmfi*?" I turn toward her, my orgasm making me feel emotional and caring. Or at least that's what I tell myself as I'm met with the tip of a blade held to my throat and Desy's dark gaze blazing with fury.

"No, no, no, no." I hold my hands up in submission. Having a knife to my throat is only one step above having one held to my cock and balls, and as I gulp and the blade knicks my skin, a flush of panic runs through my veins. "What the fuck are you doing?"

"I'm getting out of here," the nymph hisses as she grabs her chiton from the floor. She snarls at the flimsy material and tosses it away, eyeing my leather leggings and tunic.

"You can't take my clothes, Desy."

"It doesn't look like you're in much of a position to bargain with me this time, *Prince*." Her lip curls on the moniker and I attempt to rise, only to have her swipe awkwardly into the air in front of me.

"I give, I give." I fall back against the blankets and pillows, pulling the bedding over my lower half. She continues to point the knife at me as she pulls on my leggings, wobbling with unsteadiness.

"Is this about Olympus?" If my soldier training taught me anything, it was to use my skills of socializing and spewing bullshit to my advantage. "I told you I'd take you with me."

"Like I believe anything coming from your mouth."

"You came from my mouth," I add wryly, hoping desperately for a smirk. She squints at me and scowls. Shaking my head, I edge closer to her but keep my hands visible. "Just put down the knife, Desy, and we can go to Olympus in the morning. Come back to bed." I pat the spot she recently vacated, her warmth only now seeping from the fabrics.

"I'm done being held captive, being a prisoner." She cinches the leggings with one hand, tying them as tight as they'll go, and quickly pulls on my tunic. It hangs below her knees. Sticking the handle of the blade in her mouth, she quickly knots the hem of the tunic, turning my manly outfit into one showing off all her ample curves.

I blink quickly, setting aside how good she looks in my clothes, and spring for the weapon. I reach for her mouth just as she pulls the blade from between her teeth, slicing the palm of my hand wide open. Blood spurts across my naked chest, and I growl in pain. Cupping my injured palm as the blood pools, I grab her around the waist and fling her onto the bed.

"Ack!" she screeches as she whips out her leg, landing a kick to my cheekbone. Pain blasts through my eye socket, and I stumble back.

"*Fuck*!" I hold my unbloodied hand to my eye, but she's too quick. Jumping out of the bed, she throws a blanket over my head before another kick lands straight to my chest, knocking me against a desk.

Her footsteps echo down the hall, and as I pick myself up, my head throbbing and my fingers sticky with oozing blood, all I can think is that I'm in love.

And so fucked.

HECATE

Running down the hall as though I were being chased by Cerberus, I flee from the room I shared with Castor. Hot tears stream down my face, but I must hurry if I'm to magic myself out of Olympus before my husband frees himself from the restraints, or worse, he's discovered and set free by a god with a hidden vendetta against us. There are many to distrust at the palace in the sky, but ultimately, leaving him here on Olympus with the protection of Athena and Artemis, my most trusted friends, is the best thing I can do for my love.

"Hecate, wait!" The voice from behind startles me, and I stop in my tracks, my fingers tingling with fear. I turn slowly, gritting my teeth and forcing my eyes to stay open and innocent, as I begin to mutter a compliance spell under my breath.

"*Ypakoúo sti—*"

"Hecate, are you returning to the Underworld just now? We, too, must hurry home!" The approaching voice saps the spell from my breath, and I find myself pulled into the arms of the Fates. Clotho and Lachesis are missing their third sister, Atropos, who refuses to ever leave the Underworld.

The elderly women poke and prod at me.

"My dear, what have you done to your hair? It's a mess!"

"When was the last time you've eaten? You've gotten so scrawny. Look at her, Clo! She's practically skin and bones!"

"Where's that handsome husband of yours? I wouldn't mind returning to the Underworld on his arm. Am I right, Lachesis?"

I pull away, confusion knitting my brow. I pull them aside into a darkened alcove. "What are you both doing here?" I keep my voice lowered as I check up and down the hallway.

"Athena sent for us. Did Hades not inform you?"

"Of course he didn't inform her, you dolt. She wouldn't have asked if she'd known."

"Hush up, Clotho, or I'll snip your thread myself!"

"Ladies, ladies." I edge in between them and motion for them both to keep their voices down. "I must hurry back to the Underworld, so if you'd like to come with, we must go now. There's no time for arguing."

"I'm ready now. Clo, do you have your spindle?"

Clotho pats her chiton, a look of uncertainty pulling at her brows. "Ah, yes, here it is!" She digs it from beneath the folds of fabric and holds it aloft. The small handheld spindle glows with golden string, and my eyes widen as I behold the power of the Fates. To carry around the thread of life so carelessly sends a shiver of panic through my chest, but I gulp it down and pull both goddesses back into the hallway. Our footsteps echo in the emptiness.

"Which one of these doors leads to the gardens?" I ask. "You two know the palace better than I."

"Take a right and then hang a left, and we'll come to Helios's private garden."

"I'd rather not have the smell of cow shit on me, Lachesis. Go left here and then take another left," Clotho instructs as she pulls me in the opposite direction.

We stumble into a small private courtyard filled with not cows, but a single apple tree. I approach a heavy branch and pull down a golden apple. Furrowing my brow as I examine it, Lachesis approaches and smacks my hand.

"Don't touch that! We must've come upon Hera's garden!"

I look around, my heart beating loudly in my chest, as realization dawns on me. The grass is overgrown and weeds sprout between the stones of the footpath. "We need to get out of here. Now." I turn and head toward the doorway. The last place I want to be is in Hera's private garden, even if she no longer holds a place of honor at the court.

"Wait." Clotho grabs me by the wrist. "This is the perfect place to open the portal to the Underworld. No one will come upon us in here. We have privacy and peace for you."

I bite my lip, refusing to tell her that this is the least peaceful place I've ever been. It's as though I can feel Hera's spite and bitterness toward me in the way the apples shine in the sunlight. A heaviness pushes down on my shoulders, and my head begins to ache. I hope it's not another migraine, and as I take a deep breath and nod at the Fates, I recite the spell to unseal the doorway between the Land of the Living and the Underworld.

"*Anoixe tin pórta. Fos anamméno. Xekleidóste tin pórta. Steílte to fos.*"

• • • • • • • • • •

I blink in confusion. The Terranean Sea lies before me, its aqua waters glistening. The hot sun shines overhead, the top of my head burning. How did we end up on the cape?

"This isn't the Underworld," Clotho whispers to her sister, loudly enough for me to hear. Lachesis is silent, her face pale and devoid of emotion. My eyes widen as I see her fiddling with her staff.

"What are you doing?" I rush toward her and grab her by the shoulders, shaking her out of the trance.

"She's reading your destiny, Hecate." Clotho's words breathe a chill into the air, and goosebumps break out along my arms.

"Make her stop," I command. But deep down I know it's useless. The Fates have already decided my destiny. I watch in horror as Clotho holds out her spindle in her palm. It begins to turn, slowly at first and then wildly and without reason, alternating between slow and fast.

"It is time for you to learn your destiny, witch." Clotho's eyes look toward the distance, and as a shadow falls over me, I turn. My breath hitches as I look up, and up, and up until my neck is craned so far back I feel as though my spine will snap.

It's a giant.

"Get back," I call to Clotho and Lachesis as my fingers begin to tingle.

"The Fates are not my intended target, Hecate." His voice echoes around me, shaking the ground and causing rocks and boulders to tumble from the surrounding hills.

"Who is your target then, Giant?" I clench and unclench my fists, readying my powers. The beastly being wears only a leopard-skinned loincloth and has the face of a mortal man, but where two legs should be, there are only the tails of serpents.

"I am sent by Mother to absorb the powerful witch's magic," he intones, his beady eyes dead of emotion. He seems to be under some sort of spell. I circle around him, racking my brain for anything that would break the hold over him. Perhaps, if I can free his mind, I can stop this war before releasing Zeus.

"*Ta mátia tou den vlépoun tin alítheia.*" I lift my arms into the air and send the words on a breeze.

The giant inhales, the words swirling before him.

He blinks once.

Twice.

Then he lets out an ear-piercing roar. I cover my ears and turn to Clotho and Lachesis, ensuring their safety. Clotho's eyes are wide in horror, her hand covering her mouth as she cowers next to her ashen-faced sister. Gulping down my fear, I turn back to the brute before me. If spells won't work, then I'll have to use the fire in my veins, which is already begging to be released.

I grind my teeth together and curl my hands into fists, my fingernails biting into my palm. I can feel the blood seeping from between my fingers as the white-hot anger simmers just under my skin.

The giant advances and I unleash my rage, the blood burning as the heat barrels from my wounds.

HECATE

The bastardly giant effortlessly dodges the flames I throw at him, but the dry foliage in the distance is suddenly alight.

"Fuck," I mutter as a lump forms in my throat. I blink rapidly as I openly stare at the blaze spreading to the dried shrubs. I've always been the most powerful witch—the most powerful being—in any battle I've had to fight. Save for Zeus. It's probably why he felt we were so perfect together. Why he wanted all my power for himself.

Once, I was lucky enough to have all the Olympians on my side. And we were barely successful as we overpowered him. But now, as I look around at the frightened Fates, I know I'm all alone in this fight. I'm going to have to outwit this beast with something different. And I'm going to have to do it by myself.

I duck as a boulder whips past me. If he's strong enough to lift slabs of rock so effortlessly, I'll need to use my wits to counterattack. My hair sticks to my face as the burning shrubs give off an oppressive heat and the smoke clouds my vision. Clogs my throat. Swiping my brow, I grit my teeth and think.

My spells won't work. But why?

Think, Hecate.

There must be some kind of protection warding him.

Simply throwing flames at him won't work. He's too quick. I need to get closer.

I watch as he slithers, serpent-footed, toward another stone. My breathing comes in rapid puffs now. My time is running out.

"Hecate!" Clotho hisses from behind me. I keep one eye on the advancing giant as the Fate nods to a set of abandoned walking sticks. Clotho bends down and picks them up, then tosses them both to me. I catch one in each hand, assessing their weight. The heft is perfect for what I have in mind.

An explosion of pain blooms in my shoulder, and I'm knocked sideways as a piece of debris slices my skin.

I yelp in terror as the giant's body slithers toward me, the snake tails gliding across the crusty terrain. This beast is quick. Climbing behind one of the boulders, I zig and zag around several other slabs until I've found a hiding place. Backing into a darkened crevice, I wait in anticipation as the giant smashes the rocks around me.

"Hecate!" he calls, as though I'd give up my location so easily. But the way my heart pounds so loudly, I'm sure he'll find me before long.

"Come out, witch." His voice drips with need. He's parched. Thirsty for my death.

I lay the walking sticks out, one on either side of my crouched body, and try to control my breathing. I won't be able to win this fight if I can't control myself. And my magic.

I remember when, as Melinoe, my magic was so uncertain, so prone to failure when I needed it the most. As much as I know deep within myself that I'm no longer that scared girl, I can't help but worry that history is doomed to repeat itself. And if my magic fails on me now? I shake my head, unwilling to consider the thought, just as another boulder shatters. The dust and pebbles mar my view, so I know he's close. I close my eyes and hold my breath as I allow my ears to take over.

His footsteps falter next to the crevice.

I'm sure I've been spotted.

He knows where I'm hiding.

The shadows of my refuge disappear, and the sun's heat hits the back of my neck.

"Got you," he roars as he raises the slab higher into the air.

"*Kápste to fos*," I yell as my hands cup the ends of the sticks. They flare to life and I hoist the two torches aloft, all while rolling out of the way of the falling boulder. It hits the spot I just vacated and shatters, scattering shards and debris all around us. Holding my breath, I squint through the dust and drive the flaming torches home.

They hit their mark, catching him in the abdomen and upper thigh. He lets out a piercing cry of pain and stumbles backward, tripping over a stone. His threadbare loincloth lights as the fire spreads over his body, burning him as he tumbles backward down the hill. I force myself to watch, my body hunched over and shaking, as he lands at the bottom and doesn't move. The corpse is broken and still burning, the stench wafting into the air.

Picking my way carefully down the hill, I seek out the Fates.

• • • ● • ● • • •

A high-pitched scream rends the air, and I increase my pace as I leap over the remnants of boulders.

"Hecate!"

I reach the bottom of the hill and round the corner to find yet another giant, this one holding Clotho aloft by her throat. Lachesis rushes toward me, her staff discarded in the dirt.

"You must open the portal to the Underworld. Now!" The fear in her eyes demands my immediate surrender. If only to save her sister.

"We cannot let him into Hades's realm!" I respond as my brain surges to life. This giant resembles his brother-in-arms, except he's wearing steel armor instead of a flimsy loincloth. He's much broader around the shoulders, but still serpent-footed and massive.

"Open the portal, Hecate! Our sister Atropos will be on the other side waiting."

Before I can ask how another Fate will help our cause, Lachesis is grabbed around the middle and jerked backward by one of the snake tails. She shrieks as the slithery scales curl around her body, squeezing tightly.

"Fuck," I hiss to myself, hurrying away from the carnage. I must remain calm in order to open the cavernous doorway, and with my strength sapped and my nerves on edge, that's easier said than done.

I take a few deep breaths and roll up my sleeves. Closing my eyes, I intone the words again, hoping that this time they work. *"Anoixe tin pórta. Fos anamméno. Xekleidóste tin pórta. Steílte to fos."*

Nothing.

I curse and squeeze my eyes closed. Of course I can't open a doorway to the Underworld when I almost just died and two Fates are fighting for their lives just behind me.

Calm yourself, I beg. *Hurry.* I hold my palms up, my fingers visibly trembling. I fist my hands and shove them down to my sides. My back teeth grind against one another over the sounds of the two Fates struggling. Their deaths are imminent if I cannot control my emotions.

I refuse to glance backward, as I know the sight will be my undoing. Instead, I take another few steps forward and, with my eyes closed, envision Castor.

Our home, with Cerberus at our feet as we laugh over dinner.

My garden of herbs. Where Castor brings me a cool cup of pomegranate wine.

Our bed, where we spend many nights speaking of our past—and more importantly our future.

I release one last calming breath. The words sail from between my parted lips.

"Anoixe tin pórta. Fos anamméno. Xekleidóste tin pórta. Steílte to fos."

The ether before me crackles and trembles as the doorway parts, and I inhale a gasp of joy as Atropos steps through carrying two bronze maces.

"Where are they?" She tosses me a mace, and I immediately turn and start running back to the giant. Lachesis is nearly completely entrapped within the confines of the serpentine coils, her hand reaching out as we appear. Clotho, her body held aloft in the air, kicks and scratches against the giant's large hand that's wrapped around her neck.

I toss my weapon to Lachesis just as Atropos raises hers, swings it around above her head, and brings it down on the giant's outstretched arm.

As the spiked metal ball sinks into his skin, he roars in pain and drops Clotho. I race to catch her. Her weight lands heavily on me as we crash to the ground. I'm able to lift her up and carry her to safety, setting her behind one of the intact boulders, just as Lachesis drives her weapon into the meaty body of a serpentine appendage. The body part recoils and releases Lachesis, who scurries away as she heaves with heavy breaths.

"Give me the mace!" I yell to her, and she tosses it back. With her energy sapped, it lands between us on the soil. My eye catches the giant, who bends to dive for the weapon at the same time as I, but it's Atropos who hits him square in the jaw. Blood and teeth spew across the dirt. I reach the mace and bring it down on his extended hand, the crunch of his bones a glorious sound.

As the giant rises to his full height, his face mangled and his broken hand hanging limply at his side, Atropos and I make eye contact and nod, our weapons ready.

I swing the mace over my head and land it straight in his gut. With a groan, he stumbles and doubles over in pain as Atropos comes up from behind and bashes in his skull. He falls to the ground, the earth shaking, and we both make quick work of finishing him off.

My body sagging and covered in the bloody remains, I drop the weapon. I lean over my knees in an attempt to catch my breath, but instead fall to the ground.

"I-I'm so—" I begin.

And then everything goes black.

POLLUX

It takes me at least half an hour to clean and bandage my hand. I wince as I shove the sewing needle through my palm and pull tightly. Cinching the knot, I rip the thread with my teeth and angrily toss the kit back into the basket of weaving. Not only did I have to properly stitch the cut one-handed, I also now have to find men's clothing in a house of women. Searching through Desy's trunk of gowns, I toss everything aside as either too small or too sheer. Growling in frustration, I stumble down the darkened hallway to a more ornate bedroom. The bed is larger and fabric drapes from the ceiling around the sleeping area, providing privacy. This room must be Demeter's. I rummage in her trunks for something that will fit my bulk. Throwing robes and chitons left and right, I finally find a set of sea-salt-crusted leathers at the very bottom of a second chest. Holding the gear to my nose, I inhale. They smell of the sea.

I frown, realizing these likely belonged to Poseidon at some point. Curling my lip in disgust, I squeeze myself into the pants, feeling proud that I'm much bigger than him. I manage to knot the pants carefully so as not to strain the stitches in my injured hand and then toss the tunic over my head. Thankfully Desy left my boots, otherwise I'd be barefoot.

Stomping from the house toward the stables, I curse under my breath at my predicament. I should have known better. I should have heeded Castor's and Hecate's warnings, but my cock got the better of me. I enter the stable and find it barren, save for a lonely donkey. The creature brays pitifully. His stall is clean and filled with fresh hay, but I add another layer and some oats. My hands on my hips, I eye the small creature and shake my head. There's no way I could ride this sway-backed ass without killing it, so I exit the stable and look around, hoping an idea comes to me.

· · · · ● · ● · · · ·

I munch on a piece of flat bread as I walk down the dirt path toward the nearest town. Dawn is just peeking over the hill in the distance, and my body is starting to lag with lack of sleep. I'm unsure what I'll do when I get to civilization, but staying at Demeter's wasn't a feasible option. I need to send word to Hecate and then make my way to Olympus, hopefully intercepting Desy along the way. My chances of finding her are slim, but I must try.

I can't believe I fucked up yet again.

Shaking my head, I return the remainder of the flat bread to the pouch of food at my side as I come upon a small farm. I quietly approach the cottage, but don't see any movement inside or around the farm itself. The inhabitants must still be asleep. I spy a barn in the back and slink around the side of the hut.

As I enter the small shelter, I frown at the single horse standing silently in its stall. My stomach plummets at the thought of stealing this family's only horse, but the heavy bag of gold at my side is enough to buy at least a hundred more. As I enter the kennel, a row of shiny weapons catches my eye, and I pull a sword and blade down, adding them to my tab. I lead the horse quietly from its space and into the trees lining the perimeter of the farm. From here, it'll be safer to stay off the beaten paths.

Using a fallen tree to stand on, I hold the horse steady and mount. I've left the family with their leather saddle but did take a halter with reins. As I kick the horse into a trot, I use the rising sun to orient myself. If I head east, I'll have to go through Corinth and around the land route to reach Olympus. It's the

121

safer option, but something within my chest pulls me north, toward Patrae and the more dangerous Gulf of Corinth. Could it be that I'm already entrapped by Desy? That she owns my mind . . . and my heart?

• • • ● • ● • ● • • •

I'm nearly sideways when I reach the city of Patrae by nightfall. My body is stiff and my bones are screaming at the pain of riding without a saddle all day. As I enter the city proper, there is a festival underway. I'm glad that my soldiering has led me to be a sound sleeper. Whether I'm surrounded by the cries of battle or soothing crickets in the night, once my head hits a pillow, I'm out.

I find a small inn on a side street away from the revelry. The innkeeper eyes my crusty leathers suspiciously, but once he catches sight of the gold I slide across the counter, he's offering me the biggest room, a bowl of fish stew, and a whore for the evening. I accept the room and food with a smile, but shake my head at the feminine companionship, despite her deliciously plump bosom in her revealingly sheer chiton. She pouts prettily but shrugs and moves on to the next patron, whose eyes widen with glee.

"Have you come to town for the Festival of Artemis's Wrath?" the innkeeper asks as he leads me to my room.

I shake my head. "I'm just on my way through for the evening. How long does the festival last?" I worry about finding a seat on a ship across the gulf with so many visitors in the city.

"You must not be from around here if you are not familiar with the Festival of Artemis's Wrath, son." The man chuckles as he opens the door.

"No," I respond flatly, my body aching to lie down and release the stiffness from my journey. Unfortunately, the innkeeper must not take my hints and enters the room unbidden behind me, sitting in the nearest chair as he pours himself a cup of wine from the carafe.

122

"Ah, well then, I'll share the tale with you, my weary traveler. Have a seat." He motions to the chair in my room, and I rub my forehead as I lower myself stiffly, wincing in pain as my ass hits the hard surface. I'm certainly out of shape if one day without a saddle has left me so swollen and uncomfortable. He pours me a cup of wine, and I gulp the delicious sweetness down in one swig, wondering how many more I'll need to imbibe before I pass out and he leaves.

"There once was a priestess of Artemis's Temple. Her name was Comaetho. She was a most beautiful woman, and she fell in love with a very handsome fellow. His name was Melanippus. They wished to marry and sought permission from their respective families, as young lovers do." He pauses to take a sip of his wine and then refills my cup. I nod politely and toss it back. His eyes widen, but still he continues the story.

"Unfortunately, both families refused the marriage. And before you ask, my traveler friend, we shall never know why they refused. But that didn't deter the young lovers, for they continued to meet in the Temple of Artemis, pledging their love and fucking as those who are blinded by love will do." He winks at me.

I gulp down another cup, the hardness of the room becoming fuzzier as the man continues his tale. "Of course the benevolent Artemis found out and cursed the city of Patrae. The land yielded no harvest and strange diseases took the lives of our townsfolk."

I snort and smile wryly at Artemis smiting yet another city, as she was the goddess behind the Calydonian boar hunt that Castor and I participated in years ago. After the goddess of the hunt was inadvertently spurned by their king, she unleashed a terrifying wild hog on the people of Calydon and then sent her own woman, Atalanta, to slay the beast and win the prize.

"I take it by the color leaving your face that you, too, are aware of Artemis's wrath."

I nod carefully. "I, uh, participated in the boar hunt of Calydon." My jaw ticks as I remember the many men that died by the boar's tusks, and I gulp down the knot in my throat as I think of my friend, Meleager, the crown prince who was murdered by his own brethren over the hunt's prize.

"Ah, yes. Well, then you are no stranger to the wrath of our goddess. Our people went to the Oracle at Delphi and beseeched the Pythia for a way to right the wrong done by these two young impetuous lovers. The Pythia proclaimed that not only must the pair be sacrificed, but each year thereafter a sacrifice made of the fairest youth and most beautiful maiden."

My gorge rises, but I swallow it down and instead chug another cup of the cloyingly sweet wine. "That's a horrendous fate and reason for a festival."

"That it is. But it is said that Comaetho and Melanippus did not suffer, for they were successful in love."

"But the youth and maiden being sacrificed this year, do they not suffer, having never known love?"

The innkeeper is quiet for a moment, as though the thought has never crossed his mind. "Huh, I suppose they do." He laughs jovially and stands, clapping me on the back. "But it is the necessary cost for Artemis's pleasure."

He makes to leave as I stand, my legs wobbly beneath me. "I hope you'll be able to watch before you leave on the morrow. It's certainly a sight, friend."

With that, he takes his leave and I myself collapse on the mattress, the darkness engulfing me as I dream of cursed lovers and the wrath of Artemis.

HECATE

"Hecate?" The deep baritone pulls me from under the waves of sleep, and I groggily blink my eyes open. I crane my neck left and right, wondering how I got here, but as Hades stands over me in my childhood bed, I finally feel safe for the first time in days.

My brow knits in confusion. "How—?"

"The Fates brought you home after the battle with—"

"The giants," I finish for him, my voice shaky with fear. It's a fear I haven't felt since . . . I shake my head and clear away the thoughts of Zeus and what I know must be done to save both mortal and immortal lives.

"Atropos and her sisters spoke highly of your bravery, Hecate. I'm proud of you." He grasps my hand in his, and a warmth spreads through my body. It's one of comfort. Of safety and security. "She was able to provide some information about them—the giants."

I dig my elbows into the bedding and attempt to sit up, but my head spins and I crash back into the pillow, pain exploding behind my eyes. Clenching my eyes closed and inhaling slowly, I will the migraine to pass.

"How long have you had them?" Hades inquires as he releases my hand. He reaches for a small mug of wine.

There's no sense in lying. My father can practically read my thoughts with as well as we know one another. "Weeks, really. Since just before the influx of souls arrived." I lift my lips to the cup and sip, the refreshing liquid calming my nerves.

"Why didn't you tell me?"

I lie back, my body already exhausted from the exertion of simply imbibing the wine. "You had enough to worry about with Persephone gone. I didn't want to add to your trials. And then the souls began arriving in droves . . ." I sigh, too tired to provide any more excuses.

"You should have told me, Hecate."

"What would you have done? I'm the one who heals, the one who creates the potions and salves. I'm the one who knows the spells to take away the pain, to release the unwanted. And even I cannot rid myself of these migraines."

A knock at the door interrupts us, and we both look to see Atropos and Clotho enter. Clotho's face lights up and she rushes to me, sitting on the edge of the bed and immediately grabbing my hand in hers.

"I'm so glad you're feeling better!"

"Well, I'm awake, so there's that, but I don't know about feeling better. What happened?" I direct my question to Atropos, who stands awkwardly behind Hades's chair, her eyes round as concern etches her features.

She beckons to her sister, who hands her a leather-bound book. She flips it open to a page toward the back. "The giant you killed, called Clytius, was sent by someone—or something—to absorb your power."

"For what purpose?" I ask as my jaw ticks. I'm reminded of Zeus and Hera trying to use me and my power to make themselves stronger, and I won't be made a pawn again. I pull my hand away from Clotho and clench my fists.

"We're still unsure." Atropos flips the page and continues. "The giant that attacked my sisters was called Agrios, and we think he was created to replace us Fates."

"Do you think Clytius was created to replace me too? Maybe this person is creating giants in hopes of replacing all of us?"

"We don't know anything else, but it's a possibility."

I sigh heavily and lean back, closing my eyes for only a brief second before Clotho clears her throat. My gaze finds her sending a strange look to her sister and Hades.

"What aren't you telling me?" I sit up and cross my arms. I feel the adrenaline surging through my veins at the unspoken words between the three visitors.

The Fates look to Hades, who immediately turns his gaze to the floor as he leans forward. "Athena sent a message."

My stomach plummets and I swallow down the lump in my throat. Of course she did. She would be wondering why I'd left my husband tied up in our bedchamber and then fled without saying goodbye.

"She expects Zeus to be freed," Hades says as his eyes meet mine.

My shoulders sag. "Of course she does."

"Today." I stare back at the god who raised me as Melinoe. The god who taught me everything I know. Tears blur my vision as I see the hurt and regret pass over his face. "I'm so sorry, my daughter." He drops his face into his palms as the tears spill down my cheeks. My throat burns.

"Me too."

• • • ●•●•● • •

I thought the next time I returned home it would be for good. I thought I'd be with Castor, and the war would be behind us. I thought we'd return in triumph—together—as heroes.

"Are you ready?" Atropos's hand steadies me, even as the migraine's throbbing pain blurs my vision.

"No," I admit, cocking my eyebrow at her. "Not at all."

"I don't know what will happen, but I'll protect you." Hades stands tall at my other side, his chin tilted high as he stares down the oak tree in the distance.

I reach for him, and he pulls me into a hug. *This is the last time I'll feel safe,* I think. I pull away from my father and turn my gaze toward the tree. My jaw clenches, but I take a deep breath and roll my shoulders down and back. This isn't about me and my safety. This is about the safety of those in the Land of the Living. It's time I put my revenge, my past, behind me.

I turn toward Atropos and offer her a small smile before turning to Hades and dipping my chin. They know to stand back and, should the need arise, seek shelter in my cabin. I've protected the abode in case Zeus is unable to control his anger with me. I cannot have my people hurt.

I force myself to take a step. And then another. *One more*, I tell myself. Before I know it, I'm standing in front of the solemn oak, under the canopy, its branches creaking with impatience.

I reach out and run my fingers along the rough bark. I feel the grooves and jagged edges of the trunk. "You will be released," I tell the oak as I circle around the thick timber, my finger tracing a path. I step over the roots. "You are needed, now more than ever before." My rotation complete, I step away from the tree. "To atone for your crimes."

I sneak one last glance at my father. He nods his head solemnly.

It is time.

POLLUX

The shouting voices outside the inn wake me, but it's the soreness in my muscles that gets me out of bed. I stand in the middle of the room and stretch, cracking my bones and feeling every year of my age. I suppose it's a good thing I'm not going into battle anytime soon, as my aging body would likely break anyway.

A roar from the revelry in the streets sends me to the window, and I part the curtain to see a stream of people heading toward the town square. Moving to the small basin, I shake out the leathers, wishing I had stopped to buy a new pair last night, and then squeeze into them. They've stretched out slightly, and my hand isn't as painful, so I am able to lace them up easily. I rinse my face and hands with the lukewarm water in the bowl the innkeeper left, and then quickly make my way downstairs.

"Ah, I see you haven't left yet! You're just in time to witness the sacrifice."

I'm not sure if it's the lack of food this morning or the overindulgence of wine the night before, but a sour taste floods my mouth. "I think I'd rather not. If you could just point me in the direction of the harbor, I've a ship to catch." The pull to go north has lessened since I arrived in Patrae. I can't imagine that Desy's wasted her time wallowing in wait, so I need to be on my way if I hope to catch up to her.

"The harbor's just beyond the town square. You'll have to fight through the influx of visitors, mind, but you'll find many a sailor willing to trade you a place on a ship for a few coins."

I nod my thanks and make my way to the stables, where I find the stableboy brushing down my stolen horse. "Your horse is ready, sir."

I pat the creature affectionately on the snout and turn to the young lad. "Would you care to make some extra coin?"

The boy looks at me suspiciously. I can only imagine the offers he's had, what with his curly locks and dark brown eyes. "I cannot take this horse with me, but I'd appreciate it if you cared for him. I know there are those who would take an abandoned horse to the butcher, but I'll give you coin to take him to your house and keep him there as your own."

The boy's eyes widen in bewilderment, but then a slow grin breaks out on his face. He shakes his head happily. "I've never owned a horse of my own before, sir! Thank you, thank you!" He holds out his forearm and I shake it, nodding my head.

"I'm trusting you, and I'll be back to check on you and my friend here, so take good care of him." I ruffle the horse's forelock and then smack the boy gently on his shoulder.

"Good day, sir! And thank you again!" he calls as I make my way into the sea of revelers.

· · · · ● · ● · · · ·

I'm immediately sucked into the swarm of people and pulled in the direction of the town square. Luckily, I can see the harbor in the distance. I pull a piece of dried fish from the pouch at my waist and take a bite as I near the festivities. The loudness of the music increases. Banners and flags sway in the morning breeze. I continue following the crowd, but suddenly everyone stops. The music ceases and a man climbs onto a rickety stage not far from me.

"Citizens of Patrae!" he calls, and a hush falls over the crowd. I try to continue onward, but the people are packed so tightly there's no way my bulky shoulders will part the mob. So instead, I wait patiently.

"Many moons ago, a beauteous young maiden and her handsome lover defiled Artemis's Temple." The crowd around me boos and hisses as two actors reenact the innkeeper's story from the previous night. I watch as the skit portrays the young lovers begging their parents to consent to their marriage and later them pledging their troth under the garland of the makeshift temple. The townsfolk continue to catcall and throw curses as the couple's actions bring about disease and drought to the city of Patrae. When the Pythia proclaims that only a sacrifice will free the city of its curse, the crowd cheers. My jaw clenches as I eye the harbor in the distance.

"And now, people of Patrae, we must make our way to Artemis's Temple to continue our festivities in the culmination of the yearly sacrifice!" The crowd again roars and begins moving away from the town center. My route to the harbor is wide open, less than the distance I've traveled from the inn, but something stops me from taking that first step.

An ache in my chest throbs in time with the chanting revelers. It pulls me in their direction—the direction of Artemis's Temple. Looking at the sparkling water in the distance, I sigh heavily and turn with the crowd, following the thrumming in my sternum.

As we arrive on the outskirts of the city, the temple comes into view. The limestone is pristine, as though it's been washed by hand. It gleams in the sunlight, and green wreaths and garland are pinned to the structure. The same man from the city center stage climbs the steps as the crowd stops, becoming silent as they await his words.

"My people, we are here to sacrifice the fairest maiden and youth, to please our most high priestess Artemis. We ask for her protection, for her forgiveness, and for her generosity in the seasons before us." He falls silent and turns toward the temple. The crowd watches, rapt, as the door creaks open.

My breath catches and my stomach plummets as Desy, her hands bound in front of her, is escorted out first, followed by a dark-haired boy just shy of adulthood.

"We bring forth the sacrifices, the beauteous maiden and the handsome youth!" the man shouts as he raises his hand toward Desy and the boy. The crowd roars, their weapons held aloft.

I watch as Desy's face falls, her eyes gleaming with unshed tears as she quivers. I elbow my way through the crowd, trying to get closer, but it's impossible. The crowd is so thick, so tightly packed, that I can't fight my way through.

"Desy!" I yell, trying to get her attention. But she can't hear me over the din of the mob.

"Desy!" I try again, raising my hands to my mouth. She looks around at the crowd, her face a mask of terror and despair.

I continue to fight my way forward, now picking up people and moving them out of my way. I'm elbowed and punched, scratched and kicked, but none of it matters as long as I keep Desy in my sight.

"Desy!" I roar again, pleading with her to look my way. She seems to hear something, and her head snaps in my direction, but her eyes go past mine and beyond, farther into the crowd.

"I said stop!" a deep voice proclaims from behind me. I turn, along with the rest of the mob, as silence descends over us. "There will be no sacrifices today!"

"And who are you to demand we halt our sacrifice to the goddess?" the man on the stage demands as he shades his eyes with his hand, seeking out the voice in the crowd.

The revelers part, affording me a clear view.

"I am Heracles."

Hᴇᴄᴀᴛᴇ

"M*etá apó aftó to déntro tha klaíei, ta fýlla tou tha marathoún kai i ríza tou tha maratheí.*" I reverse the spell. Where once I grew a tree with leaves so lush and roots so deep, I now command the soil to weep. To purge itself of this oak. The leaves shrivel and the roots curl in on themselves. The trunk cracks and light spills forth, blinding all of us with its brightness.

I step back and shield my eyes, but my senses are on alert. I cannot allow him to escape the Underworld and go free, wreaking havoc on all of us who sent him to this prison.

The ground rumbles and I trip over a stone, falling backward. I catch myself with my palm, but a sharp pain spreads through my wrist and up my arm. I wince.

A gentle touch spans both my shoulders and I look up, startled to find my father lifting me from the ground. "What are you doing? This is not safe for you!"

"I cannot stand by and watch . . . whatever may happen. I am by your side." He brushes the dirt from my tunic and laces his fingers with mine as he stares into the light.

Tears cloud my vision and I swipe them away with my good hand before I, too, look into the light.

The trunk cracks all the way up to the sky as the tree cleaves in two. The pieces crash to the ground on either side of the lone figure who stands before us.

Hecate, the voice hisses in my mind, even as the god before me utters not a word.

I blink, my jaw clenching as the light grows brighter and brighter. Finally, as the former king of gods steps from his prison, the brightness flares and then dims.

Gleaming spots dance in my vision, and I blink over and over to quickly clear them from my sight. Unable to see clearly, my heart pounds in my throat and a roar rushes in my ears.

Where is he?

I blink furiously.

Suddenly a hand circles my throat, and on a gasp, I'm lifted into the air, my toes seeking the ground.

I claw at the hand with my nails, but the grip only grows tighter. My airway constricts, and now red and black spots dance in my vision.

"Release her. *Now.*"

I drop to the dirt, my knees buckling. I gulp in air between coughs. "You . . . bastard . . ."

Hades has his bident pointed straight at Zeus's stomach, ready to impale him. I've never seen my father's face filled with such hatred, such rage. "You're lucky I don't send you straight to Tartarus, brother."

Zeus's gaze slides from mine to my father's, and a serpentine smirk lifts his lips. "You wouldn't. Why else would you release me unless you needed me? I knew this day would come." His silky-smooth voice is like hot water on a sunburn. It burns through my bones.

He's right.

We need him.

And when he reaches his hand out, raising me up from the dirt he threw me in, I take it.

If only to save our people.

· · · ● · ● ● · · ·

"My lady, what are you waiting for?"

The voice startles me, and I turn to find Selene. Her eyebrows draw together as she leans forward. My gaze flicks around the outer chamber before I run my hands down my jewel-encrusted dress. The red gems may sparkle beautifully in the sconces' light, but I am only reminded of the rage and hatred I still feel for Zeus.

"Selene, I can't . . . I can't do this." I shake my head, my curls tickling my exposed back. My heart feels as though it's going to burst forth from my chest, and I cannot catch my breath. I gulp air but still feel as though I'm suffocating. "What is happening?"

My handmaiden reaches her wrinkled hands toward me and wraps them around my upper arms. She runs them up and down, shushing me with pursed lips. "Titaness, you are stronger than you know. Your heroics are told from one sea to the next, stories of not only your magical abilities, but of your kindness, strength, and intelligence. You are the only one who doubts yourself, my dear." She pats my arms and withdraws her touch. I'm instantly chilled, but calmer.

"How can I face him?"

"The same way Hades is." My shoulders drop and I realize that I hadn't thought about how difficult this has been for my father. To face his wife's rapist? To look his own brother in the eyes and be strong enough to restrain his hatred?

"You're—you're right." I nod and press my lips together. Hades raised me to be not only a princess of the Underworld, but also a warrior. He made sure that I was strong enough to handle anything. I turn my gaze toward the doorway and, running my hands down the dress one final time, step through.

My father has exchanged an intimate dinner in his personal chambers for the more formal dining room. The dark wooden table extends the length of

135

the space, with Hades positioned at the head. My footsteps echo loudly as I approach and take a seat to his right. Zeus occupies the chair to his left. I swallow the lump forming in my throat and force myself to make eye contact with the former king of the Olympians.

My old childhood friend, the man I spent years hiding from before finding the strength to fight back, Zeus looks haggard and weak. My gaze finds my father's, and I can tell we share common thoughts. While Hades is older, he looks years younger than the brother at his side.

"Will your queen be joining us, Hades?" Zeus juts his chin, looking to provoke his sibling.

I watch helplessly as my father's grip on the utensils tightens and his knuckles turn white. His eyes flash a deep maroon as his skin grays and crackles. I've only seen him transform this way once before, when Hermes attempted to return to the Underworld after Zeus was imprisoned. My father wouldn't accept a traitor in his midst, and the messenger god quickly retreated to the Land of the Living.

"My queen is taking care of the additional souls who appeared in our kingdom just days ago. She serves our realm well and has an equal role in ruling alongside me." The dig at Hera clearly doesn't escape Zeus, whose own face darkens with rage.

"That reminds me. Where is *my* wife?" He turns his murderous gaze on me, and I resist the urge to shrink back in my chair.

Instead, I exhale slowly and reach for the glass of wine before me. Twirling the stem between my thumb and forefinger, I raise the goblet to my lips and take the smallest sip before returning it to the table. "That I do not know, as I've spent your imprisonment here in the Underworld—my home."

"Until I know where she is, that she's safe, I'll not help anyone who colluded with you to overthrow me."

Hades's eyebrows squish together, and I smirk at him. "Brother, did you think you had a choice in the matter?"

"What do you mean? Of course I have a choice! I'm the most powerful god. Your king!"

I place both palms on the table and stand, eager to share the truth of Zeus's release. "You *were* the most powerful, but now Athena reigns in your place."

"Blasphemy!"

I shrug. "Be that as it may, the moment you were released from your imprisonment, I bound your abilities. You may notice that you haven't healed as quickly as before or that you feel nauseous and not quite right?"

Zeus narrows his eyes at me as his jaw clenches.

I glance at my father, who nods for me to proceed. "Until we have what we need from you, you belong to me." With that I plop back down in my seat and return to my meal with a smug smile on my face.

But I don't eat a single bite. Instead, I force myself to breathe in and out, in and out, as I purposefully avoid Hades's rapid blinking or the sound of my own heartbeat thrashing in my ears.

POLLUX

The muscled man—Heracles—is assailed by the crowd, their thirst for blood desperate to be satiated. I look back and forth between the two, Heracles who seems to be holding his own against the mob and Desy who's being dragged back into the temple by the man on stage, and sprint toward the steps of the temple.

I grab an axe from an unsuspecting citizen just as he's about to swing it and slice open the skull of his neighbor. "Ho there!" he shouts, but I'm pressing forward and already climbing the stairs.

"Let her go," I demand of the man as Desy's eyes light up.

"Pollux!" She tries to rush toward me, but her jailer wraps his arms around her and yanks her backward. She stumbles and smacks her head, a string of curses leaving her mouth as blood dots the stones.

I step over her and aim the axe at the man, holding it straight at his chest. "If you know what's good for you, you'll leave her. *Now.*"

His eyes widen in fear as he looks at Desy and then back to the axe. Shaking his head and holding his hands out in supplication, he turns and runs into the temple, closing the door behind him.

I bend down and lift Desy to standing, slicing the ropes at her wrist and cradling her wounded cheek in my palm. "We need to get out of here. Can you walk or do you need me to carry you?"

Her eyes look out over the sea of bodies, now enmeshed in an all-out brawl, and her gaze stops on the fair-haired Heracles. "We can't leave him behind. He needs our help."

I follow her line of vision, even as my jaw ticks with jealousy. The golden, godlike man swipes and stabs his way through the crowd of attackers. I grit my teeth and hand her the axe. "Can you use this?"

She eyes me as a smirk touches her lips. Just then a brute from the mob reaches the top step and grabs her foot. He pulls, throwing her off-balance. She shrieks, but before I can pull my sword from my belt, she's lopped the man's hand from his body with her weapon.

My eyes widen in appreciation as her face pales at the bloodied hand still attached to her ankle. She squeals and uses the axe to fling it into the crowd. Laughing, because what else can you do in a situation like this, I pull her down the stairs and into the mob.

"Stay close to me," I yell over the din of swords and cries of pain.

I make a path toward the savior, slicing and punching my way through the throng of people. As we reach Heracles, I see he's uninjured. I am able to at least appreciate his swordsmanship and technique as he quickly dispatches the remaining attackers around him.

He sees me approaching and starts to swing, but it's Desy's shrill voice that stops him in his tracks. "You have to come with us!" she yells from behind me.

He looks between the two of us, as though he has a decision to make, before nodding. "We've got to make it to the harbor," I add. "Are you injured or can you run?"

"I'm fine, mate," he responds with a bright toothy smile.

Of course he is. Not a single scratch, not a hair out of place. The damn man hasn't even broken a sweat.

"Let me carry you!" He pulls Desy into his arms before she has a chance to respond, his eyes filled with concern as he examines her cheek. "They've hurt you."

"She said she was fine," I mutter as we take off toward the harbor.

"I don't mind," Desy responds as she clutches her bruised cheek, the axe held close against her body. I roll my eyes as the flare of jealousy burns in my chest.

I suddenly wish I was back in Sparta.

· · · · ●· · ● · · · ·

My mind isn't soothed during the quick trip across the narrow channel. The choppy waters only add to my already sour gut as I watch Heracles and Despoena sit closely, a rough tarp their chaise. I stay within earshot, not that I desire to overhear their conversation, but the envy coursing through my veins won't allow me to move farther.

"Tell me, Heracles," Desy purrs as she trails her long delicate fingers up the man's muscular arm, "where are your people from?"

"My father is the famous general Amphitryon and my mother is the beauteous Alcmene."

My ears perk up at the mention of my dear old friend Amphitryon.

"I soldiered under your father once and even visited your parents when you were just a babe in your mother's belly." *Fuck*, I curse myself silently, wishing I'd said nothing. Not only is this golden boy prettier than me, but I've at least twenty-five years on him.

Heracles rises from his lounger and comes to stand next to me. "I heard tales of the battle-hardened Spartan twins at my father's knee. I always wished to grow up and meet you both, and look at me now!" He flashes me a winning grin, and I can't help but like the boy.

My lips flatten in acknowledgment. "I imagine you'll be on your way home once we dock in Naupactus then. Your parents must be worried." I add the last bit hoping a guilty conscience will send him on his way.

"Despoena has asked me to accompany her to Mount Olympus, where she'll rendezvous with her mother." He looks over fondly at the reclining nymph.

140

"Did you realize she was traveling alone? What kind of man allows such a beauty to strike out with nary a chaperone for protection? It's a wonder she made it so far without finding trouble." He tuts to himself and shakes his head.

My jaw ticks as my fists clench at my sides. Now I know what poisonous lies Desy's been dropping into the poor boy's head. "It seems she ran off from her companion, choosing to put herself in grave danger against his better judgment."

Rather than the expected astonishment, Heracles's face goes ashen. "That poor delicate goddess. To feel the only way to stay safe was to run away . . ." I nearly roar with rage when his eyes begin to glimmer with unshed tears. "I can only imagine what type of brutish loser would dare force himself on her and then—"

I've heard enough and stalk over to Desy, where I hoist her up from her reclining position by her wrist. "What other lies have you been spewing to this poor fool, nymph?"

"Now wait just a moment!" Heracles grabs Desy and breaks my hold on her. "Are you the brutish loser?" He eyes me up and down as his face turns red with barely contained anger. "I'll slice you from your navel to your throat for what you did to this woman!" He reaches for his blade, pointing it toward me.

I may be older, but I'm still nimble, and I pull my sword from its place at my waist. Holding it aloft, I point my own weapon at him. His eyes darken with rage as his teeth gnash, his temple throbbing. "Don't insert yourself into the middle of this, boy. This nymph is nothing but trouble." I dip my eyes to Desy, her face a mask of indifference.

Heracles looks between us, and I take the opportunity to disarm him of his blade. I sweep my leg behind his, and he stumbles onto the tarp. I point both swords at him.

"My orders were to deliver her to her home and then make my way to Olympus to rendezvous with my brother and his wife. Unfortunately, she snuck off in the middle of the night, stealing my horse and incapacitating me." I hold up my bandaged hand as evidence.

Heracles's face pales, but his brows lower in distrust as he locks eyes with Desy. She visibly deflates and then stomps off, flipping her hair in her wake. Shaking my head, I toss down Herc's blade and then offer him my hand.

"I'm sorry, sir," he says as I lift him up. His contrition is admirable, but unnecessary. He reminds me of myself in my own youth. Naive and easily influenced by a beautiful woman.

"Think nothing of it. But watch out for that one," I add, nodding in Despoena's direction.

He's quiet for a while. We stand together as the ship docks, but as I move to follow Despoena as she departs the ship, Heracles catches my arm. "Sir, if I may? I'd still like to accompany you to Mount Olympus."

I wrinkle my brow. "Why, now that you understand I'm fully capable of returning the nymph to her mother?"

The knot in his throat bobs. "I heard rumors in my travels that there's a war coming, and I'd like to offer my services as a soldier, like you."

I gulp down a sarcastic retort. Little does he know my only service is as a glorified nymph sitter. But, as I've already screwed up my mission, what's the harm in him tagging along?

HECATE

"Hecate?" As I leave the dining hall, my stomach neither full nor settled, I turn to find Clotho stepping from the shadows.

"Clotho? What is it? Is everything well with your sisters?" I don't bother to hide the panic in my voice as my concern builds. Has a giant managed to enter the Underworld?

"Everyone is fine, well, I suppose that's not true . . ." Her gaze dips to the floor as she bites her lip. Reaching into a tiny bag at her waist, she pulls out a scroll and hands it to me. "It's from Helios."

My brow knits as I wonder what message the Titan god of sun sends to the Fates. Untying the knotted cord, I unfurl the scroll. "It's addressed to me?"

"Yes, it was just delivered."

I skim the note. "His daughter, Circe, wishes to meet with me," I recite as I read the missive. "The giants have been visiting her island for days, harvesting an herb, and he worries for her safety." My eyes widen as I look up at Clotho. A smile cracks my lips, and I pull her in for a hug. "This is wonderful news, Clotho!"

"It is?" She quirks an eyebrow at me.

"Don't you see? We have a clue. This herb must be important to the giants. I must travel to Circe's island! Tonight!"

I turn to run to my rooms when Clotho's voice stops me in my tracks.

"What about Zeus? He cannot remain here. And he certainly cannot be trusted to return to Olympus without you as his escort."

My excitement is tampered.

Damn.

I close my eyes and my head falls back as I think of a solution—any solution—where Zeus doesn't accompany me to the island. There must be a way, right?

"He must go with you, Hecate," Clotho interrupts my thoughts, and my stomach plummets. "Would you like me to check your life thread to confirm?" She pulls the glowing spindle from her bag. Her casualness in carrying such an important item around causes my chest to heave, and I bury down how closely we all came to destruction when the giants attacked.

I flap my hands at her. "No, no. That's not necessary. And put that thing away before the wrong person sees it. Don't you think it'd be safer in your home?"

She blinks at me as though the thought never occurred to her. "What's safer than on my very person?" She chuckles and shrugs, sliding the spindle back into her bag. "You best get back in there and share the news." She tilts her head toward the dining hall.

I gulp down the dread building in my gut and look at the crinkled scroll in my sweaty palm.

"Go on now," Clotho urges as she nudges me forward.

I raise my finger toward her. "What if instead I—"

"No, Hecate. There's no way around this. Now go."

As she slips back into the shadows, I scowl at her disappearing form, but she only wags her fingers at me to proceed, so I exhale with a grumble and return to the dining hall. And Zeus.

• • • • • • • • • •

144

"I don't like it, Hecate. I demand you take Rhadamanthus with you." Hades's gaze is cold and hard as he stares daggers at Zeus, whose arms are folded as he sits back in his chair. My gaze narrows. He has not a care in the world while we struggle to form a solution and save everything.

I blink my gaze back to Hades. "Rhadamanthus? It's not possible. We will go directly to Olympus, and besides, you need the general here to assist with the judging of souls." This dinner is the first night away my father has had in weeks. Selene told me he's been nearly chained to his desk and wasn't sleeping or eating nearly enough. "The sooner we get Zeus to Olympus, the sooner we can win the war and everything will go back to normal." I don't miss Zeus's cocked eyebrow or his snort of amusement. The truth is that none of us know what the new normal will look like, or even if we will win this war with the giants. But that doesn't stop me from trying.

"How do you plan on getting to the island?"

I can't let Hades know the truth about my magic, so I shrug and avert my gaze. "We'll follow the River Oceanus. It shouldn't take more than a day or so."

"In that case, I insist Charon take you. At least to the island. Please, Hecate." Hades's eyes plead with mine. "The line is so long, he hasn't been able to carry the souls across the rivers. He's begging to help in some way."

"I forgot, brother, how much I love to watch you beg." Zeus's voice sears my skin, and I go rigid with anger.

I clench my fists, even as the tingling in my fingers becomes unavoidable. Directing my gaze to my father and avoiding eye contact with Zeus, I say, "My lord, I will abide your command and Charon will ferry us to Circe's island."

Zeus growls under his breath, as I knew he would, at my calling Hades "my lord." He always did hate to be second to the god of the Underworld.

"It's settled then. You'll leave on the morning light."

"No." I rap my knuckles on the table and raise my chin. "We leave now. On this I will not compromise. I've wasted enough time returning for him." My eyes flick to Zeus and I purposefully curl my lip. With that I spin on my heel and leave Hades to deal with his obstinate brother while I seek one last moment of peace in my chambers.

• • • • • • • • • • •

"You're simply not going to speak the entire journey, my little witch?"

My muscles stiffen at the endearment, even as I know that Zeus uses it not with love, but with spite. He's looking to get a rise out of me, to rile me up. He forgets that I know him.

"That's the idea," I finally answer as I keep my eyes trained on Charon's back. The Underworld's ferryman stands at the helm, dipping the pole into the dark water. I keep my back straight and my jaw clenched. The boat is small and too much movement will cause Charon to fall, I tell myself. In reality I won't allow myself even a moment to relax, to let my guard down, while Zeus is near.

"You could at least tell me about this war. About these giants we are to fight. I'd like to be prepared should one come along."

I narrow my eyes and slide my gaze to his reclining form on the other side of the boat. "Need I remind you that your abilities have been bound and will not return to full capacity until I allow?"

"How am I to protect myself then? I could fall into this river at any moment!"

I snort and shake my head. "You'd best be still and silent then, for your brother Poseidon despises you and wishes for your head even more than Hades." I dip my finger into the salty water and flick it at him.

I don't tell him that Poseidon hasn't been seen nor heard from since Zeus's imprisonment. He's become an undesirable, along with Demeter and Hermes, since Athena's coronation. However, the sea god's former wife, Amphitrite, regularly visits Olympus as an emissary to the ocean and its living beings. A sour feeling grows in my gut as I wonder what life in Olympus will look like when—or rather if—we win this war.

Who will survive?

Who will rule?

"Hecate." Zeus's hand on my arm pulls me from my thoughts. My lip curls in disgust at his fingers touching me. "You're shaking."

I recoil so sharply that I nearly topple the boat, and Charon stumbles. He thrusts the pole into the water and rights himself before sending me a pinched expression.

I drop my chin to my chest and attempt to compose myself. With my eyes squeezed closed, I recite a calming spell under my breath. "*To myaló sou eínai íremo, i psychí sou tragoudáei me galíni.*" Not many people realize I can use magic on my own emotions, as I rarely do. But desperate times of war require desperate measures of magic. So I repeat the spell once more to ensure it's taken effect, and then sit back and breathe easily as Charon steers us toward Circe's island.

POLLUX

"What do you mean I don't get my own room?" Desy scowls at me.

"Like I'm going to trust you in a room by yourself," I snort as I pass the innkeeper two shiny coins.

"I wouldn't be in the room by myself. Heracles can stay with me." She flicks her gaze to the man just now entering the inn. After putting our mounts in the stable, he rubs his hands together to stave off the night's chill.

"What?" Heracles asks blankly when he notices us eyeing him.

"Nothing," I growl, still frustrated at the nymph's blatant ogling. The golden boy shrugs his shoulders and takes a seat near the inn's front windows.

"You're jealous," Desy whispers under her breath as she edges closer to me. She rubs against my side like a cat in heat, and I can't help but warm at her touch.

"Certainly not, *mikrí nýmfi.*"

Her gaze darkens. "I've told you not to call me that."

I turn to her, crowding her into the counter and pressing my body against hers. I dip low and, licking my lips, whisper in her ear. "I'll call you whatever I choose, and you'll like it after all you've put me through." I tower over her, my entire length flush with hers.

She leans back as she looks up at me. "I hate you." Her lip curls over the words.

"The feeling's mutual." *But it's not mutual.* It's not at all. I want to lift her onto this counter and ruck her chiton up along her thighs before diving face-first into her pussy. My cock throbs at the thought. Her eyes widen, the pupils dilating, and I know she's felt the proof of my arousal.

She suddenly snorts out a laugh before pushing me off her. "Herc!" she calls as she heads over to his spot. She wraps her arms around his neck and climbs into his lap. She leans into his ear and whispers something, and my pulse quickens as she locks those emerald-green eyes with mine.

"Fucking nymph," I mutter under my breath as I adjust myself.

"Pardon, sir?" the innkeeper asks as he reappears with a skeleton key.

"Nothing," I grumble as he plops it into my palm. I nod my thanks and then amble over to my two companions. They're still curled together like lovers. Or, rather, Desy's sphinxlike body is curled around Heracles's while she twirls a lock of his flaxen hair around her finger. The golden god sits ramrod straight, his fingers digging into the sides of the chair. His lips are pressed so tightly together they're white.

"Time to retire," I declare to the duo. Heracles practically leaps at the chance, while Desy stands and places her hands on her hips.

"Who put you in charge?"

"We've all had a long day." *Thanks to you*, I want to add, but I keep my mouth shut. "We need to be on the road early if we're to make it to Olympus in two days' time."

"Heracles was just suggesting a drink before bed. Weren't you, Herc?" She turns to him and practically flutters her long lashes. Any idiot would see through her charms.

"Uh, I did say that, but I think we should tuck in early like Pollux said."

I raise my chin ever so slightly in a sign of thanks. Maybe the blond god isn't as stupid as I thought.

Despoena rolls her eyes and snorts, blowing us both off. "I'm thirsty. I'm sitting at the bar and having a drink—with or without you both." She saunters across the room and into the adjoining tavern. I watch with murderous rage coursing through my veins as she sidles up to the bar and pushes her tits into the barkeep's face.

"Heracles," I growl, not taking my eyes from Desy.

"Sir?"

"Our room is two doors down on the left side. Please take mine and Despoena's things. We'll be along shortly." I pass him the key, my gaze never leaving the nymph's backside, and stalk into the tavern.

I'll be damned if this nymph defies my orders again.

· · · ● · ● · ● · · ·

I step up to the bane of my existence. My entire chest presses into her side as I take the stool next to hers. She inhales my scent, and I smirk as goosebumps break out along her arm, traveling up her neck.

"I thought you said it was time to retire." She refuses to meet my gaze. Instead, she focuses on the drink in front of her.

"You wanted a drink, so let's get a drink."

She flicks her gaze to me, eyeing me suspiciously. "I don't need a nursemaid."

I crack a smile. "I beg to differ."

"I can take care of myself."

"It sure looked like it when you were nearly sacrificed."

"I knew what I was doing."

"It certainly appeared so."

"I *despise* you."

"No, you don't."

She turns to face me. A blush creeps from her neck up into her cheeks. "Oh, but I do, Pollux. I despise everything about you." Her gaze travels from my toes to my forehead. "You just can't see it because your head is so far up your own ass, you're blind to everyone else's feelings."

I shrug noncommittally and take a swig of her drink. The tartness causes my eyes to water, but I refuse to let her see so I lower my lids instead.

She huffs at my silence and shakes her head. "I can't believe we fucked."

I turn to her, but she's already turned her body back to the bar and refuses to make eye contact. I lean in, willing her to see me. "It was amazing, wasn't it?"

Her mouth falls open and she rotates toward me once again. "That's not what I meant and you know it!"

I shrug again, enjoying how easily she's agitated. "You said it, not me."

She's quiet for a moment, swirling her glass and eyeing the liquid inside. I keep one eye trained on her while I check out the tavern. It's rugged, but warm. Cozy, even. A pair of weary travelers, their clothing stained with mud, sit at a table in the far corner. They huddle over their mugs.

"Thank you." It's barely above a whisper, but my ears tingle with the words.

Even though I know she's grateful for my following her and assisting in her rescue, I crack another devilish smile, just to hit a nerve. "You're welcome. My cock thanks you as well. It was a lovely fuck, if I do say so myself, even if I was stabbed afterward."

Her jaw ticks and her eyes flash with anger. "Forget I ever said anything. Forget we even fucked. I know I will."

I knock back the dregs of her drink and slam the cup on the bar. Standing, I pull Desy from her stool.

"Hey!" she yelps in surprise.

My hand still clutching hers, I drag her into a dimly lit corner of the tavern, away from the patrons. We pass a few doors—locked—before finding one that opens. Inside is the tavern's larder. I pull her inside and slam the door behind us, shutting out the light.

"What the fuck are you doing?" she demands. Even though I can't see her, I can imagine her narrowed gaze and full pout.

"Making sure you'll never be able to forget me, *mikrí nýmfi*." One hand circles her neck while the other drops to her ass, pulling her against me. I lower my mouth to hers, but miss and hit the side of her cheek instead. I tighten my hold around her throat and use my thumb to force her chin toward me. Her eyes shine brightly. I try again, hitting my mark as I pull her lips in for a deep kiss. My other hand cups her ass, squeezing her against my growing erection. I part her lips with my tongue and taste the fruitiness of her wine.

A sigh escapes from her mouth, and it's all I need to hear to spur me onward. I use both hands to lift her and, turning us both, lay her out on a sack of grain in the corner. As hungry as I am for her pussy, my cock is weeping to be inside of her. I unlace my pants and pull my cock free, stroking it from root to tip. With the other hand, I slide up the inside of her chiton. She unhooks the pin holding her top up and her breasts bounce free.

"I want your eyes open and on me the entire time, *mikrí nýmfi*, even if it's dark in here. I don't want you to forget what I look like when I'm fucking your wet pussy. When I'm making you come all over my cock. Do you understand?"

"Yes," she whispers breathlessly as she palms her tits.

"I don't ever want to hear you say you wish you could forget this. *Us.*" I sink two fingers into her slick heat, and I know she's ready for me. She wants me. I ruck up the rest of her dress and line myself up at her entrance. I push myself in gently at first, coating my cock with her desire. In and out, in and out, until I'm completely drenched with Desy. When I'm sufficiently slick, I drive into her harder. Faster. The only noises are her sighs of ecstasy and the sound of her wet pussy taking my thick length to the hilt.

"Eyes on me," I demand when I notice her tilting her head back toward the ceiling. I reach for her throat. I tilt her chin back down, and when her eyes are back on mine, I pull her up for a deep kiss. "Are you ever going to forget this, *mikrí nýmfi?*"

"No."

"Tell me." I drive deeper. Harder. "Tell me you'll never forget this."

"I-I'll never forget this." Her legs wrap around my waist, and she rocks her hips up to meet me thrust for thrust.

Her moans come faster, but I can only focus on her breasts bouncing as my cock sinks into her wetness over and over, faster and faster. Just when I can feel she's about to come, when her muscles start to pulse all over my cock, I pull her forward, locking our eyes together as my own release spills inside of her.

Her eyelids start to flutter. "Eyes open," I demand and she complies as a shudder racks her body.

We stay connected, our eyes and bodies bound as one, as our chests heave. We rise and then fall together, collapsing into the soft sack of grain. And then, once we've each caught our breath, I pull her to standing and we walk, hands locked, back to the bar.

"Now how about that drink?" I ask with a playful smile on my face.

She rolls her eyes but tightens her hold on my hand, and I swear I catch a glimmer of a smile lifting her lips.

HECATE

"How much farther?" Zeus groans behind me as the sun beats down on our backs.

"How should I know?" My legs burn as I climb higher on the rocky trail of Circe's island. Sweat drips from my brow, and I'm sure I smell like a pigsty, but at least I'm able to restore myself easier than Zeus. With his abilities bound, he's struggling to even hike a few miles uphill. His wheezing grows shallower. "We can take a rest here on this boulder." I direct him to sit and pull out the skin of watered wine, handing it over to him.

He takes it and drinks greedily, the liquid spilling down his chin.

My lips pull down in a frown, but I bite my tongue. I'm sure Circe will be able to replenish my supply. "If you cannot go farther, perhaps you should stay here," I offer. This is already the third time we've had to pause for a rest since Charon left us on the sandbar mere hours ago. I shield my eyes and glance toward the sky, the sun on its descent to the west. I'd rather not spend the evening outdoors with Zeus. Alone. The thought makes my skin crawl. Or maybe that's the mosquitos buzzing close for their next meal.

Zeus hands me the wine, and I wipe the mouthpiece with my sleeve before taking a sip. I cock an eyebrow as his mouth falls open, daring him to chastise me. He doesn't.

Instead he says, "You know, this island reminds me of Crete."

I clear my throat as I cap the skin, saying nothing. That he would bring up our shared childhood home proves he's trying to crack me.

"Come on, Hecate. We can at least make conversation on this voyage."

I look around—anywhere but at him—and nod. "Crete also had mountains."

He exhales audibly and presses his lips into a white slash.

Before I can stop myself, I ask, "Did you ever go back?"

"I did. Once. Did you?"

I shake my head. "Asteria and Perses were gone by then." *Thanks to you*, I want to add, but don't. He has the audacity to look contrite.

"I suppose I never apologized to you for what I did. To your real parents, that is."

I huff and roll my eyes. "You never apologized for anything, Zeus. To anyone." I can't afford to think about him turning my mother into a desolate island simply because she refused his advances. About my father dying only months later, his heart broken beyond belief at the loss of my mother. My mind needs to stay focused on the giants. Using Zeus only as a means to win this war. I start to walk onward, ready to leave him behind to rot in the sun for all I care, when I feel his presence at my side.

I watch him out of the corner of my eye, and just as he opens his mouth to speak, a beast bursts forth from the shrub before us.

"Watch out!" Zeus cries as he pushes me out of the way. I stumble backward, my sandal catching on a rock, and land in the dirt.

"Baaaa!" the beast bleats, its woolly fur begging to be shorn.

I blink at the animal's horizontal pupils. The way it nuzzles into my shoulder. "A sheep? You tossed me in the dirt over a sheep?" I fume as I stand, digging the small pebbles from my palms. I glare at him, my hands on my hips as my fingers tingle with the need to spew a few flames.

"I didn't mean—"

He's cut off as a handsome older Titan clothed in a purple tunic appears behind the sheep. "You found her!" he exclaims as he raises his arms in celebration. "I'm so grateful to you!"

"Helios?" I inquire, a smile lifting my lips. His joy is infectious, as though he has an aura of sunshine around him.

"Hecate? You made it!" He reaches for me, but Zeus holds out a sturdy arm, stopping Helios in his tracks. "And you brought Zeus . . ." Helios's smile immediately falters, and the light goes from his eyes. "Follow me. I'll show you Circe's cabin, where I'm staying." He eyes Zeus suspiciously as he's finally allowed to take my arm and lead me along the path.

"You know, I saw your brother-in-law Pollux just the other day in a small town called Patrae."

I frown up at him. "You did?" I try to remember the route that Pollux was to take after seeing Despoena home safely and cannot recall a town of that name. "Was a young nymph with him?"

Helios purses his lips and holds his finger to his temple. "I don't believe so."

"Hm," I hum noncommittally, tucking this piece of information away for later. I don't have time to worry about Pollux and Despoena right now, especially as we approach Circe's cabin.

"Do see the sheep to the barn, my friend," Helios directs Zeus, who holds the sheep by a leash, to the outpost around the back of the abode.

I keep my face impassive as Zeus looks at me with murderous rage.

"Oh, and please wipe your hands and face before entering at the servant's door. You've something sticky on your chin."

I only manage to hold in my laughter until the former king of Olympians disappears around the corner, and then my mirth bursts forth like a volcano.

"What?" Helios inquires. "He's spilled wine all over himself like some kind of drunk peasant."

· · · · ● · ● · · · ·

"So when, precisely, did you first notice the giants invading your island?" I ask the willowy blond as she languishes on the kline. She rests her back against the headboard and, without lifting herself, reaches for a plump grape on the side table. Her father stands guard, his arms folded protectively over his chest, in the doorway. My head swivels as Zeus enters behind him, attempting to maneuver by the hulking form of the sun god. Helios's gaze dulls, but he nods appreciatively at Zeus's clean face and hands.

My traveling companion takes the vacant seat next to me, and I scoot as far as possible away on the sofa. My movements do not go unnoticed by Circe, and I drop my chin to my chest as her eyebrows raise in question.

"Answer Hecate's question, my child," Helios commands the beauty. She pops one more grape in her mouth and chews thoughtfully.

"Not long ago. The moon was full, which is how I spied them searching for the herb in the spot where—"

Her father releases a loud cough, interrupting Circe.

I clasp my hands together and thin my lips, but before I can voice the question bubbling up inside of me, Zeus butts in.

"What aren't you telling us, Helios?" Zeus's gaze is shrewd, and my eyes widen as he transforms into his kingly self before my eyes. Sitting taller, his chest puffed out, his voice booms. "Tell us now. Everything is at stake."

Helios's gaze darts to his daughter. "Tell them."

She sighs as she sags into the cushions of her lounger. "There was a giant. Here."

"How long ago?"

She's silent. Worrying her bottom lip between her teeth until the thick pink skin turns white. A flush creeps up her neck, and she drops her gaze.

The fire sparks within me and flares to life. "How long ago, Circe?"

She looks everywhere but at me. As though the walls or threadbare rug can help her. Finally her eyes land on her father. He sags visibly, as though his favorite pet cow has died.

"Many months ago," she finally admits quietly. But still she won't meet my stare.

"Why have you told no one?" I manage between clenched teeth.

"My father didn't want the prophecy to come true. He did it for you, Hecate!" Circe's eyes are filled with unshed tears, and I feel the edge in her voice as she speaks the truth.

"For me?" My accusatory gaze darts back to Helios.

The sun god drops his chin and rubs along his hairline. "No matter how much we wanted your imprisonment of Zeus to succeed, we Titans knew it wouldn't last. We tried to protect you. To protect Athena and the other Olympians. But we failed." His shoulders sag.

"And what happened to this giant?" Zeus's voice is surprisingly calm, although I suppose he's always been hated by the Titans.

"I killed him, but in his place of death grew these—"

"White blooms with black roots," Circe finishes for her father. "We didn't even notice until the sheep got into them."

"What's special about the herb? What did the sheep do?"

"They died," Helios answers quietly. His throat bobs and he blinks slowly. If there's one thing I know about Helios, it's how much he loves his animals.

I turn back to Circe as I stand, my hands smoothing the wrinkles from my outfit. "We're going to need to see them. The blooms."

She nods and, with a handful of grapes, leads us out the door and into the rocky terrain of her island.

POLLUX

"**I** can't go past Calydon without paying my respect to my friend," I tell Heracles and Desy again.

"But it's out of our way, Pollux. I'm sure the deceased will forgive you just this once." Desy sits pertly atop the new horse we purchased in town, its sleek coat brushed to a glossy sheen.

"I'd rather not take our chances with the dead and our current situation, wouldn't you agree?" I direct my question to Heracles, who's tightening the girth on his own mount.

"I'm staying out of this," he says, dutifully ignoring the question. I huff at the golden boy's neutral nature. He's been awfully quiet this morning, no doubt noticing the flirtatious banter between Desy and me over breakfast. I shrug. After all, he is tagging along with us as a third wheel.

"We're stopping at Meleager's tomb, and that's the end of it."

Desy rolls her eyes as her jaw ticks in frustration.

The sun has hardly moved by the time we ride into Calydon. The town has flourished since my last visit, during the boar hunt that took the life of my friend the crown prince Meleager. The beastly boar was unleashed by the bitter Artemis after Meleager's father forgot to honor her at the annual harvest. It destroyed crops and farmland, leaving the villagers starving and terrorized. Meleager's father finally sought to eradicate the monster and offered the best hunters in the land a prize for slaying the boar. Unfortunately, his own son would lose his very life for giving the prize to his lover, Atalanta, as she was the first hunter to draw blood before Meleager himself slew the beast.

"So his own uncles murdered him because he chose Atalanta to receive the boar's tusks and hide over them?" Heracles question hangs in the air as we pass the forest where, it seems only days ago, tents were erected during the hunt. In my mind, the ghost of Atalanta stands in shock, her hands and chest covered in Meleager's blood. The coppery scent still burns my nostrils.

I gulp and nod, my eyes searching the forest for my friends seated around the fire, an annoying weasel stealing scraps of fish from us. The sounds of our carefree laughter echo on the breeze that tickles the trees. Hecate and Castor snuggle under a blanket while Atalanta and Meleager make eyes at one another. I smirk to myself. Both couples were clearly in love to all who witnessed their behavior, but neither knew it yet.

My gaze slides to Desy. Her horse has slowed as though it, too, can feel the memories, the importance, of the forest. I spy the makeshift memorial where Meleager's tent once stood. The place of his death has been decorated with mementos and trinkets to honor the Calydonian prince. My companions and I tether our horses a distance away and solemnly approach the sacred space. Even Heracles is quiet, his constant questioning about the infamous boar hunt finally exhausted.

Desy and Herc stay back as I close in on the shrine. My eyes widen as I take in the gleaming tusks and brushed hide of the very boar that caused my friend's death. I reach out to touch them, as though they have the power to transport me back to a simpler time, when a gasp from behind a tree startles me.

I pull back and reach for my dagger, but as Atalanta tentatively steps from behind the oak, my rigid stance softens and a smile breaks out on my face.

"Pollux?"

"Atalanta." I reach for her. "It's been so long!" I pull her in for a hug, and it's not until she's pressed against me that I feel the roundness of her belly pressing uncomfortably against my own stomach. I pull back and look down as my mouth falls open. "You're—?"

She nods wordlessly as her fingers delicately trail over the bump beneath her chiton. "My father bade that I must marry." There's an edge to her voice, a hardness that wasn't there before.

"Congratulations are in order then!"

She winces but her eyes remain dull. The spark of defiance, the strength, is gone. "He cheated to best me, to win my hand."

"I'm afraid I don't understand."

She sighs heavily. "My father demanded I marry, but I couldn't betray *him*." She looks longingly at Meleager's memorial. "He was my one true love, after all."

I swallow the lump forming in my throat. "Atalanta, I'm sure he would understand. Life must go on for the living."

Her chin juts forward, and her eyes finally sparkle to life with anger. "Not for me. I knew no one would ever hold my heart as he did. So I commanded that I'd only marry the man who could best me in a footrace."

"But you're the fastest person I've ever met!" I exclaim. "Even Meleager wouldn't have beat you."

"Precisely. I knew no man could match my speed and my father would leave off the idea of marriage. But that bastard Melanion tricked me by tossing out golden apples given to him by that bitch Aphrodite."

I pale and glance around, terror spreading through me at Atalanta's blasphemy.

"There's no need to be afraid, Pollux," Atalanta sneers as though she can smell my fear. "The gods of Olympus have failed us, and thus the giants seek to destroy them. I only pray they succeed."

"I know you're hurt, but you cannot possibly believe the giants are righteous. They're killing mortals—the people you've always fought to protect."

She simply shrugs, her face devoid of any emotion.

My mouth opens and closes, and I'm crushed that my once-strong friend is now a shell of her true self. I look around, grasping for something—anything—to say. "Are you the one who's shined the tusks and brushed the hide?"

Her gleaming eyes meet mine, unshed tears threatening to spill over. "I come when I can. When my husband is busy and won't notice my absence. But it'll be harder once the babe comes. I worry who will tend to his memorial." She swipes at her cheek as the tears trace a river down her face.

I reach out and grasp her hand. "I'll come more often. I'll honor him as you've continued to do these years." Her chin wobbles but she nods as she sniffles. I pull her in for a hug, wishing her heart would heal of the hatred and bitterness she feels toward the gods at the loss of her lover.

As we pull apart, my heart wrenches inside my chest as my eyes flick to Desy, her and Heracles now tending to the horses. "She's lovely," Atalanta smiles softly as she follows my gaze. "And I pray you never know the pain of losing her, Pollux. Of watching her be taken before your very eyes. I would've done anything to keep Meleager with me."

I take her hand and pull it to my lips. "He's always with you, Atalanta. With us."

I watch wordlessly as Atalanta turns and, pressing a kiss to her fingers, touches one of the boar's tusks. She kneels, and I silently step back, giving her space for her benedictions. I finally turn and make my way back to my companions, their eyes full of questions. But instead of answering, I simply untether my horse, hoist myself into the saddle, and with a swift pull on the reins, set my horse to canter away from Atalanta, Meleager, and the possibility of a love lost.

POLLUX

"You've been quiet since we left Calydon, Pollux. Aren't you going to tell me what Atalanta said?" Desy's been trying to make conversation since we reached the outskirts of Thermos, and my silence has not deterred her. If she knew what I was really thinking, she'd stop speaking to me altogether.

But I can't stop reliving the pain in Atalanta's eyes. Imagining the suffering she's been through these years since losing Meleager. She couldn't protect her lover any better than I could protect my father. Does she feel responsible for her lover's death the way I feel responsible for my father's?

It was all my fault.

My mouth goes dry and the pain in my chest returns, so I rub my sternum through my gear. I keep telling myself that my feelings for Desy are pointless. I don't deserve her. I can't protect her, but I can't stop thinking about her. Her supple body breaking out in waves of ecstasy as I drive into her. The way she challenges me, making me crazy with worry and frustration. Her wry smile and mischievous emerald-green eyes flashing with desire or deceit depending on her mood. The chest pain grows stronger, and I hunch over in the saddle.

"Pollux, I want you to know..." My father's voice pulls at me. It tugs me down into a darkness that I'll never escape.

"Sir, are you all right?" Heracles pulls his mount close and reaches for my reins. My vision goes hazy, and I let him lead both our horses to a copse of trees. He dismounts and then catches me as I slump from my own horse.

"I'm fine," I proclaim as he lifts me easily and then plunks me down with my back against the trunk of a large oak. I lean my head back against the rough bark and take deep breaths, willing the pain in my chest to subside.

Delicate fingers caress my cheek, and I open my eyes to find Desy wetting the hem of her chiton with water from our pack. She raises the fabric to my forehead and applies the cool compress. I try to keep my gaze focused on her concerned features, but her dress is rucked up high enough that I can see her sun-kissed thighs, and I wonder how they became so tan. I imagine her body spread out in the fields behind her mother's home, naked as the day she was born, as the sun's rays warm her skin.

The pain in my chest suddenly subsides, and I instantly feel better. I gently untangle myself from Desy and pull her chiton down, cursing myself as I cover her.

"I'll find a stream and refill our water," Heracles states as he grabs the skins and trots off through the trees.

Desy watches his retreating form before returning her gaze to me. She narrows her eyes and frowns. "What are you keeping from me?"

I look anywhere but at her. "I don't know what you're talking about. I was simply overcome with thirst. Possibly overheated."

She stands and places her hands on her hips, glaring down at me. "Bullshit, Pollux. What did Atalanta tell you that has you so flustered?"

I bring my knees up and fix my gaze on her. "I'm not a woman. I don't get flustered. I told you, I was thirsty and overheated."

"It's not even overly warm, you liar." She huffs in annoyance. She stares daggers at me for another moment before giving up and, grinding her teeth so loudly I can hear, stomps to the other side of the oak tree. I hear her plop down onto the ground and kick her feet out before she's silent.

We stay that way for a while. She on her side of the tree and me on mine. I fiddle with my fingers, wishing I had something intelligent or witty to say, but for once my words elude me. It's like I can't speak the truth to her. Can't tell her that, since meeting her, my life finally has meaning and purpose. She challenges me and drives me insane all at the same time.

Suddenly I know what I must do. It's the same thing Castor, and now Hecate, does when he's unsure about life and needs answers. I stand abruptly and rush around the other side of the tree. Desy looks up in surprise as I pull her to stand.

"We've got to go," I yell in excitement. The promise of answers has me eager to get back on the road.

Her brow furrows as she brushes the dirt from her clothing. "We need to wait for Herc to return. And besides, what's the rush? Only a moment ago you were practically faint with thirst. Your delicate constitution needs more time to mend."

I ignore her jabs, even as my heart swells at her banter, and yank her to the horses. "We're going to Dodona."

Desy rolls her eyes. "Another detour? Pollux, our destination is Olympus. Not some ancient oracle. If you wanted to stop and have your fortune told, we could've traveled to Delphi. It's much closer anyway."

Without asking, I grab her around the waist and hoist her into the saddle of her horse. She yelps in surprise and kicks her foot out at me, but I manage to dodge it in my mania as I circle around to my own mount. "I've been to Delphi, and Dodona is on our way to Olympus," I lie. Technically it is a day's detour northwest, but after Hera was able to infiltrate the Delphic oracles and disguise herself as a Pythia, I'm not sure I trust any but the original seers at Dodona.

I take Heracles's horse's reins and, with Desy following, head into the trees. We move slowly, dodging the bramble and fallen branches. I'm deep in my own thoughts of the trip to Dodona when I realize that Desy is no longer behind me. I turn in my saddle, but don't see her.

"Desy?" I call as my stomach drops. Has she run off again? My mind spirals as my heart rate increases. I thought we had moved past that. I thought we were on this journey together. Anger courses through my veins, and my lips thin as I delicately turn the horses around, careful not to get caught in the shrubbery.

"Desy!" I holler, louder this time. I retrace the path, moving at a brisker pace than before. My mind is full of the curses I'll spew at her when I find her. My trust is broken, my heart hardening.

I catch a flicker of black horse tail in my periphery and rein in the horses. She likely got lost trying to evade me, I think to myself wryly as I quickly knot Heracles's horse to a thick branch above my head. I slow my own mount to a crawl. My jaw tightens each time the horse crunches on the leaves underfoot, as I'm sure Desy will hear us approaching. But, for whatever reason, we sneak up behind her horse without her turning and noticing.

"What the fuck do you think you're doing running away from me again?" I demand as I sidle up beside her. But she doesn't turn to me. Her rigid body is shaking, her very hair trembling as it cascades down her back in a thick braid.

I reach out and grab her upper arm, and she flinches as she turns, her face pallid and her eyes wide.

"Desy?"

It's only then I notice the giant in front of her, his roar drowning out her name on my tongue.

POLLUX

I'm off the horse and pulling Desy down beside me before the giant's roar fades through the trees. "Heracles is back there!" she hisses as I yank us behind a thick trunk.

"Golden Boy can fend for himself at the moment. I need to figure out how to get you out of here and then I'll deal with him."

She smacks me across the jaw, the sting surprising more than painful, and stalks out from behind our hiding place.

"Oh no you don't!" I yell, pulling her back. She lets out a growl of frustration and fights against my chest, but I hold her arms at her sides and pin her against the trunk with my body.

"Let me go! Heracles is out there alone!" She continues to wriggle against me, thrashing her head back and forth and tangling her hair against the bark.

"Stop fighting! Calm down!"

She refuses.

"Fine, you can stay and help, but you have to stop so we can come up with a plan."

Her eyes narrow as though she's suspicious of my promise, but she stills nevertheless. I pull back and help her untangle her locks. "Careful," I whisper as my fingers work deftly. She winces as a few hairs catch, but she's free and beside me in no time. Together we peer from behind the trunk.

Heracles and the giant stand across from each other in a glen. A stream burbles between them. The giant, his head in the shape of a lion and his legs the bodies of snakes, roars at Heracles.

"What the fuck is that?" Desy whispers.

We both duck back behind the tree, our breaths heavy as the panic settles over us. "I think that's a giant."

"There's no way Herc can defeat that thing—whatever it is."

I nod, squeezing my eyes closed as I come to terms with what I must do. My hands feel clammy, and I wipe them on my pants before I pull my blade from its scabbard. The sound of my own heartbeat thrashing in my ears drowns out the roars of the beast.

"What are you doing?" Desy's voice echoes in my head as though I'm underwater. I blink slowly, taking her in for possibly the last time. A smile lifts my lips, and her brows furrow in confusion.

"No," she mouths to me, but I can't hear the words as I start to nod, as though to convince myself that this is the only way. She's grabbing my shirt, shaking her head as her eyes fill with tears, but I bring my free hand up and unclasp her fingers, shushing her.

"Don't do this." Her face cracks and she's blubbering, her arms going around herself as she continues to shake her head.

I continue shushing her. This could be the last moment I ever spend with her, and I don't want her to feel sadness. I want her to know I was brave, a fighter who wasn't afraid of a battle. I pull her into my chest, her face buried in leather. She pulls back. Tears and snot coat her face, but she's never been more beautiful. I lean down and place a gentle kiss on her lips.

I break free, even as my heart stutters, and run toward Heracles.

This time, even as the giant roars, the sounds of Desy's sobs fill my ears.

• • • • ● • ● • • • •

I yell as I run toward Heracles, hoping to distract the lion-headed beast. My sword raised overhead, I grab my dagger from my hip with my free hand and charge forward. Heracles, still on the other side of the stream, stares wide-eyed for just a moment before springing into action. He nocks an arrow into his bow and aims, but it sails wide and misses. The giant doesn't even notice, instead advancing toward me.

"Fuck," I mumble as I turn away from the stream. I dip into the trees. If I lure him toward me, Heracles can attack from behind. I keep running parallel to the beast but slow my pace to dodge behind trees and stay out of sight. I clang my weapons together, moving forward and then doubling back. The giant crashes into the trees, his roar shaking the branches and sending a blast of wind that nearly knocks me on my ass.

I keep moving, making as much noise as possible. "C'mon, Herc," I whisper just as an arrow flies past me, nicking my shoulder. "Fuck!" I hiss as I pull back against the tree.

The leather is torn but my skin is saved, thank the gods. I get to moving, circling back toward the stream just as a feminine voice sends an arrow of ice to my heart.

"Over here, you lion-headed fucker!"

"Despoena!" Heracles growls loudly and I pause. "What are you doing? Get out of here!"

I move around and try to see through the foliage, but the forest growth is too thick. I curse under my breath and realize that, not only can I not see Desy or Heracles, I've also lost sight of the giant.

I keep still and listen, but my ears can't focus on anything but Desy and Herc arguing.

"Come on out, you ugly beast!"

"Shut your mouth, nymph, or you're going to get us all killed!"

"I'm trying to lure him away from Pollux since you're a lousy shot!"

The snap of a twig to my right sends me sprinting from my hiding spot—straight into the chest of the beast. He grabs me by the throat and lifts me, my feet dangling, as he roars in my face. I swipe with my sword and slice his exposed chest. He emits a screech of pain and drops me. Luckily, I land on my feet and take off, running straight toward the stream. As much as I don't want this beast to see Desy, I need him out in the open so Heracles can finally sink a shot.

I break through the tree line and both Heracles and Desy light up with relief, but their features soon change to twin looks of terror as the giant stumbles after me, his torso covered with blood.

"Run!" Desy screams as I leap over the stream. I crash to the ground, and my knees give out. Heracles nocks another arrow and takes aim. He's got a clear shot, and I watch in awe from the ground as the reed arcs through the air and sinks into the beast's neck. I cover my ears as the giant's screech of pain echoes through the valley, but Herc manages to sink two more arrows in quick succession into the monster's throat, piercing its vocal cords.

Blood spurts from the wounds and covers the ground as the lion-headed creature falls to his knees and then keels over. Not trusting two measly arrows to the throat, I hobble over to the beast and stick my blade through his chest, just to be safe. The last breath leaves the giant, and his eyes dim. I sag to the ground, my energy depleted. I manage only a brief sigh of relief before Desy and Heracles are lifting me up into a group hug.

"I was so worried about you both!" Desy exclaims giddily as she glances between us, but her face falls as she realizes what she's done. Herc's nostrils are flaring, and a vein is twitching in his forehead. I'm flexing my fingers, thinking about wrapping them around Desy's neck for what she's done, and grinding my teeth down to nubs.

"How could you have been so stupid, Despoena?" Heracles starts.

"You could've been killed!" I finish.

Her gaze hardens as she crosses her arms and lifts her chin. "Don't you think I felt that way about you both?"

I rub the back of my neck while Heracles pulls at his earlobe.

I don't miss the look that he gives Desy, or the look that she gives to me.

And I gulp, wondering what it all means but more determined than ever to find our way to Dodona and get answers.

HECATE

"**S**low . . . down," Zeus gasps behind us.

Even as I keep my gaze trained on Circe's back, I sense Helios pause and turn. "We're going downhill. How are you so exhausted?"

"Ask . . . the witch!"

I snort and continue plodding along even as I shake my head.

"What've you done to him then? A lovers' spell?" Circe turns and slows so that we're walking shoulder to shoulder.

"No, nothing like that. I've bound his abilities so his powers are more along the lines of, say, a demigod instead of the former king of Olympus."

Her eyes widen in awe. "How'd you manage to accomplish that without binding him to your powers, thus making yourself weaker?" As a witch herself and the goddess of sorcery, Circe *would* ask about my methods. We'd communicated in the past, via letters, about our own personal attempts and discoveries.

I give little away and simply shrug. I'd rather not admit aloud, especially within earshot of Zeus, that I had in fact bound the prisoner's magic to my own and *did* make myself weaker. Even Hades didn't know the true extent of the spell I'd cast. It was best to keep the knowledge to myself.

"Hm," Circe responds as she slides her gaze back to the trail. "Did you know that my name actually means *to loop around*? It's an homage to binding magic."

"Is it now? How lovely." I carry on, my secret sealed. If she thinks I'll spill anything, she's sorely mistaken.

"I'd love to learn the spell you used, Titaness."

My lips press firmly together, even as I'm honored by her deference. "Perhaps after we secure the herbs." I slow my steps, only to get away from her, not because I'm draining myself in this heat—or so I tell myself—and fall in line with Helios. "How much farther, do you think?" I ask him as I wipe a drop of sweat from my brow.

He lifts his hand and begins to point, but then quickly grabs me before making a hissing noise to alert Circe. Ahead of us, she stops in her tracks and immediately drops low onto the ground. I follow suit as Helios waves his arms at Zeus, still lagging behind us. He frowns slightly before he complies. Zeus begins to crawl toward us, but then freezes. Silent, not moving a muscle, we all hear it.

The sound of digging and dirt being tossed around.

Giant, Helios mouths to us, and as Circe grows pale, my stomach plummets.

• • • ● • ● • ● • •

The three of us backpedal quietly to Zeus.

"Are you sure?" Zeus asks, even as I shake my head and Helios rolls his eyes.

"Yes, I'm sure." Helios's tone brooks no argument. I cock my head to listen more closely but am interrupted by Circe's trembling.

"Get her out of here," I command Zeus. I grab Circe's elbow and try to guide her toward him, but she's rooted to the spot.

"I think it'll be better if I stay here and fight. You should take her to safety." I stare at him and grind my teeth.

"Coming from someone who's actually fought a giant and lived to tell about it, I'll be the one to decide who stays and who doesn't."

"Silence, both of you!" Helios commands, and I immediately clamp my mouth shut. He turns to his daughter, her bottom lip wobbling in terror.

"Circe, pull yourself together, girl. We need you, and we all must stay together. We don't know if more lurk in the woods."

At that Helios stands, knees bent and back stooped, and slips into the thicket. So much for staying together. We're silent as we await his return. I reach out and rub circles into Circe's back.

"The giant who came before . . . he wasn't like others who have come to this island. I can defend myself from trespassers, unwanted visitors. I usually simply turn them into pigs," she huffs. "This giant, though, entered my dreams. He became my nightmare."

I look to Zeus, his face a mask of concern as the column of his throat works. "Circe, tell us what happened," I prompt.

She looks into the forest, as though willing her father to reappear. When he doesn't, she whispers so softly that I have to lean in to hear. "I was certain that I was awake. The walls of my house were streaming with blood and a fire devoured my potions, my life's work. I had to stop the flames, but nothing I did or used calmed the blaze. I had a visitor, a gentleman, staying with me, and as I took the blade to his throat, I knew his blood was the only way to satiate the fire's hunger."

I swallow thickly and work to keep my face impassive, my hand steady as I continue the slow circles around the bones of her back.

"I walked down to the sea to wash the blood from my hands, to bathe in the refreshing saltwater, but the water was filled with the limbs of the man I murdered." Her voice cracks as tears fill her eyes. "I kept cleaning myself, hoping the blood would wash away, but it wouldn't." She releases a sob and covers her eyes as a shudder racks her body. "It felt so real."

"But it wasn't?" I confirm.

"No." She shakes her head as she raises it to look at me through wet lashes. "But by then I was such a mess, my head and heart so shattered, that I was unable to fight off the beast. I hid for days while he ravaged my island, my home, looking for me. If my father hadn't arrived when he did, I—" She goes silent, simply shaking her head.

"This time we have four of us. A single giant cannot best us, Circe." My gaze flicks to Zeus, who only lowers his eyes to the ground and says nothing. Even as I clear my throat and kick a pebble toward him, he never looks up or adds to the sentiment. *Useless as always*, I think.

It's only when Helios bursts through the thicket that he finally lifts his face. "There's just one," the sun god says.

I smile wryly. It's the best news I've had in days.

"Circe, are you with us?" He looks expectantly at his daughter, his hand outstretched. Zeus and I both rise and glance at the goddess's tear-streaked face.

"We need you. *I* need you." My plea is soft. I don't explain that my magic is weak, that there's no way I can produce the type of power Zeus and Helios would expect from me. I don't explain that I need to keep up this farce, that I'm terrified of taking on the giants at half capacity and with a god I abhor by my side.

Even as Circe accepts her father's outstretched hand, it's me she looks to.

"I'm with you."

POLLUX

"I still don't understand why you're wearing that disgusting thing," Desy admonishes Heracles as she wrinkles her nose.

The golden boy looks down in confusion at his lion-skin cape. "Why wouldn't I wear the hide of my triumph?"

I chuckle to myself, shaking my head at his naivete. Only the young find the need to flash their victories about so arrogantly.

"There's blood dripping down your shoulders. It's gross." She flips her hair and looks away from him, her chin tilting up, before spurring her mount away from us.

She may miss his crestfallen face, but I don't. A lump forms in my throat. Poor kid. Against my better judgment, I feel sorry for the youth. "Perhaps you should put away the cape and clean yourself at the nearest stream before we reach Dodona."

He nods, but his eyes are dull, his facial features blank.

"Listen, Heracles," I add on an exhale. "You can be proud of your conquest. Killing that giant was quite the feat." His face brightens slightly at the compliment. "However, women don't necessarily enjoy the smell of death and the reminder of a traumatic event." I raise a single brow at the grisly lion-headed hood that covers Heracles's long locks.

He blinks slowly before giving a half-hearted shrug. "I suppose you're right. You likely know more about women than I do, given your age."

I gulp down a snarky retort. I won't kick a man when he's down, and Heracles is clearly embarrassed by his inability to impress Desy.

We travel for no more than a mile before spying a peaceful and deserted river. We tether the horses near the bank, and they begin to drink their fill. Desy watches from a seat on the shoreline, fingers pressed to her smiling lips, as Heracles discards the cape and then wades into the water. He begins rinsing the dried blood from his shoulders and neck.

"Thank you for getting him to rid himself of that horrid thing." She looks at me with steady eyes.

"Go easy on the boy, *mikrí nýmfi*. He's clearly enamored of you."

She rolls her eyes and lets out a snort. "He's clearly enamored of *you*, Pollux! Always calling you *sir* and waiting for your wisdom with bated breath."

"At least someone listens to me." I chuckle, but the laughter dies on my lips as I meet her gaze, deep and steady. Her lips part and she trails a finger down her forearm. Then she runs her hand further down her thigh. I fist the dirt as my hands ache with need. The need to grab her chiton and pull it over her thighs. The need to sink into her.

"I'm suddenly overly warm. I think I'll cool off. With Heracles," she adds with a sigh as she stands.

My throat tightens as she rolls up her dress, exposing the very skin I was just thinking about.

She dips a toe into the river and gasps at the temperature. She wades farther in, going slowly, and Heracles stills as he watches her, a look of pure lust on his face.

"I thought I'd help you wash your hair," she tells him, twirling her finger for him to turn around. He smiles goofily and follows the instruction like a dog as he leans back and wets his hair once more in the cool water.

I feel antsy with an overwhelming desire to join in, but I remain rooted to the riverbank and simply watch as Desy massages his scalp and then untangles his golden locks.

"That feels nice, Despoena."

She giggles breathily and then glances over her shoulder, cocking an eyebrow at me. A flush of warmth spreads from my groin outward, but I simply tilt my head toward the sun and close my eyes.

"Join us, Pollux." Desy's demand breaks through my thoughts.

"The water feels perfect," Heracles adds. He splashes her and she squeals with happiness. Only I should be the one making her scream. My indecision shatters. I hoist myself to standing and discard my weapons and heavy leathers.

Desy's eyes darken as Heracles lets out a jubilant whoop, and I strike a few poses, my face cracking open with laughter.

"This does feel amazing," I concede as I step into the depth. I splash farther out and float on my back, letting the sun warm my bare chest. If only for a moment, my mind is clear and my worries are gone, but I know it's only temporary.

· • • ◦ • ◦ • ◦ • • ·

As we approach Dodona, I can't help but think back to my last trip to a seer. When I visited the Oracle at Delphi with Hecate, Castor, and Helen, I hadn't wanted to know my future. I was content with a life of women and fucking. What a cocky bastard I was, believing that knowing one's destiny was only for those who couldn't make their own decisions. I shake my head and snort at my naivete.

"Will you seek out answers with the oracles?" Heracles asks Desy shyly. I listen to their exchange but keep my own answers close to my heart. It's clear that Heracles has feelings for the nymph—*my* nymph—and I'm still not sure how I feel about it. Desy *should* be with someone like him. A hero in his prime. Not a has-been with no prospects. But it doesn't stop the jealousy biting my insides.

"Of course I'll meet with the oracles." I'm not surprised that Desy will want her future told. Besides her annual trips to the Underworld with her sister, she's never been farther than her mother's estate; she will want to experience everything.

"Didn't you know they're not called oracles in Dodona?" I finally butt in. "They're actually called doves."

Desy turns to me, her head tilted to the side.

"The Oracle at Delphi is a seer for Apollo. The Doves at Dodona are seers for Zeus," Heracles adds as he puffs out his chest. My lips thin, but I nod in acknowledgment.

"Have you been?" Desy asks him, her eyes full of wonder.

"No, but my parents went before I was born. They were desperate to know my future and were told that I was destined to rule all those around me."

Desy lets out a soft giggle, but the mirth falls from her lips at Heracles's hurt expression.

"Clearly that prophecy didn't come to pass," he adds quietly.

"You're young yet," I say, trying to make him feel better.

"What about you, Pollux? Have you ever visited the Doves at Dodona?"

I shake my head. "The closest I've ever come to the infamous doves is when I traveled with Jason on the *Argo*. He claimed a piece of the ship was from a tree taken from Dodona."

Heracles's gaze becomes more focused as his lips part. "What was it like? Being one of the Argonauts?"

Just behind him, Desy smirks and cocks an eyebrow. *He's clearly enamored of* you, her look says.

I turn my attention back to the golden boy. "Ah, it's been such a long time. I'm sure you've heard all the good parts already."

"I've heard tales, but never from someone who was actually *there*. Please, tell me what it was like!"

A warmth radiates over my face. I clear my throat, embarrassed that I'm blushing at Heracles's admiration. In all honesty, it feels nice to be esteemed and revered. It's been a long time since I felt the respect and praise of others. "Castor and I met Jason while under Chiron's tutelage. He's the centaur who—"

"—mentored noble youth," Heracles finishes giddily.

"Yes, so my twin and I knew Jason from an age, and when he needed a crew on his quest for the Golden Fleece, we of course volunteered."

"Why was he looking for a Golden Fleece?" Desy asks.

"Jason's uncle stole the throne of Thessaly, and Jason sought to gain it back. His uncle sent him on an impossible task—to get the gifted fleece from the king of Colchis," Heracles adds before I can answer.

I nod, impressed with his knowledge but not surprised. The story of Jason and his Argonauts, as we've been called, has been bandied about for years since we were successful in our endeavor. "Unfortunately, the king tasked Jason with even more impossible labors, all of which our leader accomplished. It was only then that Jason was able to locate and return the fleece, claiming his rightful seat on the throne."

"Ah, but you left out one vital piece of the story, sir," Heracles adds with his finger pointed haughtily in the hair.

I frown at him, but Despoena looks on in awe.

"You forgot about the part his lover, Medea, played in his success." He winks at Desy.

A gleeful smile breaks out on her face.

"Medea was the daughter of the king of Colchis, and after falling in love with Jason, she helped him through each of the improbable chores. She and Jason were married shortly after he returned to his rightful place as king."

Desy's cheeks flush pink. It's clear she wants adventure. A hero. She's enraptured with Heracles's version of the events, and I don't have the heart to tell her the true ending to the fairy tale. That, as a trained witch, none of us Argonauts were certain Medea hadn't tricked Jason into loving her. That their perfect union later collapsed, and she brutally murdered her children as revenge for Jason falling in love with someone else.

So instead I swallow down the truth and look at the road ahead as Dodona and its temple come into view. Desperate for the answers I need to feel whole again.

HECATE

"**S**tay close to me," Circe mutters under her breath as we creep through the thicket. Helios and Zeus have looped around the giant's backside while we have taken the front. Now, as we lay eyes on the beast, his fingers deep in the silty soil, my throat goes dry with fear.

"Circe." My voice trembles as I struggle to swallow.

"You don't need to say what you've done, Hecate. I'm not dense. There's no way you were able to bind Zeus's magic without sacrificing your own in the process."

"You can't—"

She turns to me, her aqua eyes darkening as her pupils dilate. "Your secret is safe with me."

We both return our focus to the giant as we await the signal from the sun god. "Why would you do that for me? You could easily tell Zeus the truth. You'd be rewarded a thousand times over just for helping him return to power."

Her eyes never leave the target, but her words are filled with emotion. "Hecate, everything I know about magic I've learned from you. As a young goddess, I grew up hearing stories of your bravery. How you reincarnated yourself just so you could seek revenge on a god who harmed both mortals and immortals alike. I would never betray you."

My eyes sting with unshed tears, but I blink and sniffle, refusing to let them fall.

"I know it must seem impossible right now, having freed him against your will. But you have my support, and clearly the support of my father, too." We both chuckle quietly. "I don't know what will come of this war, or where all the pieces will land afterward, but my island will always be here should you need a safe place."

"Thank you," I manage over the tightness in my throat. A feeling of calm washes over me. Even as my power is weaker than ever, I've forgotten what it feels like to rely on, and trust in, those around me. It's one thing I had to learn as Melinoe. I had to use my own strength, but also the strength of others, to succeed. I've spent so long in the Underworld with unlimited ability and power that I forget there are those who have heard my story and will support and help me.

"There's the signal!" Circe snaps to attention. She leaps to her feet, and I follow as quickly as possible in her wake.

I grab two thick sticks from the ground as we run, and for the first time in a long time I think, *What would Melinoe do?*

• • • • ● • ● • • •

"*Kápste to fos,*" I breathe out as I hold the branches in front of myself. If using torches worked on the giant at the gate to the Underworld, I'm confident they will work again. The ends of the sticks flicker.

"Please light!" I beg the lumber. Just one stick barely blinks, but finally the tip ignites. I breathe a shaky sigh, my body already feeling drained and depleted, and marry the two torches together. The second finally flares to life.

I step behind Circe, my chest heaving with even the smallest exertion. As I'm surrounded on all sides by greenery, I needn't worry about igniting the island, only the beast who growls and grunts before us. Helios and Zeus appear on the opposite side.

"Look away," Circe mutters to me as the aura around her father brightens. I lower my gaze, but still feel the heat on my forehead and cheeks. The intensity grows so strong that my eyes close of their own accord, shielding me from the sun god's aureole, but even the insides of my eyelids burn a bright red.

"Go!" Helios yells, and my eyes flash open. Splotches of light dance in my vision, and I struggle to focus on the giant.

"Hecate, move!" Circe chastises me, and I blindly rush forward with my twin torches aloft. My foot catches and I stumble, tripping over a protruding root. As I crash to the dirt, my weapons tumble to the ground, the flames stuttering. *Please stay lit*, I beg. I reach for a torch just as a serpentine tail wraps around my forearm. I gasp and pull away, but the scaly muscle wraps tightly around my limb. It pulls me forward, my shoulder popping painfully as my torso drags across the rocky terrain.

"Hecate! Catch!" Zeus lobs a torch through the air. I pull my other arm from under me and snatch it. I sink the flaming end into the giant's wiggling, serpentine appendage. The creature hisses and shrieks as I stab over and over.

"Fuck. You," I growl each time the end hits the meaty flesh. But then a second tail whips out and strips the branch from my hand. I scream as my palm is shredded, blood and skin coating the dirt, and watch helplessly as my weapon is thrown into the trees.

My bloodied hand works to grab onto something—anything—as the beast pulls me closer. My entire right side is wrapped within its viselike grip, and yet another snake tail inches toward my throat.

"Zeus!"

He's the only one I see, and as he hears my plea, he stops and looks at me—really looks at me—and *hesitates*. I see the look of uncertainty pass over his features. He gulps, and I instantly know what he's thinking. Does he save me? Or free himself?

"Help me!" I scream, making the decision for him, as the muscular appendage circles my neck and tightens. His features harden and he throws his shoulders back before running toward me, my second torch in his hand.

But before he can reach me, Circe's intonation crackles in the air. "*Ypakoúo stis entolés mou!*" she commands the beast.

His body stiffens as his eyes glaze over. Then, he complies, the thick, scaly ropes loosening before freeing me from their grasp. My breathing stutters and I crawl clumsily to my feet, my arm dangling limply from the popped shoulder socket.

I slice my gaze to Zeus and glare as I hold my injured palm against my chest. "I'm—"

"*Save it,*" I seethe as I turn back to the swaying giant under Circe's control. She approaches him with an outstretched hand, her eyes glowing an unearthly yellow. Like the sun.

"Why are you here?" Circe demands of the giant.

"The herb."

"What do you need with the herb?" I ask, but the giant doesn't react to my inquiry. I thin my lips in consternation.

Circe repeats my question.

"It will . . . It will save . . ." The giant fights against answering, but Circe's magic of compliance is too strong. " . . . us from being killed by mortal hands."

I furrow my brow and look around at my companions, their eyes mirrors of my own and filled with only one question. Which mortal will aid us in killing the giants?

POLLUX

"Welcome, Prince Pollux." An elderly woman's voice carries from somewhere inside the giant oak tree situated in the open-air temple. My jaw drops as my eyes circle the sanctum before me. The temple itself is built into the side of a mountain and is protected by marshes surrounding the outer shrine. Beyond the wetlands lie rich meadows filled with abundant flocks of sheep and oxen. Inside the sanctuary, the wide-trunked oak tree rises from the ground in the middle of the temple. A curved doorway is carved into the base, from which exits three doves. Only one approaches while the other two stand back.

I gulp and immediately drop to my knee, lowering my gaze to the ground. The three elderly women are small, smaller than my own nymph who awaits beyond the marshes with Heracles. They both insisted I enter first. Whether from fright or respect, I'm not sure, but I thinned my lips and stalked into the temple without a word or backward glance. Now, as I stand here ready to hear my fortune—my future—all I can think is that I'm the one frightened.

A melodic tinkling comes from the branches of the monstrous oak. I raise my eyes, but no wind chimes or hanging decorations are visible.

"The future is impatient, my son."

I swallow and dip my head again. Should I apologize? I keep my gaze averted, but my ears tingle as the dove's footsteps crunch quietly on the softened clay.

Her gnarled fingers touch my chin, tilting it up. "Look at me, Prince, for I am the lover of the god you and your kin condemned for eternity."

My breath hitches as I look upon the once-beautiful features. Seafoam eyes, once clear, are now cloudy and surrounded by parchment-thin skin. But the resemblance is still there, even with age. "Aphrodite?"

She smiles slowly, the wrinkles deepening along her mouth. "My daughter."

"Your lover—?"

"Zeus."

My stomach plummets. "I— We didn't—"

"Say no more, Polydeuces."

I clamp my mouth shut at the formal use of my name.

"Zeus's destiny was woven in the Fates' fabric. You and your kin were simply the soldiers carrying out the orders from those above you."

I release the breath I didn't realize I was holding.

"But I am sorry to say I cannot tell your future." She moves to turn, and my instinct is to reach out, to grab her thin wrist, before I realize what I'm doing. I recoil as though burned, even though my fingers did not touch her divine skin.

Her eyes widen. "You are bold, Prince."

"I'm so sorry, Dione . . . er, Dove?" I'm unsure how to address her now that I know who she really is.

"I see what troubles you, but there is nothing for me to share. You were right, we oracles cannot yet see your destiny. You have decisions to make."

My body sags. Of course my future cannot be told. I have no prospects. No future. Nothing.

"I will share one thing with you though," the dove adds. I perk up slightly. "With you is a means to end this war. While my own mother, Gaia, is the one who birthed the giants as punishment for entombing her grandson Zeus, your witch has released him. But it's actually—"

"Hecate released Zeus?" I'm incredulous, my body going cold. How could Hecate just decide to release Zeus after all the pain and suffering he's caused so many?

"It was necessary," the dove says, interrupting my spiraling thoughts. "But he cannot win the war alone. Even he is not enough to defeat Gaia's giants." Her pupils dilate as she focuses on me.

I swallow the lump in my throat. I'm honored to be needed. "I will do what I must, Dove."

She blinks, and a look of amusement passes over her features. "You misunderstand me, Prince. It is not you who will help defeat the giants."

Oh.

Oh.

I drop my head on a sigh. "Heracles." The feeling of worthlessness washes over me.

"Yes, Zeus's very own son by Alcmene. Your half brother. It is his turn for glory."

I should be proud that one of my kin is tasked with such an important feat, but Zeus spread his seed far and wide. I'm related to nearly every god and demigod. I'm not surprised I've one more sibling. But this brother rivals me in everything that matters—strength, looks, and youth. My ribs grow tight as I fight to breathe. I blink back the embarrassment and offer a weak smile. "I understand."

Her smile is wide. "I trust you to do the right thing, Polydeuces, and help him become the hero he is meant to be. Guide him. Give him what he needs to be great."

As you were once, but not anymore, rings in my mind.

I nod, just wanting to leave this place, to get away from here.

"You may go." She turns, her footsteps sinking into the orange clay as she pads away. This time I don't stop her.

What's the point?

My foot taps as I wait impatiently for both Desy and Heracles to exit from their own prophecies. Unlike the single Oracle at Delphi, the doves are numerous, with many rooms available. I suppose it was luck that I was allowed to visit with Dione, the once-consort of Zeus. I pace back and forth, my future—or lack thereof—echoing in my mind as I attempt to sort out the information laid at my feet.

Zeus is released from his Underworld binds. He's free.

Heracles is a means to end this war. He's to be the hero. Not me.

I serve so little purpose in all this that the seer had nothing to predict, saw nothing in my future.

I mean so little that I'm to serve as merely a tutor, a chaperone, to Heracles. The golden boy. Zeus's heroic son.

My head drops into my hands as my feet still. I want to rage at the Fates, scream and curse them. Ask them why I've been relegated to the empty chasm of obscurity.

"Pollux?"

Heracles's voice pulls me from my inner torment, and I immediately snap to attention. Clearing my throat, I scrub my hands down my face and then take a deep breath, mentally composing myself even if I look a mess on the outside.

"How was your visit?" I ask. My hands itch to destroy something. Someone.

A wide smile breaks out on his face, transforming his entire aura. It's like seeing a king being crowned—seeing an important historical event as it unfolds. And I've got a front seat.

Lucky me.

"Oh, sir, my dove foretold of my future wife and our three beautiful sons."

I swallow, waiting for him to continue.

Just then Despoena exits the temple. Heracles turns, his eyes drinking her in as though he were a man dying of thirst.

He can't possibly think—

She's *mine*.

My hands fist at my sides as my jaw tightens. Desy's face brightens as she meets Heracles's lovestruck gaze, and my teeth grind to stumps.

The golden boy reaches for her, and my insides turn to lava as she takes his hand. Smiling up at him as her emerald eyes flash in the sunlight, I see a flush of lust crawl up his neck to his cheeks. He rubs his chin before his tongue flicks out to lick his bottom lip.

Her own face turns rosy, and her fingers trail down her sternum.

I watch with fury in my veins as his eyes trace the path of her hand.

And that's when I realize I'm not going to help Heracles. I'm going to murder him.

HECATE

"He makes a lovely pig, Circe."

I cock an eyebrow at Helios, who's leaned into the pen and is patting the giant-turned-swine on the head.

The island sorceress shrugs. "I suppose I get my love of farm animals from you, Father." They share a grin before turning away from the animals. Helios ambles to the hut while Circe looks at me expectantly.

"Now that you know why the giants have been harvesting the mysterious herb, will you continue on to Olympus to share your findings?"

I nod but keep my lips pressed firmly together. Now that I also know I cannot trust Zeus in battle, I need to make arrangements for a way to protect myself. Without magic. Without Zeus. "I may need to stop and visit a friend along the way, but yes—Olympus is our destination."

Circe gives me a conspiratorial smile, her pink lips parting to reveal perfectly straight teeth. "I hope you will return to the island soon. It's been a pleasure hosting you, even under such strange circumstances."

I take her hands in mine and return her smile. "Thank you. For everything." *For keeping my secret*. I pull her in for a hug and inhale her coconut and saltwater smell.

"After you and the gods win this war, you'll definitely need a vacation. Perhaps a second honeymoon?" She waggles her eyebrows at me. "Where is your gorgeous Spartan prince anyway? I'm afraid I didn't get a chance to ask before."

I gulp, the guilt of abandoning Castor in Olympus returning. "He's safe."

She chews her lower lip and nods. I appreciate that Circe knows when to pry, and more importantly, when to leave something alone.

I follow her into her cabin to say my goodbye to Helios, with a promise to summon him if I need help. "Of course I'll do that." I gulp down the fact that I'm currently unable to summon anyone, but as I eye Zeus warily, his large form standing imposingly by the door, I know that I cannot share the truth of my lack of magic with anyone.

· · · · ● · ● · · · ·

"No."

"*Yes.*"

"I said *no*, Hecate."

"It doesn't matter what you want or don't want, Zeus. You're my prisoner, and we are most definitely stopping in Athens for more supplies."

Even through his full beard, I spy Zeus's scowl beneath the multiday growth of facial hair. I match the look of anger with one of my own, and it's only when Charon informs us that we are out of fresh water that I smirk in victory.

"It will do you good to see Athens, the city that honors our Queen Athena above all others." I am nothing if not petty, and if rubbing in how much Athena is beloved by the people is a reminder to Zeus of his failings, then so be it.

"She is my daughter, so of course she is the epitome of greatness."

My lip curls in disgust, and I shake my head before crossing my arms over my chest. I lean back, refusing to even acknowledge the cocky bastard across from me, and instead look out at the approaching Athenian shore.

The argument over whether or not to stop in Athens has been the most Zeus and I have spoken since leaving Circe's island. If he is annoyed at being unable to best a giant without his abilities, then I am even more annoyed at his hesitancy to help me when my life was hanging in the balance. And therefore, the impasse. Which is perfectly fine with me. After all, the less he says, the easier it is to pretend I am on a pleasure cruise. The only thing missing is a skin of strong melogion, my favorite drink from the Underworld, and a plate of grapes, smoked fish, and crusty bread.

"What the—?" Zeus's obnoxious grumble invades my personal space, and I glare at him.

"Oh, that?" I nod toward the giant golden statue of Athena, visible even now as we prepare to dock. A glittering crown of gems and a human-sized owl adorning the effigy. "The people of Sparta donated that to the city upon the goddess's ascent to the throne of Olympus."

His brow crinkles in confusion. "But Sparta and Athens hate each other. They always have. Don't tell me your perfect prince had anything to do with this?"

"Actually, without the Olympians inciting unnecessary drama between the mortals, it turns out the two cities are able to live harmoniously. And no, Castor wasn't involved in the gift. It was actually Leda who commissioned the statue."

Zeus's mouth hangs open as he digests the information I've imparted. His victim purchasing a bespoke sculpture to honor his downfall? I chortle with glee.

"But the cost . . . ? Surely the stingy Spartans didn't enjoy the tax increase to pay for such a monstrosity?"

"The Spartans live rather frugally, yes, but they were more than happy to donate in honor of their beloved Leda. They do despise you, though, once word got out of your . . . crimes."

The former king snarls and grinds his molars so loudly that I can hear them gnashing together over the splashing of the waves against our boat.

As we pull into the dock, I turn to Zeus, expecting him to refuse to set foot in the city that honors his downfall so openly. But as he pushes past me gruffly, I raise my eyebrows at Charon and shrug, the magic that binds our powers pulling me along in his wake.

• • • ● • ● • ● • • •

"This place is an abomination!" Zeus snarls as he stomps along the street toward the agora. With his hood drawn up over his white locks, he's practically invisible to the Athenian people. Not that they would stop to honor him anyway. Not after what he's done to the women of the Land of the Living.

Since his entombment, word of Zeus's atrocities spread like the fire in my veins. From the Cape of Taenarum to Mount Olympus, every living soul was made aware of his misdeeds. Men questioned their wives and eyed their offspring with apprehension. How many sons and daughters had the king of the gods sired on their women? Nobody even attempted to keep count. Now, as we traipse closer to the town square, I, too, pull up my hood to hide my identity. While I'm an honored Titaness and celebrated across the land, drawing a crowd would not keep my prisoner safe. He's likely to be torn to shreds by those he wronged.

"I should reveal myself to these ingrates—show them that their king returns!" He makes to whip off his hood, but before he can expose his identity, I drag him into a darkened alley.

"You will keep your existence hidden," I hiss with a scowl on my face. My forefinger digs into his massive chest.

"And why should I? What's in this for me, my little witch?"

My blood boils at the endearment, once said in love by my childhood friend, but now used by my enemy to taunt and berate me. "There is *nothing* in this for you, Zeus," I spit at him. "But for the first time in your long life, perhaps you

194

might think of those who need you. Who need you to be their hero and their savior."

Something flashes over his features, but before I can catch it and examine it, turn it over in my hand and prod it into existence, his face transforms into fury. "And why would I want to help those who overturned my rule? Those traitors who imprisoned me in the Underworld and—"

"Enough!" I shout. My fingers tingle to spill what little magic is within me. "This is exactly why you were overthrown, Zeus. You became a monster, a supreme being who only brought pain and suffering to his people. And if you cannot see that this is one *small* way to make amends, to change people's perception of you, then this whole charade is useless." I turn and stalk away, my rage growing even as I put greater distance between us.

"Foolish narcissistic . . ." I mutter to myself as I push through the crowds. Without realizing, I've reached the agora. I've gone the wrong way, as I meant to return to the boat and tell Charon to proceed without our prisoner. I curse under my breath and work to reorient myself. It's been quite some time since I've been in a city so large, and as I look to the sun and my surroundings to figure out which direction to go, an overlarge statue catches my eye.

It's the only statue I've seen that is not of Athena. Instead, it's of a man. Gulping down the lump in my throat, I approach the figure and search for a dedication plate. As I elbow my way toward the small sign at the feet of the statue, a voice behind me reads it aloud.

"Cecrops, the earthly born king of Attica and founder of Athens."

I recognize Zeus's timbre without having to turn around. My eyes travel up the effigy. Two serpent tails for legs turns into the waist and upper body of a man. "H-he was a giant?"

"No, he was born from the earth, an autochthon, but is a *diphuês*."

"Dual form," I repeat. "Like the giants, though." I turn to him, my mind working at the implications of finding another serpent-like human, one who is honored as a king among men.

Zeus nods slowly as the conclusion takes root in his brain.

"Who were his parents, Zeus?"

I tap my foot impatiently while his eyes flick up and to the right as he thinks. "Gaia was his mother."

"And his father? Who was his father?" I clench my fists to keep my fingers from reaching out, grabbing his cape, and shaking the information from his brain. I bounce on my toes.

Zeus's eyes lower, and at first I think he's trying to recall, but as he continues to hesitate, I know there's something he's not telling me.

"Tell me who's the father." I grind my teeth impatiently, ready to wring his neck.

"Hephaestus. It's Hephaestus." My mouth drops and my gaze goes hazy, the noise from the agora mutating into a dull roar in my ears. It can't be. My friend Hephaestus? He sired this—this creature? My mind goes wild as I remember the bronzed man from Sparta. Talos. He was also created by Hephaestus. Could the god of metalworking also be the father of the giants?

"We need to go. *Now*." I stomp off without waiting for my companion, only trusting that he'll catch up if he wants to continue this journey. And if he doesn't follow? Well, I've got another god in my sights.

The path back to the boat is quick, and both Zeus and I are gasping for breath when Charon assists us into the small hull.

"Take us to Mount Pelion. We're going to Hephaestus's forge."

POLLUX

The headache that forms along my temples from grinding my molars to a pulp is nothing compared to the pain I'm going to inflict on Heracles.

"I cannot believe the doves told you that!"

"My seer was so old, but she was so kind."

"I know exactly how you feel!"

"Can you believe they knew so much about my past?"

Desy and the golden boy haven't stopped gushing over their shared experience since we left Dodona hours ago. As we traipse through the foothills, I lead the group in stoic silence. My mind is still on how exactly I can strangle my half brother and dump his body without Despoena being any the wiser.

I've yet to come up with a viable plan.

"Pol?" I startle as Desy's horse edges next to mine. Blinking in confusion, I meet her worried gaze. "Didn't you hear us calling your name?"

I shake my head, unable to speak, my teeth likely fused together at this point.

Desy chuckles softly. "Herc thinks we should stop for the night before it gets too dark. He knows of a small village close by."

"Hm," I mumble to myself. *Herc thinks.*

"We aren't more than a mile away," Heracles adds from behind us.

I turn, a sneer lifting my lip, and rein in my horse to allow him to pass.

Might as well let him lead before I put him in the ground.

· · · ● · ● · ● · · ·

"No. Absolutely not," I repeat. Desy's lips are pinched together and her arms are crossed in front of her chest.

"It's the only inn in town, Pollux." Heracles rubs the back of his neck.

"I'm telling you, it's not happening. We'll keep going."

Desy shakes her head. "Herc says the next town is easily three hours away. It's getting darker, and I'm exhausted."

My eyes bounce back and forth between the two of them. They cannot possibly be serious. "And where will we all sleep exactly? Hm?" My foot taps impatiently as I raise my eyebrows at them.

"The lady should have the bed, of course," Heracles says gallantly. A blush creeps up into his apple cheeks as he glances sheepishly at Desy.

I grind what's left of my teeth and drop my head into my hands. "Are you certain there's nothing else available? We have plenty of coin."

The innkeeper shakes his head and shrugs.

My stomach hardens as the pain in my head begins to throb again. So much for sleeping it off. "Fine," I growl as I storm out of the inn's foyer.

I might as well unsaddle the horses and bring in the gear.

After all, that's all I'm good for.

· · · ● · ● · ● · · ·

"Where's *Herc*?" I release the saddlebags. They clatter to the floor. Desy startles from her perch on the side of the tub, where she's braiding her wet hair. I inhale her clean scent. A fluffy linen towel is wrapped around her breasts, but all I want to do is tear it away with my teeth.

"He's helping bring up the cauldrons of water. The servant they sent to do it was no more than a child!"

I start to roll my eyes but realize I'd probably have done the same thing in his position. Who forces a child to carry heavy buckets of scalding hot water? I press my lips together and, instead, turn toward rearranging the saddlebags from where I'd carelessly dropped them in the middle of the floor.

Anything to get my mind off Desy and her flushed skin, still pink from the bath.

I pretend to busy myself but can still feel her gaze on my back. Watching me.

"The water's still plenty hot if you'd like to wash."

"Hm," I mutter noncommittally. A hot soak would do wonders for my sore muscles. Unfortunately, the last thing I want to do is sit in a tub like an old woman while the golden boy uses his strength to hoist buckets of hot water into the bath.

My ears prick as her footsteps approach, and I feel her press her breasts against my back. I gulp down the lump in my throat and slowly turn. My eyes drop to her naked form, the towel now pooled at her feet. Droplets of water trail down her shoulder, but my gaze focuses in on her full lips.

"You've been quiet since we left Dodona, Pollux."

I wince and try to recover bravely, but words escape me.

"What did the dove tell you?"

"Nothing."

She huffs in annoyance. "You can tell me."

I blink. "No, I mean the dove told me nothing."

Her brow furrows in confusion.

"I met with Aphrodite's mother, and she told me that I have no destiny. My future isn't even worth describing." I scrub my palm over my face.

"Oh, Pollux." Her voice is full of pity, which is the last thing I want from her right now.

"It's as expected." I shrug and force out a laugh. I don't want to talk about this right now. I don't want to talk at all. I force my gaze down her naked body. I just want to feel better. Feel something. Anything.

She starts to shake her head as her hand flutters to her heart. Pitying me. I grab her fingers and bring them to the front of my trousers.

"Pol—" Her voice stills when I grind against her palm.

"I don't want to talk about Dodona or the doves, Desy." My voice is gravelly. Her nipples harden and goosebumps break out along her damp skin.

She brings her other hand up and begins unlacing my leathers. I sink into her, seeking her warm lips and pulling her in for a deep kiss. My bottoms drop to the floor, and she grabs my thick length and begins stroking as I palm her breast.

"*Mikrí nýmfi?*" I pull away and lick a line down her neck.

"Huh?" Her mouth falls open in pleasure.

"You need to be reminded of who you belong to, don't you?" At least I can pretend to be the big man with my cock in her hand. Still palming her breast, I bring the other hand up and around her neck. I grip her jaw, forcing her eyes on me. "I want to make it clear, Despoena. *Very* clear," I enunciate.

Her lashes flutter and she bites her lip while arching her back. I slide my palm from her breast and trail it down her stomach to her heat. She opens her legs slightly and her gaze darkens.

"You're mine, *mikrí nýmfi. Mine.*"

I tighten my grip around her delicate throat and sink my fingers into her wet flesh. A moan escapes her lips as her eyes shutter.

"Say it," I demand roughly, walking her back against the wall. When it hits her backside, she wraps a leg around my hip, and I add another finger to her core. "Tell me you're mine."

"I'm yours," she repeats between gasps as I curl my finger inside her pussy. "I'm *yours!*"

She's coming undone on my hand, her breaths turning into quick gasps. I withdraw my fingers, licking each one clean. "You taste delicious," I whisper in her ear.

She huffs, her pleasure coming out as a moan of desire.

Smiling, I line up my cock at her entrance—

"What the fuck are you doing?"

POLLUX

Desy's eyes go from rolling back in her head with ecstasy to an intent and focused gaze that suggests the impossible.

I try to pull away, to cover myself—or her—but she sinks her nails into my ass and squeezes. I hiss in pain. Or arousal. I'm honestly not quite sure.

"I want you," she states flatly. I swallow the lump in my throat, already knowing what's coming. "And I want him too." She flicks her gaze to Heracles, who's standing in the doorway, his mouth gaping.

He leans toward us.

"Stop," I command without looking his way. My cock is rapidly softening as the situation settles in my mind. I shake my head at Desy, my jaw clenching.

"Please," she begs, thrusting her chest against my naked torso.

"I don't share." My voice is low. There's no room for discussion. Or so I thought.

She sticks out her lower lip in a pout, her green eyes growing larger as she looks up at me.

I inhale deeply, my eyes closing just for a moment of their own accord, before turning to Heracles. As I exhale and focus my gaze on him, I notice his own brown eyes are shining with desire. He clenches his fists and then quickly releases them when he sees me notice. A slight flush creeps up his neck, and his lips part.

He moves carefully, and I immediately put out my hand to stall him. "You can sit over there. And watch," I add, indicating the chair in the corner of the room.

I turn my attention back to Desy, ignoring Heracles as he quickly moves across the room. She's touching her own throat, gliding her fingers up and down the smooth column of her neck. Taking the hint, I wrap my hand around the soft skin just below her jaw. I tilt her chin up as a small breathless whisper escapes her lips.

"I want you to take me to the bed. Where he can watch us." Her pupils dilate with desire, and she flicks her tongue out to lick her bottom lip.

"I told you. You're *mine*. And I don't share," I repeat quietly. But there's a hunger in her eyes, and the word no isn't in my lexicon when it comes to Despoena.

She stands on her toes and devours my mouth with deep sweeping strokes of her tongue.

My heart thuds loudly in my chest as my cock springs back to life. I grab her ass and lift her up. She wraps her lithe legs around my hips, and we turn in tandem to the bed.

As I carry her to the fur-lined mattress, she releases my lips and nuzzles her face in my neck, kissing and licking along the underside of my jaw. I crack a smile as she hits a sensitive spot just as my gaze meets Heracles's. His eyes have darkened to almost black, and he's biting his lower lip. His legs are spread wide, and he's slouched down in the chair. I swallow heavily as my gaze travels down his torso to his fisted cock. He strokes himself from base to tip, his gaze never leaving me.

"Focus on me," Desy whispers in my ear when she senses me stalling. "We'll go slow." She nibbles the soft skin of the lobe and I blink, lowering her to the bed.

She immediately grabs my length and, situating herself on all fours, greedily takes me into her mouth. I hiss as heat travels to my groin and my stomach muscles tremble. She alternates between licking along the shaft and firmly stroking, her saliva lubricating me.

"Enough." Heracles's voice breaks the silence and my gaze flicks to him. He's focused on Desy's bare ass. The perfect view from behind as she sucks me down.

She releases me and wipes her mouth on the back of her hand. She glances over her shoulder. "What do you want me to do, Herc?"

My heart skips a beat, and that familiar ache returns to my chest. "Des—"

"Hush, Pollux. I want to know what Herc wants now."

My jaw hardens and I clench my fists.

Heracles meets my eyes. "I want to watch you fuck her. Hard. From behind."

Glad that he isn't joining and taking what's mine, I exhale a sigh of relief and nod as Desy adjusts her position. She faces Heracles, her heavy breasts swaying as she crawls across the bed. I climb onto the mattress and pull her ass against my stomach.

Desy wiggles against me and my cock throbs to be inside her. I run my hands over her back and to her hips as she groans with pleasure. Moving my warm palms to her rear, I massage her cheeks and pull them apart, taking my fill of the gloriously wet pink flesh.

A hiss from Heracles draws my attention. He holds his palm out, almost as though he's reaching for me. My heart thrums loudly. But then he presses his lips together and, jaw working, spits into his hand. My own jaw ticks as I watch him slather the moisture up and down his engorged length, his brown eyes darkening to midnight black.

A sigh escapes from Desy, and I know she's watching too. "I want you inside me, Prince. Now." Her head swivels around. Her demanding eyes are feverish.

Tired of being commanded like a lowly hoplite, my muscles tense with anger.

I reach forward and squeeze her breast. She yelps but pushes her ass against me, seeking my cock. "I'll fuck you when I'm ready." I'm careful not to call her *mikrí nýmfi* in front of the golden boy. As though using the term of endearment would make it less special, I keep it hidden. Just for us.

Instead, I reach under her and feel for her clit. Her ass clenches when I find it, and I take my time running my thumb and forefinger over the bud. I work the sweet spot until she's panting, her excitement drenching my palm. Moving to her cunt, I insert a finger and, when she starts to bounce against me, add another. Her muscles pulse against my digits, and I quirk my fingers. She gasps and throws her head back.

"Not yet," I hiss as I withdraw from her. I reach around and hold out my dewy fingers. She pulls two into her mouth and sucks. My balls tighten as Heracles bites his bottom lip.

"Fuck," he mutters. He wants a taste of what's *mine*.

Just to spite him, I pull my hand up to my mouth and lick my fingertips clean. "You taste delicious."

"I know," she responds huskily. She reaches behind and grabs my cock, her shoulder dipping into the mattress. I run my palms up and down her thighs as she notches me at her entrance and eases back onto me. Our bodies simultaneously relax as I am coated in her wetness. I grab her ass and move slowly, watching my erection slide in and out of her cunt. I pull all the way out and then sink back into her with more force. She pants and sighs before reaching down and touching herself.

I ignore Heracles's grunts from the chair, keeping my eyes on Desy's bouncing backside. Our speed increases as I thrust harder into her, our bodies smacking loudly in the otherwise quiet room.

"Don't stop," she moans as I continue to plunge into her. She's soaked me with her desire. Her hand fists the bedding while the other punishes her clit. I can feel her muscles pulsing around my cock, and I grit my teeth as my breathing increases.

She throws her head back, and Heracles's body goes rigid with trembles. They're both so close, but so am I. I keep going, sweat beading on my brow and dripping into my eyes. Desy's moans grow louder, and as her cunt pulses around my cock and she screams my name, I come undone. My body shudders its release, spilling into her as I spasm. Heracles, too, hisses as his seed spills on his stomach in long pearly ropes.

My breathing slows, and I reluctantly withdraw from Desy. She collapses onto the bed, a sigh of pleasure complementing her delirious smile. I use the tub's cooled water to clean myself, and then wet a corner of Desy's discarded towel.

I return to her side. "Turn over, *mikrí nýmfi*," I whisper in her ear for only us to hear. She moves languidly, and I proceed to clean her myself. Her heavy-lidded eyes are dulled from the exertion, satiated by me.

"Ahem."

I don't even bother looking as I toss the used towel to Heracles. Instead, I sink down next to Desy, who immediately wraps her arms around me. Then I pull the covers over both our naked bodies and quickly fall asleep nestled against my nymph.

Hecate

“My lady? My lady!” The gentle rocking of the boat is interrupted by Charon’s violent shaking, and my eyes snap open as I gasp for breath. “My lady, we are here.” The boat is already tied to the dock, and as I sit up and brush my hair from my eyes, the edge of a brown blanket falls to my waist. No, not a blanket. Zeus’s hooded cape. I’m covered in the fabric, protected from the chill that’s taken over as we’ve sailed north.

“Ahem.” My gaze flashes to the dock and Zeus’s outstretched hand. He wiggles his fingers in a beckoning manner. Flustered and still a little drowsy from my nap, I stand and take his hand, the palm smooth. Giving me an odd look, he jerks me from the boat. I stumble, but manage to step onto the wooden planks without falling. “I wanted my cape, witch.”

“Oh, of course.” I blink slowly. How stupid of me to think he was being chivalrous. Before I can step back into the boat and retrieve the cape, Charon has already passed the brown material to him. I flash the captain a grateful smile and return my focus to Zeus.

“I think it best that you remain here,” I say first to Zeus. I turn my back to him and address the Underworld’s shipman. “Charon, I’m sure you’re welcome at the house. I’ll meet you back there before nightfall.”

Charon nods and strides up the hill without a backward glance. I start to follow in his wake, but Zeus grabs my arm and pulls me back. My sandal catches on the dock's warped wooden planks, and I nearly fall into the water. I yelp as he catches me before pulling me into his chest. I immediately shove away from him, pushing with all my might.

"I would've rather fallen into the sea," I sneer and proceed to stalk away.

"I should've let you fall, but that's beside the point. I'm not staying here, Hecate. I'm coming with you."

"No. I highly doubt either Thetis or Peleus wish to see you. Let alone Hephaestus. Don't you get it?" When he doesn't respond, I continue, "Everyone *despises* you for what you've done."

He has the audacity to look contrite, despite never once apologizing for his actions. I narrow my eyes at him and clench my fists, wanting to smack that remorseful look off his face.

"Thetis and I have always gotten along, and there are things that I need to say to Hephaestus."

I blink at him.

"And I'm certainly not allowing you to speak with him alone."

I snort, my mouth falling open in surprise. "Allowing me?"

"Hephaestus is . . . a person of interest in this war. We do not know his motives or how he's connected to the giants. You aren't safe around him without protection." He crosses his arms over his chest and dips his chin at me.

I stare at him. A string of curses nearly burst from my mouth, but I snap it shut and, instead, take a few calming breaths. When I'm sufficiently calm—or at least calmer than I was a few seconds ago—I finally unleash the rage that's been building throughout this entire trip.

"Who do you think you are?" I yell as my fingers begin to glow. The color is more of a dark maroon rather than the bright red I'm used to. But even with my magic dulled, its appearance makes me feel powerful enough to say what needs to be said.

Zeus's jaw clenches, but he keeps his arms crossed and just stares at me.

"You may have once been the king of the gods, but you were overthrown. *By your own daughter*," I grit between my teeth. "Do you remember why you were overthrown, or have you conveniently forgotten your crimes too?"

When he doesn't say anything, I continue my tirade.

"You were overthrown for being a *rapist*, Zeus. You took something precious that wasn't yours, and you used your power to hurt people. You lied, you cheated, and you *assaulted*—for years—without any remorse or consequence." I'm quiet for a moment, letting my words sink in. "And you think to lord yourself over me *now*?" An angry laugh bursts from my chest. "Piss off."

I turn and trudge up the hill, a headache forming at the base of my skull but my chest feeling lighter than it has in days.

· · · · ● · ● · · · ·

Before I reach the entrance of the abode, Thetis throws open the door and runs out to greet me. "Charon just informed Peleus that you arrived!" She throws her arms around me. "It's been too long, my friend." It feels good to be hugged, and even with the world falling apart around me, here in Thetis's arms I feel protected. Safe.

"I'm so sorry, Thetis. Hades has kept us busy."

"Is Cas with you?" She looks behind me, searching for my husband, but when she doesn't see him, she takes note of the frown dotting my face and releases me from her embrace. "What's happened?"

"I really need to speak with Hephaestus, They," I say, using her nickname.

She scoffs and pulls me toward the cabin. "You have time for a glass of wine. Besides, I have someone to introduce to you!"

I follow her inside, the pop of color alarming my senses. As a sea nymph who's traded the water for land, she's brought the ocean to her decor. Bright blue, the color of the Terranean, covers the walls. Giant seashells dot the tables while the furniture is made of sanded driftwood and coarse linen. Despite the chill of the air outside, the temperature inside is practically tropical.

"Achilles!" she shouts as we both plop onto the chaise. "You must meet my son!"

"You have a son?" I gape, only now realizing how long it's been since I visited.

Her eyes gleam with pride as a toddling baby boy runs into the sitting room, his chubby legs carrying him so fast he nearly crashes into his mother's knees. "Whoa there, m'boy!" She lifts him up and sets him on my lap.

The tot reaches for my tangled curls and grabs a fistful. "Ouch! Careful," I say as I disentangle my locks from his iron fist. "He certainly is strong!"

"Just like his papa," Thetis responds with a look of adoration on her face.

"Where is the proud father?"

"He's seeing that Charon is fed and catching up on the Underworld gossip." Her voice drops as she leans in. "We've heard the rumors . . . about the line of souls. Is it true?"

I nod my head and frown. "Yes, but as we track down the giants and learn of their origins, we hope to find a means to rid of the earth of their kind and return order."

Thetis blinks at me and drops her hand to my forearm. "That's a very well-rehearsed answer, Hecate. Quite the emissary you still are. But we are friends, are we not? What is the truth?"

I sigh, my shoulders sagging as I allow myself to feel the weight of this journey. "The truth is that we don't know where the giants came from or why they're here. But we've clues. That's why I'm here. To speak to Hephaestus."

Her brow crinkles. "You believe Hephaestus has the answers you seek?" Thetis has always been like a stand-in mother for the god of metalworking. That she would worry about her adoptive son is honorable, but I'm wary of what I say, nonetheless.

"I believe Hephaestus can help me, as he once did long ago." My fingers trace the place where Hephaestus's golden necklace once sat. It saved me from Hera, and I gulp down the guilt I feel at questioning Hephaestus's loyalties in this war.

Baby Achilles rubs his eyes and yawns audibly. Thetis tuts as she reaches for her son. "I need to get this one to bed, but I'm sure you can find your way to the forge. Will you stop by on your way back? To say goodbye?"

"Of course." I smile as I hand her the beautiful child. I plant a soft kiss on his forehead and disentangle his fist from my hair once more. Watching as Thetis rocks the tot, I tiptoe out the door and down the path that will take me to Hephaestus's forge.

POLLUX

"So you two just aren't going to speak to one another the rest of the way to Olympus?"

Annoyed with Desy's questioning and already feeling awkward as fuck, I keep my mouth shut.

"I, for one, had fun. I'd love to do it again. Maybe tonight?"

Heracles's playfulness grates on my nerves. I'd like to throw him into the pit of Tartarus. If he needs someone to play with, I'm sure one of the brutish Hecatoncheires could oblige. Even thinking of the multiheaded Underworld giants torturing the golden boy lifts my spirits slightly. Perhaps, when we get to Olympus, Hecate would be willing to do me a small favor . . .

"What was that?" Heracles brings his horse to a quick stop and tilts his head.

My gut tightens, and I crane my neck, listening. Heracles may need some roughing up at the hands of Hades's prisoners, but he's an excellent warrior. If there's danger ahead, there's no one I'd rather have fighting by my side.

A bloodcurdling scream reaches my ears, followed by a loud crash, and then a rumble shakes the earth. Heracles and I lock eyes.

Giants.

"Stay here," I order Desy, my voice low. Not waiting for her response, I spur my horse after Heracles, who's already taken off at a gallop.

We tear through the trees toward the source, the ground continuing to quake every few moments. The screams increase in volume and then go silent. I don't have to voice to my companion what this means. We both already know.

If I allowed it, my blood would run cold with fear. Instead, I force the adrenaline to take over and squash the negative thoughts and terror from my mind.

We break through the forest and into a clearing, our horses coming up short and rearing onto their hind legs. I quickly dismount, and my horse immediately flees back into the tree line while Heracles attempts to rein in his beast.

"Get off. He won't go any farther if he senses danger ahead," I order, drawing my sword.

Heracles obliges with a swift nod, and his horse quickly follows mine, abandoning us to the unknown. "Oh, fuck."

I follow his gaze and my stomach plummets. An entire village burns in the distance. We both break out in a run, me sheathing my sword and pumping my arms faster as Herc pulls his bow out. I nod, knowing he'll cover me and protect us both.

As we reach the outskirts of the village, we crouch behind several tree hollows. We peek from behind the stumps, quickly assess the situation, and turn back to one another.

"We need to go left." I begin.

"We're surrounded by beehives."

My mouth goes dry as a lazy fat bumblebee appears next to my face. I make to stand, but Heracles grabs my forearm and pulls me down.

"We need to stay here until we can figure out what's out there, and if there are any alive we can help."

I swallow down the lump in my throat, not ready to admit that I'm terrified of something as simple as a stinging insect. My body goes cold and my hands feel clammy, so I close my eyes and take a few deep breaths.

"What's wrong with you?"

"The bees," I admit on an exhale.

He rolls his eyes. "You're afraid of bees?"

"Not afraid," I gasp. "Got stung once and swelled up like a pig's stomach."

His eyes widen. "You didn't die?"

"My father, err, King Tyndareus, sent for a healer. They applied a salve and removed the stinger." I stiffen as two bees swirl in the air in a deadly dance. I flinch away from them, my hands beginning to tremble as they move closer, sniffing out my fear.

Heracles peers around the stump once more. "There's a smoldering hut a distance away. If we stay low, we can make it without being detected. But we can't get too close."

It doesn't sound promising, and the smoke may impair our sight while also seeping into our lungs, but it's better than sitting here and waiting for a bee to send me to the Underworld.

I don't hear him count down until he yells the word "One!" Grabbing me roughly by the collar, he yanks me away from the hive and toward the burning village.

• • • • • • • • • • •

We're nearly halfway to the soot-covered hut when a blast rocks the air around us and the ground bulges beneath the grass. I stumble and drop to my knees, the pain shooting straight up my spine, while Heracles stills and holds out his arms to steady himself.

Once the quake has passed, Herc continues on his way, arriving safely at the hut. I, however, am stuck, incapacitated with a throbbing ache in my legs. I'm rooted to the spot, hissing through my teeth as I try to sling my foot out and rise.

"Pollux! Can you get up?"

I grit my teeth and use all my energy to stand, but my back spasms and I fall to the ground. I hold in frustrated curses. "I'm fine," I lie as I keep to my belly and begin slithering along the ground like a snake.

"Shit," he mutters. I think he's cursing at my injury, but as the ground begins to tremble again, I look up and see his eyes widen as he stares behind me.

Knowing the giant must be behind me, and fast approaching by the quake of the ground, I crawl on my belly faster, refusing to give up. I'll not die on this field. Not when I have a mission to accomplish.

Get Heracles to Olympus.

Win the war.

"What are you doing?" Heracles exclaims as the ground shifts beneath me. I growl and dig my forearms into the ground, pulling myself along faster and faster, before the darkness settles over me.

The noisy world is muffled as the smell of death overcomes my senses. I gag and flail my arms and legs, light peeking through as my appendages claw at the dirt.

"What the fuck?"

"Pollux! Move!" Heracles's voice reaches my ears, and I rise to my hands and knees, the pain miraculously gone. Something heavy still covers me, and as I reach up and yank the smelly blanket off, I realize it's the lion skin of Heracles's giant.

I gag at the stench, but quickly rise to my feet and hold the fur in my outstretched hand as I sprint toward my companion.

Tossing it at Heracles, I bend at the waist and gulp deep breaths of the smoke-filled air. "Where—? How—?"

The golden boy's jaw works as he peers around the hut. "Fuckin' Despoena," he mumbles under his breath.

I shake my head, sure that I've misheard. "What?"

"Despoena," he repeats, trading places with me. He points in the distance, and my heart stops.

Desy, *mikrí nýmfi*, is standing in the middle of the village square, completely unarmored and weaponless, staring down a massive giant.

HECATE

It's been many years since I've visited Hephaestus at his personal forge. Not since Thetis's wedding have I seen the god at work, although we've come in contact many times on Olympus. Hephaestus is one of the few gods from the old regime allowed to continue to serve the throne. As half sibling to Athena, and also son of Hera, he is one of her most trusted advisers. He's also the resident blacksmith with his own workshop just outside the palace walls.

I approach the hot, smoky building with trepidation. The last time I was here, Hephaestus revealed the truth of my marriage to Castor—that my husband had made a deal with Zeus in exchange for immortality. Regardless of the nightmares this place holds, I grit my teeth and move toward the heat.

Hephaestus's back muscles glisten with sweat as he holds a metal creation over the forge. The flames lick the tool, turning the shiny iron black with soot. I tiptoe into the light and take a moment to assess my surroundings for clues. I see no herbs. No swords or weapons that would lead me to believe my friend has been disloyal or dishonorable.

On an inhale, I open my mouth to announce myself when Hephaestus speaks first. "How long were you planning on standing there?"

As he turns and cocks an eyebrow at me, I offer him a sheepish smile. He limps over and throws a burly arm around my shoulders, pulling me in for a side-hug. "You should know by now that my other senses are incredibly heightened to make up for . . . well . . ." He nods at his deformed foot, a birth defect that resulted in his banishment from Hera's motherly love.

"I wanted to surprise you." The lie slips through my lips and tastes like the soot covering the god. I widen my eyes and my smile.

Hephaestus looks at me, his face impassive. "Did you find what you were looking for then?" If there's ever been an immortal to call me on my mistruths, it's the god of metalworking.

I sigh, knowing I should never have attempted to trick Hephaestus. "Tell me about your time with Gaia." I slyly move away from his grip and wander around the workshop, picking up and discarding odds and ends.

"What do you care to know?" He crosses his arms over his chest and leans against a tabletop. "I'm an open book about my former lovers."

"You created a son together. The Athenian king Cecrops?"

Hephaestus hums in assent. "Cecrops was an intelligent and wise child, not unlike myself," he jokes.

My lips flatten and the god's face falls.

"Enough with the inquisition, Hecate." He pushes himself from the bench and grabs a hammer. As he flips it from hand to hand, my heart flutters in my chest and my fingers tingle, ready to protect myself should I need it. Hephaestus eyes my faintly glowing digits and slams the hammer onto the tabletop. "Tell me why you're here and what you want to know."

Startled, I back up and raise my hands, my body warming as the little magic I still have thrums through my veins.

"You're afraid of me now, friend?" His eyes betray the despair I feel simmering in my own gut.

"No, it's not that—well, I don't know what it is, actually. But—"

As I struggle to complete my thought, to tell Hephaestus why I'm really here, a boulder smashes through the side of his workshop. It hits the open fire pit in the middle of the forge and breaks apart into a million shards that fly through the air.

I duck and cover my face, the bits slicing my arms. I hiss with pain as each one cuts deeper. Bloody rivers run down my limbs, and I collapse onto the ground, shielding my life veins from the onslaught.

A heavy form settles over me, the warmth soothing my fear. Before I realize what's happening, Hephaestus has picked me up and carried me behind his workbench. Blocked from the next boulder that shatters, I look into the god's eyes and immediately know that he's innocent of my accusations.

"It—it's Gaia," I stutter as the boulders continue to fragment into shards. "It's Gaia. She created these—monsters. Hephaestus! No!" I shout as he grabs a sharp tool and launches himself over the workbench. As he steps through the hole in his forge and disappears into the blackness of the night, my heart thuds in my chest.

I look around for something—anything—that I can use to fight. I spy two long spears, and a smile breaks out on my face. *No need for sticks this time*, I think. I find a discarded tarp under some rubble and, using my teeth, tear two strips and then quickly wrap them each around one of the spears. I dip the cloth-covered ends of the spears into the oil that Hephaestus keeps away from the fire and then hold them over the flames. I wince as the spears flame to life, my face immediately breaking out in a sweat.

"Hephaestus!" I call as I step through the hole in the wall. It takes a moment for my eyes to adjust to the darkness, and then my heart stops. There's not one giant. There're not two giants.

Three fucking giants.

My mouth goes dry, and I pause for a moment as my brain catches up with my eyes. Hephaestus stabbing one of the beasts in the throat as thick blood spurts all over the god. He immediately swipes the ichor from his eyes and turns to me.

"Move!" his mouth says, but I can hear nothing over the roar in my ears. The second giant reaches out a slithering tail and grabs my hair, yanking me flat onto my back. The wind is knocked out of me, and I gasp for breath. Luckily, I keep my torches held tight and, crossing them over my chest, use them to protect my upper body as the giant's serpent appendage strikes over and over, searching for my heart.

Hephaestus comes out of the darkness and slices the limb from the giant. The beast shrieks and withdraws into the night. I yelp in disgust as the wiggly appendage smacks me in the face and then rolls to the ground and goes still.

"Where did they go?"

"One went that way." Hephaestus nods behind his forge. "The other disappeared over the ridge." He's quiet, his eyes bouncing back and forth between the two locations. "You think Gaia created them?"

I nod silently, and then, realizing he likely can't see me in the dim light, say, "Yes. Your son Cecrops, he—"

"He had a serpent's tail, too." Hephaestus's eyes go flat in the flickering torchlight. "And you thought . . . ?"

"I'm sorry. I didn't know what to think, Hephaestus. And when Zeus and I saw the statue in Athens—"

"Zeus? He's here with you?"

I clamp my mouth shut as something rustles in the distance. I inch forward, holding a torch away from my body, but there are only trees and shrubs. No monsters.

"Hecate! Is Zeus here with you?" Hephaestus grabs my arm and I flinch, not realizing he'd moved so close.

"Yes, he's at the dock. Or he was," I mutter as I keep my gaze trained on the dark depths of the night.

"Fuck," he hisses as he takes off running.

"Where are you going?" My voice is shrill as the fear slithers up my spine. I don't want to be left out here alone.

"To Thetis!"

Oh no. She, Peleus, and the babe are all alone—unprotected. "The giants!" I scream as I sprint after him, the torches nearly dying as I pump my arms faster to catch up with Hephaestus. My breathing comes easier now as the adrenaline kicks in, and I easily propel myself past the god.

Please don't let us be too late.

POLLUX

"**N**o!" Heracles pulls me forcefully back just as I take a step into the open.

I immediately withdraw my blade, holding it to his throat as I clutch his collar, my body on fire with rage. "I'll not let her die out there for my sake. For our sakes."

He gulps and lowers his eyes, nodding in agreement.

Still scowling, I peer around the corner again. Something sharp stabs me in the chest. Whether it's love or fear, I don't know. But when I look at Despoena, standing there before the giant after riding in like a goddess and throwing the cloak over my broken body, I know she must feel the same. Right?

I turn to lay out a plan for Heracles, but he's already gone. "Over here!" I hear him yell, and when I return to my post, he's running in between the burning huts, his bow notched and pointed at the giant.

I run in the other direction, clanging my blade along the sides of the huts to disarm the creature. The giant roars and swipes at Desy, knocking her aside like a rag doll, and then takes off toward Heracles. The air leaves my lungs in a whoosh as I sprint toward my fearless lover.

I skid to a stop and drop onto one knee. I'm careful not to move her in case of broken bones and curse myself for leaving the lion skin behind.

"Desy?" I shake her shoulders gently, and my heart stills as she blinks open her eyes. She winces as I try to get her to sit upright. "Are you hurt badly?"

She clutches her side. "I think he cracked a rib."

"Can you walk?" She nods and I help her stand. I glance around, not seeing Heracles or the giant, and blood rushes to my ears. "Do you see them?"

Her eyes dart back and forth, but between the roaring fire burning the cottages and the smoke, neither of us have a good view of anything.

"We need to move. Now." With her arm around my shoulder, we hurry behind the first hut. I find the discarded lion skin and wrap it around Desy.

She crinkles her nose. "Somehow it smells worse than the first day Herc wore it."

My lips crack into a smile. "I know."

Her breathing becomes less ragged as the cape begins to work. "I didn't—I didn't realize it could heal when I threw it over you. I thought to hide you from the giant."

"Is it working?"

She nods. Holding the cloak open, she sways her hips and rolls her shoulders seductively. "I feel fine now." She blinks slowly at me as a smile lifts her lips.

I sigh with relief. "Good." I pull her in quickly for a kiss. "If we weren't in the middle of a war zone, I'd want you to roll those hips again while you rode my cock."

A laugh bubbles from her throat as her eyes flash with hunger.

"Stay here this time. I mean it." I pull away regretfully, but I know that I need to get to Heracles. I sling the cloak over my own shoulders just in case, and with one last glance at Desy, run into the flames.

"Heracles!" I call into the smoke-filled village. I withdraw my short blade and bang it against my other sword. "Heracles!"

The ground rumbles and begins to shake. This time I'm prepared, and I crouch low, ready to ride the wave of the quake. It passes underfoot just as a loud screech shatters my ears.

I run toward the noise, staying as close as possible to the huts, which have by now begun to smolder as the fires die away. My eyes burn from the smoke, and my breathing has become ragged, but I continue onward.

"Heracles!" I yell again. Nothing.

I round the corner of a burned-out hut and spot the giant, his back to me. Slinking back out of sight, I reroute myself. I move to the next hut, my footsteps halting as I have a clear view of the giant's side. He's focused on something, and my stomach drops when I realize Heracles is being held down with the giant's serpentine lower body. One slithering appendage wraps around Heracles's midsection while another slides toward his neck.

I sneak slowly toward the giant, my gaze bouncing back and forth between Herc and the beast. I pick up my pace as Heracles's lids become heavy, and I slice into the closest limb.

An ear-piercing shriek rattles the cottages' bones, and several collapse in the distance. Blood spurts on the dirt as the cut-off tail wriggles around uselessly on the ground. I move quickly toward the other limb that holds my companion, then stab and cut into it in an attempt to free its prisoner.

A thick hand grabs my neck from behind, and I'm lifted into the air. Heracles struggles to find his footing, and as he gasps for air on the ground, his eyebrows rise as I'm flung into the burned hut. I crash through the still-smoldering timber, landing flat on my back.

"Fuck," I mutter to myself as I struggle to breathe. Ashes rain down over my face, getting into my mouth and mixing with the smoke, creating a charcoal slurry. I roll to my side, coughing and hacking as the sludge slides down my throat. I swipe my fingers into my mouth, pull the gunk from my gullet, and finally manage to sit up and spit out the remaining burned offerings of the village.

I shake out my hair and brush off my face just as Heracles's head pops into view. *Flying above the cottage's missing roof.*

The giant's few remaining appendages are coiled around Heracles's neck again, squeezing so tightly that my companion's eyes are bulging from his skull. His face is so red it's nearly purple. The man scratches at the scaly tails and kicks his legs futilely.

Tossing aside rubbish, I search in haste for my blades, but they're gone. Likely flung into the distance. I mutter a curse as I pull my smallest weapon—a mere bone knife—from my boot. It'll cut nothing thicker than a steak, but it's all I've got.

I rush from the destroyed building just as a flash of light blinds me. I blink, my vision blurry, and shake my head to clear the dancing lights from my eyes.

Still unable to see clearly, I hear a loud thud followed by a wet squelch. *Oh fuck*, I think. *Please don't be Heracles. Please don't be Heracles*!

"Herc!" I shout as I rush in the direction of the giant. Even blind, I'm willing to throw myself at the mercy of the giant if it saves my friend.

"Pollux." The quiet whisper comes from the ground. I wave my hands and move in the general area until I feel Heracles's body.

"I can't see shit! Are you hurt?"

"I'm . . . fine," he mumbles in between breaths. "Ath—Athena. She's here."

I keep blinking and finally my vision is clear enough. "I'm going to her. She'll need help."

He nods, his throat fast turning into a giant bruise. I toss the cloak over him, its healing powers beginning to work quickly as his breathing evens out and his neck returns to its natural color.

"Desy's behind the outer cottage. Get her out of here," I command as I stand and sprint toward the giant, its head bobbing overtop the huts as it seeks out another victim.

Holding my measly bone knife and one of Herc's arrows I grabbed from the ground at his feet, I pick up my pace. I move swiftly but stop short when I spot Athena battling alongside another female.

Desy.

My eyes bounce back and forth between the two women. One, the ruler of the gods and goddesses on Olympus. Our queen. The other, my sassy and independent lover who *simply will not listen to me*. I grit my teeth and storm into the view of the giant, his face full of rage as he catches a glimpse of me. An evil smile quirks his lips as his eyes narrow.

The beast turns his full force on Desy, completely forgetting about Athena. I release a roar as I charge toward him, but a serpentine limb whips out and coils around my ankle. I trip and land in the dirt, Heracles's arrow snapping in two while the bone knife slices my thumb.

"No!" I hear Athena shriek. I hop to my feet just as Desy is flung into a cottage. "Go to her!" Athena yells at me as she continues to attack the giant.

I cannot reach Desy fast enough, but when I do, my blood pools in my feet. Her eyes are glassy and she's trembling.

"Pollux?" she whispers as blood spurts from her lips. "Am I . . . ? Am I hurt?" She coughs and red splatters my vision.

My jaw clenches. I refuse to look down. Refuse to look at the carnage I know will be there.

But when I do, when I finally lower my gaze to her wound and see the wooden spike sticking through her chest, I break.

HECATE

"Thetis? Peleus?" I burst through the door to the large cabin just before Hephaestus, who immediately stomps through the different rooms as he echoes their names.

"In here!" Thetis calls cheerily. My stomach plummets as a bright aura shines from the kitchen. My body flames hot and I stop in my tracks, my hands trembling as I bring them up to my line of vision.

Glowing so brightly that they're as white as Helios's disk in the sky.

My ability to run—to surpass Hephaestus—wasn't adrenaline. It was my magic. Surging back to life. To full capacity.

"Thetis, what have you done?" I whisper as my gaze travels to hers.

"Zeus mentioned that you were both working together to fight these awful giants, and that his magic was under a binding that couldn't be broken. So I broke it." She shrugs as her eyes flick to the glowing god in the corner of the room. His chest heaves as his abilities roar back to life. His dulled eyes flashing to their stormy blue as he bares his teeth in a hungry smile.

"*No!*" I manage to scream before everything tilts and the world crashes around me.

The cabin—and all of us inside it—go flying as the two giants smash into the sides. The wooden planks snap in half, and Hephaestus and I topple over one another while Zeus and Thetis are thrown to the ceiling and crash back down to the floor.

"Thetis!" Hephaestus untangles himself and rushes to the woman who raised him as a youth. His mother in all but blood. She's unconscious, her body broken on the ground and bleeding from a gash along her temple.

"The baby!" I cry, scrambling to my feet and rushing down the hallway, searching for the nursery. I climb over furniture and slide through cracked pieces of wood, opening and closing doors until I reach the babe's room. The door remains firmly closed, and I breathe a sigh of relief as I crack it. The tot sleeps peacefully in his crib, the entire room unfazed by the chaos beyond its door. I quickly cast a protection spell over the doorway, breakable only by Thetis, Peleus, or Hephaestus, and then make my way back to the nightmare in the kitchen.

"Is he—is he—?" Hephaestus's eyes are crazed with worry as he catches me in the hallway.

"He's safe. I protected the room. What of Thetis?"

"She's breathing. Healing."

I exhale in relief. Even if the nymph unbound Zeus with her ability to transform herself into anything, including a witch, I am glad she is alive. "Where's Peleus and—and Zeus?" I glance around at the carnage of the destroyed rooms and my lip begins to tremble. How will I contain Zeus now that his binding has been broken? How will I protect us? I shake my head and focus on Hephaestus, who's speaking words that I don't hear.

" . . . feeding the chickens and Zeus ran down to the forge."

"We can't let him get close to any of your weapons, Hephaestus!" I make for the door, but Hephaestus's hand whips out and grabs me.

His eyes narrow as he looks me up and down. "What is going on, Hecate?"

I bite my lip, my cheeks heating as tears fill my eyes.

"Tell me. Otherwise I can't help you fix this." He looks around at the damage to the home. *His* home.

"We need Zeus to win this war with the giants, but I bound his magic—to my own—so that he was weakened. It was the only way to get him to Olympus. And now . . . and now . . ." The tears spill and fall down my cheeks as my chest heaves. "What am I going to do now? This is all my fault!"

Hephaestus pulls me in for a tight hug, his warmth soothing my frayed nerves. I sob for only a moment before he releases me from his grip. "We don't have time for this. I can help."

Grabbing my hand and tugging me out the doorway, or what was left of the doorway, Hephaestus and I race back down the hill to his forge.

· · · ● · ● · ● · · ·

"Zeus! Stop!" Hephaestus roars as we reach the forge just in time to see the king of gods grabbing a jagged spear from the workbench.

With his back to us, Zeus's muscles ripple as he inhales. His hair, only moments ago dry and frizzy, has turned silky and now covers the back of his neck. He releases a laugh, or a growl, I'm not sure which, and finally turns to us.

"We need your help." I hold my hands out in front of myself, my fingertips glowing bright as I bring my magic to the surface. It pulses in my veins, ready to be released on a whisper.

"And I need *nothing* from you now. Funny how that works." He tosses the lightning-bolt-shaped spear into the air and catches it deftly in his hand.

"You do, actually. Need us. At least me." Hephaestus adds with a shrug. While I have my battle stance down to an art form, Hephaestus stands with his hands on his hips and his lips pursed. The picture of nonchalance.

"*You*?" Zeus snarls, his eyes flicking to Hephaestus's crippled foot. "You think I need *you*?" His laugh crackles in the air around us.

"That weapon there?" Hephaestus nods to the spear in Zeus's hand. "It's useless without *my* magic touch. Plus it's not been heat sealed yet." The god of metal cocks an eyebrow at Zeus as a smirk touches his lips.

"*Fuck!*" Zeus tosses the piece to the ground just as a rumble knocks us all sideways.

"If you help us get rid of the giants, I'll be your personal blacksmith. I'll make you whatever you need. Any weapon, Zeus. It can be yours." Hephaestus holds out his hand.

"Hephaestus . . . no," I plead with him.

His sad eyes meet mine. "We all do what we have to, Hecate, to win this war." His throat bobs as he swallows.

"You're paying with your life. You're promising to be his servant. Forever."

"I know." He turns back to Zeus. "So what do you say, Zeus?"

The forge's fire flares in the background as Zeus's face transforms and he smiles. His dark eyebrows stretch across his face and his lips part, showing his sharp, wolfish teeth. His eyes seem to glow yellow as he reaches his own hand out. "Deal."

As they shake, my throat tightens, and the hair on the back of my neck stands up. "We need—" I try, but my voice breaks with emotion. "We need to get rid of these giants." I eye Zeus, then add, "For Thetis's sake."

"Easy enough," the god says smoothly. "Now that I'm whole again." He eyes me darkly before picking up the discarded spear and, with a nod at Hephaestus, stalks out of the forge and into the tree line.

The moment he's gone I snap my gaze to Hephaestus.

"Before you start, Hecate, I did what needed to be done. Just like you did when you released him from his prison." He grabs a variety of weapons, sticking them in the various slots of his belt and boots.

"But Hephaestus, you belong to him now."

"Yes, I do. But that means I will always—always—know his plans. And we can use my position to stay one step ahead of him."

I'm quiet as the implications sink in. "I hate that you had to sell yourself for my mistake."

Hephaestus hands me two more spears, already lit with oil, not that I need them now that my magic has returned. "Gaia made the mistake when she thought she could fight us and win, Hecate." He tosses me a loose smile, and with a nod, we leave the forge and enter the darkness of the night.

POLLUX

"*F*ather, you called for me?" I enter his darkened study to find him hunched over his desk, a parchment scroll in his hand. He's silent, as though he hasn't heard me. "Father?"

The paper flutters to the ground as the king, the man who raised me as his own, clutches his left arm and slumps farther over in his seat.

"Father!" I rush to his side and catch him before he slips to the floor. His eyes shutter as his breathing becomes ragged.

"Help!" My plea echoes off the walls, and I hear the footsteps of the king's protectors approaching. I'm pulled away from my father as his guards carefully pick him up.

"Father! Father!" My keens fall on deaf ears, and I'm further restrained by Menelaus, my sister's new husband.

"Control yourself, Prince!" he demands, grabbing my jaw to force me to look into his beady eyes. They narrow to mere slits. I shove him aside and follow in the guards' wake.

· · · ● · ● · ● · · ·

"What news, Mother?" Days have passed since Father's episode, as it's now known around the palace. The staff have been told to keep quiet, to keep the king's health concerns hidden. All in the name of Sparta and the safety of our country.

"Nothing new, I'm afraid." She wearily turns to look at me. The circles beneath her eyes have darkened since yesterday.

"You should get some rest. I'll sit with him for a spell." Her lips thin as the muscles in her neck tighten, but as I move and gently usher her up and out of the room, she doesn't argue. After nodding to the guards to make sure she goes straight to bed, I softly close the door.

I return to the chair and sink into its plushness. Brushing my hair from my eyes, I reach for my father's calloused palm.

Please wake up, Father, *I mentally beg.* Sparta isn't ready to let you go. I'm not ready to let you go. We still need you.

As though he can hear my pleas, he inhales deeply and slowly blinks open his eyes. My heart stutters and my mouth falls open.

"Father?"

He turns to me slightly, his brow knitting together as he meets my worried gaze. *"Polydeuces."* His voice is gravelly with disuse; his tongue licks dry lips.

"You've had an episode. How are you feeling now?"

He takes a few more breaths and lets the news sink in. *"That bastard brother of mine caused this,"* he finally mumbles as his face reddens.

A panic spreads across my chest at his coloring. Still too pale. *"Calm down, Father. We don't want to lose you again."*

His jaw works and his face contorts. His nostrils flare as his lips curl. *"I feel fine, boy. We must get to work to ensure the throne is safe."* He whips the blankets from his body and swings his legs to the floor. I hold out my hands in an effort to stop him, but it's no use as he stands and then staggers against me.

"Sit down!" I command as I shove him back to the bed. *"Guards! Send for the healer!"* The door creaks open, and the soldier's eyes widen as he sees the king is

awake. He immediately turns and exits the bedroom, his footsteps echoing down the hall.

"How dare you disobey me?" my father rages as he attempts to stand again.

"Father, if you are truly well then please wait for the doctor to assess your condition. I will do whatever you ask of me, but your health comes first."

With a dejected grumble he relents, leaning back and crossing his arms over his chest. I bring the soft blanket back over him. "The least you can do is retrieve my correspondence from my bureau. Bring it to me while I await the doctor's arrival."

I narrow my eyes.

"I promise I'll stay here," he huffs indignantly.

I bow stiffly, an ache spreading from my neck to my temples, and quietly close the door behind myself.

· · · ● · ● · ● · · ·

"What in Hades's name are you doing in here?"

Menelaus stiffens in his seat at my father's desk. Spread out before him are the country's ledgers, correspondence, and—sitting at his right hand—my father's official seal.

"Who do you suppose has been running Sparta while you and your family hold court at your father's bedside?" He settles back in the chair with exaggerated casualness.

"That duty should have fallen to me. His son." I push against the desk, my arms splayed wide as I lean into his hard smile.

"I see no true *heir of Sparta here. Your brother resides in the Underworld with the witch, too busy to attend to his duties here in the Land of the Living."*

I refuse to be baited by this ogre. As a family we decided to keep Father's episode a secret, even from Castor, until more information about his condition was forthcoming. I sweep my arms out and gather the parchments, corralling them together hastily. "Guards!" I holler over my shoulder. A stout soldier with dark brown curls enters the room and stands at attention. "Expel Menelaus from the king's office."

The guard hesitates, his eyes flicking to Menelaus. Something passes between them, and I freeze, my stomach plummeting even before the words are out of the soldier's mouth.

"Prince Pollux, I cannot do as you direct, for Menelaus has been named the regent while the king is in ill health." The soldier's eyes are steely as he holds my gaze, his shoulders rolled back and his weapon ready at his side. Ready to defend his regent. Menelaus. Not me. Because I'm not his true-born son. I turn slowly to my brother-in-law, the papers rough in my hand.

"The king has requested his correspondence be sent to his bedchamber, where he's awake and ready to resume the duties of the realm."

A flash of surprise crosses Menelaus's face before it's tamped down with an indifferent nod. "Ah, that is very well. My duties are done then." He clasps his hands in front of his ample girth and widens his stance. "For now." Menelaus cackles behind me.

I skirt around the soldier, taking my leave even as rage courses through my veins.

• • • ❋ • ❋ • • • •

"Pollux! We've got to go. Now!"

Desy's lifeless body lies in a cart we found abandoned next to one of the burned houses. The lion skin covers her wounds, its magic apparently useless when the injury is fatal.

Fatal.

"Pollux! Listen to me." Heracles enters my line of vision, but even though I sense him grab my shoulders and shake me, I'm completely numb. "We. Have. To. Go!"

"He's in shock. Just lift him up and settle him in the back with the nymph. We don't have much time." Athena's voice breaks through the haze and I snap.

235

"Where are you taking her? What are you going to do to her?" My hands clench into fists, ready to brawl with anyone—man or goddess—who touches Desy.

Athena appears before me and slaps me. Hard.

"We told you. We're taking her to Asclepius. But we don't have much time, so you need to get your ass in the cart or on a horse. Now!"

Without another question, I climb into the cart and kneel down next to Desy. Crossing my legs, I pull her into my lap, my arms wrapped around her, clutching her closely.

"Hurry. Please," I beg.

The cart lurches forward, and I hold Desy even tighter.

• • • ● • ● ● • • •

"You cannot be serious, Father." My jaw drops at the man seated on his horse in full Spartan regalia just weeks after being cleared by the court healer.

"Polydeuces, you either come with me as my second-in-command or you stay here to protect your sisters and mother. Either way, I'm going to war." He stares down at me from his mount, his shield in one hand and a long spear in the other. Even his horse, a black stallion with a white forelock, wears the blue, red, and yellow of S parta.

"This is preposterous!" I grit my teeth but still take the horse that's been saddled and readied for me. "I cannot believe this is why you sent me to the Underworld for a visit with Castor. To go behind my back and ready an army for war." My jaw aches as the tension spreads to the base of my skull.

"I told you before, my brother's sons have declared the throne of Sparta theirs to take. I will not tolerate such disrespect to our family, our country, and the crown. It's time they learned that I am the rightful heir."

I keep my mouth closed despite the fact that I want to question his appointment of Menelaus as regent—official court paperwork that was drawn up and signed by the nobles shortly after the marriage with Helen was consummated.

"So, my son, are you with me?" Even as he calls me his son, despite the fact that I'm not his by birth, a lump forms in my throat. By all measures he appears healthy. The healer himself stated the king had never been stronger—physically and mentally. I bite my lower lip and glance at the soldiers surrounding us, their weapons ready as the carts are loaded with food and other supplies.

I turn my gaze up, the day dawning bright without a cloud in the sky.

I finally relent as I drop to my knee in a bow. "I'm with you, my king."

A satisfied smile lifts his lips, but it's the gleam of pride in his eye that warms the icy fear in my veins.

POLLUX

We roll into the small city of Tricca just as night falls, the stars peeking from behind the clouds to twinkle in the darkened sky. If I wasn't clutching my lover's dead body in my arms, this moment would be the epitome of romance. Instead, Desy has grown cold, even as I tried to give her my own body's warmth.

"We're here." Her dark braid whipping over her shoulder, Athena turns to look at me from atop the horse. I swallow with difficulty, my mouth as dry as the arid climate, as Heracles opens the cart's hatch.

I try to move, but my limbs have locked up from the hours spent rigidly clutching *mikrí nýmfi*. "Stay there, I've got her." Heracles hops easily into the cart, the motion jarring my frozen muscles. He takes her reverently in his arms.

I stand on shaky legs and ease myself down from the cart. Athena watches silently as Heracles passes the body back to me. "Asclepius is expecting us." Her eyes dart to an owl atop the temple, its yellow eyes seeking me in the darkness, silently boring into my soul.

You failed again.

I clench my teeth and follow my queen up the stone steps. A group is gathered at the doors, but as their eyes light up in recognition, I know they're friends.

"Pollux, these are Asclepius's daughters." She rattles off their names, but I ignore everything as my heart pounds in my ears.

De-sy. De-sy.

I have no time for pleasantries; I only want to see the god of medicine. Finally, at the end of the line stands an aged man. He holds a thick serpent-entwined wooden staff, and my mind reverts to the snake-legged giant whose body now rots in a village hours away. The one who tore my nymph from me.

"My son, bring the girl to my examination chamber." For someone so old, he moves rather quickly, and with Desy in my arms, I struggle to keep up. We wander past an open-air pool where bathers luxuriate in heated baths. "Once I've examined your friend, I invite you to take advantage of the healing properties of the waters."

I blink slowly, not quite comprehending what he's saying. He acts as though Desy isn't dead. As though she's merely ill and needs a salve or tonic. I open my mouth to speak, to admonish this charlatan, but Athena's grip on my shoulder stops me.

"Trust, brother. Asclepius works wonders."

I bite my tongue and, as we finally come to a well-lit chamber, allow my fears to slip away for the first time all day.

"Please, lay the girl on the table."

I oblige, and as his daughters immediately begin fluttering around, I step back. Standing between Heracles and Athena, I press my fist against my lips and watch as Desy is stripped to the waist, her fatal wound on display. My blood freezes as I force myself to look at the violence done to the beautiful body that, just last night, I worshipped.

Asclepius turns from his patient and loudly picks through a batch of intimidating instruments. Each *clink* and *clang* slices my skin as I tap my foot impatiently. Finally, the barbaric tools held in his hands like weapons, his gaze flickers to mine.

"Let's begin."

· • · • ● • ● • •

"We will not negotiate or parley with pretenders to the throne!" my father shouts as he rides back and forth between the legions. They roar in approval, banging their spears against their shields. The noise is deafening, a true testament to the power the king has over his people. Loyalty. Admiration.

I bow my head as I realize why my father didn't choose me as the successor. I don't inspire those qualities in the people. His people. Even Castor was beloved during the many times he served as regent, though he hated being left behind while Father and I went to war. But now, as my twin has chosen the Underworld and his wife over the Land of the Living and our people, my father has chosen a new heir, has a new son to reign in his absence. Menelaus.

I tuck my bitterness aside and, with a heavy sigh, turn to the troops. Tyndareus nods to me. It's my turn to speak. I always hate this part. I despise riling up men to kill one another. But, as my father's expectant gaze settles on me and the soldiers wait with bated breath, I tap my finger against the horn of my saddle and begin to speak.

"Soldiers of Sparta, we have a mission before us. On the other side of this ridge lie in wait men who would steal the crown from your king. My cousins believe they are the rightful heirs to the throne. They wish to control our lands and demean our customs and livelihood with their own ways of life. But we are Sparta, and our history is rich with rulers and soldiers who fight to the death against anyone who would seek to quell our traditions and heritage. Therefore, we fight. We fight for our freedoms from tyrants. We fight for loyalty. For king and crown. We fight and we win, or we die—our place in Elysium secure to those honorable enough to earn it. For Sparta!"

The crowd cheers as the first legion takes off at a run, headed for the hill in the distance. At the same time, the enemy army spills over the ridge like ants to a picnic.

"Set!" I call out as a horn blares at my direction. The soldiers on the front lines crouch, their shields before them. "Now!" The horn toots twice in succession, and the hoplites behind the shields hoist their spears while the archers in back aim and loose their arrows toward the hill.

The cries of death signal the battle has truly begun, as men from the other side are impaled, falling to the ground in screams of agony. My father and I make eye contact, and at his nod, I race toward the front line on my mount. My sword aloft, but my spirit despondent.

. . • ● • ● • • . .

The sun moves behind a dark cloud, casting a pall over the battlefield. I'm worn out. My horse is panting and slowing his pace. My shoulder and side both burn with the exertion of slicing through the enemy lines. My tunic, once red, is now brown with the spray of dried blood. I hoist my heavy helmet from my head and look around, the battle quite done. My stomach plummets at the carnage. Bodies litter the sodden earth—more of the enemy than our own—and I dismount in a small area clear of carcasses.

"Prince!" The call comes to me on a gentle breeze, the tone at odds with the salty smell of the sea in the distance. I look around and find my father's personal guard waving at me in earnest from a way, and I immediately take off at a run.

I stumble clumsily over bodies, my gut churning as they beg me for help. One even grasps tightly to my calf.

"Help . . . me . . ." The plea slips from blood-crusted lips.

"Forgive me," I beg, pulling his wrist away from my leg and continuing on my path. My foot catches and I fall, my palms landing in the bloody entrails of a Spartan soldier, his organs spilled out into the wet muck. My stomach roils and I swallow down the vomit, forcing my eyes up to the sky as I wipe the mess onto my trousers.

I continue my climb, but my heart stops as my father's form, motionless on the ground, his once-yellow vest now soaked with blood, comes into view. I drop to my knees as my eyes seek the guard's. "What happened? You were to protect him!"

"My prince, I have failed in my duty." Tears flood his eyes and trickle down his grimy cheeks as he bows his head. "I know my fate, sir." He surrenders to the

soldiers who have followed me, their faces mirrors of my own. They force him down to his knees and grab his chin, raising it up to expose his throat.

"Wait, my son."

I startle as my father lifts his hand and holds it out to me.

Everyone stops.

"Father!" I grasp his outstretched hand and bring it to my chest. "Father, you're going to be well. The healers will stitch you up and—"

"No, Pollux. No." He inhales raggedly, the death rattle burning my ears.

My vision blurs as tears collect and then slide down my face in rivulets.

"I want you to know . . ." He coughs and blood sprays from his mouth. "I want you to know that I chose Menelaus so that you could be free."

My throat tightens. I open and close my mouth, but no words come out.

He struggles to breathe. "Like your brother, I want—I want you to be free to choose your destiny. Free to find her, the woman you are meant to be with."

"I-I—"

But it's too late. His eyes shutter, the light gone from them as his chest stills.

"Prince?" The guard startles me, and I blink in confusion as I look at the sword held out to me. "You may do the honors, sir." He flicks his chin toward the guard partly responsible for my father's death, his throat still exposed. Muscles flex as he swallows. His hair shaking as he trembles with shallow breaths.

Instead, I shake my head and knock the blade from the guard's hand.

"There will be no more death today, soldier."

HECATE

With two gods and a witch, we make quick work of the giants. Zeus uses the bolt-shaped weapon to decapitate the giant with the missing tentacle, while Hephaestus drags the second monster into his forge. As he pours molten iron over the beast's head, the snake-tailed appendages pulse and throb, trying to find purchase on Hephaestus's lame foot.

I watch both deaths with a fire in my belly. "We can win this war," I shout, holding a torch aloft.

Hephaestus, the dead creature slumped on its side next to him, discards his pot of melted ore and pulls me in for a hug while Zeus uses his weapon to pick soot from beneath his nails.

"We must make haste for Olympus." I eye Zeus, expecting pushback. But he only juts out his lower lip and shrugs nonchalantly. "Hephaestus, will you come with us?" I try to convey the uncertainty I feel at traveling with Zeus—alone—with his powers fully returned.

The god of metal blinks once. Twice. As he swallows, the cords in his neck tighten. I hold his stare, pleading, until he finally relents. "Yes, Hecate. I realize where I'm needed more. With you . . . and the gods of Olympus," he adds with a sideways glance at the Zeus.

The former king's eyes bore deeply into Hephaestus, as though judging his true intentions, before flicking to me. He snorts and shakes his head before stalking out of the destroyed forge, the iron weapon still held in his white-knuckled fist.

"I need to check on Thetis and Peleus first."

"I'll come with you," I say. As we walk in silence to the cabin, I bite my lip as I look at the destruction of the property. Did the giants follow me to Mount Pelion? Is this all my fault?

"No, it's not."

My gaze snaps to Hephaestus as he continues to stride toward the larger abode. "What?"

"I know you, Hecate. I know what you're thinking. None of this is your fault. I know Gaia, too, and I'm sure she's been planning this onslaught for years."

"How do you figure?"

"These giants are trained. They're trained to fight and likely trained to attack certain gods."

I wrinkle my brow, trying to connect the pieces of the puzzle. Unfortunately I don't know of all the attacks throughout the realm. Which gods are targeted and which are left alone? I need more information. I need to get to Olympus and speak with Athena.

"The sooner we speak with the queen, the sooner we will have our answer, Hecate."

· · · · · · · · · · ·

"What do you mean, we need to make a quick detour?" Hephaestus pulls his mount up short at Zeus's statement.

"Just what I said. And I don't expect questions from the likes of *you*." His malevolent gaze flicks to Hephaestus's foot.

"We haven't time for this, Zeus," I admonish. We'd already spent extra time making sure Thetis, Peleus, and baby Achilles were safe. After helping clear the debris from the forge, Hephaestus and I moved the family's belongings into

Hephaestus's hut, including the baby's crib. As we turned to leave, Thetis's eyes fluttered open and she beckoned both of us forward. With an apology on her lips for me, and a motherly hug for Hephaestus, we were nearly on our way when the nymph held me back and asked for privacy.

"I truly am sorry, Hecate," she said as tears gathered in her eyes.

"I know. I understand that you thought you were doing what was right."

"Zeus and I were close once, and he never treated me poorly like those other women. I believed he was truthful with me, but now I know better."

I nodded. "He is a pathological liar."

Her lips thinned. "Please be safe. And take care of Hephaestus."

I turned toward the flickering candle on the bedside table, unsure if I should inform her of Hephaestus's deal with Zeus. As I looked at her expectant face, a mother's face full of anxiety and fear for her adoptive son, I swallowed down the words and, instead, took her hand in my own.

"I promise," I said with a smile on my face.

Now, as I watch Zeus gallop off into the dawn, I wonder if I've made one more promise that I'll never be able to uphold.

"We have to follow him," Hephaestus states bluntly. He canters after Zeus with his shoulders slumped. We still have hours until we reach Olympus, and a detour adds at least another day to our journey.

I press my heels into the horse and quickly catch up with Hephaestus and Zeus. "If we're to follow you, you can at least tell us where we're going."

"Something isn't right. I felt it suddenly, as though a spirit was pulled from its travails into the Underworld."

"Can't something like that wait until after we've saved the world?" Hephaestus cracks a smile, but immediately wipes it off his face at Zeus's glare.

"No. Order must be restored in this realm. Clearly in my absence all manner of senseless behaviors have been allowed. Perhaps this is why the giants have attacked." His lips flatten into a white slash as he glowers at us.

I grind my teeth together and face forward, refusing to be baited by someone so pompous.

"You of all, Hecate, should know what happens when souls are allowed to be resurrected without consequence." His snipe hits me square in the chest, and as my fingers start to tingle and turn a blinding white, it's only Hephaestus's question that saves the day.

"Isn't the business of souls Hades's domain, Your Majesty?"

I audibly gasp at Hephaestus's deference, but as he winks at me, I know he clearly understands how to ply Zeus.

The kingly god sits straighter, charmed by his new servant, and addresses Hephaestus with a gleam in his eye. "I handle the souls above and he deals with them below. Plus, as he's currently preoccupied with yet another mess, the job falls to me."

"In that case, where are we headed?" Hephaestus flicks his reins to keep up with Zeus's increased speed.

"Tricca," he replies and spurs his mount onward.

POLLUX

"Pollux?" A warm hand shakes my shoulder. "Pollux?" The voice pulls me from my nightmare, and as I blink my eyes open, a stream of sunlight blinds me.

I glance around, unsure of my location, but my stomach drops when I remember where we are.

Tricca.

Asclepius.

Desy.

I launch to my feet. "Where is she?"

Athena steps back, her hands held out as though she's attempting to tame a wild beast. "Asclepius wishes to see you. In his chambers." She adds.

My gut wrenches and I double over. I start to shake as the sobs break free from their prison.

I've lost her.

I couldn't save her.

I've failed again.

"Pollux! Get ahold of yourself!" Athena yanks me up from my prostration by my hair, and I gasp. "Compose yourself!" She raises her hand as though to slap me—again—but as I flinch, she must think better of it because she drops her open palm to her side. "Desy's fine. She's recovering. But we cannot see her yet, so Asclepius would like to speak with all of us in his private study."

I rub my eyes, certain I've misheard. "Desy's—Desy's healed?"

"Yes, you fool. He finished the procedure hours ago. You needed sleep, so we didn't wake you."

I glare at her, but after a few hours of rest my body does feel better, so I thin my lips and move past her toward Asclepius's study.

"Wrong way," she calls and I stop. Backtrack. "It's to the left."

I turn the knob, and with Athena on my heels, we enter the well-lit rooms. I'm awed by the inner sanctum of the healer. I would have expected dark wood and the smell of leather, but instead Asclepius's chambers are filled with terrarium after terrarium of . . . snakes.

"You were expecting a more dour study, I presume?" Asclepius asks, likely due to the fact that my face is full of disgust. I now hate snakes almost as much as I hate bees.

"What on earth—?"

"Asclepius uses these nonvenomous snakes in his healing rituals," Heracles provides from his place on the lounger in the corner. "In fact, these particular snakes are called Aesculapian snakes. Did I say that right?"

The healer turns a proud smile toward Heracles. "You did, son. Very well." He turns his gaze back to me. "Come, Pollux, sit. I'd like to discuss Despoena's condition with you and your companions."

I drop into the nearest chair, refusing to get any closer to the reptiles.

"Her body has experienced quite a lot, and it needs time to heal. I recommend she stay here—with me and my daughters—for a minimum of two moons."

I burst out laughing.

Heracles's lip quirks up at the corner while Athena and Asclepius don matching confused expressions. "I don't understand. What is so humorous?"

"You think that Despoena—Desy—will stay here to heal for two months?" I howl with laughter. "Asclepius, the nymph stabbed me, nearly got herself sacrificed in some ancient ritual, and then threw herself in front of a giant multiple times against our wishes."

Heracles nods in confirmation.

"And you think she's going to listen to you?" I snort and lean back in my seat, the snakes the least of my worries now.

"She must if she is to heal properly. I command it."

I shake my head and wipe a tear of mirth from my eye. "I wish you the best of luck when you tell her. You're going to need it." I hold up my scarred palm as proof.

Asclepius is silent, his mouth pursing as he digests the information. "Perhaps if you and your companions left—without Despoena—she would have no choice but to remain here to heal?"

Heracles and I exchange glances, and it's evident from his furrowed brow that he likes the option no better than I.

"We'll not abandon a member of our party here without her consent." Heracles speaks up before I have the chance, but I nod in agreement.

"You two can stay here as long as you wish, but mind there is a war going on outside these temple walls. One that cannot be won without all of us working together." Athena's reminder crashes over me, the weight of her words a pall over the good news. We cannot dally here, and we cannot leave Desy either.

My gaze turns to Heracles, and just as I'm about to voice the dilemma we both surely feel, a rumble shakes the corridor. The tapestries fall to the ground as the sky darkens outside the windows. A bright flash of light flares in the distance, and Athena gasps.

"What's happening?" Asclepius runs to the doorway, his sandals slapping on the ground as his tunic billows behind him.

Before he can fling it open, the giant wooden door splinters to bits, spraying all of us with fragments. I duck as Athena raises her forearm to protect her eyes.

Heracles's intake of breath and stuttered steps pull me from my squat, and I turn to the entryway.

My stomach plummets and my mind goes blank.

Zeus.

I pull my gaze from his enormous form and turn to Athena, but she's gone.

"Asclepius!" the king of gods roars at the healer who shrinks before him.

"Zeus, my lord!" Asclepius drops to his knee and bows his head, but even I can see his shoulders trembling.

"How dare you defy the balance of the realm?"

Asclepius startles, his eyebrows knitting together as his mouth pulls down. "Sir?"

"You've fiddled with the Fates—and for the last time at that!"

"I-I'm afraid I don't understand." He makes to rise, but Zeus slams his own palm down on Asclepius's scrawny shoulder. The healer buckles under the weight and crashes to the ground in forced supplication.

"How many times have you been warned, Asclepius? You've been resurrecting again, and you thought I wouldn't find out."

Fuck, I mouth to Heracles, whose eyes are as wide as bowls. I flick my chin and begin to move backward, trying to blend in while Zeus focuses his anger on the healer. Heracles remains rooted in place, clearly in thrall of his father's rage. "Herc! Move! Now!" I whisper at him.

"My lord, you've been gone for so long. I-I didn't know—"

"*Silent!*" Zeus raises his arm, his long fingers waiting for the pull of his lightning bolt.

Fuck fuck fuck fuck fuck. An alarm goes off in my head, and I know it's time to go. *Now.* I pick up a stray fragment of the door and flick it at Heracles. It pricks him in the arm, and he finally glances my way.

"We. Have. To. Go. *Now*," I emphasize in tight whispers. With one last look at Zeus, he finally tiptoes over to me. As we round the corner out of sight, the flash of lightning and crackle of energy makes my hair stand on end.

"Please! I didn't know!" Asclepius's screams drown out the sound of our footsteps running down the adjoining hall.

We've got to get to Desy.

• • • ● • ● • • • •

"*Mikrí nýmfi.*" I lean down and tuck a strand of hair behind her ear. Her breathing is shallow, but her color is back to normal. I pull down the sheet and check her wound. A fresh bandage covers her chest.

"Pollux!" The voice from the window is Heracles's, signaling that he's found what we need to escape. I stride over and he dismounts from the single horse.

"I'll pass her through to you, and then I'll place the bedding in the cart." I eye the contraption hitched to the horse and then scurry back to the bed and Desy's inert form.

I lift her gently, cradling her against my chest, then carefully pass her through the window into Heracles's waiting arms. He hugs her tenderly as he gazes down, a look of yearning passing over his features. I gulp down my own jealousy as a realization dawns on me. The golden boy would be a much better suitor for her. He's everything I'm not. He's young, with his whole life ahead of him. He has a promising future and can safely protect and care for her. I bite my lip as I eye the bandage across her chest. I couldn't protect her any better than I could my own father. I wasn't good enough to become the king of my family's land, and I'm certainly not good enough for Despoena either.

"Pol, the blankets!" I blink back to the here and now and turn to the bed. Grabbing the pillow and bedding, I wiggle out the window. In a matter of moments, we pull away from Asclepius's temple. I guide the horse around divots and bumps in the road while Heracles sits with Desy in the cart, his fingers brushing along her shoulder as he glances into the forest. My own hands grip the reins, my knuckles turning white.

I avert my gaze and focus on the road ahead. We need to get to Olympus before Zeus.

POLLUX

"Pollux, wake up!" A sharp pain thrums through my arm and I groan. "Wake up! We're here!"

I blink, my blurry vision coming into focus on the stables of Olympus. I stretch and simultaneously release a sigh of relief. It had been a long two days of riding, Heracles and I rotating duties, but we finally made it to the safety of Olympus.

A roar followed by a rumble startles me fully awake. "What the fuck is that? Did Zeus beat us here?"

Herc shakes his head. "No, I don't believe so. Those are two giants that are attacking the palace. I managed to sneak us through the gates, but it doesn't look good out there. I'm going to help." He unhitches the horse and then seamlessly eases the cart into an empty stall. Desy's unconscious form is unchanged. "I think you should stay here. With her."

I shake my head, my jaw tightening. "No, she'll be safer tucked away in the stables." *Away from me.* I don't add that my protection is utterly useless. Instead, I avert my gaze from *mikrí nýmfi*'s sleeping form and look around the barn for anything that could be repurposed for a weapon. I find a whip and a falx, a curved blade used for clearing fields. Perfect.

When I look back at Desy, Heracles is gently tucking the blankets around her. He plants a kiss on her forehead. I gulp and avert my gaze.

Finally, Heracles drapes the lion skin over his shoulders and grabs a second falx from the wall of tools. I pull my hair back and secure it with a leather cord while Heracles allows his to hang around his face. With another roar, we take off at a run and leave the barn—and Desy—safely behind.

The stable of Olympus sits behind the palace proper, and as we leave the security of the building, my gorge rises at the same time my heart stills. The two twin giants are laying siege to the golden gates of Olympus, throwing boulders as the metal trembles.

"They're going to bust through!" Artemis yells at Ares, who stands ready, his shield and helmet gleaming in the sunlight.

"I'd like to see them try."

I roll my eyes at Ares's cocky mannerisms. It's hard not to smirk when, with one last boulder, the gates crack, the golden spindles breaking. One of the creatures seizes the opportunity and wrenches the hole even wider. He maneuvers the metal as though it were nothing more than thread.

"Oh, fuck." Heracles's face pales as first one then the other climbs through the hole. More Olympians rush from the palace, charging toward the intruders.

Ares is the first to strike, his sword slicing the outer thigh of the larger of the two. Unfortunately, the giant's twin slams his fist into Ares's helmet and the god of war falls to the ground.

Heracles joins Artemis and the two rain arrows down on the twin creatures, but the giants simply swipe them from the sky. I meet Apollo in the field as we both run, our weapons ready.

"What's the plan?" I ask between breaths.

"Kill them." He skirts away, running to the left flank while I take the right. We loop toward the creatures, pushing their backs against one another, and attack. I'm able to slide my blade under the giant's armor and sink into the soft meat between his ribs as I strike true. I pull my blade back and then raise the whip and fling it toward his eyes, where it slashes a cut across his cheek. The giant grabs the leather whip and yanks, pulling it from my hand.

"Fuck," I hiss under my breath as I flee toward a crop of shrubs. The giant raises the whip and circles it in the air, then cracks it toward me. The leather hisses behind me, and I jump and roll behind a bush, the thong of the whip tangling in the shrubbery.

A storm of arrows showers the giant, and he turns away from me as they pepper his back. As he advances toward his twin and Apollo, I catch my breath and look around for something—anything—to use. Finding several small stones, I fling them one by one at the giant's back, but it does no good.

"Pollux, we've got to work together and take one out at a time." Ares's voice startles me as he appears from behind. I'm quiet as we both think, formulating plans in our heads. He sighs heavily—brawn always his forte over brains—and adjusts his shield. The sun glints off it, blinding me.

"I've got it!" I draw out the idea in the dirt as Ares bites his bottom lip.

"I think it will work," he says with a slow smile.

Only then do we race out into the field, ready to save Apollo from the onslaught.

• • • ● • ● • • • •

"Ho, you big ugly beast!" I flail my arms around, jumping up and down as I attempt to get the giant's attention. When he doesn't respond, I grab a handful of gritty dirt and fling it at his back. "I'm over here!" The creature stills and then clenches his fists. I wait, holding my breath, only swallowing the lump in my throat as the giant slowly turns toward me. His face is a mask of fury.

He approaches at a run, the ground beneath me shaking as his footsteps thunders toward me. I widen my stance to steady myself and hold the falcata with both hands. "Come and get me," I whisper under my breath. I don't move, even as the giant gets closer. The quakes grow stronger, and I struggle to keep my balance. But I won't flinch; I won't move. That's the plan.

Just when I think the giant will crush me with his foot, Ares pops out from the shrub and, with his shield in hand, catches the sun's light and shoots it straight into the beast's eyes. The giant winces, slowing just enough that I can roll out of the way. Underfoot, I slice at the serpentine appendage. Slice it clean off. A shriek spews from the beast's mouth as he stumbles, blind and injured, backward onto his twin.

Hearing his brother's pain, the other giant turns away from Apollo and, a scowl on his face, shoves his twin. The two begin grappling with one another, their mission against me, Ares, and Apollo forgotten.

Wordlessly, we circle around the beasts, their blows raining down on one another sounding like boulders being crushed. Ares advances first, too quickly, and startles the giants out of their destruction of one another. Before Apollo and I can distract them, one of the creatures catches Ares by the throat and sends him hurling into the mangled gates.

I flinch as his body collides with the metal and collapses on the ground. Looking around, I spy the second giant reaching for Apollo, whose own blade is out of reach.

"Apollo!" I break into a run, my legs crackling with energy as I sprint forward.

Suddenly, a blur whooshes past me. I skid to a stop before searching for the archers. Only Heracles is still stationed on the overlook, his bow ready to be loosed as his mouth hangs agape.

My head swivels back toward the giants, their attention now attuned to a diminutive doe who prances between them.

Artemis.

"Sister, no!" Apollo roars as the two beasts circle the helpless creature. Their eyes are hungry for a kill. The deer skirts in between their legs, drawing them closer together until they're within arm's reach. Ready to crush her to bits. Only then does she stop.

"Artemis!"

The doe stands perfectly still, her wet nose twitching and her tiny tail flicking, as each giant lifts his closed fist. Only then does she transform back into her human form.

"Now!" she screams to Heracles, who looses an arrow straight for the giant's eye. It pierces the orb, and as he screeches and flails, his meaty fist knocks his twin right in the jaw, sending him flying through the air.

The blinded giant falls forward, where Artemis climbs atop his prostrated form and shoves a blade through his back and into his heart.

In the distance, Apollo stands over the second giant, its skull broken. I wipe my forehead of the sweat that drips into my eyes.

"Ares!" Artemis reminds us, and we dash toward the gate. The god of war sits against the metal columns, blood matted into his golden curls. I breathe a sigh of relief until I look down and notice the odd angle of his leg.

"It's right busted, but at least I'm alive."

Apollo and Artemis work together to get Ares to standing, and he leans on me as we hobble back to the palace.

Where I'll have to tell them that not only do we have to contend with the giants, but also the return of Zeus.

HECATE

"You will answer for your crime, Zeus!" I snarl, my feet slapping the granite floors of Olympus. "You can't expect to murder an innocent healer and get away with it."

Zeus stops short and I slam into his muscular back. Pulling away, I rub my nose and find a trickle of blood in my palm. Fuck.

"How dare you speak to me thusly, and in my own palace?" He hovers over me, his long finger pointed at my chest.

"Step away from my wife."

My heart stops and both Zeus and I turn toward the voice. Standing not five feet away is my husband, my Castor, his face a mask of pure fury as he glares at the scene in front of him. Zeus hovering over me, his finger shoved in my face as blood drips from my nose.

My eyes widen. "Cas—"

Zeus roars, "Perhaps I should continue my murderous streak and take out one more pawn on my way back to the throne."

"Quiet! The lot of you!" booms from the opposite side of the hall. All three of us swivel our heads and meet the exalted stare of Athena, our queen.

"Your Majesty." Castor and I dip our chins in respect.

"Usurper," Zeus growls between clenched teeth.

Athena turns to my husband and me, her face a mask of reticence. "You two are dismissed. I must speak with my father. In private."

Neither of us need to be told twice, and as we entwine our fingers, we quickly scurry back to our chambers.

• • • • ● • ● • • • ·

"I've missed you so much." Castor exhales as his lips meet mine in the hallway.

"I've missed you, too, my love." I breathe in his scent as my fingers dance over his broad chest and find their way to his smooth-shaven jaw. My lips part and invite his tongue in. I melt as he licks along the back of my teeth, both of us ready to devour one another.

He pulls back with a hiss, running his hand along his chin.

I don't need to ask what's wrong, I already know. "I'm sorry I left you here." The heat leaves my cheeks. "But I had to do this on my own."

His jaw ticks. He stares past me into the deserted hallway. "I wanted to protect you. Be there for you."

"I didn't know how to keep you safe and—"

"I don't need you to keep me safe, Hecate."

I swallow down the truth, that no matter how dangerous the situation may be, I will always see him as he was in the throne room. Struck down by Zeus.

I didn't know I would be throwing away the life we were meant to have . . .

I get it now.

I get it.

Living forever means nothing without you by my side.

"I couldn't let it happen again." My throat tightens and my bottom lip trembles uncontrollably. "I couldn't let it happen again."

His hands move to his brow, his fingers rubbing the ridge there, and then swipe back his hair. "*Fuck*, Hecate, I'm immortal now. It'll never be like that again."

I lower my eyes and rub my sweaty palms over the leather skirt that barely reaches to my thighs. "I'm sorry," I whisper. The sting in my eyes lessens as the tears lick down my cheeks. "I love you so much, and I didn't want to lose you again."

"Don't apologize. Don't ever apologize for loving me too much." He pulls me against his chest and strokes my hair. The tension I've felt over the last weeks immediately dissipates as I listen to his heart beating and press myself further into him.

"Are you two done yet?" Pollux's voice comes through the closed door, and I snort while Castor groans.

"Yes, we're done." My husband releases me, but keeps our fingers linked, and turns to open the door, pulling me along.

• • • ● • ● • • •

"What do you mean, you brought her back to life?" The words dance in my brain as I stare down at Despoena's lifeless body in the bed.

"In Tricca, Asclepius, he—"

My mouth falls open as my eyes shoot to Pollux's. "You mean you were the reason Zeus . . . ?"

Pollux swallows, the column of his neck working as his jaw clenches. "I didn't mean for any of it to happen. Athena brought us there. It was her idea. I didn't *know*."

I see the struggle in his eyes. "You love her." It's an accusation. I *warned* him.

"Yes, I do." He doesn't hesitate. The air hangs thickly around us. "You resurrected Castor when—"

"That was *different*, Pollux," I hiss as anger simmers beneath my skin. How dare he bring up the worst point in my life while we stand in the same palace where it occurred? "I'm a witch and you were just as involved as I was."

259

"I'm not accusing you. I'm asking you to put yourself in my position. You couldn't lose him. I couldn't lose her." His gaze drops to the nymph's peaceful form. It's so tender and loving that I feel as though I'm intruding on a private moment.

I press my lips together and inhale loudly. "I'll speak with Hades and smooth it all over when . . . if . . ." *we win this war* hangs unsaid between us. As though saying it, uttering the words and giving them life, will make it less likely to happen.

Pollux strides toward me and wraps me in a hug. "So who's the golden boy?" I ask, my question a garble of nonsense as my face is smooshed against him.

A chuckle rumbles up through his chest. He pulls away as a blush creeps up his throat. But then, as he meets my gaze and his pupils dilate, he deflates, his shoulders sagging. "I think . . . I think he's the hero of this war, Hecate."

POLLUX

As nightfall descends on Olympus, I lie next to Desy's inert form. My fingers trace her features. Across her forehead, down her temple, over her brow ridge, and descending along her nose.

"Wake up," I plead quietly, the strands of her hair vibrating with my breath.

"Nothing's changed?" Heracles's voice snaps across the room as he walks over the threshold.

"No," I sigh, carefully pushing myself to sitting. I pull her warm hand into my lap. "How did it go, meeting our father? Was it everything you imagined?" Sarcasm spills into my question.

Heracles shrugs as he pads to the bed and then takes a seat on the other side of Desy. He pulls her other hand into his own lap and begins mindlessly running his fingers up and down her arm. "I always knew I was different. Not like my brother."

I nod, understanding his feelings more than he knows, but keep silent. This is his story, not mine, I realize with a stutter in my heart.

"My mother knew I was different too. And though she never said it aloud, Athena and the other gods visited often enough that I soon learned I was not the mortal child of Amphitryon."

"Did your fath— Did Amphitryon know, do you think?"

Heracles stares off for a moment as his lip cocks up slightly on the side. "I think he did. I was much stronger, more agile, than my brother. But he never treated me any differently. He never held my birth against me nor my mother. He was a good man."

"I soldiered with him a long time ago. He was the best general. A great man."

The golden god leans back, taking Desy's hand and pulling it to his chest. He closes his eyes for a moment, and I wonder if he's fallen asleep, when suddenly he speaks again. "I don't know how to not hate him, Pollux. For what he did to my mother. And the other women."

I exhale loudly, not because his question is bothersome, but because I, too, have yet to learn how to not hate Zeus. "I, like you, was lucky to have a father, King Tyndareus, who loved me as his own, who treated me as though I were his and his alone." I lean against the headboard, releasing Desy's hand but instead turning toward her and Heracles. "To be fair, I hardly ever think of Zeus anymore."

"I suppose that's easy when you're surrounded by family . . . and love." Heracles sighs. Even though I could feel bad for the youth, I know he has his own life, his own adventures, ahead of him. I scoot farther down on the bed, careful not to pull Despoena's hair in the process, and stare into the darkness of the room. My thoughts wander to my childhood, to my father, and for the first time in a long time, I don't fear the dreams that come as I close my eyes. Like Heracles, I was lucky. Sired by one but raised by another who loved me just the same. This time, I wish for the dream, so I can see my father once more. And thank him.

· · · ● · ● · ● · · ·

"Pol?" The scratchy voice pulls me from the peaceful slumber, and I blink my eyes open. It takes only a moment, the span of a breath, to realize that Desy is awake.

"*Mikrí nýmfi*," I whisper as my chest expands.

Her dry lips crack into a small smile. "Don't call me that." I sit up, thinking to fetch some watered wine, but she pulls me back to the bed. "Stay."

It's all I need to hear. Her arms loop around my neck as she drags my face mere inches from hers. I tentatively press my lips to hers, but she immediately pulls away.

"Perhaps I will take that watered wine," she mutters as she holds her hand over her mouth. "And some mint leaves, too, if you please."

Chuckling, I grab the necessities, along with a plate of pastries, and return to the bed. After chewing the mint leaves, she swills some watered wine and then takes a huge bite of the flaky bread. She moans as she swallows.

"I thought only I could make you moan like that, love."

A blush tints her cheeks, and she lowers her lashes. She reaches for the hem of her night dress and lifts it to expose the gash through her chest.

I swallow down the desire that flares in my groin and, instead, examine the wound for signs of infection. "It appears to be healing quickly."

"How long have I been out?"

"About three days."

She lowers the hem and covers herself up again. "How did you—?"

I take her hands in mine, holding them to my chest. "Don't ask questions you don't want the answer to. We did what we had to do. To save you."

Moving slowly, she turns and catches a glimpse of a sleeping Heracles on the other side of the bed. "You didn't get rid of him, then?"

I cock a sly grin. "I couldn't. He just wouldn't leave your side."

Adjusting her body so she's fully facing him, she moves a tendril of his hair out of his eyes and tucks it behind his ear. "He's so young," she whispers.

I gulp, desire flaring in my gut again. "So are you."

Her head whips around and her eyes flash to mine. "Don't do that."

"Do what?" I tilt my head.

"Push me away."

"How could I push you away when I just got you back?"

Her lips thin and she turns back toward the golden god.

As I swallow the lump in my throat, I stare at her profile, wondering how I'm ever going to get through the rest of this war without losing her or Heracles.

· · · · ● · ● · ● · · ·

My eyes scan the room full of the preeminent gods and goddesses of Olympus and the Land of the Living. Aphrodite sits next to her paramour, Ares. His injuries have yet to properly heal, and she helps him raise a cup to his lips. Athena, Artemis, and Zeus crowd the top of the table, with the latter tapping his thumb impatiently. Hecate, Hephaestus, and Castor are seated as far as possible from the former king. The only Olympian who doesn't seem upset by her nearness to Zeus is Demeter. She whispers in his ear, a mischievous smile pulling at her lips.

"I've called you all here so that we can discuss our strategy," Athena announces from her place at the head of the table. At her right hand sits Zeus. His meaty arms are crossed over his chest while a frown pulls down his features.

"I wonder how their meeting went," I whisper to Hecate, who sits to my left.

"Hush," she hisses at me as Athena sends us both a warning glare.

"As I was saying," the queen continues, her eyes perusing the long table, "After visiting Circe's isle, Hecate and Zeus were able to collect and destroy the herbal remedies the giants were using. Without access to the herb, the giants can be killed by mortals. Now, in terms of strategy . . ."

I clear my throat, ready to add to the tally of giants killed that Artemis is tracking, when Despoena enters the chamber. Her hair hangs limply past her shoulders and her lips are pale. She holds her hand protectively over her chest, as though protecting her heart from its injury.

"I'm well enough to be used as—as bait again," she croaks from the entryway. I flick my gaze toward Demeter, and I see the rage I feel mirrored in her face.

"Nymph, please join us." Athena motions for Desy to take a seat at the foot of the table next to Castor.

"Return to your rooms, daughter." Demeter's voice booms over the queen's. Desy's eyes flash to her mother's, but she raises her chin.

"I will not. I have been out there, fighting against the giants, and my story is worth telling." She slumps into the seat proffered for her.

"You're clearly not yet well, Despoena. You need time to heal." Hecate's face is a mask of worry.

"While I do not normally agree with *the witch*, I will echo her words. You are to remain here with me while the others ride out to battle." Demeter's voice is cold, her gaze darkening as she stands and makes her way toward her progeny.

"Demeter, sit! Despoena is of age to make her own decisions." Athena's clipped tone snaps like a whip at the goddess, who hisses and recoils to her seat. Out of the side of my eye, I catch Zeus's surreptitious smirk as he revels in the discord.

"He's loving the chaos this war is creating among the Olympians," I mutter under my breath to Hecate.

"Hm," she grumbles noncommittally, but I can see the agreement flash in her eyes.

Eyes that narrow as she watches Zeus like a hawk.

HECATE

"The status of our fleet, so to speak?" Athena turns to Artemis, who flips back a few pages in her notes and clears her throat.

"Ares . . . injured," Artemis reads aloud before glancing around the room.

"And I will remain behind to tend his wounds," Aphrodite adds from her seat next to Apollo.

"Of course," Hephaestus mutters under his breath. He rolls his eyes and then crosses his arms and leans back in the seat. The large brute sits to my left, while on my right sits Pollux. Neither man can take his eyes off his intended. Pollux's eyes are fixated on Despoena, while Hephaestus hasn't diverted his gaze from Aphrodite since we entered the room.

"Focus, please," I murmur to my friend. He grunts in agreement as Artemis reads the next names.

"Hecate and Hephaestus, you are both able and willing to fight?"

Eyeing the god of the forge, I sit up tall. "We are."

"And your powers, Hecate? They are . . . ?" Athena's question hangs in the air as every eye in the room turns to me.

"My powers are well." I nod and press my lips together. I can feel both Pollux's and Castor's eyes boring into my right side, but I keep my gaze trained on Athena and Artemis at the head of the table. Only when Zeus's eyes narrow at me do I allow my mask to slip. Hephaestus's hand covers mine, and I shutter my emotions again just as Artemis moves on.

"Pollux and . . . is this Heracles I see listed?"

My husband's twin clears his throat and then speaks. "Yes, Artemis."

"And who is this mere mortal to us?"

Before Athena can answer, Pollux stands and addresses the assembled gods. "On my travels, I visited the oracles at Dodona and was told that he is the hero of our war."

A cry of dismay circulates through the crowd before Athena herself stands and addresses the group. "Enough! If my brother-in-arms states that Heracles is the hero, then let it be so."

"And where is this mortal, Pollux?" Artemis holds her feathered stylus to her cheek, her eyes wide. Waiting.

Pollux glances briefly at Despoena, who swallows and lowers her eyes to the floor. Her cheeks redden. "Heracles is likely asleep. In my bedchamber."

• • • • ● • ● • • • •

Nobody cares that Heracles is in Despoena's bed. The entire court of Mount Olympus spends much of its time hopping from bedfellow to bedfellow. It's only Demeter that's upset, so after Athena dismisses us to rest before dinner, the goddess of the harvest angrily drags her nymph daughter into an alcove.

Pollux follows like a lovestruck fool, but before Castor can go after him, I pull my husband from the stratagem room.

"Where are you taking me, wife?"

I'm quiet, my lips quirking, as I lead him back to our shared chamber. His face falls slightly but then perks up again as he follows me into the bathing chamber. Inside, the servants have drawn a hot bath fragrant with chamomile and lemon balm. The scent wafts over us, and as I inhale, my muscles relax as the calming oils work their magic.

"A bath? But I'm not yet dirty." A single eyebrow flicks up in challenge.

"You're about to be." I smile wickedly, unclasping the pin at my shoulder that holds up my chiton. It falls in a heap to the cold tile floor. I step away from the pooled fabric as my husband's eyes drink me in. He's parched from my absence. Dying of thirst.

As I approach him, I reach for his lightweight tunic first. I yank it out of his leathers and pull it over his head, my fingertips lightly trailing his skin as I go. I toss it with my discarded dress and then run my palms over his chest and down his abdominals. The muscles flex under my touch, jumping and quivering against my hands.

"I missed you so much." He leans in, but I pull away and shake my head.

"Not yet," I whisper as I kneel. I untie his pants and work the fabric over his muscular thighs. He carefully steps out of them, and to the pile they go.

Eye level with his cock, I work the flesh with my hand until he's hard. Standing at attention like a good little soldier. I cup his balls, rolling them in my warmed palm until he's hissing between clenched teeth.

"More," he pleads with me as his heavy-lidded eyes watch.

I run my tongue along the underside of his length, barely touching the tip to his skin. His thighs pulse with need, trembling beneath my fingertips as I hold him steady. I pull him into my wet mouth and suck greedily. I lick up and down from root to tip. I've missed this. The taste of him. His need for me.

His cock falls from my open lips, and I push him back onto the edge of the tub. He sits and I lean my chest into his lap, pressing my breasts together around him. I rock on my knees as he slides himself into and out of my cleavage.

I dip my hand into the tub and slide it over his cock. The oils glide over him and coat my skin. The water's heat and the slickness of the oil have me dripping onto the tiles with desire.

"Let's get in the bath before the water grows cold." He climbs in first and straightens his legs as I step in after. I stay standing, straddling him. He grabs hold around my backside and pulls my core to his face. Parting my flesh with his fingers first, he licks his lips.

I watch, my skin glowing. Ready and wet for him.

"I've missed my favorite meal, wife."

I gasp as he tongues the apex of my thighs. That torrent of nerves that has my knees buckling and almost collapsing into the water. His other hand plays with my backside, his oiled fingers sinking into the puckered flesh.

I grip his hair and run my fingers through the length as my body throbs and hums. I ache to be full of him. Yanking back on his strands, I pull his mouth away from me as I drop into the water.

"I need you. Inside of me." I grab hold of his hard cock and notch it at my entrance before sinking down slowly. Our eyes locked, we begin moving in tandem as the water sloshes around us. I grind up and down, my nipples peaked as my breasts bounce.

Castor roughly pulls a taut bud into his mouth, and I release a squeal as the pain turns to pleasure. He releases it with a pop. "Turn around so I can watch your ass."

I oblige, pushing my rear end into his stomach as I sink back onto his oil-slicked length. Gripping the tub's lip, I bounce up and down. "Touch me. Back there," I beg, wanting to feel the fullness from all angles. He parts my cheeks and lazily draws circles with the pad of his thumb while I continue riding him. But it's not long before he's pushed into that entrance. The pressure builds and I work faster. Harder. I take his cock in fast strides, not stopping when the water spills over the edge of the tub or my damp and matted hair gets in my eyes. The pleasure starts at the base of my spine. The heat spreading inward and lower. Deep into my core. I dip my hand beneath the water and touch myself, working my clit until it's throbbing.

Castor enters me fully with his finger and I lose all control. Breathlessly gasping and rocking wildly, stars flash behind my eyes as he roars with release too. Our bodies slow, but we stay connected. Locked together and slick with our own sweat and the bathing oils.

I sweep my long locks away from my face and sag against my husband's wet chest. He coils my curls around his hand and pulls me close, our chests heaving as our breathing begins to slow.

His lips find the nape of my neck, and my eyes close as I run my own hands over my body. Sated and sleepy, I lean back and enjoy the safety of my husband's arms.

POLLUX

"**Y**ou cannot be serious, Despoena!" Demeter's voice echoes in the hallway outside the war room. My footsteps still and I hang back, allowing them some privacy. However, I'll not leave my woman alone and unsupervised. Unprotected. Not in this den of vipers. I lean against the wall and wait patiently.

"I've had enough of you telling me how to live my life, Mother." Desy's voice is full of emotion, but I know she's fighting to remain calm.

"I am your mother, and I know what's best for you. You'll not spend any more time with that—that worthless prince of Sparta."

I gulp down the pain that flares in my chest as my head drops. Folding my arms over one another, I shake my head and wait.

Demeter continues to badger her daughter. "You're better off with the hero of this war. What's his name again? Hercules?"

"It's Heracles."

"Exactly!" I hear the way Demeter's voice lights up as she speaks of the golden boy. "He's the one for you. He has prospects. It's settled. You'll pursue him."

"I won't." My chest flares, this time with warmth, at Desy's determination.

"You will, Despoena."

Desy's voice goes feral. She's losing her control of the situation. "You tried the same tactic with Persephone and look what happened, Mother. You pushed her toward your own goal so hard that she ran away from you. From us. Is that what you want to happen again?" Her voice cracks. I clench my fists, holding myself back from running to her and soothing the hurt.

"I won't let something like that happen again. In fact, if you choose to align yourself with Pollux over Heracles, I'll be forced to take matters into my own hands."

Desy's voice falters. "What does that mean?"

"Well, daughter, you have a choice. You can choose Heracles, the hero of this war . . . or you can be sold off to Zeus. After all, he's likely to need a new queen once he regains his throne."

"I . . . I can't believe you, Mother."

"I'll not have another daughter throw away her life on some degenerate unworthy of you."

"Pollux is worthy of me! It's I who am unworthy of him!"

Fabric swishes and Desy cries out in alarm. As much as I want to interrupt, I restrain myself from rushing forward and taking my dagger straight to Demeter's neck. This isn't my fight.

"If the threat of Zeus as your betrothed isn't enough for you, then perhaps I'll just tell Pollux the truth of your powers, my dear," Demeter hisses.

My ears perk up as a rush of heat sears my face.

"You wouldn't. You know there's no truth to that."

"Isn't there? Everyone knows when a nymph sleeps with a man, she owns him, heart and soul. That's the only reason he believes himself in love with you, darling. Because you parted your thighs and allowed him to taste your sweet nectar. Now he's under your spell."

"No, that's not true!" Despoena's voice is shrill now.

"How would you know what's true and what's not? You're just a silly little nymph, not a real goddess." I peek around the corner and watch as Demeter reaches tenderly toward her daughter and tucks a honeyed tendril behind her ear. "Now, daughter . . . who will it be? Zeus? Or Heracles?"

I fling myself back behind the partition and, shaking my head, stomp off before I can hear Despoena's answer. Not that any of it would matter anyway.

• • • • ● • ● • • •

"Pollux? May I come in?" Athena's voice through the closed door startles me, and I rush to answer.

"How can I help you?" I step back and allow her to walk through the doorway and into the room. She eyes the rumpled sheets on the bed with curiosity, her eyebrow raised only slightly.

Turning to me, she clasps her hands in front of her belly. "I've come to ask a favor, Polydeuces."

"If it's to return a nymph to her mother's home, I refuse."

"No," she says slowly, her gaze raking up and down my frame. "I've come to ask if you'll assist in training the gods and goddesses for battle."

I'm surprised, but as I clear my throat, I can't help but feel honored. "Ar-are you sure?"

Her lips thin and she thrusts her chin out. "Pollux, I have been kept apprised of your time in Sparta, training the soldiers there while you . . . lay about. As Ares is injured and unable to participate in this battle, we need you."

Suddenly everything that Helen, Demeter, and the oracle at Dodona said about me comes rushing back.

Degenerate . . . unworthy of you.

It is not you who will defeat the giants.

I've had to deal with your mess again.

My chest tightens, and I struggle to draw breath. Rubbing my sternum, I work my jaw. I can't possibly be good enough to train the most powerful gods and goddesses against a species of beast that could wipe us all out, could I? What if I fail? What if—

"Pollux? I need an answer. Now. If you cannot assist, then I'll have to ask Castor."

"You didn't ask him first?" I'm astonished that Athena came to me before going to my twin.

"Of course not. His talents lie with his ability to train horses and other . . . beasts. Yours are with fighting, soldiering, and training for battle. Anyone with eyes can see that."

The tightness in my chest dissipates, and I fill my lungs completely as a chuckle overtakes me.

Athena eyes me warily. "So? Is that a yes?"

"Yes, that's a yes, Your Majesty. I'll get right to work." I dart around the room, collecting my weapons and corralling my shoes and leathers.

"Pollux!" Athena holds her hands out with a laugh. "Tomorrow! Training begins tomorrow."

I stop dead in my tracks, suddenly feeling sheepish. "Of course," I say as I drop the items to the plush rug. "Tomorrow."

Athena opens the door, and as she steps through the entry, she stops and turns. "Pollux?"

Oh no, she's changed her mind. I gulp down my disappointment, but square my shoulders and prepare to be let down easily. "Yes?"

"Make sure you get a good night's rest." She winks and closes the door behind her.

. . . .

I avoid Despoena for the next several days, not that it's challenging. With me leading the training from dawn until dusk, and her spending her days avoiding her mother, we rarely cross paths. I've even moved out of the shared chamber and am bunking with Hecate and Castor, much to their chagrin.

"Sorry . . . I'm so very sorry," I mutter, my hand over my eyes, as I sneak into the room to grab a clean shirt. I stumble over a discarded boot on my way to the bathing room but quickly right myself and slam the alcove's door behind me.

"Why, exactly, did you allow him to stay on our chaise?" I hear Hecate ask Castor.

"Something happened between him and Despoena, but he won't speak about it. He needed space. I couldn't deny him, wife."

"The sooner this battle is over, the better. I can't wait to get back to our home. *Alone.*"

My brother growls and Hecate squeals. If I don't exit the washing room now, I'll be stuck in here for goodness knows how long. With an inhale and slow exhale, I toss open the door and, clearing my throat while averting my eyes, step into the bedroom.

Hecate's cheeks turn pink as her hands work to tame the bird's nest atop her head. I shoot my brother a wry grin, but he meets my look with a tight-lipped glare.

I rub the back of my neck. "I am heading to the dining hall. Are you both coming, or—?"

"We'll be down shortly," Castor answers me curtly. He's madder than the time I hid his favorite saddle. It took him a fortnight to find it, and his ass was chapped from riding bareback the entire time because he refused to use our sister's pink flower-embroidered concoction.

"Cas." Hecate's eyes bounce back and forth between me and my twin. She lays her hand on his forearm, and I see the frustration leave my brother's body at his wife's touch. I bite my lip and lower my eyes before the jealousy eats away at my appetite. I can't afford to think of Desy—her touch—when I have a battle to prepare for.

Castor sighs and stands. "I suppose I could eat. Let's go then."

I smile gratefully at the duo. Grateful that, even if just for tonight, I won't be alone at dinner.

Hecate

"Attention, my compatriots!" Athena's voice rings out from her place at the head table in the dining hall. She's surrounded by her closest advisers. Artemis, as usual, sits at her right side, while Apollo sits next to Artemis. The twins share a quick glance before turning their attention to their leader.

Castor, Pollux, and I stand in the entryway. We wait for the voices and noise to settle down and for Athena's announcement, and also look for an empty table. Unfortunately, there isn't one.

"Fuck," Pollux murmurs under his breath. I follow his line of vision and exhale a growl as I spy the only available table where just one goddess sits.

Demeter.

"I'd rather sit with—"the room goes silent, and I snap my mouth closed.

"The Fates have gleaned more information of our enemies, the giants." A murmur goes through the crowd, but Athena continues on. "They reside on the Phlegraean Plain, the place of burning. It lies just across the Thermaic Gulf, which we cross on the morrow."

A mighty roar echoes around the chamber as the gods and goddesses alike holler their excitement. My hand seeks Castor's, and our fingers entwine. He tenses beside me, and I squeeze his palm.

"Feast tonight and enjoy each other's company, for tomorrow we sail for Phlegra and do battle with the giants!" Athena raises her cup in one hand and her sword in the other. She's a magnificent leader, and as my eyes scan the gods and goddesses howling their appreciation, I only hope that after this war—after this battle that will decide all of our fates—she's still our queen.

• • • ● • ● • ● • • •

"How sweet of you and your Dioscuri to join me," Demeter oozes sweetly as we take our seats at her abandoned table. It's no wonder that she sits alone, what with her allegiance to Zeus, Hera, and Hermes.

"Where's Zeus?" Castor asks as he takes a bite of his salted meat.

"You mean *His Majesty*?" Demeter blinks at him and cocks her head.

"I mean what I said. *My* Majesty is just there." He juts his chin toward Athena's table.

"You and yours will rue the day you took down the true leader of Olympus." Her eyes blaze yellow, and I recoil as her gaze lands on me, flashing pure hatred.

"That's enough." Pollux tosses down his food and stands abruptly, the bench jostling as his strong thighs push it away from the table. "I've heard just about enough from you."

The goddess of the harvest snickers. She reaches for her wine and takes a sip. She sets the cup down, but her fingers linger on the stem, twirling the glass as her gaze flicks to Pollux's looming figure. "Funny you should say that, Polydeuces. I *heard* you'd finally slunk off to lick your wounds after my daughter sought affection elsewhere. From a real hero."

I sense Pollux's body sag in defeat at the mention of Desy. My blood boils, but I restrain myself from launching across the table and lighting the wheat lover's dry hair on fire. This is Pollux's battle, not mine, so I bite my tongue and grind my teeth to dust.

"My liege, if I may interject?" Heracles appears before our table, his golden hair shorn and a look of consternation dampening his beautiful features.

Pollux's jaw ticks and he slumps down to the bench. I pat his leg and offer a small smile as Heracles assesses Demeter with cool eyes.

"I only wish I was half the hero this man is. I grew up hearing stories of the infamous Polydeuces, the Dioscuri twin who battled with Jason's Argonauts and was an integral part of the defeat of Zeus. Not only has he saved me from giants countless times, he's taught me to be a better man. I'm not the hero without him." Heracles widens his stance and clasps his hands behind his back. "Now if you'll excuse us, I have an important, *private* message for Pollux and his family." He nods curtly at Demeter and, as we three stand from the bench, ushers us out into the foyer.

· • · • ● · ● • • ·

My eyes are on Pollux's back as I follow him into the smaller chamber. I glance nervously at Castor, but his gaze is trained on the tiny creature in front of Pollux.

Despoena.

Heracles leaves our trio and moves to join the nymph standing before us. He puts his arm around her, and Pollux's jaw tightens.

"I understand you overheard my mother's lecture, Pollux," Despoena begins as she fidgets with her fingers. She's unnaturally pale given her browned skin and honeyed hair. Dark circles ring her eyes, and if possible, she seems even smaller than usual.

"Yes." Pollux's body vibrates with adrenaline and energy. As I glance up at him, I can see the fight behind his eyes. What is he battling over?

"She's a *liar*," Despoena hisses between gritted teeth. "I don't have that ability—the power over your heart and soul. None of it is true."

Pollux turns to me, his eyes full of questions that I can't answer. I swallow slowly, recalling what I'd said.

If Desy successfully seduces you, you're no longer your own man. You belong to h er.

I shake my head. "I was always told—"

"So you don't actually know, and you just made it up." Despoena levels her anger at me. The rage pushes me back, and I startle that something so strong can come from someone so small.

"I didn't make anything up, nymph. It's legend that your kind seduces and uses all for your own gain."

Pollux's face hardens. "I trusted you, Hecate. I thought you were protecting me."

"I was! I wanted to protect you from *her*." I point my finger at the smug woman and a flame shoots across the room, hitting her in the arm. She yelps and dodges into Heracles's side.

"What do you think—"

"Fuck you—"

"How dare—"

"Enough!" Pollux roars and we all cease our fighting, mouths snapping shut. "I can't do this, Despoena. Hecate." He turns and storms from the room and my stomach drops.

I've hurt the only brother I've ever known. And as I flick my gaze to the nymph and her golden boy, glaring at me from across the chamber, I realize that I am the only one who can fix this mess too.

• • • • • • • • • •

"Go away, Castor." Pollux's defeated voice drifts through the washroom door.

"It's not Castor," I respond quietly, my hand pressed against the wooden barrier.

"I don't want to talk to you either."

"Please, Pol. Please let me in." The thickness in my throat makes it hard to swallow. I wait, my stomach feeling heavy. When he doesn't open the door I sigh, my shoulders sag, and I begin to turn just as the door clicks open.

Pollux stands there, his broad shoulders taking up the entire frame. His white-knuckled hands grip his hips as he stares down at me. "Well?"

The backs of my eyes burn and I sniff. "I'm so sorry. I didn't mean—"

"But you did," he interrupts gruffly as he pushes past me. He crosses to the window and places both hands on the sill, leaning out into the failing sunlight. His head falls to his chest, a single strand of white-blond hair hanging loosely over his face.

I study his profile, the first time I've really looked at my brother-in-law, my best friend, in years. Whereas my husband may be his twin, Castor's face remains unlined, his hair cut short and kept neat. Pollux's wavy silvery strands hang to his shoulders, and lines of worry have etched his features. When did he start to look so tired? So sad and lost? Have I done this?

Suddenly I realize that Pollux's anger with me is bigger than my lie about Despoena. "I abandoned you."

His head snaps up as his eyes find mine. He pushes away from the windowsill and stands in front of me, his arms crossed over his massive chest.

"You helped me save the world. You were the only one to stand by my side against Zeus, and I abandoned you after Tyndareus died."

Pollux's eyes shine, and he makes a sound with his throat.

"I'm so sorry. I'm sorry Castor and I didn't come back, didn't visit, didn't invite you to come to us. We—"

"You were newlyweds, Hecate. I wasn't welcomed. I get it." He stalks over to the bed and sits down at the foot. His elbows dig into his knees as his head drops into his hands. "But I was all alone. For so long."

I go to him, standing because I don't deserve to sit. "And with Desy, you're not alone."

He nods and then runs his big hands over his face and into his hair. "All this time, in the back of my mind, I wondered if I felt this way only because of her . . . powers."

I drop to my knees and meet his tortured gaze. "I shouldn't have said that about her. I didn't truly know, and I just wanted to protect you from—"

"From what? The chance to find something like you and Cas have?"

My mouth goes dry, and I lower my eyes. "I didn't think she was good enough for you, Pol." My chin trembles.

He huffs in annoyance. "You think she's not good enough for me? Hecate, do you hear yourself? I'm the one that's not good enough for her. I'll never be good enough for her."

I shake my head. "No, that's not true. You're the best, Pollux. And if she can't see that . . ."

"I see it."

I snap my head to the doorway, where Despoena stands, her green eyes flashing with fire.

"I see it, Hecate." She may speak to me, but her eyes haven't left Pollux. His face brightens and then turns a shade of pink as she approaches. He stands and, as she falls into him, wraps his arms around her and pulls her against him.

I avert my gaze as they kiss, their lust for each other warming the room. When Pollux finally releases her, Desy's cheeks are flush with desire. Her eyes full of hunger.

I gulp down my pride and hold my hand out to the nymph. "I-I'm sorry, Despoena. For spreading an untruth about you."

She takes my hand and nods. "I understand you were just trying to protect someone important to you. Someone who's grown important to me too." She smiles up at her lover. The look he gives her could burn the world down.

"Hecate?" Pollux asks, his gaze trained on Despoena's lips.

"Yes?"

"Can you help me move my things back into Desy's chambers?"

POLLUX

After wishing them both a goodnight, I close the door behind Castor and Hecate. Knowing what's on the horizon—the battle with the giants—I should get some sleep, but Desy's half naked form lying on the bed sends a bolt of energy straight to my cock.

"I missed you," she says as her bare legs writhe in the blankets, her chiton rucked up around her knees.

"I didn't go anywhere, *mikrí nýmfi.*"

She pouts as she sits up and then knee-walks toward me. "You did. You got stuck in there." She taps my forehead.

I nod, swallowing the thorns that line my throat. "About tomorrow—"

"Hush," she says as she puts her forefinger up to my lips. "There's plenty of time for tomorrow, tomorrow. Tonight we enjoy ourselves."

My eyes widen as she releases the clasp of her toga. The material falls to her waist, leaving her topless. I drink in her perfect breasts and then reach for them, my hands burning to touch her. "Where's Heracles?" I ask, not wanting to be interrupted.

She inhales on a gasp as my fingers gently pull at her taut nipples. I roll the buds between my thumb and forefinger and lower my face to her neck. "He's in the bath, so we have to be quiet." She moans and leans back, exposing the column of her throat, and I lick my way along the cords and up to her jaw, nipping delicately as I go.

"I can't promise anything." My fingers tangle in her braid, and I release her hair from the style, combing my fingers through the strands. She grabs my ass, pulling me flush against her, her tits pressing against my chest. "Touch yourself," I beg as I take her hand and guide it to her stomach. "Please."

She blinks, biting her lip, and her hand disappears beneath the fabric that sits loosely on her hips. Her gaze darkens. Her lips trembling slightly. She groans and I'm instantly hard, my erection pressing painfully against my leathers.

She glides her other hand along my cock and palms me through my pants. I lean down and pull a hardened nipple into my mouth, using my other hand to run my fingers delicately along her ribs. Goosebumps break out along her soft skin, and I switch to the other breast, leaving a trail of kisses and licks in my wake.

"I need to see you. All of you," she whispers.

I oblige, pulling my loose tunic over my head and depositing it on the floor.

She dips her chin at my bottom half. "The pants too."

I pull her in for a long, slow kiss as I unlace the trousers. Then, moving away and standing at the edge of the bed, I drop them to the floor, kicking them off. My throbbing cock springs free, and she eyes it hungrily.

My balls feel heavy as I climb into the bed. I grab her by the hips and pull the chiton down over her ass, revealing her glisteningly wet pussy. "You're ready for me?"

She hums her assent and then slowly pulls away.

· · · ● · ● · · ·

"What did you say?" I'm certain I haven't heard her correctly.

She repeats herself, but my hearing stutters out once more, so I kneel there, staring at her. Spread out before me. Wet with need. Her breasts heaving as she waits for my response.

"Come again?"

"That's the plan." The voice from the washing room cuts through the murky waters in my brain, and I snap my gaze to Heracles, naked as the day he was born. I avert my eyes and return to Despoena's pout.

"I want him to join us." Desy's eyes blink heavily with need. Want. Desire. I can't say no to her. She must notice my discomfort because she reaches up toward me and grabs my chin. "If you don't want this too, then say the word and he'll leave."

"It's you I want." I lean in and take her mouth, pulling her into my orbit. I grab her ass and press against her, my desire turning painful.

"It's you I want. *Always.* But I want him, too, while he's here."

"We won't be here—like this—ever again, *mikrí nýmfi.*"

"Exactly, Pollux. I can be his tonight. While he's still here. And yours forever." Tomorrow isn't promised, and none of us knows who we'll lose in the battle. Heracles?

Me?

Desy?

"He can join, but only I get to fuck your sweet pussy." She vibrates against me and, with a smile, bites her bottom lip. I turn to Heracles. "Did you hear that, golden boy? You'll give my nymph all the pleasure she deserves, but only I get her cunt."

He nods, his eyes landing hungrily on the woman who's now knee-walking toward him. She steps out of the bed and goes to Herc. Her bouncing breasts make my mouth water. She rises to her tiptoes and whispers something in his ear, all while keeping her gaze on me. As he pulls away, his mouth cracks into a smile.

"Wha—"

"Hush," Desy admonishes me. She pulls him toward the soft bedding, and Heracles sprawls out on his back on the bed. His feet touch the headboard. With a flare of jealousy tightening my chest, I watch as Desy climbs his large form, sliding herself over his chest and shoulders. His arms flex as he grips her hips and pulls her into place. Right over his face. Her breath stutters as she lowers and he rises, meeting in the middle. Then she sinks her pussy down onto Heracles's mouth. Her nipples pucker.

Without even realizing, I've started to fist myself, pumping my cock as Desy grinds over the golden boy.

"You didn't think we'd leave you out, did you?" She beckons me closer, begging for my length. When I'm within reach, she drops to her hands, her breasts tickling the top of Herc's head, and pulls me into her mouth.

My body relaxes in the warm wetness of her mouth. I pump in and out slowly while she rides Heracles's face. His hands grip her waist, and mine soon cover his as I thrust faster.

"Fuck, Des," I hiss as she rolls my balls in her hand. She moans against my cock and then pulls out and begins to stroke me with her fist. She works the head in sharp, short movements, adding spit to keep it smooth. "If we don't switch it up, I'm going to come before I get to sink into that pussy."

Her eyes darken as a smirk lifts her lips. What is she thinking? How will she fit our puzzle together? She pulls away from Heracles. His face, covered in her desire, shines in the candlelight.

"I could eat you all night."

"Good," she mutters. "That's what I want you to do." She reverses herself, angling her ass toward me, and grips Heracles's cock. He's still got access to her clit, and he adds two fingers to his mouth before fingering her.

Something within me snaps into place, and my cock grows harder. I push his hand out of the way and tip her pelvis so that the apex of her thighs is within reach of his mouth. "Lick her," I demand as I lean in. "I want to watch you suck on her while she sucks your cock."

He grips her thighs and leans up into her flesh, his tongue flicking out. I insert a finger into her pussy and peek around her ass. She's licking the base of him, her spittle dripping from his length. I add another finger, pushing deep into her. Her walls pulse around my digits. She's getting close.

"*Mikrí nýmfi,*" I manage through the desire, "while he eats your front, I'm going to taste the back." Her muscles tighten over my fingers, and I lean down and tongue her from my digits up to her backside. She squirms, pushing her ass toward me, and it's all I need to keep going. I lick around her hole, tonguing the pucker until she's begging to be fucked.

"I want you inside me, Pollux," she pleads. I give her one last lick and withdraw my fingers and mouth.

"Hurry, sir," Heracles begs as his thighs vibrate.

"I won't be long," I assure him as I enter Desy. She groans as I slide in, seating myself completely. I see stars as Heracles's golden locks tickle the underside of my cock and balls. My hands cover Herc's again, and we work together. All the pieces of the puzzle fitting together. She's sliding her fist up and down his cock, he's licking her clit, and I'm fucking her from behind.

"I'm already so close," Desy says when I briefly push the pad of my thumb to her back hole. She hums with pleasure, and a thrumming begins at the base of my own spine. I fuck harder, grateful for Heracles's extra muscle as he pulls and pushes her hips along with me.

They come almost in tandem. Herc roars with release first, his body shuddering and his toes curling. Then Desy releases a high-pitched moan, her pussy clenching over my cock while she simultaneously sucks down his seed. I aim for a few more thrusts—almost there—but when Desy reaches around and runs her fingers through Heracles's hair and squeezes my balls, I'm lost. I spill into her with a groan, releasing the tension of the last few days on a curse. My speed slows and, with one last thrust, I pull out and prop one knee next to Heracles's face.

Desy climbs off the golden boy and he immediately stands and returns to the washing room. He comes out with a wetted cloth. He hands it first to Desy, and we take turns cleaning each other. She then snuggles under the furs, smack in the middle of the bed. I eye Heracles, and we nod as one takes the left side and the other takes the right.

Our nymph is sated, and with the looming battle on the horizon, I pull the fur over our naked bodies and fall into a dreamless sleep.

HECATE

I divert my gaze from the direction of the sun and our destination. Phlegra lies straight east of Olympus, and as we boarded the ships nearly two hours ago, we should make landfall shortly. I turn my back to the open water and lean against the ship's railing, my eyes trailing over the various gods and goddesses as they mentally and physically prepare for battle.

Pollux strides through the melee, his relaxed gait a welcome change from the past few days. His smile comes freely now, his eyes lighting up at a young fellow asking for assistance with his blade. Together they wander below deck.

I catch a whiff of briny air and turn my face in the direction of Heracles. He's leading a guided meditation on the deck of the ship. Surrounded by several gorgeous goddesses, they fawn over his muscular form and windswept golden locks. He gently unclasps their wandering hands and directs them back to a cross-legged position, but most don't take the subtle hint and stare at his handsome face with doe eyes and heaving bosoms.

"He is beautiful." Desy's lilting voice snaps me from my innocent ogling.

"I didn't mean . . ." I try to get out an apology, knowing that my fingers would be burning from the inside out should I find some harlot salivating over Castor, but she waves her hand in the air.

"It's no mind. You may look your fill, and taste if you'd like." She flashes a wicked smile at me, but I don't miss the spark of jealousy in her eyes either.

"I would never. I love Castor completely." I turn back to the water, putting the buff, golden man out of my mind as I allow the wind to dry the nervous sweat on my brow.

"You can love someone and still enjoy another's company. Together."

I gulp, my face feeling impossibly hot even as the cool air blows against it. I fan myself as the flush creeps down my neck and across my chest. Even with the compulsion to flee from this conversation, my mind picks up on one word she said. "You love Pollux."

Her green eyes seem to glow with pleasure. "Yes, I love Pollux."

Suddenly all the distrust I had for her increases tenfold. How can she love Pollux and share her body with another? "Have you shared this with him? Or do you just share your other lovers?" The venom in my voice doesn't go unnoticed, and she reels back as though I'm a snake ready to attack.

"What Pollux and I do in the bedroom is no one's business but ours, Hecate."

"And do you love Heracles too?"

Her features tighten as spots of color tint her cheeks. "That's none of your concern," she spits at me without hesitation.

I wince, chastened by my inappropriate outburst. "I'm sorry, you're ri—"

"No," she says, her lips flattening as the word hangs between us.

"No?"

"No, I don't love Heracles. Or Orphne. Or the guard at Persephone's castle that Castor found me with."

"You don't?"

"I don't love any of them. Not the way I love Pollux."

There's a prickle in the back of my eyes. I blink against the gusts of wind and push away my judgment of Despoena. "If you love him, truly love him, you need to tell him. Before this battle begins."

"It's not the time." Her nostrils flare and she turns away from the ocean. "Maybe after—"

I grab her arm, my fingers already feeling hot. She recoils at their heat. "Do it now. There may not be an after, Despoena." For any of us.

She moves farther from me, a frown pulling at her lips as she stares at my reddened digits. "There has to be an after, Hecate. If not for me, then for him." Her eyes jump to mine, her expression blinking to cheerful as Castor comes to my side.

My husband wraps his arm around my waist and plants a kiss on my temple. "Everything all right?"

"Yes," I mutter as I watch Despoena walk away. "Yes, everything will be fine." My heartbeat quickens as I formulate a plan. There's no way I can allow Despoena out onto that plain and into the path of the giants.

• • • ●•●•● • • •

"My brethren, today we battle the giants. Today we break them as they have broken us and the mortals we protect." A battle roar goes up around the ship as the gods and goddesses raise their shields and spears. "Remember, we are all strong in our own right, but we are stronger together." Athena snaps her eyes around the group. Her gaze lands on Hephaestus and me. Then Pollux and Heracles. Finally, on Zeus. "We must work together, despite our differences, to defeat the beasts and take back our land from their tyranny and destruction!"

The clang of metal against metal rings out, and I push through the crowd to get to our queen. Artemis, as always, stands at her side, a scroll unfurled. The soldiers fall silent as they await instructions from their leader. Athena reads out the squadrons and their leaders from the scroll.

When she gets to Pollux's troop, I butt in. "Despoena stays on the ship."

A murmur moves through the group, but it's Pollux's glare that leaves me cold.

"How dare you?" The nymph pushes through the melee, her tiny body struggling to navigate around the taller gods and goddesses.

I sneak a look at Athena and she nods, even as her eyebrows draw together. She knows to trust me, even if she doesn't understand the reason just yet. "Take her below deck and cuff her if she cannot contain herself."

Pollux's voice rings out from the back of the crowd as he yells for his lover, but it's Castor who restrains him this time, pulling him away. When my husband can't handle his twin, Hephaestus steps in to assist and shoves Pollux away from the group.

"You can't do this to me!" Despoena cries as she's carried away by two large brutes. She's held aloft between them, kicking and clawing as she writhes in their grip. "*Hecate*! You can't do this!"

"Release them!" Heracles demands as his eyes bounce back and forth, his two bedfellows carried away.

"*Silence*, mortal, or you'll join her in the hull." Athena's voice slices through Heracles's rage, as do the two burly guards that appear at his back, and he falls silent.

The queen turns to me, her voice dropping to a whisper. "I hope you know what you're doing. The nymph can stay locked away for all I care, but we cannot afford to lose the golden Heracles or Pollux."

Closing my eyes, I inhale, knowing that this is for the best. I cannot let Pollux lose one more person close to him. Or worse, allow him to blame himself should Despoena be mortally injured on the battlefield.

Like his father.

"Lower the row boats. I'll speak with Pollux and have him battle ready by the time we reach the shore."

· · · ● · ● · · · ·

Pollux is squared up against Castor and Hephaestus when I approach the group. His eyes cut to me like daggers. He reaches for his blade, and my husband steps in between us.

"Draw a sword on my wife and I'll knock you over the side of this ship, brother."

"Rein in your wife and I wouldn't have to use weaponry to deal with her, *brother*," Pollux grits through his teeth.

Hephaestus snorts and surreptitiously coils a chain around Pollux's sword-fighting hand, locking him to the railing of the ship. "Now you're stuck, so listen to the witch before I have to knock some teeth out of your head."

I wait for Castor and Hephaestus to leave, but when they don't, I thrust my chin toward the row boats. They both saunter off, but Castor looks back with narrowed eyes.

"I'll be fine, husband."

"It's not you I'm worried about."

I turn toward Pollux, his teeth grinding so loudly I can hear them through his mouth. "She stays here."

"Why are you doing this?"

"It's for the best. She cannot be a distraction. To you or Heracles."

"You know *nothing*, Hecate."

"I know enough," I respond. "One, or both, of you will get hurt. We cannot afford that. We need the distraction contained."

"She's not a distraction. She's not something you can contain, putting it away out of sight."

"She is, and I have already done so."

He shakes his head as he flexes against the restraint. His bicep curls as he pulls, the metal clanging against the railing. "You don't know what you've done. Locking her away like her mother did for years."

"Do you want her to die? Do you want to lose her, Pollux?" I bark the questions at him, startling him to silence.

He gulps slowly, his eyes flicking back and forth over my face. "No, but I—"

"Don't you even remember what happened to Castor? How close we were to losing him?"

His mouth hangs open, but no words come out. His shoulders sag. He's defeated.

"She stays here. For her own safety—and yours. She'll be restrained and confined. If needed, I'll ward the door to the hull."

His eyes widen at my tone. "No, that won't be necessary. I'll follow orders. She stays." The fight leaves his body.

"Good. Now pass along the message to your—to Heracles." I flick my wrist and the cuff falls to the floor of the ship. "We depart in five. Be ready. And focused."

Pollux stalks off, his boots mirroring the pounding of my heart as I close my eyes and breathe the villain out of my body.

POLLUX

I stare ahead as our rowboat hits the wet sand. I'm focused. *I'm* focused. I'm *focused*.

In reality my focus is on the ship that's dancing out in the waves and the nymph who's restrained in the hull.

"I'm thinking about her too, sir," Heracles mutters under his breath next to me. Our squadron consists of the two of us plus Apollo and Artemis. Even with an entire other group in our boat, Heracles and I are at the front. Secluded from the others. "She should be here with us. We could protect her, keep her safe, and keep our wits about us."

I shake my head. "It's never been about protecting her, Heracles. All she's ever wanted was to see the world, not be left behind. Not be restrained. And we've let it happen." I can hardly live with myself.

I jump from the vessel, the sand a welcome respite from the rocking ship. I take a moment to get my bearings. The sun beats down on us, and without the covering of trees or shrubs, we're completely visible on the beach. I catch Athena's eyes as her own boat slides up the sand, and as I point toward a shallow cave between the rocks, she nods.

"To the cave!" The gods and goddesses jump from the vessels and high-knee their way over the sand and rocky terrain to the hideaway.

It's tough fitting everyone inside, but we make room. Athena's the last one in, and she gestures to me. "From here on out, General Pollux is in charge. We all take orders from him. Myself included." As she bows to me, all eyes swivel to mine, and I gulp at the power. The chance to prove myself.

I've been waiting my entire life for this.

And yet, I can't stop thinking about Desy.

· · • · • ● · ● · ● · ● · ·

"Brethren." My eyes scan the faces of my siblings, my friends and acquaintances. "We have one goal today, one outcome for which to strive: kill them!" The fighters nod and beat their chests as they look around at one another. "But in order to do that." I pause and they quiet down. "We must watch out for each other. Be aware of your surroundings. Look out for your sisters. Your brothers. Your kin." A murmur of agreement runs through the group. "While we want to win—we *will* win," I amend, "we cannot allow casualties of our own—"

A rumble shakes the cave. Sand and detritus fall from the ceiling. A few of the goddesses yelp in surprise before a hush falls over the cavern.

Another rumble.

Athena's overly bright eyes snap to mine.

My leg muscles tighten as my body prepares for what's coming.

"They know we're here," Zeus hisses from somewhere within the crowd.

I gulp down breaths to quiet my heart, even as it pounds so loudly it could give away our hideout.

I catch Heracles's gaze. He lifts his chin, his expression neutral. *I'm ready*, he conveys without words.

I scan the crowd for Hecate and, finding her eyes already on me, give her a curt nod.

My brother looks impatient, his shoulders back and chest out.

295

"It's time!" I call out as the ground shakes once more. Larger stones roll down the walls. "Follow me!" I roar, raising my blade overhead.

Small pebbles continue to fall from the ceiling, hitting my back as I lead the troops out of the cave and into the light. Artemis, Apollo, and Heracles are with me. I afford a brief glance behind us and am glad to see the other squadrons breaking off into their formations.

I quickly assess the area of the flat peninsula. Large tree-covered mountains lie in the northern distance, but otherwise there are no places to hide or retreat for safety.

"Fuck," I yell at Heracles, whose own face mirrors my own at the lack of forestry.

"Look out!" Apollo roars as a boulder flies past us, narrowly missing Artemis. It hits the crusty soil and smashes into a thousand pieces. I stare toward the mountains and see at least five beasts squirming toward us, their serpentine legs slithering over the rocky terrain.

I corral my group together. "We haven't much time. We need to draw one to us and away from the others. Get him isolated."

"Apollo and I will use arrows if you and Artemis can get him within our range," Heracles says as he starts to check his quiver and bow.

Apollo nods at Artemis. He grabs her by the back of the neck and, pulling her in forehead to forehead, reminds her to shift forms should the need arise. "You're faster as a doe, sister."

With a visible pulse in her neck, she nods once, biting her lip. "Don't worry, brother. I know how to handle myself in a battle. Aim true." They hug once more and then Apollo and Herc are off and running toward the beach.

Artemis and I begin banging our swords and shields together. "Over here!" I holler to the creatures. One spots us and I watch transfixed and disgusted as his snake legs propel him closer.

Artemis scowls. "I forgot how fast they are."

I try to swallow, but something catches in my throat. I blow out a ragged breath. "Get ready." I toss my sword back and forth, palm to palm.

"I'm ready." Artemis's gaze never leaves the giant.

We both take off at a run, our lungs burning with battle cries and our weapons slashing through the salty air. Artemis, her legs long and lean, reaches the beast first. She slides through the dust and dirt and slices at a serpentine tail. The giant shrieks, the call alerting his brethren, and blood coats the ground. His meaty face transforms as his maw gapes, roaring and spewing a gray goo at Artemis.

"Did he just spit at me?" Artemis looks livid, her nostrils flaring as she bares her teeth.

"What the fuck is that?" I yell as she dodges the liquid, but keeps the beast engaged. I'm able to skirt around the other side and land a blow to his arm.

I backpedal and allow myself a smile of triumph, but one of the snake appendages swipes my leg out from under me and I'm down on my back. "Fuck!" I yell as the wind is knocked from my lungs. I dig my free hand into the dirt, trying to find purchase, as my body is pulled in toward the beast. It does no good, and once I'm within reach, I begin thrashing and kicking. I swipe with my sword wildly, but the giant's second limb wraps around my free hand.

Both appendages work, and I'm pulled farther under the creature. "Artemis!" I yell, but the tension of the muscular limbs cuts off my breathing. "Art—"

Suddenly the appendages shudder, and the beast screeches in pain. I have just enough room to roll out from underneath the giant's girth and, as I gulp in air and struggle to my feet, watch as another arrow strikes the creature in his eye. There's already one lodged in his throat, and now a third catches the beast in the cheek.

A volley of arrows sends the giant crashing backward, his shrill cries of death going unnoticed by his brethren still embroiled in battles across the Phlegra.

I shield my face from the sun as Apollo and Heracles run from their position on the beach. Their triumphant smiles are a welcome sight, even as the battle rages on behind us.

HECATE

"Castor!" The shard of boulder pierces his arm. I quickly look around and then run to him, my torches deserted on the ground. "Let me heal you," I demand, but he brushes me off.

"I won't have you sapping your energy on a tiny cut."

I frown at the blood dripping down his arm. "The wound needs healed else you lose too much ichor and become faint."

"I'm fine, wife. Enough!" he growls at me, but then seeing my face, softens. "I promise, it's nothing but a small nick. Here." He tears a strip off his tunic and, with one end of fabric held between his teeth, he wraps the wound and secures the bandage with a knot.

I blink back the tension, the distraction, of having him here on the battlefield.

"Return to your post. Now." His voice is stern, demanding. My nipples pebble beneath my breastplate.

"Yes, sir," I whisper with a cock of my eyebrow and a slow grin spreading my lips. New kink unlocked.

"Good girl." As I turn, needing to wring out my undergarments before focusing on the battle, he grabs me and plants a brief kiss to the exposed skin along my temple. Our helmets clank together. "Go!" He pushes me away and I return to my discarded torches, the fires licking the dirt.

"He is beneath you," Zeus says as I approach our shared post. We are hidden among the beach's dunes.

I ignore him and settle onto the warm sand.

"You should have been my queen."

I keep my gaze trained forward, refusing to look at the fool beside me, but my lips flatten as he continues his tirade.

"I should never have left you in Crete."

My mind shudders as I'm transported back to a simpler time. A time when I spent my days with my best friend on a beach not unlike this one. Swimming in the warm Terranean Sea and wishing for nothing more than his hand to find mine beneath the salty water.

"We can rule together. Just me and you. The king of gods and the queen of witches. How powerful we will be."

He's slipped into the present tense, and my body stiffens. "Shut your mouth. I can't focus with so much of your blathering."

Zeus follows my directive. For only a moment. "Think of all the good you could do as my queen. Ruler of Olympus. Beside me. Your power unmatched."

"I'd rather be eaten by a giant."

A loud screeching roar startles me to standing. I stare into the distance, shielding my eyes with my hand, as Pollux is pulled along the ground by a giant's serpentine tail. I dig my hands and feet into the sandy dune and begin to climb out of my hiding spot when I'm yanked back, landing on my ass.

"Let me go!" I exclaim as Zeus stands over me.

"No, you have orders to remain here. At your post. No matter *what*," he emphasizes.

"Pollux is—"

"My son can handle himself." He holds out his hand, and I take it weakly. He pulls me up but doesn't immediately release me. We stand together, the former king and his childhood companion. "We could—"

"No." My voice is cold. Like the waters of the sea beside us. Because we aren't in Crete anymore. And Zeus is no longer the god I once believed him to be. He hasn't been that for a long time. I push away from him. Put distance between us.

Even as I stand and pace, my ribs feel too tight. I need to focus on the battle. I pop my head over the dune and scan the plain. My brethren are fighting and I'm not there helping. I'm sitting here being propositioned by a traitorous deviant who, only weeks ago, was imprisoned in the Underworld.

It's only as my eyes land on Castor, Hephaestus, and Athena facing away from the ocean, that I catch sight of a giant on the beach. He's moving slowly. So slowly. As though he's trying to sneak up behind them, using the crash of the waves on the rocks to silence his movements.

"They're in trouble!" I yell as I climb over the dune, this time wiggling out of Zeus's grasp. I'm beyond his reach before he can call my name to return. I pump my arms and sprint through the dry sand, my legs burning with exertion.

"Athena! Castor! Hephaestus!" I yell, calling their attention to me. But it was the wrong thing to do, and as they're distracted, watching me battle the sandy dune, the giant rises from behind and strikes.

The beast bears down on Athena, Hephaestus, and Castor just as I hit the solid dirt. My gaze is trained on my husband. My mind completely focused on getting to him to help when—

Something knocks me sideways, and I careen into the rocky soil.

Pain shoots through my side, up my stomach, and to my neck.

Fuck.

"Hecate? Look out!"

I blink away the dirt from my eyes and raise my hand to swipe the debris from my cheek as an arrow shoots past me. It sinks into the giant's belly. The giant who's mere feet from me.

"Move!" Artemis grabs me around the middle and lifts me, and I hobble out of the way. "What were you thinking?"

I blink between her and the giant behind her. Then crane my head to the left and notice that Athena, Hephaestus, and Castor are still fighting off their own beast.

Artemis exhales loudly. "I should've known." She brushes the pebbles and debris from my skin and holds me at arm's length. "I know what it's like having someone you care about on the battlefield." Her eyes seek out Apollo. "But you need to stay out of your head and in the moment."

She bends down and hands me my torches, which have gone out.

"We could use your help." She looks beyond me at Hephaestus, Athena, and Castor. "That giant is handled well enough with the three of them. We already took down one, but this guy is different. No matter how much we strike him, he doesn't bleed. His injuries heal too quickly. Can you help us?"

I glance back at my husband, Hephaestus, and Athena, who do seem to be handling their giant. *Where's Zeus?* He should be helping them.

"Hecate?"

I blink at her.

"Snap out of it. We need you!"

I inhale deeply. Right. "Let me see what I can do. Keep him distracted."

Artemis nods and, with a snap of her finger, transforms into a beautiful fawn. I'm speechless, but as I watch her flick her tail and bounce toward the giant, I come to my senses.

I circle around the giant. Heracles, his bow and arrow discarded, slashes the beast's tentacled appendages, but they regenerate almost as quickly as they're cut. Pollux breathes heavily, sweat dripping from his brow, as he dodges out of Artemis's way. Even Apollo's arrows fail to break the giant's leathery skin.

I need to immobilize the beast. I set the torches at my feet and close my eyes, focusing only on my breathing. I push away the sounds and images of the battle. I put aside the smells and cries of death. I just breathe.

"*Lýthikan ta névra,*" I intone once. I take my time, my tongue tasting each word as it leaves my mouth. I exhale, allowing the spell to waft on the breeze and land on its target.

Cracking an eye, both widen when I am met with the same giant. Still moving. Still fighting. Still unable to be wounded.

"*Lýthikan ta névra.*" I whisper the words again and watch as the salty air carries them to the beast, where they fall at his feet. Useless.

"He's protected!" I scream, the realization hitting me like one of the shattered boulders. "He can't be injured!"

Heracles and Pollux hear me, their bodies sagging just noticeably, but only Apollo runs to me. Bow in hand, his quiver is nearly spent. "What can we do? How do we kill him?"

My mouth open and closes, but I shake my head. "I-I don't know. Even my magic won't reach him. It dies on the plain."

Apollo blinks at me, his gaze going distant. "You said your words died on the plain?"

I nod, my chest tightening as I struggle to calm my mind enough to search for an answer.

"What if he wasn't on the plain?"

"What do you mean?"

Apollo nods to the shore. "What if this one is protected when he's on land? Would he still be protected if he was in the water?"

I bite my lip and blink against the harsh glare of the sun. "I-I don't know. It's worth a try."

"Artemis can lure him toward the beach. I'll use my arrows to send him running after her. You tell Herc and Pollux," Apollo nods at my torches and then takes off toward his fawn-formed sister.

"*Kápste to fos,*" I breathe out. My torches ignite on the spell, further confirmation that my magic works fine and that the giant himself is protected.

"Pol! Herc!" I yell, running toward them with my weapons flickering on the breeze.

Pollux's words echo in my mind.

We have one goal today—one outcome for which to strive.

Kill them.

POLLUX

"We need to get him to the water!" Hecate yells as she approaches.

"What?" I can't hear her over the roar that the giant sends into the air as he pummels his chest, dodging another swipe of Heracles's sword.

"Push him toward the ocean—the water!"

"Why?"

"Just do it!" She circles around the creature and swings her torches toward him, causing the beast to take two steps back. Away from us and toward the water.

Artemis darts by, her tail flicking as she prances past the swipes of the giant's serpentine tails.

The giant takes three more steps as he chases the animal goddess.

"Keep pushing him back!"

Heracles catches on and cuts left and then right. Then he parries, pushing into the giant's chest.

Two more steps.

Apollo looses an arrow and it knocks against the giant's forehead. Even as it doesn't break skin, the beast stumbles backward at the onslaught.

Another step.

"Keep going!"

As I continue slashing and slicing, I catch Athena, Hephaestus, and Castor in the distance. They've taken down yet another giant. As they stand over it, their chests heaving in the heat, they see what we're doing and join in.

Between the lot of us, the giant is quickly approaching the water.

As he reaches the drop off to the beach, he stumbles and falls back. The ground shakes as he rolls toward the waves. We cheer collectively, even as our triumph is short-lived. In my periphery, the beast that Athena, Hephaestus, and Castor felled rises with a growl, the gash in his head healing before our eyes.

"Fuck!" I shout as Hecate's eyes go wide and her mouth drops open. "Did you see that?"

"Split up! But keep pushing!"

Castor, Athena, Hephaestus, and Artemis charge to the healed giant while Hecate, Heracles, Apollo, and I continue the barrage on the original beast.

I high-knee into the surf, distracting the fallen giant as Heracles grabs a serpentine appendage in each hand. The beast struggles to right himself, but Herc pulls, hauling the beast farther into the water. Apollo joins him and holds the beast's head under the waves.

"We've got him!" I catch Artemis's fawn darting in and out of the waves as the other giant stumbles and crashes into the surf. The tidal wave he causes covers the animal, who struggles to keep her head above the water. "Apollo!" I yell, but it's Athena who hauls the deer from beneath the waves. She shivers in the queen's arms, blinking the salt from her long-lashed eyes.

"Bring the beasts to me!" A voice roars from the depths of the ocean. Our eyes snap in tandem to Poseidon, who rises from the waves as a god from his kingdom.

Athena's jaw tightens and she sets Artemis, now back in her human form, on the sand. "King of the sea," she acknowledges haltingly. Her shoulders are back, and even with her hair a salty, sweaty mess, she's the image of royalty.

"Queen of Olympus." Poseidon dips his chin. "Allow me." He towers over the giants as his feet walk on the waves.

Heracles mutters, "How—"

I smack him in the arm. "Hush."

The king of the sea grabs each giant under their chin with his thumb as one would a fish. Heaving them farther into the surf, Poseidon holds them under the water as their snake appendages writhe. We all seem to hold our breaths. It takes only a moment before the limbs go still. Lifeless. Poseidon then floats each body out into the sea.

"The ocean life will feast on their remains." His eyes meet Athena's, and she nods in gratitude. "My apologies that I was unable to help sooner. Hera came to me—"

"Hera?" Athena's lip curls in disgust over the traitor's name.

Poseidon blinks, confusion knitting his brow. "You do not know then?"

"Know what?" Apollo asks, stepping forward to Athena's side.

Poseidon's eyes travel along the line of gods and goddesses. We each take a step forward, in line with our queen. Our sister. Our kin.

"You really don't know." Poseidon repeats, his face falling.

"Know what exactly, Uncle?" Athena's deep timbre dances on the waves as the cold sea settles into my bones.

"It was Hera. Hera released the giants."

A shriek pierces the air, and while at first I think it's coming from Athena, I soon realize that the cry is coming from the plain.

Heracles is the first to take off at a run, but I'm not far behind.

Because I know that cry.

My nerves stand on end as the terror rips through my skin, tearing me to pieces.

I'm the first one over the sandy dune, but Heracles is there with me in an instant. He stands beside me as we scan the Phlegra, our eyes finding her at the same time.

Desy.

Mikrí nýmfi.

Her arms and legs are restrained by the snake appendages of a giant, this one larger than the others. At his side stands Hera, her arms crossed over her chest. And next to her—

"Zeus," Heracles hisses.

"No," Athena exhales on my other side.

"Brother!" Zeus shouts up at us from his place on the plain. I turn and find Poseidon at my back, his gaze full of challenge as he glares down at his brother. "How nice of you to join us!"

"Let my daughter go, Zeus." The sea king's voice booms, echoing off the mountains in the distance.

Even as far away as we are, there's no mistaking the chortle that Zeus releases at the demand, but it's Hera who speaks for him.

"Come down here and talk like civilized gods and goddesses. Perhaps we can arrange a fair trade." She directs her words to Athena, whose own sharp jaw is tight.

"We have to do something," I mutter under my breath at Heracles. My eyes travel from his legs up to his chest. Each muscle vibrates with tension.

"You'll hold until I speak with him," Athena manages through gritted teeth. "Artemis. Apollo. Hecate. Poseidon. Come with me."

I make to join, to be included, to follow in their path. "Wai—"

Castor holds me back. "Be still, brother. Be still, but ready." His gaze darkens as he watches Hecate, who turns back to him and swallows, nodding. She's holstered her torches, but as she turns forward and walks down the sandy dune, she pulls them from their place across her back and they flare to life.

"Heracles?" Hephaestus leans across me and pushes against the golden boy's arm. "Heracles?"

My soldier has gone catatonic, but as I elbow him in the rib, he snaps to life.

"Be ready." Hephaestus nods to Herc's quiver of arrows. Heracles's eyes flash to the bow he's holding in his other hand and he swiftly drops to his knee, nocking an arrow and aiming it straight at Zeus's heart.

"You might want to aim it at the woman behind all this." I make to adjust his bow and point it toward Hera, but he pulls away.

"No. He's the one I'm aiming for when all this goes wrong."

The hair lifts from the back of my neck. Whether from the ocean's breeze or because I'm restless, I don't know. But as I stare down at Desy, her face tilted up to find me, time slows to a stop.

HECATE

"You bastard!" I get within feet of Zeus and lunge, but it's Apollo who restrains me, pulling me back against his bare chest.

"Control yourself, cousin," he whispers, his hands tight around my biceps.

Athena, not commenting on my outburst, glares at Hera. "What do you expect to come of this parley? Do you expect your position to be restored? Do you expect your king to take the throne again?" Her eyes flash to Zeus's and darken even further as her jaw ticks.

"You forfeit your crown, your place on Mount Olympus, and we'll spare you and your kin. You may scamper off to Athens, the city where you'll rot in obscurity. And that's being more fair than you ever were with me."

"I should've turned you into a weed when I had the chance," I spit from Apollo's arms. "So you could live in the shadow of your beastly king!"

Hera stalks over, her steps slow and steady. "And the witch." She stands in front of me, her arms crossed as she eyes me up and down. "You, on the other hand, will serve as my servant. My slave. To do with what I choose." A cruel smile spreads her mouth until I can see all her teeth.

This time it's Artemis who speaks up. "None of us will kowtow to you or him." I can smell her rage as she seethes.

Hera ignores her and instead looks behind us at Poseidon. My stomach plummets at the real possibility that the sea king will defect, taking our hopes with him. "Brother Poseidon, how kind of you to join your nieces and nephews. This haphazard army of youth. You turned me away before, but now I suspect you may reconsider my offer."

Poseidon's eyes turn a dark navy and his fists clench at his sides. "Release my daughter, hag."

Hera recoils at the slur, her hand coming to her sternum in mock offense. "And to think I was going to warn you."

"Warn me about what, exactly?"

Her eyes flash brightly. "The youth overthrew us. Don't you think they'll do the same to you and your kingdom?"

He swallows once. Twice. The cords in his neck working.

"Ah, I see I have your attention. Unfortunately, the girl is mine. You should've aligned yourself with me before it got to this point." She snaps her fingers and the giant hoists Despoena in the air. The nymph shrieks and Poseidon lunges.

He's caught around the throat by a slithering appendage. The tentacle squeezes and the sea king's face turns beet red.

"You see, Poseidon. This is Porphyrion, the greatest of the giants. And he needs a bride."

"Let. Her. Go," Poseidon hisses as he struggles to free himself from the giant's entanglement.

"Enough!" Athena roars as she pulls her blade from its scabbard. She holds her shield in front of her and widens her stance.

Hera just laughs, her eyes so wide that the white shows all around the iris. She pounds her fists against her thighs and then raises her hands to her hair, pulling at the roots as she violently shakes her head from side to side.

"She's gone mad," I whisper to myself.

Then she suddenly stills. Eyes me up and down. A vein stands out on her forehead. Pulsing.

One.

Two.

Three.

Then she releases a bloodcurdling maniacal shriek.

"Kill them. Kill them all."

The giant tosses Poseidon across the sky, and his body crashes in the distance.

"Go!" Athena yells. Apollo releases me from his grasp and unsheathes his weapon.

I sprint across the plain, my boots catching on pebbles and dried twigs. Yet I remain upright against all odds as I lick my lips and inhale puffs of air. Pollux, Castor, Heracles, and the others stream down the sandy dunes like ants, their weapons ready.

Faster, I tell myself.

I slide to the ground at Poseidon's lifeless body. My hands search for injuries, but it's only his skull that's broken. Pink meat seeps onto the ground, and I gulp down the vomit that bubbles up in my throat.

"You once tried to poison me. To use me against your brother, but I forgive you." I talk to him as I roll him onto his stomach. My hands shake with adrenaline and fear, but I need to get a better view of the injury. The wound is horrendous; it'll take all my focus just to heal him enough to speak, let alone fight. Frowning, I hold my hands out, my fingers vibrating.

"I forgive you for your evil deeds against me, but not for how you treated Amphitrite. I'm only healing you because it's the right thing to do. But you had better bless the union between Pollux and Despoena," I add for good measure.

I glance back at the battle raging behind me. Hera's run off, and as Castor and Apollo fight with Zeus, Pollux and Heracles are battling the giant.

Fuck. I need to hurry.

I breathe in through my nose, shutting out all of the rage and pain around me.

Breathe it out, I think as I exhale.

The world goes quiet and I feel the thrum of energy pulsing through my fingers. They grow hot as I channel the spell in my mind. I form the words, their taste bitter and medicinal.

"I pligí epoulónetai. Gia aftá, parakaló, giatrépste tis pligés. Kánte ton ygií. Éna ygiés sóma."

I release the spell on a breath, the words tumbling from my mouth on a cold breeze.

Blinking my eyes open, I assess my work. Poseidon's skull, though soft and bruised, has reformed. He's still pale, but he's now breathing, albeit shallowly.

I lean down and listen for his heartbeat.

Lubdub.

Lubdub.

I let out a sigh of relief.

Unfortunately, I can't drag him anywhere, so I stand and stare down at him.

"Remember what I said. You'll bless their union or else." I shake my fist at his unconscious form and then, grabbing my torches from their holster at my back, run into the melee.

POLLUX

T he moment Poseidon's body flies through the sky, I know this won't end well. How can it when the king of the sea lies dead and broken in the distance?

"Fuck!" Castor roared as we watched Poseidon crash to the ground. I must have blacked out because moments later I'm on the plain, the sandy dune behind me, my sword slicing through a thousand snake muscles.

Through it all, Heracles is by my side. We battle next to one another as though we've done it for years. He swipes right and I swipe left. We pivot and turn, dancing around one another in an intricate, choreographed routine that we never practiced.

It's second nature to fight alongside him.

The hero.

And the hero's general.

"Sir! Watch out!" Heracles's words catch up to me just as another appendage darts out and licks along my cheek. My helmet goes askew, and I'm momentarily blinded before Herc is beside me, righting the metal headpiece and moving on faster than I can say thank you.

The golden Heracles jumps as a limb reaches for his ankle, and I slash, cutting the muscly fiber at the root. The giant roars and flails his arms.

I keep one eye on Desy and another on Heracles, who's also watching her body be flung around by the beast. "We need to get her down!" he yells at me. "Before she snaps her neck!"

I step away and turn. Castor and Apollo are tied up in a battle against Zeus. No help there. Hecate's sprinting across the plain toward us, her torches flickering in the breeze, her sweaty braid bouncing off her back.

We don't need magic. We just need those torches.

And good aim.

"I have an idea!" I call to Heracles and then nod at Hecate. He briefly meets my gaze, the sweat licking down his face under his helmet.

"Make it quick then."

"Hold him off for another moment."

I run to meet Hecate and explain the plan to her. Her mouth twists in uncertainty as her brow furrows, but I smack her on the back and assure her that she can do this.

She nods, her eyes still wary, and hands me a torch.

We rush to Heracles's side. "Listen for my signal," I tell him. His breathing is labored, but I catch a nod under his helmet and move around next to Hecate.

The three of us take position. Hecate and I are together on the left, and Heracles stands in front of the beast.

I nudge Hecate, and she dodges around a bit. Then she throws her torch at the creature's arm that holds Desy. The flame hits the target, scorching his bicep. He shrieks at the burn and drops the nymph just as I send the second torch sailing over his head.

I catch Desy and fall to my knees as she clutches my shirt.

The giant watches as the flame flares through the sky, straining his neck and good arm to catch it.

"Now!"

Heracles leaps, his muscular legs propelling him toward the beast. He grabs the giant's outstretched neck and slashes. Cuts straight through the esophagus and sinew. Blood sprays all over us, the world becoming a haze of red. The giant stumbles backward—backward into Hera. He trips over her and falls, crushing her completely.

A gasp leaves Athena as she stands before the decapitated giant. She turns, blinking slowly at all of us, as her eyes widen. She shakily drops her sword.

"Wha—"

"I guess the Fates were watching out for us," Hecate says wryly.

We all turn as the continued clanging of swords draws our attention to Zeus, Castor, Hephaestus, and Apollo. With Desy leaning her weight on me, our group forms a circle around Zeus, our blades drawn and weapons ready.

Zeus's eyes dash around the group. I see the moment he realizes it's over. His breathing stutters and his movements slow.

He sags.

There's no way he can beat all of us again.

The light disappears from his eyes.

And he drops his weapon for good.

. . . ● . ● . . . .

"So what's my punishment this time, eh? Turn me into a stone? A thorn bush? What do you think you can do to me now, witch?"

Hecate's hands glow red and her forearms twitch. Castor's chest heaves beside her, his gaze darkening as the traitor addresses his wife. Hephaestus cracks his knuckles.

"Fuck you," the former king murmurs as his eyes scan around the circle. At his children. His family. "Fuck all of you. You wouldn't be here if I hadn't created you! Made you who you are!"

From behind him, Athena steps forward into the circle. He flings around, eyes wild. "And you," he growls as he points at her. "Who are you to take over my throne? Nothing but a hapless female. Oh, if only you'd been born a man, you'd have been my heir. But I was cursed with you for a daughter!"

Her face remains impassive as she assesses him. Eyes him up and down as her lip curls.

"Come on then. Dole out your punishment, daughter. *Oh wise one.* Have you not realized that I created you, and I'll simply return to take my place once more? The next time you need me."

She smirks at him and looks around at us. Her family. Her loyal subjects. "This time, the punishment will be permanent." She nods first to Hephaestus and Castor, both of whom grab the old king by the arms and shove him to the ground. Then she turns to Apollo and Artemis. Without saying a word, the twins pull Hera's broken body from beneath the giant and drag it to the center of the circle.

Zeus's eyes widen with horror as he watches Artemis take one of Hecate's discarded torches and, with a simple spell from Hecate, ignites it.

"She'll never again torment us," Athena roars as her eyes fall on Hephaestus. Then Hecate. Then Artemis and Apollo. She grabs the torch from Artemis and holds it to Hera's chest. The former queen's body is set alight.

Zeus struggles against Hephaestus and Castor, as though he could break free and save his co-conspirator.

"Hecate. Bind him." Athena blows on the torch, the flame dying on her breath.

As Hecate begins intoning the binding spell, Zeus continues to thrash against his captors. "No! You fucking witch!"

"*N Aftó to froúrio kratiétai, kaneís den tha perásei.*" Hecate's fingers glow brightly at her sides.

Something behind me stirs, and I am shocked as Poseidon enters the circle. I scoot over, making room for the sea king. He, too, eyes his brother without emotion.

Athena spins within the circle, her eyes catching each of ours. "We will not be threatened by him anymore." She leans down and hisses into his ear. Loud enough for us all to hear, but soft enough that it sends a shiver up my spine. "You die today, Father."

Zeus snaps to attention, struggling to stand against the two burly men that restrain him. "No, no!"

Ignoring his pleas, our queen continues. "Your reputation will be ruined. We, your children, will tell the truth of your crimes. Your misdeeds and mistruths."

She eyes Castor and Hephaestus, and they pull Zeus's hands behind him. Then they shove his head down, exposing his neck.

"We will ensure the stories that you and your wife tried to hide from the mortals are all that is remembered of you."

"No, please, no! Don't do this, daughter!"

Athena slowly pulls her blade from its scabbard with a long, drawn-out hiss. Everything goes silent. Even the waves in the distance cease their crashing onto the shore. My heart stops beating. Holding the sword with both hands, she presses it to the back of Zeus's bare neck. The hair on my own neck stands at attention as I, too, feel the cold steel against my skin. The sharp edge bearing down on my nape.

"Daughter! I beg of you—"

"They will come to learn that the best thing you ever did was to create us, the Olympians."

Zeus looks around at his offspring, but none meet his eye. Only Hecate, his former friend, holds her gaze steady as she watches him. But gone is the fire and feistiness I'm used to seeing in her eyes. Instead, their blue hue is icy. Cold. Frozen.

"Hecate! Don't let them do this to me!"

Hecate swallows, her throat bobbing slightly. Her fingers clench at her sides and then shakily flex open. Her lips part, and for just a moment, Zeus's features transform as his eyebrows raise and his own mouth tilts up at the sides.

But just as quickly, Hecate's gaze flicks to Castor, holding Zeus down as sweat drips from his brow at the exertion. Her eyelids drop to half-mast and her lips thin, pressing together as a sharpness cuts through her jaw.

She, too, looks away.

As though Hecate has signed her mark on Zeus's death warrant, Athena rears back and slices downward with a roar. The squelch of meat and bone cuts through the silence.

And then Zeus's head rolls.

HECATE

I don't recall how I came to be back in the palace, but as I blink the room into focus, I'm lying in a bed and the bright yellow sun is just dipping below the horizon.

My eyes scan the room even as my body remains inert on the soft mattress.

The giants.

War.

Zeus.

Castor.

My heart constricts. I sit up and whip my head wildly as I search for my husband.

"Cas?" My voice cracks, rising an octave. "Cas?" I cry out louder this time as the urgency coils around my throat.

"Sweetheart, you're awake." His form darkens the washing room doorway. In his hands are the unguents and creams we'd originally brought with us. Before I deserted him here, all alone.

I try to swallow over the tightness in my throat and then cough as my body rebels against itself. With a worried look on his face, Castor tosses the salves onto the bed, grabs a cup of wine from the bedside table, and hands it to me.

I drink greedily as my eyes trail over his face. The scratches and bruises are shiny with ointment.

I place the cup down. "What? How?" I can't seem to form a cohesive question. My brain is foggy. I shake my head and take a deep breath. My face must show my consternation because Castor reaches for my hand and perches on the edge of the bed.

"You were so exhausted after . . ."

"After the execution," I finish for him.

He eyes me warily. Then nods. "Luckily Pollux caught you before you hit the ground."

I relive the moment. Zeus's face as his eyes pleaded with mine. Begged me to save him once again. The crunch of bone and sinew as Athena sliced—

Castor's hand tightens on mine, pulling me from my thoughts. "Don't."

I raise my eyes to his and slowly nod. He's right. "I just can't believe he's really gone."

My husband releases my hand and stands abruptly. He stalks to the open window and stares out at the dusky evening, his body rigid. His jaw working.

"All this time and he's finally gone," he says quietly. "I never thought we'd be free of him."

I rise on wobbly legs and pad to his side. I don't touch him, but rather frown in his direction. "What do you mean?"

Castor is quiet for a moment. The muscles in his neck tick, and I know he's reliving the terror Zeus put both of us through. I feel it as much as he does, but I need to hear him say it. To say that it's okay to be relieved that someone is gone. Dead.

"All these years, even after he was imprisoned, there's been something hanging over you. Over us."

Hearing him put it into words, knowing he felt it too, makes me come undone. The bottled-up emotions burst forth, and tears flood my vision.

"Every fucking morning, I'd rise from the bed to find you staring at that oak tree. Wondering what you were thinking. Wondering if you missed him. *Wanted* him." Castor finally turns to me. His eyes are red rimmed as he runs his fingers through his hair, making it stand on end. He's in pain. The agony seeps from his pores. "Wanted him," he repeats. "Instead of *me*."

The tears spill down my cheeks, and my chin wobbles. "I *never*—" My voice quakes, unable to utter the words. The tightness in my throat is unbearable as it cuts off my breathing. But I push through the pain, my heart ripping in two. "I never wanted him the way I've *always* wanted you."

"Then why—every morning—did you stare at that tree, Hecate?"

I swipe at the wetness coating my cheeks. "I woke up to that reminder, that damn oak tree prison, and knew he was coming back. For you. He'd hurt you to get to me. I was waiting all these years. Just waiting for the time to come. And every morning I told myself that if he dared to touch a hair on your head, I'd kill him once and for all."

Castor sags, catching himself on the windowsill. The fight and hate and worry gone from his body. His color returns, and after taking a deep breath, he rights himself and finally pulls me to him. Wraps his bulk around me and holds me tightly as I sob against his bare chest.

His sternum shudders on an inhale. "I'm sorry. I never knew you felt that way."

"I should have told you."

"I should have asked."

I breathe in his clean scent. The spicy smell of the camphor and healing ointments tickling my nose. For the first time in years, I finally feel safe.

I pull away as Castor releases me, his thumb coming to wipe the last tear from my cheek. "As it was happening, I kept asking myself why I needed to release him. What was the reason for it all? Why did the Pythia force me to bring him back?"

Castor's gaze flicks to the darkening sky. "It was the Fates," he finally says. "The Fates realized that we'd never heal, never truly be happy, with him just beyond our door."

I follow his gaze and stare at the twinkling stars, their presence a reminder of something bigger. Something beyond our understanding.

Fate.

EPILOGUE

"We'll miss you." Desy pushes to her toes and plants a kiss on Heracles's cheek.

He wraps his arms around her waist and swings her around.

"Put me down!" she squeals. When he deposits her back on the grass, she's teary-eyed.

"I never knew you to be so emotional," I whisper in her ear as I wrap my arm around her waist.

She playfully smacks me and swipes under her eyes.

I step forward and hold out my hand. "It's been an honor, golden boy."

Heracles stares at my hand and slaps it away, pulling me in for a hug as well. His attempt to spin me around doesn't go so well, and he groans with exertion before giving up and dropping me to my feet. "The honor is all mine, sir."

We step back and join the group of siblings that Heracles has already bid goodbye to. Artemis and Apollo. Athena. Ares and Aphrodite. Hephaestus.

Our next family reunion should be loads of fun.

The golden Heracles climbs atop his horse with nary a bit of exertion and seats himself comfortably in the saddle. As he looks down on us, the sun's rays peek through the treetops, and a golden aura outlines his profile.

"Good luck on your journey," I say, my throat tightening.

"Thank you, sir. For everything." He dips his chin and flicks the reins. As the horse canters off down the mountain trail, we all stand and wave at the hero.

• • • ● • ● • • • •

Despoena and I return to our shared chamber, the room seeming much bigger without Heracles's hulking form taking up so much space.

"We should pack," I tell her as I toss a clean shirt into my bag.

Her brow furrows. "Where are we going?"

"Wherever your heart desires, *mikrí nýmfi*."

She smiles. "Don't call me that."

I hum a tune, ignoring her, and toss another item into the bag.

"Seriously, where are we going?"

I cock an eyebrow at her as a smirk dances along my lips. "We have some unfinished business."

• • ● • ● • • • •

"I still don't understand why we are returning to the Underworld with Hecate and your brother." Desy's hand flexes in mine as we make our way across the hall.

"I think it'd be nice to spend some time together. As a family. Unless you don't—"

"No, I do. I'll go anywhere with you." She tilts her chin up for a kiss, which I gladly bestow upon her just as the door to Castor's room opens.

"Gross," my twin mutters.

"Now you know how we all felt at the boar hunt."

I catch Hecate's pinked cheeks from across the room where she's buckling her bag. "Has everyone said their goodbyes?"

325

Desy and I both nod, and Castor shrugs. "We'll be back soon enough if I forgot someone."

We each grab our packs and hoist them onto our shoulders. Standing away from us, Hecate closes her eyes and breathes deeply.

"What's she doing?" Desy whispers under her breath.

"Shush," I admonish, pushing my forefinger to her lips. She gives me a mock frown and I lean down with a growl.

"Could the two of you contain yourselves for just a moment?" I'm not sure how she accomplishes it, but Hecate's glaring at us with one eye cracked open.

"Sorry," I mutter.

"Sorry," Desy echoes.

Our stubborn witch restarts her breathing. Before long, she exhales a string of nonsensical words which none of us comprehend. "*Anoixe tin pórta. Fos anamméno. Xekleidóste tin pórta. Steílte to fo*s."

I blink as the air goes thick and then thin. A hazy ring of red light shines through the circular opening in the middle of the room.

"Ladies first." Castor gestures to Desy, who refuses to release my hand.

I offer her a comforting smile and tug her through the portal. My body feels woozy, as though I've just stood up too quickly, but it's over before I'm too uncomfortable.

We walk through the portal and are greeted by the red sun of the Underworld, where Hades and Persephone sit atop their horses.

Three horses and a carriage await.

Castor pulls Hecate to the first horse and, with his hand held out, assists her in mounting. He then climbs onto the second horse.

I sneak a glance at Desy. "Carriage . . . or horse?"

She squishes her lips to the side of her mouth and taps her chin. "Horse," she states. "But only if you're behind me. I'm not such a great rider."

I lean into the whorl of her ear. "We'll just have to remedy that, won't we, *mikrí nýmfi*?" A blush blooms across her cheeks, and I escort her to the third horse.

"Sister." Persephone cocks her eyebrow at Desy and nods.

"Your Highness." Desy dips a shallow curtsy and then steps into my palm to mount her horse.

"Prince Pollux." Persephone's eyes meet mine, their cold green a vast difference from the warm, inviting emerald I've come to cherish with her sister.

"Your Highness." I offer a short bow and then launch myself behind Desy, pulling her hips against my semihard cock. I can't get enough of this nymph, and I still can't believe she's all mine.

"You'll follow us to the castle, where we'll have a family dinner together. We have much to discuss." The queen slides her gaze over all of us, holding for a breath longer on me, but as she turns her horse and leads the party, I steal the reins from Desy and guide us off the path.

"Where are we going?" she shrieks as we gallop across the open fields of Elysium.

"You'll see," I whisper seductively in her ear.

· · · ● · ● ● · · ·

The reddened sun has darkened to a deep maroon as it slides down toward the horizon. I pull up to the small hut and bring our horse to a stop. Desy's softly snoring in front of me, her body pressing deliciously against my chest.

"We're here, Des."

She breathes awake and, as I hop to the ground, blinks in confusion at the surroundings. "This is Orphne's cabin," she says slowly, her eyes sliding to mine.

"It is." I nod as a mischievous smile tilts my lips.

She climbs down and I catch her, my hands lingering on her waist and sliding up to cup her breasts. "What are we doing at Orphne's, Pollux?"

"We have some unfinished business."

Her eyes narrow as a wide grin breaks out along her lips. "What business would that be, precisely?" She plants her hands on her hips.

"Why, we have to fix her door, of course."

Her smile falls. "Oh."

"Were you hoping we were here for something else, *mikrí nýmfi*? Perhaps a little . . ." I lean down and whisper in her ear, "Fucking?"

Goosebumps break out along her temple and travel to her neck. I trace my eyes along her collarbone and down to her tunic. Leaning in, I pull her lips to mine.

"Desy! Pollux! You're here!" Orphne flings open the door and I pull away reluctantly.

Desy eyes the wooden entrance, the hinges replaced and attached to the hut. "I guess we do have some unfinished business then."

"You can be hers tonight. While we're here visiting the Underworld. And *mine* forever."

She bites her bottom lip and, with a wink, laces her fingers with mine and pulls me into the hut.

THANK YOU!

If you enjoyed reading *Daughter of War & Witchcraft*, please consider leaving a review or recommending it to a friend. Your support, through reviews, word of mouth, and social media shares, helps readers find my story.

Follow Jenn Lynn Adams on social media:

Instagram @jennlynnadams

TikTok @authorjennlynnadams

On the web www.jennlynnadams.com

ACKNOWLEDGEMENTS

Anything is possible when you have the right people to support you.
Misty Copeland

I've been blessed with a tribe of women who have encouraged me, laughed with me, cried with me, cussed with me, and kept me sane on the absolute worst days. They say to find your tribe and love them hard. As a middle school teacher, nothing could be truer. A solid support system is a must, and my tribe of itchy biscuits supports me without exception.

My alpha reader Sarah, thank you for sticking by my side throughout this journey. I couldn't have created the *Daughter* series without your help. Even if it's not motorcycle club or mafia smut, I appreciate you reading something outside of your comfort zone simply for my sake. You're the best friend, work wife, and fake sister I've ever had.

To my beta reader Anne, thank you for taking a chance on a new indie author and reading *Daughter of the Underworld*. I'm so lucky that you reached out, and even luckier you offered to beta read for me. Your suggestions and advice made my story stronger, and I hope this version met your expectations. I hope you'll stick around for more!

I could not have created my versions of Hecate, Castor, and Pollux without the help of my editor, Anna Corbeaux (@corbeauxeditorialservices). Spending months perfecting a story and then sharing it with a stranger can be terrifying, but Anna consistently goes above and beyond to not only edit, but teach me the difference between further/farther (which I still don't know), and still keep my author's voice. If you're ever in the market for an editor, I cannot recommend her enough.

Of course I'm saving the best for (almost) last, but I'm forever grateful to my husband and two beautiful children. They may not understand why I write— the need I feel to get the puzzle in my head onto the page— but they give me the time and peace to do so. They are proud of me, support me, and love me.

And to you, the readers, thank you from the bottom of my heart for continuing to read and share my stories. I appreciate your kindness, reviews, and thoughts more than you know. It's the bright part of an otherwise lonely profession. I hope you continue to support indie authors and our writing dreams.